THE JUDAS TREE

*Also by A. J. Cronin and available
in the NEL series:*

HATTER'S CASTLE
SHANNON'S WAY
THE STARS LOOK DOWN
A SONG OF SIXPENCE
THE SPANISH GARDENER
THE CITADEL
THE KEYS OF THE KINGDOM
THE NORTHERN LIGHT
BEYOND THIS PLACE
THE GREEN YEARS
GRAND CANARY
THREE LOVES

The Judas Tree

A. J. CRONIN

NEW ENGLISH LIBRARY
TIMES MIRROR

First published in Great Britain in 1961 by Victor Gollancz Ltd.
© by A. J. Cronin 1961

*

FIRST NEL PAPERBACK EDITION MARCH 1973
This new edition February 1977

*

NEL Books are published by
New English Library Limited from Barnard's Inn, Holborn, London EC1N 2JR
Made and printed in Great Britain by Hunt Barnard Printing Ltd., Aylesbury, Bucks.

45003131 4

PART ONE

CHAPTER 1

THE AUTUMN MORNING was so brilliant that Moray, judiciously consulting the rheostat thermometer outside his window, decided to breakfast on the balcony of his bedroom. He had slept well: for an ex-insomniac six hours was a reassuring performance: the sun shone warm through his Grieder silk robe, and Arturo had, as usual, prepared his tray to perfection. He poured his Toscanini coffee – kept hot in a silver Thermos – anointed a fresh croissant with mountain honey, and let his eye wander, with all the rich, possessive pleasure of a discoverer. God, what beauty! On the one hand, the Riesenberg, rising to the blue sky with heaven-designed symmetry above green, green grasslands lightly peppered with little ancient red-roofed peasant chalets; on the other, the gentle slopes of Eschenbrück, orchards of pear, apricot and cherry; in front, to the south, a distant ridge of snowy Alp and beneath, ah yes, beneath the plateau of his property lay the Schwansee, beloved lake of so many, many moods, sudden, wild and wonderful, but now glimmering in peace, veiled by the faintest skein of mist, through which a little white boat stole silently, like ... well, like a swan, he decided poetically.

How fortunate after long searching to find this restful, lovely spot, unpolluted by tourists, yet near enough the town of Melsburg to afford all the advantages of an efficient and civilised community. And the house, too, built with precision for a famous Swiss architect, it was all he could have wished. Solid rather than striking perhaps, yet stuffed with comfort. Think of finding chauffage à mazout, built-in cupboards, tiled kitchen, a fine long salon for his pictures, even the modern bathrooms demanded by his long sojourn in America! Drinking his orange juice, which he always reserved for a final bonne bouche, a sigh of satisfaction exhaled from Moray, so blandly euphoric was his mood, so sublimely unconscious was he of impending disaster.

How should he spend his day? – as he got up and began to dress he reviewed the possibilities. Should he telephone Madame von Altishofer and go walking on the Teufenthal? – on such a morning she would surely want to exercise her weird and wonderful pack of Weimaraners. But no, he was to have the pleasure of taking her to the Festival party at five o'clock – one must not press too hard. What then? Run into Melsburg for golf? Or take out the boat and join the fishermen who were already hoping for a run of felchen in the lake? Yet somehow his inclination lay towards gentler diversions and finally he decided to look into the question of his roses which, suffering from a late frost, had not fully flowered this summer.

He went downstairs to the covered terrace. Laid out beside the chaise longue he found his mail and the local news sheet – the English papers and the Paris *Herald Tribune* did not arrive until the afternoon. There was nothing to disturb him in his letters, each of which he opened with a curious hesitation, a reluctant movement of his thumb – strange how that ridiculous phobia persisted. In the kitchen Arturo was singing:

> 'La donna è mobile . . .
> Sempre un' amabile . . .
> La donna è mobile . . .
> E di pensier!'

Moray smiled; his butler had irrepressible operatic tendencies – it was he who had chosen the blend of coffee once favoured by the maestro on a visit to Melsburg – but he was a cheerful, willing, devoted fellow and Elena, his wife, though stupendous in bulk, had proved a marvellous if temperamental cook. Even in his servants he was decidedly lucky . . . or was it merely luck, he asked himself mildly, moving out upon the lawn with pride. In Connecticut, with its stony soil and unconquerable crab grass, he had never had a proper lawn, at least nothing such as this close-cropped velvet stretch. He had made it, determinedly, uprooting a score of aged willow stumps, when he took over the property.

Flanking this luscious turf, a gay herbaceous border ran, following a paved path that led to the lily pond, where golden carp lay motionless beneath the great sappy pads. A copper beech shaded the pond, and beyond was the Japanese garden, a rocky mount, vivid with quince, dwarf maples, and scores of little plants and shrubs with Latin names defying the memory.

The further verge of the lawn was marked by a line of flowering bushes, lilac, forsythia, viburnum, and the rest, which screened the vegetable garden from the house. Then came his orchard, laden with ripe fruits: apple, pear, plum, damson, greengage – in an idle moment he had counted seventeen different varieties, but he owned to having cheated slightly, including the medlars, walnuts, and large filberts which grew in great abundance at the top of the slope, surrounding the dependence, a pretty little chalet, which he had converted to a guest house.

Nor must he forget his greatest botanical treasure: the great gorgeous Judas tree that rose high, high above the backdrop of mountain, lake and cloud. It was indeed a handsome specimen with a noble spreading head, covered in spring with heavy purplish flowers that appeared before the foliage. All his visitors admired it and when he gave a garden party it pleased him to display his knowledge to the ladies, omitting to reveal that he had looked it all up in the *Encyclopaedia Britannica*. 'Yes,' he would say, 'it's the *Cercis siliquastrium* . . . the family of *Leguminosae* . . . the leaves have an agreeable taste, and in the East are often mixed with salad. You know, of course, the ridiculous popular tradition. In fact Arturo, my good Italian, who is amusingly superstitious, swears it's unlucky and calls it *l'albero dei dannati*' – here he would smile, translating gracefully, 'the tree of lost souls.'

But now he discovered Wilhelm, his gardener, who admitted seventy years and was seventy-nine at least, nipping buds by the cucumber frame. The old man had the face of the aged Saint Peter and the obduracy of a cavalry sergeant. It took tact even to agree with him, but he had proved his worth in knowledge and labour, his one drawback an embarrassing, if useful, propensity for making water on the compost heap. Straightening his green baize apron, he removed his hat and greeted Moray with a grimly impassive:

'Grüss Gott.'

'Die Rosen, Herr Wilhelm,' said Moray diplomatically. 'Wollen wir diese ansehen?'

Together they went to the rose garden where, once the old man had scattered blame in all directions, the number of new varieties required was discussed and determined. As Wilhelm departed, a delightful diversion occurred. Two diminutive figures, the children of the village piermaster, aged seven and five, were observed breasting the steep path with that breathless speed and

9

importance which denoted the delivery of an invoice; Suzy, the senior, clutched the yellow envelope, while Hans, her brother, carried book and pencil for the receipt. They were the most attractive, bright-eyed children, already smiling, glowing actually, in anticipation of the ritual he had established. So, after glancing at the invoice – it was, as expected, from Frankfurt, confirming the arrival of two cases of the special 1955 Johannisberger – he shook his head forbiddingly.

'You must be punished for being such good children.'

They were giggling as he led them to their favourite tree, a noble Reine Claude loaded with yellow plums. He shook a branch and when a rain of juicy fruit descended they burst into shrieks of laughter, scrambling down the slope, pouncing on the ripe rolling plums.

'Danke, danke vielmals, Herr Moray.'

Only when they had filled their pockets did he let them go. Then he looked at his watch and decided to be off.

In the garage, adjacent to the chalet, he chose to take the sports Jaguar. For one who had attained the age of fifty-five and had from choice retired to a life of leisure and repose, such a vehicle might possibly have been judged too racy, the more so since hs other two cars, the Humber estate wagon and a new Rolls Silver Cloud – obviously, he favoured the British marque – were notably conservative. Yet he felt, and looked, he had often been told, far far younger than his years: his figure was slim, his teeth sound and even, he had kept his hair without a thread of grey, and in his smile, which was charming, he had retained an extraordinarily attractive quality, spontaneous, almost boyish.

At first his road ran through the pasture land, where soft-eyed, brown cows moved cumbrously, clanging the great bells strapped about their necks, bells which had descended through many generations. In the lower fields men, and women too, were busy with the eternal cycle of the grass. Some paused in their scything to lift a hand in greeting, for he was known, and liked, no doubt because of his kindness to the children, or perhaps because he had taken pains to interest himself in all the local junketings. Indeed, the rustic weddings, made dolorous by the final sounding of the Alpenhorn, the traditional processions, both religious and civil, even the brassy discords of the village band, which had come to serenade him on his birthday . . . all these amused and entertained him.

Presently he came to the outer suburbs: streets which seemed to have been scrubbed, green-shuttered white houses, with their front plots of asters and begonias, their window-boxes filled with blooming geraniums and petunias. Such flowers – he had never seen the like! And over all such a clean quiet air of neatness and efficiency, as if everything were ordered and would never break down – and indeed nothing did; as if honesty, civility and politeness were the watchwords of the people.

How wise in his special circumstances to settle here, away from the vulgarity of the present age: the hipsters and the beatniks, the striptease, the rock-and-roll, the ridiculous mouthings of angry young men, the lunatic abstractions of modern art, and all the other horrors and obscenities of a world gone mad.

To friends in America who had protested against his decision, and in particular to Holbrook, his partner in the Stamford company, who had gone so far as to ridicule the country and its inhabitants, he had reasoned calmly, logically. Hadn't Wagner spent seven happy and fruitful years in this same canton, composing *Die Meistersinger* and even – this with a smile – a brilliant march for the local fire brigade? The house, now a museum, still stood as evidence. Did not Shelley, Keats and Byron spend long periods of romantic leisure in the vicinity? As for the lake, Turner had painted it, Rousseau had rowed upon it, Ruskin had raved about it.

Nor was he burying himself in a soulless vacuum. He had his books, his collection of beautiful things. Besides, if the native Swiss were not – how should he put it nicely? – not intellectually stimulating, there existed in Melsburg an expatriate society, a number of delightful people, of whom Madame von Altishofer was one, who had accepted him as a member of their coterie. And if this were not enough, the airport at Zurich lay within a forty-minute drive, and thereafter in two hours, or less, he was in Paris . . . Milan . . . Vienna . . . studying the rich textures of Titian's *Entombment;* hearing Callas in *Tosca*; savouring the marvellous *Schafsragout mit Weisskraut* in Sacher's Bar.

By this time he had reached the Lauerbach nursery. Here he made his selection of roses, resolutely adding several varieties of his own choice to the list Wilhelm had given him, although wryly aware that his would probably perish mysteriously while the

11

others would survive and flourish. When he left the nursery it was still quite early, only eleven o'clock. He decided to return by Melsburg and do some errands.

The town was pleasantly empty, most of the visitors gone, the lakeside promenade, where crisp leaves from the pollard chestnuts were already rustling, half deserted. This was the season Moray enjoyed, which he viewed as an act of repossession. The twin spires of the cathedral seemed to pierce the sky more sharply, the ring of ancient forts, no longer floodlit, grew old and grey again, the ancient Mels Brücke, free of gaping sightseers, calmly resumed its true identity.

He parked in the square by the fountain and, without even thinking of locking the car, strolled into the town. First he visited his tobacconist's, bought a box of two hundred of his special Sobranie cigarettes, then at the apothecary's a large flask of Pineau's Eau de Quinine, the particular hair tonic he always used. In the next street was Maier's, the famous confectioner's. Here, after a chat with Herr Maier, he sent off a great package of milk chocolate to Holbrook's children in Connecticut – they'd never get chocolate of *that* quality in Stamford. As an afterthought – he had a sweet tooth – he took away a demi-kilo of the new season's *marrons glacés* for himself. Shopping here really was a joy, he told himself, one met smiles and politeness on every side.

He was now in the Stadplatz where, answering a subconscious prompting, his legs had borne him. He could not refrain from smiling, though with a slight sense of guilt. Immediately opposite stood the Galerie Leuschner. He hesitated, humorously aware that he was yielding to temptation. But the thought of the Vuillard pastel drove him on. He crossed the street, pushed open the door of the gallery, and went in.

Leuschner was in his office looking over a folio of pen-and-ink sketches. The dealer, a plump, smooth, smiling little man, whose morning coat, striped trousers and pearl tie-pin were notably *de rigueur*, greeted Moray with cordial deference, yet with an uncommercial air which assumed his presence in the gallery to be purely casual. They discussed the weather.

'These are quite nice,' Leuschner presently remarked, indicating the folio, when they had finished with the weather. 'And reasonable. Kandinsky is a very underrated man.'

Moray had no interest in Kandinsky's gaunt figures and simian faces, and he suspected that the dealer knew this, yet both

12

spent the next fifteen minutes examining the drawings and praising them. Then Moray took up his hat.

'By the way,' he said offhandedly, 'I suppose you still have the little Vuillard we glanced at last week.'

'Only just.' The dealer suddenly looked grave. 'An American collector is most interested.'

'Rubbish,' Moray said lightly. 'There are no Americans left in Melsburg.'

'This American is in Philadelphia – the Curator of the Art Museum. Shall I show you his telegram?'

Moray, inwardly alarmed, shook his head in a manner implying amused dubiety.

'Are you still asking that ridiculous price? After all, it's only a pastel.'

'Pastel is Vuillard's medium,' Leuschner replied, with calm authority. 'And I assure you, sir, this one is worth every centime of the price. Why, when you consider the other day in London a few rough brush strokes by Renoir, some half-dozen wretched-looking strawberries, a pitiful thing, really, of which the master must have been heartily ashamed, brought twenty thousand pounds. . . . But this, this is a gem, worthy of your fine collection, and you know how rare *good* Post-Impressionists have become, yet I ask only nineteen thousand dollars. If you buy it, and I do not press you, for practically it is almost sold, you will never regret it.'

There was a silence. For the first time they both looked at the pastel which hung alone, against the neutral cartridge paper of the wall. Moray knew it well, it was recorded in the book and it was indeed a lovely thing – an interior, full of light and colour, pinks, greys and greens. The subject too, was exactly to his taste: a conversation piece, Madame Melo and her little daughter in the salon of the actress's house.

A surge of possessive craving tightened his throat. He must have it, he must, to hang opposite his Sisley. It was a shocking price, of course, but he could well afford it, he was rich, far richer even than the good Leuschner had computed, having of course no access to that little black book, locked in the safe, with its fascinating rows of ciphers. And why, after all those years of sterile work and marital strife, should he not have everything he wanted? That snug profit he had recently made in Royal Dutch could not be put to better use. He wrote the cheque, shook hands with Leuschner and went off in triumph, with the pastel carefully tucked beneath his arm. Back at his villa, before Arturo announced lunch, he had time to hang it. Perfect . . . perfect . . . he exulted, standing back. He hoped Frida von Altishofer would admire it.

CHAPTER II

HE HAD INVITED her for five o'clock and, as punctuality was to her an expression of good manners, at that hour precisely she arrived – not however as was customary, in her battered little cream-coloured Dauphine, but on foot. Actually her barracks of a house, the Schloss Seeburg, stood on the opposite shore of the lake, two kilometres across, and as she came into the drawing-room he reproached her for taking the boat, holding both her hands. It was a warm afternoon and the hill path to his villa was steep; he could have sent Arturo to fetch her.

'I don't mind the little ferry.' She smiled. 'As you were so kindly driving me I thought not to bother with my car.'

Her English, though stylised, was perfectly good, with just a faint, and indeed attractive, over-accentuation of certain syllables.

'Well, now you shall have tea. I have ordered it.' He pressed the bell. 'We'll get nothing but watery vermouth at the party.'

'You are most thoughtful.' She sat down gracefully, removing her gloves; she had strong supple fingers, the nails polished but unvarnished. 'I hope you won't be too bored at the Kunsthaus.'

While Arturo wheeled in the trolley and, with bows that were almost genuflections, served the tea, Moray studied her. In her youth she must have been very beautiful. The structure of her facial bones was perfect. Even now at forty-five, or six . . . well, perhaps even forty-seven, although her hair was greying and her skin beginning to show the faint crenellations and brownish stigmata of her years, she remained an attractive woman, with the upright striding figure of a believer in fresh air and exercise. Her eyes were her most remarkable feature, the pupils of a dark tawny yellowish green shot with black specks. 'They are cat's eyes.' She had smiled once when he ventured a compliment. 'But I do not scratch . . . or seldom only.'

Yes, he reflected sympathetically, she had been through a lot, yet never spoke of it. She was horribly hard up and had not many clothes but those she possessed were good and she wore them

15

with style. When they went walking together she usually appeared in a faded costume of russet brown, a rakish *bersagliere* hat, white knitted stockings and strong handsewn brogues of faded brown. Today she had on a simple but well cut fawn suit, shoes of the same shade, as were her gloves, and she was bareheaded. Taste, distinction, and perfect breeding were evident in every look and gesture – no need to tell himself again, she was a cultured woman of the highest class.

'Always what delicious tea you give me.'

'It's Twining's,' he explained. 'I had it specially blended for the hard Schwansee water.'

She shook her head, half reproachfully.

'Really . . . you think of everything.' She paused. 'Yet how wonderful to be able to give effect to all one's wishes.'

A considerable silence followed while they savoured the hard-water tea, then suddenly, an upward glance arrested, she exclaimed:

'My dear friend . . . you have bought it!'

She had seen the Vuillard at last and rising, excitedly, though still skilfully, retaining cup and saucer, she moved across the room to inspect it.

'It is lovely . . . lovely! And looks so much better here than in the gallery. Oh, that so delightful child, on the little stool. I only hope Leuschner did not rob you.'

He stood beside her and together, in silence, they admired the pastel. She had the good taste not to over-praise, but as they turned away, looking around her at the mellow eighteenth-century furniture, the soft grey carpet and the Louis XVI tapestry chairs, at his paintings, his *Pont Aven* Gauguin, signed and dated, above the T'ang figures on the Georgian mantel, the wonderful Degas nude on the opposite wall, the early Utrillo and the Sisley landscape, his richly subdued Bonnard, the deliciously maternal Mary Cassat, and now the Vuillard, she murmured:

'I adore your room. Here you can spend your life in the celebration of beautiful things. And better still when you have earned them.'

'I think I am entitled to them.' He spoke modestly. 'As a young man, in Scotland, I had little enough. Indeed, then I was miserably poor.'

It was a mistake. Once he had spoken the words he regretted

them. Had he not been warned never to look back, only forward, forward, forward. Hastily he said:

'But you . . . until the war, you always lived . . .' he fumbled slightly, '. . . in state.'

'Yes, we had nice things,' she answered mildly.

Again there was silence. The half-smiling reserve she had given to the remark was truly heroic. She was the widow of the Baron von Altishofer, who came of an old Jewish family that had acquired immense wealth from state tobacco concessions in the previous century, with possessions ranging from a vast estate in Bavaria to a hunting lodge in Slovakia. He had been shot during the first six months of the war and, although she was not of his faith, she had spent the next three years in a concentration camp at Lensbach. On her eventual release, she had crossed the Swiss border. All that remained to her was the lakeside house, the Seeburg, and there, though practically penniless, she had striven courageously to rebuild her life. She began by breeding rare Weimaraner dogs. Then, while the ignominy of an ordinary pensionnat was naturally unthinkable, friends – and she had many – came to stay and to enjoy, as paying guests, the spaciousness of the big Germanic schloss and the huge overgrown garden. Indeed, a very exclusive little society had now developed round the Seeburg, of which she herself was the centre. What fun to restore the fine old place, fill it with furniture of the period, replant the garden, recondition the statuary. Had she hinted? Never, never . . . it was his own thought, a flight of fancy. Selfconsciously, rather abruptly, he looked at his watch.

'I think we should be going, if you are ready.'

He had decided to take her to the party in full fig: Arturo wore his best blue uniform, a lighter shade than navy, and they went in the big car. Since this was the only Rolls in Melsburg its appearance always made something of a spectacle.

Seated beside her, as they glided off, his sleeve touching hers on the cushioned armrest, he was in an expansive mood. Although his marriage had been a catastrophic failure he had, since his retirement, seriously considered the prospect of – in Wilenski's vulgar phrase – *having another go*. During the eighteen months they had been neighbours their friendship had developed to such an extent as to induce gradually the idea of a closer companionship. Yet his mind had hitherto dwelt on young and tender images. Frida von Altishofer was not young, in bed she would not prove so succulent as he might wish, and as a man in whom the intensive demands of his late wife had induced a prostatic hypertrophy, he now had needs that should, if only for reasons of health, be satisfied. Nevertheless, Frida was a strong and vital woman with deep though concealed feelings, who might be capable of unsuspected passion. Such, he knew from his medical training, was often the case with women who had passed the menopause. Certainly, in all other respects she would make the most admirable aristocratic wife.

But now they were in the town and sweeping round the public garden with its high central fountain. Arturo drew up, was out in a flash to remove his uniform cap and open the car door. They mounted the steps towards the Kunsthaus.

'Some of my friends in the diplomatic corps may have come up from Bern for this affair. If it wouldn't bore you, you might care to meet them.'

He was deeply pleased. Although not a snob – good heavens, no! – he liked meeting 'the right people'.

'You are charming, Frida,' he murmured, with a sudden quick intimate glance.

CHAPTER III

THE PARTY HAD been in progress for some time: the long hall
was filled with noise and crushed human forms. Most of the
notables of the canton were there, with many worthy burghers of
Melsburg and those of the Festival artistes who had performed
during the final week. These, alas, were mainly of the old brigade
since, unlike the larger resorts of Montreux and Lucerne, Melsburg
was not rich, and between sentiment and lack of funds, the
committee fell back year after year upon familiar names and
faces. Through the haze of cigarette smoke Moray made out
the aged and decrepit figure of Flackmeister, who could barely
totter to the podium, held together by his tight dress coat, green
with the sweat of years beneath the arm holes. And over there
stood Tuberose, the 'cellist, thin, tall as a beanpole, and,
through long clasping of his instrument, very gone about the
knees. He was talking to the superbly bosomed English contralto,
Amy Rivers Fox-Finden. Well, it made no odds, Moray reflected,
gaily edging his way into the crush with his companion, the
applause at the concerts was always rapturous and prolonged,
reminding him, much as he loved his neighbours, of row upon
row of happy sheep flapping their front legs together.

They were served with a beverage of no known species, tepid,
and swimming with fragments of melting ice. She did not drink
hers, merely met his eye in a humorous communicative side
glance which plainly said, 'How wise you were, and how glad I
am of your delicious tea' – almost, indeed, 'and of you!' Then,
with a gentle pressure of the elbow, she steered him across the
room, introduced him first to the German, then to the Austrian
minister. He did not fail to observe the affectionate respect with
which each greeted her, nor her poise in turning away their
compliments. As they moved off Moray was hailed exuberantly
across the press by a sporty British type, all amiable plastic
dentures and alcoholic eyeballs, dressed in a double-breasted,

19

brass-buttoned blue blazer, baggy fawn trousers and scuffed suede shoes.

'So nice to see you, dear boy,' Archie Stench boomed, waving a glass of actual whisky. 'Can't move now. Keep the flag flying. I'll be giving you a ring.'

His face clouding slightly, Moray gave a discouraging answering wave. He did not care for Stench, correspondent of the London *Daily Echo*, who also 'on the side' did a weekly social column for the local *Tageblatt* – airy little items, often with a sting in the tail. Several times Moray had been stung.

Fortunately they were near the far end of the big room where, by the wide bay window, a group of their own particular friends had gathered. Here were demure Madame Ludin of the Europa Hof and her delicate husband, standing with Doctor Alpenstück, grave addict of the higher altitudes. Tall, erect, a noted yodeller in his youth, the worthy doctor never missed a Festival. Beyond, beside the ugly Courtet sisters, at a round table from which, short-sightedly, she had cleared all the cocktail biscuits within reach, sat Gallie, the little old Russian Princess Galliatine, who was stone deaf and rarely spoke a word but went everywhere to eat, even to remove food expertly in the large cracked handbag she always carried, bulging from over-use, and containing papers proving her relationship with the famous Prince Yussapov, husband of the Tsar's niece. A pale, limp little creature with a straggle of worn sable on her neck, whatever the past had done to her it had given her a smile of docile sweetness. Not altogether presentable perhaps – still, an authentic princess. A rather different figure occupied the centre of the group, Leonora Schutz-Spengler, and as they drew near Madame von Altishofer murmured humorously:

'We shall hear the full story of Leonora's hunting trip.'

Pausing in the act of narration, Leonora had already acknowledged them with a brilliant smile. She was a vivacious little brunette from the Tessin, with a red laughing mouth, enterprising eyes and pretty teeth, who some years before had nibbled her way into the heart of Herman Schutz, the richest cheese exporter in Switzerland, a large, pallid, heavy man who seemed fashioned from his own product. Yet Leonora was herself worthy of affection, if only for her splendid and amusing parties, junketings which took place at her hilltop villa above the town, in a candle-lit, red wood outbuilding, the walls bristling with contorted mammalian horns, amongst which scores of budgerigars flew, fluttered, perched and twittered while Leonora, wearing a paper hat, prodigally dispensed bortsch, melon soup, goulash, caviar, cheese blintzes, Pekin duck, truffles in port wine, and other exotic foods; before initiating wild and improbable games, all produced out of her own head.

Moray seldom gave much heed to Leonora's excited ramblings, and his thoughts wandered as, speaking in French, she went on describing the trip from which she and her husband had just returned. Vaguely Moray had heard that Schutz, who late in life had developed ambitions as a *jäger*, was renting a shoot, somewhere in Hungary he believed.

Nevertheless, as Leonora irrepressibly continued, his ear was caught by certain phrases, and with a sharp tightening of his nerves, he began to listen with attention. She was not speaking of Hungary but describing a stretch of Highland countryside in terms which suddenly seemed to him familiar. Impossible: he must be mistaken. Yet as she proceeded, his strained suspicion grew. Now she was speaking of the road uphill from the estuary, of the view of the moor from the summit, the river rushing between the high walls of the corrie into the loch, the mountain dominating all. Suddenly he felt himself tremble, his heart turned over and began to beat rapidly. God, could he ever have imagined this turning up again, so unexpectedly. For she had named the mountain, and the river, and the loch, she named lastly the moor her husband had rented, and these utterly unforeseen words sent a painful shock of shame and apprehension through all his body.

Someone was asking her:

'How did you reach this outlandish place?'

'We went by the most fantastic railway – one narrow line, three trains a day – to an adorable little station with such a pretty name. They call it . . .'

He couldn't bear to hear that name, yet he did hear it, and it brought back, though unspoken, the last unavoidable name of all. He turned, muttering some excuse, and moved off, only to discover Stench good-naturedly at his elbow.

'Not going already, dear boy? Or can't you stand the weirdies any longer?'

Somehow he brushed him aside. In the foyer a draught of cool air revived him, brought some order to his confused mind. He mustn't rush off like this, leaving Madame von Altishofer to

21

return alone. He must wait, find a less crowded place – over there, beside that pillar, near the door. He hoped she would not stay long. Indeed, even as he moved to take up his new position she was beside him.

'My dear friend, you are ill.' She spoke with concern. 'I saw you turn quite pale.'

'I did feel rather queer.' With an effort he forced a smile. 'It's fearfully warm in there.'

'Then we shall go at once,' she said decisively.

He made as if to protest, then dropped it. Outside, Arturo stood talking with a group of chauffeurs. They drove off. She wished to take him directly to his villa but, less from politeness than from a desperate need to be alone, he insisted on leaving her at the Seeburg.

'Come in for a drink,' she suggested, as they arrived. 'A real one.' And when he refused, saying that he should rest, she added solicitously: 'Do take care, my friend. If I may, I will telephone you tomorrow.'

At the villa he lay down for an hour, trying to reason with himself. He must not allow a chance word, a mere coincidence, to wreck the serenity he had so carefully built up. Yet it was no chance word, it was a word that had lain hauntingly, tormentingly in the depths of memory for many years. He must fight it, beat it down again into the darkness of the subconscious. He could not do it, could not seal his mind against the buffeting of his thoughts. At dinner he made only a pretence of eating; his depression filled the house, affecting even the servants, who saw in this unusual mood something reflecting upon themselves.

After the meal he went into the drawing-room, stood by the window opening on the terrace. He saw that a storm was about to break, one of those swift, dazzling exhibitions when, shouting to Arturo to put on a Berlioz record, he would watch and listen with a sense of sheer exhilaration. Now, however, he stood moodily viewing the great mass of umbered cloud which had been gathering, unperceived, drifting above the Riesenberg. The air was deadly still, sultry with silence, the light unnatural; a brooding ochre. And now there came a sighing, faint, as from a distance. The leaves trembled and on the flat surface of the lake a ripple passed. Slowly the sky darkened to dull impenetrable lead, masking the mountain, and all at once from the unseen a fork of blue flashed out, followed by the first crashing detonation. Then came the wind, sudden, searing, a circular wind that cut like a whiplash. Under it, with a shudder, the trees bent and grovelled, scattering leaves like chaff. At the garden end the tall twin poplars scourged the earth. The lake, churned into spume, writhed like a mad thing, waves lashed the little pier, the yellow flag swung up. Lightning now played incessantly, the thunder echoing and re-echoing amongst the hidden peaks. And then the rain, large, solitary, speculative drops, not soothing rain, but rain warning, ominous of what at last struck from above, straight sheets of hissing water, a flooding from the sky – the eventual deluge.

Abruptly he turned from the window and went upstairs to his bedroom, more agitated than ever. In the medicine cupboard in his bathroom he found the bottle of phenobarbitone. He had imagined he would never need it again. He took four tablets. Even so he knew he would not sleep. When he had undressed, he threw himself upon the bed and closed his eyes. Outside the rain still lashed the terrace, the waves still broke upon the shore, but it was her name that kept sounding, sounding in his ears . . . Mary . . . Mary Douglas . . . Mary . . . Douglas . . . bringing him back through the years, to Craigdoran and the days of his youth.

PART TWO

CHAPTER I

IF BRYCE'S ANCIENT motor-cycle had not broken down they would never have met. But as though fated, on that dusty April Saturday afternoon, when he swung back from a spin round the Doran Hills, the driving belt of the near-derelict machine disintegrated, a flying fragment whipping sharp across his right knee. He skidded to a stop, got off stiffly and inspected the damage to his leg, which was less than he had feared, then looked about him. No promise of assistance in the surrounding unpopulated, bracken-covered hills, the wild rush of the river Doran, the wide stretch of moorland threaded by this lonely road and the narrow single-track railway. Even the small station known as Craigdoran Halt, which he had just passed, seemed deserted.

'Damn,' he exclaimed – it couldn't have been more awkward. Ardfillan, the nearest town, must be at least seven miles away; he would have to try the Halt.

Turning, he pushed and limped uphill to the solitary platform, drew the heavy bike back on its stand. The little station was embellished with a border of whitewashed stones, its proud sign 'Gateway to the West Highlands' showered with trailing honeysuckle, a hawthorn hedge shedding blossoms on the track, but he was in no mood to admire. Not a soul in sight, the waiting-room locked, the booking-office closed as for eternity. He was on the point of giving up when in the frosted glass ornamental window stencilled with the words 'Refreshment Room' he caught signs of life: on the inner window-sill a black cat was contentedly washing its face. He pushed on the door, it opened, and he went in.

Unlike the usual station buffet, this was unexpectedly well-ordered and arranged. Four round marble-topped tables occupied the scrubbed boards, there were coloured views of the Highlands upon the walls and, at the far end, a polished mahogany counter behind which hung an oval mirror advertising Brown and Polson's self-raising flour. Before the mirror a young woman was standing with her back towards him, surprised in the act of putting on her hat. Mutually arrested, immobile as waxwork figures, they gazed at each other in the glass.

'When is the next train for Winton?' He broke the silence, addressing her reflection in a tone which failed to conceal his annoyance.

'The last train's gone. There's nothing now till the Sunday-breaker.' She turned and faced him, adding mildly: 'Two o'clock tomorrow afternoon.'

'Where's the porter then?'

'Oh, Dougal's away home this good half hour. Did you not meet him on the road?'

'No . . . I didn't . . .'. He suddenly felt stupidly faint and leaned sideways to support himself against a table, a movement which brought his injured leg into view.

'You've hurt yourself!' she exclaimed, coming forward quickly. 'Here now, sit down and let me see it.'

'It's nothing,' he said, rather dizzily, finding his way to a chair. 'Superficial laceration of the popliteal area. The motor-cycle . . .'

'I thought I heard a bit of a bang. It's a nasty gash, too. Why didn't you speak up at once?'

She was hurrying to get hot water, and presently, kneeling, she had bathed and cleaned the wound and bound it neatly with strips of torn-up napkin.

'There!' On a note of accomplishment she rose. 'If only I had a needle and thread I could stitch up your trouser leg. Never mind, you'll get it done when you're home. What you could do with now is a good cup of tea.'

'No . . . really . . .', he protested. 'I've been a complete nuisance. . . . You've done more than enough for me.'

But she was already busy with the taps of the metal urn on the counter. He had undoubtedly had a shake, and the hot strong tea made him feel better. Watching him with interested curiosity she sat down. Immediately the cat jumped into her lap and began to purr. She stroked it gently.

'Lucky Darkie and me weren't away. There's few enough folks around Craigdoran this early in the year.'

'Or at any other time?' He half smiled.

'No,' she corrected him seriously. 'When the fishing and shooting are on we have a wheen of fine customers. That's why my father keeps this place on. Our bakery is in Ardfillan. If you like we could give you a lift there. He always fetches me at the weekend.' She paused thoughtfully. 'Of course, there's your bike. Is it badly smashed?'

'Not too badly. But I'll have to leave it here. If they'd put it on the Winton train it would be a big help. You see, it's not mine. It belongs to a fellow at the hospital.'

'I don't see why Dougal couldn't slip it in the guard's van as a favour. I'll speak to him first thing Monday. But if your friend's in the hospital he'll not be needing it for a while.'

Amused at her conclusion he explained:

'He's not a patient. A final year medical student, like me.'

'So that's it.' She laughed outright. 'If I'd known I wouldn't have been so gleg at the bandaging.'

Her laughter was infectious, natural, altogether delightful. There was something warm about it, and about her, due not only to her colouring – she had reddish brown hair with gold lights in it and soft brown eyes, dark as peat, set in a fair, slightly freckled skin – but to something sympathetic and outgiving in her nature. She was perhaps four years younger than himself, not more than nineteen, he guessed, and while she was not tall, her sturdy little figure was trim and well proportioned. She wore a tartan skirt, belted with patent leather at the waist, a home-knitted grey spencer, smart well-worn brown brogues, and a little grey hat with a curlew's feather in the brim.

A sudden awareness of her kindness swept over Moray, for him a rare emotion. Yes, she had been decent – that was the word – damned decent to him. And, forgetting the nagging discomfort of his knee and the greater calamity of the damage to his only suit, he smiled at her, this time his own frank, winning smile, that smile which had so often served him through hard and difficult years. Although he had a good brow, regular features, and a fresh skin, with fine light brown naturally wavy hair, he was not particularly good-looking in the accepted sense of the word; the lower part of his face lacked strength. Yet the smile redeemed all his defects, lit up his face, invited comradeship, was filled with promise, expressed interest, understanding and concern at will, and above all radiated sincerity.

'I suppose you realise,' he explained, 'how grateful I am for your extreme kindness. As you've practically saved my life, may I hope that we'll be friends? My name is Moray – David Moray.'

'And I'm Mary Douglas.'

A touch of colour had come into her cheeks but she was not

displeased by this frank introduction. She took the hand he held out to her in a firm clasp.

'Well now,' she said briskly, 'if you like to wheel your bike in here I'll take Darkie and lock up. Father'll be here any minute.'

Indeed, they had barely reached the road outside when a pony and trap appeared over the brow of the hill. Mary's father, to whom Moray was introduced, with the full circumstances of his mishap, was a slight little man with a pale, perky face, hands and nails permanently ingrained with flour, and the bad teeth of his trade. A wisp of hair standing up from his forehead and small, very bright brown eyes gave him an odd, bird-like air.

After turning the pony with practised clickings of his tongue, and studying Moray with shrewd, sidelong glances, he summed up Mary's recital.

'I've no use for these machines myself, as ye may observe. I keep Sammy, the pony, for odd jobs, and I've a good steady Clydesdale to draw my bread van. But it might have been worse. We'll see ye safe on the eight o'clock train from Ardfillan. In the meantime, ye maun just come back and have a bite with us.'

'I couldn't possibly impose on you any more.'

'Don't be ridiculous,' Mary said. 'You've got to meet the rest of the Douglases – and Walter, my fiancé. I'm sure he'll be delighted to get acquainted with you. That's to say,' as a thought occurred to her, 'if your folks won't be anxious about you.'

Moray smiled and shook his head.

'No need to worry. I'm quite on my own.'

'On your own?' Douglas inquired.

'I lost both my parents when I was very young.'

'But ye've got relations, surely?'

'None that I have any need of, or that ever wanted me.' The baker's look of sheer incredulity deepened Moray's smile, caused him to offer a frank explanation. 'I've been alone since I was sixteen. But I've managed to put myself through college one way and another, and by being lucky enough to win an odd bursary or so.'

'Dear me,' reflected the little baker, quietly but with real admiration. 'That's a maist commendable achievement.'

He seemed to ponder the matter as they jogged along. Then, straightening himself, he began with increased cordiality to point out and describe the features of the countryside, many of which, he asserted, were associated with the events of 1314 that preceded the battle of Bannockburn.

'Father's a great reader of Scots history,' Mary confided to Moray in apology. 'There's few quirky things he can't tell you about Bruce, or Wallace, or the rest of them.'

They were now approaching Ardfillan and Douglas drew on the shoe brake to ease the pony as they came down the hill towards the old town lying beneath on the shore of the Firth, shimmering in the hazy sunset. Avoiding the Esplanade, they entered a network of quiet back streets and pulled up before a single-fronted shop with the sign in faded gilt: *James Douglas, Baker and Confectioner*; and beneath, in smaller letters: *Marriages Purveyed*; and again, smaller still: *Established 1880*. The place indeed wore an old-fashioned air, and one that seemed scarcely prosperous, since the window displayed no more than a many-tiered model of a wedding cake, flanked by a pair of glass urns containing sugar biscuits.

Meanwhile the baker had sheathed his whip. He shouted:
'Willie!'

A bright young boy in an oversized apron that reached from heel to chin ran out of the shop.

'Tell your aunt we're back, son; then skep round and give me a hand with Sammy.'

With considerable skill Douglas backed the pony through the adjacent narrow pend into a cobbled stable yard.

'Here we are then,' he announced cheerfully. 'Take your invalid upstairs, Mary. I'll be with ye the now.'

They went up by a shallow curving flight of outside stone steps to the house above the shop, where a narrow lobby gave entrance to the front parlour, furnished in worn red plush with tasselled curtains of the same material. In the centre of the room a heavy mahogany table was already set for high tea, and a coal fire glowed comfortably in the grate, before which a black sheep-skin rug spread a cosy, tangled pelt. Darkie, released from Mary's arms, immediately took possession of it. She had taken off her spencer, now seemed at home in her neat white blouse.

'Sit down and rest your leg. I'll run down for a wee minute and see to things. We close at six this evening.' She added, with a touch of pride: 'Father doesn't go in for the Saturday night trade.'

When she had gone Moray eased himself into a chair, acutely

aware of the strangeness of this dim, warm, alien room. A coal dropped quietly to the hearth. From a dark corner came the measured tick-tock of a grandfather clock, unseen but for the glint of firelight on its old brass dial. The blue willow-pattern cups on the table caught the light too. Why on earth was he here, rather than bent strainingly over Osler and Cunningham in the cramped attic that was his lodging? He had taken a spin to clear his head – his one practical concession to leisure – before settling down to a long weekend grind. But with his final examination only five weeks away it was lunacy to waste time here, in this unprofitable manner. And yet, these people were so hospitable, and the food on the table looked so damned inviting. With his money running out it was weeks since he had eaten a proper square meal.

The door opened suddenly and Mary was back, carrying a tea tray and accompanied by a stout, dropsical-looking woman and a tall, thin man of about twenty-six or seven, very correct in a dark blue suit and high stiff collar.

'Here's some more of us,' Mary laughed. 'Aunt Minnie and,' she blushed slightly, 'my intended, Mr Walter Stoddart.'

As she spoke her father appeared with the boy, Willie, and after the baker had muttered a quick grace, they all sat down at table.

'I am led to believe,' Stoddart, who, while Mary poured the tea, had been served first with cold ham and great deference by Aunt Minnie, now addressed himself to Moray with a polite smile, 'that you have had a somewhat trying experience. I myself had a somewhat similar adventure on the Luss road when a boy. When was it now, let me see, ah, yes, in nineteen oh nine, that hot summer we had. I was just thirteen years of age and growing fast. A push bicycle, naturally, in that era, and a punctured tyre. Fortunately I sustained nothing more serious than an abrasion of the left elbow, though it might well have been a tragedy. May I trouble you for another sugar, Mary. You know, I think, that my preference is for three lumps.'

'Oh, I'm sorry, Walter dear.'

Stoddart, evidently, was regarded, not only by himself, but by the family, as a person of definite importance. And presently Aunt Minnie, who seemed his chief admirer, conveyed to Moray in a whispered, wheezy aside that Walter was the Town Clerk's son, with a splendid position in the accounts department of the

Gas Department – a real catch for Mary, she supplemented with a meaning, satisfied nod.

The situation intrigued Moray, provoked his sense of humour. Walter's excruciating mannerisms, his condescension towards the Douglases exercised with all the stiff assertiveness of the small-town bureaucrat, even the ostrich-like convulsion of his long thin neck when he drank his tea – all these gave promise of entertainment. While doing full justice to the good things on the table, it amused him to cultivate Stoddart, playing a little on his vanity, and at the same time defining his own position, as co-equal, by relating, in a racy style, some of the more interesting aspects of his work in the out-patient's department of the Infirmary. It was not long before he was rewarded by indications of Walter's growing esteem. Indeed as the meal drew to its close, Stoddart took out his gold watch and clicked it open – this was another and frequent mannerism – meanwhile favouring Moray with a toothy smile.

'It's a great pity I am obliged to leave you so soon. I'm escorting Mary to the Band of Hope Social. Otherwise I should have been delighted to have more of your company. However, I have a suggestion. I am of the opinion that it would be highly irregular for you to convey your motor-cycle to Winton without a ticket, sub rosa, as the saying is, in the manner indicated to me by Mary. It might expose you to all sorts of pains and penalties. After all, the North British Railway does not frame its code of by-laws for fun! Huh, huh! Now what I propose,' he smiled hospitably around the table, 'is that our friend Moray secure the spare part in Winton, travel down next weekend, fit the part, and drive the machine back. This, naturally, will afford us the opportunity of meeting with him again.'

'What a good idea,' Mary glowed. 'Why on earth didn't we think of it.'

'*We*, Mary?' queried Walter, repocketing the watch with dignity. 'I fancy that I . . .'.

'Ay, ye're a knowledgeable chap, Walter. I don't know what we'd do without ye,' interposed the little baker, glancing towards Moray with an ironic twinkle, which indicated that he did not altogether subscribe to the prevailing view of Stoddart's accomplishments. 'Come by all means, lad. Ye'll be verra welcome.'

It was settled, then, and when Mary rose to put on her hat and coat and, accepting the invitation of Walter's crooked arm, was led off by him to the Church Social, she smiled at Moray over her shoulder.

'We'll see you next Saturday, so I won't say goodbye.'

'Nor will I.' Walter bowed. 'I hope to have the pleasure of your further acquaintance.'

Half an hour later Moray left for the station. Willie, who had listened with bright eyes to his stories of the hospital, insisted on accompanying him.

MORAY'S LODGING was a small room at the top of a back-to-back tenement near the Blairlaw Docks. The neighbourhood, shut in by a disused city dump known locally as the Tipps, was undoubtedly one of the poorest in Winton. Ragged, rickety children played on the broken, chalk-marked pavements while the women stood gossiping, in shawl and cap, outside the 'close-mouths'. On every street there was a pub or a fish-and-chip shop, while, through the Clydeside fog, the three brass balls of the pawnbroker beckoned irresistibly. Tugs hooted from the river and incessant hammering came from the repair yards. The district was certainly not a pleasure resort, but by cutting over Blairhill into Eldongrove it was within reasonable walking distance of the University and the Western Infirmary. Above all, it was cheap.

The brief though striking account Moray had given Baker Douglas of himself was thus, in some respects, though not in all, the truth. The first twelve years of his life, as an only child of indulgent middle-class parents, had been normal; never affluent, but easy and comfortable. Then his father, local agent of the Caledonia Insurance Company in Overton, had come down with i fluenza, contracted, it was thought, during his door-to-door collections. For a week his wife nursed him while he grew worse. A specialist was called in, and abruptly the diagnosis was altered to typhoid fever, but not before she, too, had contracted the disease. Within the month David found himself thrown upon a distant relative, the widowed half-sister of his mother, a burden accepted unwillingly, an unwanted child. For four years young Moray had undoubtedly suffered neglect, eaten the bitter bread of dependence, but at the age of sixteen an educational policy, prudently taken out by his father, had come into force. It was not much, sufficient only for fees, and a bare subsistence, but it was enough and, helped by a sympathetic schoolmaster who recognised unusual possibilities in his pupil, he had entered for the medical curriculum of Winton University.

But this providential provision was something which Moray, from motives of expediency, or a natural tendency to dramatise his own efforts, sometimes conveniently forgot. With his diffident charm that made most people take to him on sight, it was agreeable, and often helpful, to hint at the tight corners he had been in, the shifts and evasions he had been forced into, the indignities he had endured – shaking the fleas from his trouser ends, using the public convenience on the stair-head, washing his own shirt, eating chips from a greasy newspaper, sustained only by a heroic determination to raise himself out of the ruck and attain the heights.

Admittedly there had been diversions, occasional meals at the home of his friend Bryce, or, through the kindness of one of the Infirmary staff, a free theatre or concert ticket would come his way; and once, in the summer vacation, he had spent an exceptional week at the seaside house of his biology professor. Certainly he had made the most of his opportunities, not only by the profusion of his gratitude when anything was done for him but by a particular earnestness of manner, quite touching, that inspired confidence and affection. 'So good of you to give me a leg-up, sir,' or, 'Jolly decent of you, old chap.' With that modest, self-disparaging expression and those clear, frank eyes, who could help liking him? He was so absolutely sincere. The truth is that, when he was in the mood, he believed everything he said.

But entertainments are never a conspicuous feature of Scottish universities and in recent months they had been few. For this reason alone his encounter with the Douglas family held the attraction of the unusual. During the week, while he attended the Infirmary by day and studied late at night, it remained agreeably at the back of his mind. He found himself looking forward to his visit on the following Saturday.

The morning came grey but fine. After attending out-patients in the forenoon, he took the one o'clock 'workman's special' from Winton Central. This was a low-fare train – the price of the ticket, unbelievably, was fourpence – which ran down the Clyde estuary, serving the shipyard workers en route. He had the new belt with him – Bryce, anticipating trouble, had actually bought it as a spare some weeks before, and had willingly turned it over to him in his easy-going style. At Levenford Junction he changed to the single line, and just after half-past two, as the sun was breaking through the clouds, drew into Craigdoran.

The little white station with its flowering hawthorn and tangle of climbing honeysuckle now wore a familiar aspect. The scent of the honeysuckle filled the air and he heard the hum of an early bee. Two youths, dressed for climbing, with packs on their backs, got out of the train before him. They went into the refreshment room where, peering through the ground-glass window, he saw Mary wrap in waxed paper the sandwiches they bought. Then the youths came out and Mary, following them to the door, looked searchingly along the platform.

'It's you.' She smiled. 'I was beginning to be afraid you'd not come. Is your knee better?'

She beckoned him in, made him sit down. The cat approached and rubbed against his leg.

'I'm sure you've not had your lunch. I'll fetch you some sandwiches and a glass of milk.'

'Please don't,' he said. 'I've had a snack . . . in the . . . the buffet at Levenford Junction.'

'Dear me,' she said quizzically, rather like her father, raising her brows. 'That's extraordinar' peculiar. There never has been a buffet at the Junction.' From the glass bell on the counter she took a plate of sandwiches, then poured a frothing glass of milk. 'There'll be scarcely another soul in here over the weekend and I can't see good food go to waste. You'll just have to oblige me, this once.'

A moment later she seated herself opposite him, struggling, it seemed, against some inner effervescence which grew suddenly beyond control.

'I have news for you,' she exclaimed. 'You've made a most tremendous hit.'

'What!' He drew back, misunderstanding her.

'Walter,' her lips twitched, 'has taken the greatest notion of you. Ever since you left he's done nothing but sing your praises. You're such a nice young fellow.' She fought down laughter. 'He's quite cut up at missing you tonight – he's attending a meeting of the Municipal Officials' Guild in Winton – and I'm to give you his best regrets.' She went on before he could speak. 'He's fixed up a rare jaunt for us tomorrow. We're to sail round the Kyles of Bute, stop for lunch at Gairsay, then back home.'

He stared at her with a blank frown.

'But I can't possibly come down again tomorrow.'

'No need to,' she said calmly. 'Father says you're to stay over with us. You can sleep with our Willie.'

Still he frowned at her; then, gradually, his brow cleared. Never had he met such simple, open-hearted people. He had no out-patients at the Infirmary tomorrow, and surely would not lose much by missing just one day's work. Besides, Sunday in Winton was an unspeakable day which he had always loathed.

'You'll come?' she queried.

'With pleasure. And now I must mend the bike.'

'It's in the left luggage. Dougal put it there out of the way.'

For the next hour he worked, fitting the new belt, which had to be cut and riveted. She came in occasionally to watch, not saying anything, just watching companionably. When he had finished he wheeled out the machine and started it up.

'How about a spin?'

She looked at him doubtfully, a hand on her ear against the frantic blast of the exhaust.

'It's quite safe,' he reassured her. 'You just sit on the carrier and hold tight.'

'I can't get away till the four-thirty comes in. But afterwards, maybe you could take me home. I could ring up Father from the booking office and spare him coming out.'

'That's settled then,' he said gaily.

An unusual mood of lightheartedness took possession of him. Whether due to his escape from work, or the fresh green country-side, he felt lifted up, as though breathing a rarer, brighter air. Until she should be free, and to test the machine, he took a fast run over the hill to Tulliehewan. When he returned, she was all ready to leave. Since Darkie must stay behind she had set out a saucer of milk for his supper.

'So this is where I get on,' she said, perching side-saddle on the carrier.

'You can't sit like that. You'll fall off. You must sit astride.'

She hesitated, then swung one leg across, modestly, yet so inexpertly that before he averted his eyes a sweet prospect was momentarily revealed to him. Blushing, she said:

'I'm not quite up to it yet.'

'You're doing famously.'

Quickly he got into the saddle and set off. At first he went slowly, carefully avoiding the bumps, then, as he felt her gain confidence, he opened the throttle. They tore along, over the moors, the wind whistling past their ears. Her arms were clasped round his waist, her head, turned sideways, was pressed against his shoulder.

'Are you all right?' he shouted.

'Fine,' she called back.

'Enjoying it?'

'It's . . . it's glorious. I've never gone so fast in all my life.'

They were doing at least thirty miles an hour.

When he pulled up at the shop in Ardfillan her cheeks were glowing, her hair blown and burnished by the breeze.

'What a treat.' She laughed into his eyes, swaying a trifle unsteadily, still drunk with speed. 'Come on up. I must run and tidy. I'm sure I'm a perfect sight.'

His welcome by the baker was cordial, and by Willie even more enthusiastic than before. The aunt, however, seemed to accept him with fresh reservations, her eye speculative, at times tending coldly towards suspicion – though he softened her later by listening attentively to her symptoms and suggesting a cordial that might help her shortness of breath. The meal she set before them was macaroni cheese, a wholesome repast though lacking, inevitably, in those refinements that had been produced for Walter. Thereafter the evening passed quietly, Moray played draughts with the baker and was handsomely beaten three times in a row, while Mary, on a low stool by the fireside, worked on a piece of crochet which was clearly intended for her trousseau. Watching it develop, he could not help wondering if it was an edging for a nightdress – a warm, indulgent thought, not lewd. From time to time she would look at the clock and remark, with sedate concern, wholly unlike the girl full of humour and high spirits who had whirled gaily through space with him only an hour ago: 'Walter will be at his meeting now.' And again: 'Surely he'll get a chance to give his speech. He wrote it all out so careful, and was so set on making it.' And finally: 'He should be on his way to the train by this time. I hope he remembered his overshoes, he's such a martyr to cold feet.'

They all retired early. In Willie's back room, which overlooked the yard, Moray had his first real talk with the boy, whose shyness had hitherto kept him silent. It appeared that as a school prize he had recently received an exciting book on David Livingstone, and soon they were in the wilds of Africa together, discovering Lake Nyanza, deploring the ravages of beri-beri and the tsetse fly. Moray had to answer a spate of eager questions, but at last he turned out the light and presently they were asleep.

CHAPTER III

NEXT MORNING WALTER arrived punctually at half-past nine, greeting Moray like an old friend, full of his success on the previous evening. Although a number of ill-bred bounders had left the hall before the conclusion of his address, he had spoken extremely well, and for a good three-quarters of an hour. Having fully earned this day of relaxation he was in the mood to enjoy it. Nothing had pleased him more, he added, than to organise the expedition.

This bumptious effusiveness puzzled Moray. Was there a streak of the woman in Walter or did he, as a man consistently rebuffed by his fellows, so lack male companionship that he fastened on to the first newcomer who came along? Perhaps the prestige of a future doctor attracted him, for he was patently a snob. Or it might be that through vanity he was simply bent on demonstrating his own importance to someone new to the town. With a shrug, Moray gave up.

Mary and her brother had been ready for some time and now they set out, Walter leading the party along the Esplanade towards the pier, obviously determined to do things in style. At the steamer booking office he demanded first-class return tickets, adding casually:

'Three and a half: the boy is under age.'

The booking clerk turned a practised eye on Willie.

'Four full fares,' he said.

'I believe I asked for three and a half.'

'Four,' said the clerk in a tired voice.

An argument then ensued, brief yet fierce on Walter's side, ending when Willie, interrogated by the clerk, truthfully gave his age, thus disqualifying himself from the reduced rate. Not a good start, thought Moray, ironically observing Walter slap down the extra coins with an injured air.

The little red-funnelled paddle-boat came spanking down river and alongside the pier. She was the *Lucy Ashton*. Walter, somewhat recovered, explained to Moray that all the North British boats were named after characters in Scott's novels, but he seemed disappointed that they were not to have the *Queen Alexandra*, the new two-funnelled Caledonian turbine; its absence seemed a slight impairment of his prestige.

The gangway was skilfully run out, they went on board, and, looking around, he selected seats in the stern. Then the paddles churned and they were off, across the sparkling estuary and out towards the open firth.

'Delightful, is it not?' Walter murmured, settling back. Things were going better now.

But it was fresh upon the water and before long it became apparent that the situation he had chosen was exposed.

'Don't you think it's a little breezy on this side, dear?' Mary ventured, after several minutes. Head inclined to the wind, she was holding on to her hat.

'Not a bit of it,' Walter answered curtly. 'I want to show Dr Moray all our local points of interest. This gives us an uninterrupted view.'

The view – undoubtedly unimpaired, since most of the other passengers were in the lee of the cabin – was quite lovely, perhaps the most beautiful in all the Western Highlands. But Walter, though complacently owning its charm with all the proprietorship of a cicerone, was more concerned with the commercial import of the towns which fringed the shore.

'That's Scourie over there.' He pointed. 'A thriving community. They put in a new gasholder last year. Twenty thousand cubic feet capacity. There's progress for you. And they have a new sewage disposal project up before the town council. My father knows the Provost. And across on the other side is Port Doran. Can you make out the municipal buildings behind that steeple . . . ?'

They were all steadily getting colder. Even Willie had turned blue, and had departed, muttering that he was going to look at the engines. But Walter went remorselessly on. What a goddam bore, thought Moray, with his legs stretched out and hands in his pockets. Scarcely listening now, he was watching Mary who, though very silent, occasionally put in a dutiful word of support. He saw that her entire nature changed in the presence of her fiancé. Her sparkle died, all the fun went out of her, she became reserved, sealed up, conscientiously obedient, like a good pupil

42

in the presence of her teacher. She'll have a hell of a life with that fellow when they're married, he reflected absently – the wind and Walter's monologue were making him drowsy.

At last they threaded the Kyles, swung into Gairsay Bay, and manoeuvred to the pier. Willie, after a search, was retrieved from the warmth of the engine-room and they went ashore.

'This is nice,' breathed Mary, with relief.

The town, a popular resort, had an attractive and prosperous air: a circle of good shops on the front, the hotels mounting up on the wooded hill behind, moorland and mountain beyond.

'And now for lunch,' Walter exclaimed, in the manner of one who has something up his sleeve.

'Oh, yes,' Mary said cheerfully. 'Let's go to Lang's. There it is, quite handy.' She indicated a modest but promising-looking restaurant across the road.

'My dear,' Walter said, 'I wouldn't dream of taking Dr Moray to Lang's. Or you either, for that matter.'

'We always go there when we come with Father,' Willie remarked dourly. 'They have rare hot mutton pies. And Comrie's lemonade.'

'Yes, let's, Walter dear.'

He stilled her with a raised, gloved hand and calmly produced his *pièce de résistance* of the day.

'We are going to lunch at the Grand.'

'Oh, no, Walter. Not the Grand. It's so . . . so snobby . . . and expens . . .'.

Walter threw an intimate, confidential smile at Moray, as though to say, These women!

'It's the best,' he murmured. 'I have reserved a table in advance from my father's office.'

They began to climb the hill towards the Grand, which towered majestically, high above them. The footpath was long, through woods carpeted with bluebells, and steep, in parts excessively so. Occasionally between the trees they caught sight of expensive cars flashing upwards on the main driveway. Moray perceived that the ascent, which Stoddart led like a deerstalker, was tiring Mary. To allow her to rest he stopped and picked a little bunch of bluebells which he tied with a twist of dried grass, and handed to her.

'Exactly the colour of your dress.' He smiled.

At last they reached the summit and Walter, sweating, breathing heavily, brought them on to the broad terrace of the hotel where a number of guests were seated in the sunshine. An immediate silence fell as the little party appeared, some curious stares were turned towards it, and someone laughed. The main entrance was on the opposite side of the hotel and Walter had some difficulty in finding the terrace door. But finally, after some wandering, they were in the rich, marble-pillared foyer and Stoddart, having asked directions from an imposing figure in a gold-braided uniform, led the way to the restaurant, a huge, overpowering affair done in white and gold with enormous crystal chandeliers and a rich red pile carpet.

It was absurdly early, only just gone twelve o'clock, and although the waiters were on duty, gathered in a group round the head waiter's desk talking amongst themselves, no one else was in the room.

'Yes, sir?'

The head waiter, a stout, red-faced man in striped trousers, white waistcoat and cutaway, detached himself and came dubiously forward.

'Lunch for three, and a boy,' Stoddart said.

'This way, please.'

His hooded eye had taken them in at a glance: he appeared to lead them off to a distant alcove in the rear, when Walter said pompously:

'I want a table by the window. I have a reservation in the name of the town clerk of Ardfillan.'

The major domo hesitated: he smells a tip, thought Moray satirically, and how wrong he is!

'By the window did you say, sir?'

'That table over there.'

'Sorry, sir. That table is specially reserved for Major Lindsay of Lochshiel and his party of young English gentlemen.'

'The one next it then.'

'That is Mr Menzies' table, sir. A resident. Still, as he rarely comes in before one fifteen, and you'll doubtless have finished by then. . . . If you care to have it . . .?'

They were seated at Mr Menzies' table. The menu was handed to Walter. It was in Anglicised French.

'Potage à la Reine Alexandra,' he began, reading it through to them, slowly, remarking complacently, in conclusion:

'Nothing like French cooking. And five courses too.'

While they sat in solitary state the meal was served, rapidly, and with veiled insolence. It was atrocious, a typical Grand Hotel luncheon, but below the usual standard. First came a thick yellowish soup composed apparently of flour and tepid water; next, a bony fragment of fish which had probably travelled from Aberdeen to Gairsay by the long way through Billingsgate, a fact only partially concealed by a coating of glutinous pink sauce.

'It's not fresh, Mary,' Willie whispered, leaning towards her.

'Hush, dear,' she murmured, struggling with the bones, sitting very straight, her eyes on her plate. Moray saw that under her apparent calm she was suffering acutely. For himself, he did not, in his own phrase, care a tinker's curse – he was not personally involved – but strangely it worried him to see her hurt. He tried to think of something light and gay that would cheer her but it would not come to him. Across the table Walter was now chewing his way through the next course, a slab of stringy mutton served with tinned peas and potatoes which cut and tasted like soap.

The sweet was a chalky blancmange accompanied by tough prunes. The savoury, which followed swiftly, for now they were really being rushed, took the shape of a stiff, spectral sardine, emitting a kind of bluish radiance, and impaled on a strip of desiccated toast. Then, though it was not yet one o'clock and no other guests had as yet appeared, the bill was brought.

If Stoddart had paid this immediately and they had departed forthwith all would have been well. But by this time Walter, through his unfeeling hide, had become conscious of a sense of slight, scarcely to be tolerated by the son of the Ardfillan town clerk. Besides, he had an actuarial mind. He withdrew one of the pencils with which his waistcoat was invariably armed, and began to make calculations on the bill. As he did so a tall, rakish-looking, weatherbeaten man, grey-haired, with a clipped moustache, wearing a faded Black Watch kilt, strolled in from the bar. He was followed by three young men in rough tweeds who had all, Moray immediately perceived, had more than a few drinks. As they took possession of the adjoining table they were noisily discussing how they had fished a beat on the River Gair – apparently the property of the man in the kilt. One of the three, a flashy-looking article, with blond hair and a slack mouth, was rather less than sober, and as he sat down his eye fell on Mary.

Turning, he lolled over the back of his chair, began ogling her while the waiter served their first course, then, with a nudge and a wink, diverted the attention of his companions.

'There's a nice little Scotch trout, Lindsay. Better than anything you landed this morning.'

There was a general laugh as the other two turned to stare at Mary.

'Come now, get on with your soup,' said Lindsay.

'Oh, hang the soup. Let's have the little lady over to our table. She doesn't seem too happy with her Scotch uncle. What do you say, chaps? Shall I do the needful?'

He looked at the others for confirmation and encouragement.

'You'll never chance it, Harris,' grinned one of his friends.

'What do you bet?' He pushed back his chair and got up.

Walter, disturbed at his mathematics, had been nervously aware of them from the moment they entered the room. Now, extremely grey about the gills, he averted his head.

'Take no notice,' he muttered. 'They won't let him come over.'

But Harris was already advancing and with an exaggerated bow he leant over Mary, took possession of her hand.

'Pardon me, my dear. May we have the pleasure of your company?'

Moray saw her shrink back. She had at first blushed deeply but now all the colour had drained from her face. Her lips were colourless and quivering. She looked pleadingly at Walter. Willie too was staring at Stoddart with wide, frightened, yet indignant eyes.

'Sir,' Walter stammered, swallowing with difficulty, 'are you aware you are addressing my fiancée? This is an imposition. I shall be obliged to summon the manager.'

'Quiet, Uncle. We're not interested in you. Come along, dearie.' He tried to draw her to her feet. 'We'll give you a ripping time.'

'Please go,' Mary said in a small, pained voice.

Something in the tone struck home. He hesitated, then with a grimace released her hand.

'No accounting for tastes.' He shrugged. 'Well, if I can't have you, I'll take a lee-itle souvenir.' He picked up Mary's flowers and, pressing them affectedly to his lips, wavered back to his place.

46

There was a hollow silence. Everyone seemed to be looking at Walter. In particular the man in the weather-stained kilt was observing him with a cruelly satiric twist of his lip. Walter, indeed, was pitifully agitated. Forgetting his intention to query the bill, he fumbled in his pocket-book, hurriedly threw down some notes, and rose like a ruffled hen.

'We are leaving now, Mary.'

Moray got up. There was nothing heroic in his nature, he had no strong leanings towards mortal combat, but he was angry – most of all perhaps at his own wasted day. And a sudden nervous impulse, almost predestined, sent him over to the other table, down at Harris, who did not seem greatly to relish his appearance.

'Weren't you told to get on with your soup? It's a little late now. But let me help you.'

Taking him by the back of the neck, Moray pushed him forward, ground his face hard once, twice, three times into the plate of soup. It was the thick soup, the Potage â la Reine Alexandra. which in the interim had nicely set, so that Harris came up for breath dripping with yellowish glue. Dead silence from the others while, with a swimming motion, he groped for his napkin. Moray picked up the bunch of bluebells, gave them back to Mary, waited a minute with a fast beating heart, then as nothing seemed to happen, except that now the man in the kilt was smiling, he followed the others from the restaurant. Outside, on the steps, Willie was waiting for him. The boy wrung his hand fervently, again and again.

'Well done, Davie. Oh, man, I like ye fine.'

'There was no need for you to interfere,' Walter broke out, as they started down through the woods. 'We were completely within our rights. As if decent people couldn't have a meal in peace. I know about that Lindsay – a kailyard laird – not a fish or a bird on his property, he'll rent to the lowest cockneys from London, but I'll . . . I'll report the matter . . . to the authorities. I won't let it pass, it's a public scandal.' He continued in this strain until they reached the pier, dwelling largely on the rights of the individual and the dignity of man, and concluding with a final vindictive burst. 'I shall certainly put the entire affair before my father.'

'And what will he do?' Willie said. 'Turn off your gas?'

The return journey was sad and silent. It had started to drizzle and they sat in the saloon. Nursing his injuries, Walter had at last ceased his monologue, while Mary, who gazed fixedly ahead, uttered scarcely a word. Willie had taken Moray away to show him the engines.

At Ardfillan, Walter, with a forgiving air, offered his arm to Mary. They walked to the bakery and into the yard, where Moray started up his bike.

'Well,' Walter moodily extended his hand, 'I don't suppose we'll meet again . . . '.

'Come again soon,' Willie cut in quickly. 'Be sure and come.'

'Goodbye, Mary,' Moray said.

For the first time since they left the hotel she looked at him, breathing quickly and with moist eyes. She remained silent, quite silent. But in that steady glance there was something lingering and intense. He saw too that she was no longer holding the little bunch of bluebells: she had pinned them to her blouse and was wearing them upon her breast.

CHAPTER IV

AT THE END of the following week Moray had a real stroke of luck. By special favour of the registrar he was moved from the out-patients' department of the Infirmary and given a month's appointment as house assistant in Professor Drummond's wards, which meant, of course, that he could leave his wretched lodging and live in hospital until his final examination. It was Professor Drummond who, after listening to Moray interrogate a patient, had once remarked, though somewhat dryly: 'You'll get on, my boy. You've the best bedside manner of any student I've ever known.' Moreover, Drummond was one of the examiners in clinical medicine, a significant fact that did not escape Moray and which he intended to make the most of during the next four weeks. He would be alert and assiduous, available at all hours, a demon for work, a regular fixture in the ward. For an eager and willing young man there seemed little hardship in this prospect. Yet in one sense it caused Moray an unaccountable vexation: he would be unable to take sufficient time off to make the journey to Ardfillan.

Ever since that moment of departure after the return from Gairsay, strange forces had been at work in his absorbed and ambitious soul. Mary's final glance, so quiet and intense, had struck him like a wounding arrow. He could not escape the vision of her strained little face, nor – and this was most ominous – did he wish to do so. Despite all his precautions, at odd moments of the day, in the ward or the test room, he would discover himself gazing absently into space. It was she whom he saw, in all her sweetness and simplicity, and he would then be seized by a longing to be with her, the wish to win a smile from her, to be acknowledged as her friend – he did not so far permit himself to frame a stronger and more compromising word.

He had hoped there might be news from her, or from her father, perhaps another invitation which, though he could not accept it, would give him the opportunity to get in touch with the family again. Why did he not hear from them? Since all the attentions had come from their side he had no wish to impose himself further without some hint that he would be welcome. Yet surely he must do something . . . something to clear up this . . . well, this uncertainty. At last, after ten days, when he had brought himself to a state of considerable tension, a postcard, showing a view of Ardfillan, arrived for him at the hospital. Its message was brief.

Dear David,
    I hope you are well. I have been reading more about Africa. There's been some ructions here. When are you coming to see us? I've been missing you.
                                    Yours ever,
                                        Willie.

That same day, immediately the evening round was over, he went into the side room and telephoned Ardfillan. After some delay he was put through to the Douglas shop. Aunt Minnie's voice came to him over the humming line.

'This is David Moray,' he said. 'I had such a nice card from Willie, I thought I'd ring up and see how you were all getting on.'

There was a slight, though definitive pause.

'We are quite well, thank you.'

The coldness of her tone took him aback. He hesitated, then said:

'I have a new job here which keeps me on the go. Otherwise I'd have been in touch with you before.'

She did not answer. He persisted.

'Is Willie there? I'd like to thank him for his card.'

'Willie is at his lessons. I'm afraid I can't disturb him.'

'Mary, then?' He plunged on, almost desperately. 'I would like a word with her.'

'Mary is out at present. With her young man. She has been a trifle poorly lately, but now she has quite recovered. I don't expect her back till late.'

Now he was silent. After a moment, he said, very awkwardly:

'Well, I wish you'd tell her I rang up . . . and give her my best regards.'

He could hear her sharp intake of breath. Her words came with a rush, as though she found them difficult, but felt constrained to get them out.

'I cannot undertake to give any such message, and I hope you won't attempt to repeat it. Furthermore, Mr Moray, although I've no wish to hurt your feelings, it will be best for everyone, including yourself, if you refrain in the future from forcing yourself upon us.'

The receiver at the other end went down with a click. He hung up slowly and turned away, blinking, as if he'd been hit in the face. What was wrong? Forcing himself upon them! What had he done to deserve such an unexpected and stinging rebuff? Back in the resident's office at the end of the corridor he sat down at the desk and tried to find the answer.

The aunt had never been too favourably disposed towards him, and because of her frequent headaches – due, he suspected, to a chronic nephritis – her temper was often, and understandably, short. Yet surely the cause lay deeper – probably in her devotion to Stoddart, coupled with the sudden dislike which Walter had apparently developed towards him. Reasoning in this fashion, though rather dejectedly, Moray still could not believe that Mary was a party to his abrupt dismissal, and on an impulse he took a sheet of prescription paper from the drawer and wrote her a short letter, asking if there might not be some opportunity of meeting her. As he was on emergency duty that night he could not leave the hospital even for a moment, but he got one of the probationers to go out and post the letter.

During the next few days, he awaited an answer with increasing impatience and anxiety. He had almost given up when, towards the end of the week, it arrived.

Dear David,

I shall be coming to Winton with my aunt to do some shopping on Thursday the 9th. If you can manage to be at the clock in the Caledonian Station about six o'clock I believe I could meet you there, but only for half an hour, since I must take the half-past six train home. I do trust that you are well and not working too hard.

Mary.

PS. Willie hopes you received his postcard.

The letter was as lifeless as a railway timetable, yet beneath

51

its dullness ran an undercurrent which stirred Moray deeply. The absence of that animation which she had displayed, which indeed marked everything she had ever done in his company, was painfully evident to him. But he would see her on Thursday next. This at least had been gained.

When the day came his plans were already made. He had arranged with Kerr, another houseman, to take over for two hours in the evening. Professor Drummond never made his evening visit until eight o'clock, so with luck he would be safe. The afternoon had turned wet and a fog was settling on the city as he left the hospital and boarded a yellow tram at Eldongrove. He feared he might be late, but well before the appointed time he was in the Caledonian Station, standing beneath the big central clock. The rush hour was in progress and under the high glass dome, impenetrably coated with the grime of years, crowds were streaming towards the local trains. The place reeked of steam, fog and sulphur fumes, echoed with the shrill blast of departing engines. From the underground platforms of the 'low level' a poisonous smoke welled up in snakey coils as from the inferno.

The clock struck six. Searching amongst all those unknown faces, Moray at last caught sight of her. His heart throbbed as she came towards him, carrying a number of parcels, looking unusually small and unprotected in that thrusting mob. She was wearing a dark brown costume with a short jacket, a thin necklet of fur and small brown hat. Nothing could have better suited her. He had never seen her so formally dressed. It gave her an unsuspected distinction and suddenly he coveted her.

'Mary!' He relieved her of her parcels, untwisting the string from her small gloved fingers. She smiled at him, a trifle wanly, for she seemed tired. The fog had smeared her cheek and marked faint shadows under her eyes.

'So you managed to get away?'

'Yes,' he said, looking at her. There was silence between them, then he added: 'You've been shopping?'

'There were some things I had to get. Aunt Minnie's had a regular field day.' She was making an effort to speak lightly. 'Now she's gone to see a friend . . . or I couldn't have got away.'

'Can't you stay longer?'

She shook her head, with lowered gaze.

'They'll be meeting me at Ardfillan.'

Was there a hint of surveillance in her answer? Whether or

not, her apparent fatigue troubled him, as did her listless tone, the manner in which she hesitated to meet his eye.

'You look as though you needed your tea. Shall we go in there?'

He pointed with some misgivings to the buffet which, flaring with light and packed to the doors, bore slight resemblance to the quiet refreshment room at Craigdoran. But she had already shaken her head.

'I had tea with my aunt at Fraser's.'

He knew this as the big household furnishing emporium. He felt the blood rush to his head.

'Then let's not stand here in this confounded rush. We'll take a walk outside.'

They went out of the main exit and took the back street that led to Argyle Place and the lower end of the station. The fog had thickened. It swirled about them, blurring the street lamps and deadening the sound of the traffic. They seemed to move in a world of their own, but he could not reach her, did not dare to take her arm. Even their words were stilted, formal, utterly meaningless.

'How is the study going?' she asked him.

'All right . . . I hope. And how have things been with you? All well at home?'

'Quite well, thank you.'

'And Walter?'

She did not immediately reply. Then, as though resolved to reveal and explain beyond all question of doubt:

'He's been upset, but he's better now. You see . . . he wanted to fix the date of our wedding. I felt it was a little early . . . I thought we ought to wait a bit. But now it's all settled . . . for the first of June.'

A long pause followed. The first of June, he repeated dully to himself – it was only three weeks away.

'And you're happy about it?' he asked.

'Yes,' she reasoned, in a tone of practical common sense, and with words that seemed to him to have been instilled in her. 'It's the right thing for people to settle down early and get used to each other's ways. Walter's a good man and he'll make a good husband. Besides . . .'. She faltered slightly but went on, '. . . his connections in the town will help our business. Father's not been doing near so well these last few years.'

A few large drops fell upon them and in a moment it was raining heavily. They sheltered in the entrance to a shuttered shop.

'I'm sure I wish you the best of luck, Mary.'

'And I do you, David.'

It was completely dark in the narrow passageway. He could not see her but with all his senses he felt her near him. He heard her breathing, quietly yet quickly, and the scent of her wet fur came to him. A frightful weakness came over him, his mouth was dry, and his joints so loosened they barely supported him.

'I mustn't miss my train,' she said, almost in a whisper.

They went back to the station. There was only a minute to spare. Her train was at the platform. He found her a corner seat in a third-class compartment. While he stood on the footboard she lowered the window. The whistle shrilled, the engine emitted a hiss of steam. She leaned out of the window. She was fearfully pale. The rain had streaked the smut on her cheek and draggled her little necklet. The pupils of her eyes were wide and dark. A little vein in her neck was pulsing frantically.

'Goodbye then, David.' Her voice trembled.

'Goodbye . . . Mary.' The hurt in his side was unendurable. She was leaving him for good, he would never see her again.

Then as the train began to move, together with an instinctive irresponsible, predestined movement, each reached out towards the other. They clung together, closely, blindly, passionately, and their lips met in a wild, delirious, exquisite kiss. Drunkenly, at the end of the platform, the train now moving fast, he jumped from the footboard, staggered and almost fell. Still leaning from the window she was borne into the darkness of the tunnel. His heart was beating like mad with delight, tears had formed under his eyelids and, to his consternation, were running down his cheeks.

CHAPTER V

SUDDENLY, AS FROM a great distance, he remembered that his chief was due at eight o'clock to perform a lumbar puncture – a case which had come into the ward that afternoon. He must rush to the hospital to relieve Kerr. Dashing out of the station into the fog he was fortunate in finding an Eldongrove tram which, though its progress was laborious, took him back in time. Yet how he got through the next two hours he never fully understood. Speech and movements were automatic, he was barely conscious of his own presence in the ward. Once or twice he felt Drummond glancing at him oddly, but he made no comment, and at last, towards ten o'clock, Moray was able to go to his own room and give way to his feelings.

He was in love and, with the ecstasy of her kiss still lingering he knew that she loved him. It was an eventuality which, even remotely, had never entered his mind. All his thoughts, his energy and endeavours, had been concentrated exclusively on one objective, his career: to lift himself out of the swamp of poverty and make a dazzling success of his life. Well, he reasoned, with an upsurge of emotion, if he could achieve this alone, could he not do so with her, encouraged and fortified by one who, despite her modest social status, possessed all the qualities of the perfect helpmate? He could not lose her – the mere idea made him wince, like the prospect of sudden death.

He knitted his brows: what was to be done? The situation in which she was placed, with the date of her wedding fixed, and no more than three weeks off, demanded immediate action. Suppose by some fearful mischance he could not stop it. The thought of Walter, painstakingly precise, exacting the full resources of his connubial rights to their most intimate extent came to him with horrifying vividness. It was enough to drive him frantic. He must write to Mary, write at once, and send the letter to her express.

Suddenly, as he reached towards his desk for paper, the

emergency phone rang. With an exclamation of annoyance he took up the receiver. Macdonald, the switchboard night operator, was speaking.

'Mr Moray . . . '.

'Damn it, Mac – what is it? Another false run?'

'It's a personal call for you. I'll put you through.'

There was a whirring on the line. Then:

'David . . .'

He caught his breath sharply.

'Mary, is it really you?'

Her voice came to him, guarded yet intense.

'I've come down to the shop. . . . The others are asleep and I'm all in the dark. . . . But I simply had to speak to you. . . . Dearest David, I'm so happy.'

He had a swift, sweet vision of her in her nightdress and slippers in the darkness of the little shop.

'I am too, dearest Mary.'

'Ever since that first minute at Craigdoran, when I saw you in the mirror . . . I *knew*, David. And when I thought you didn't care, it fair broke my heart.'

'But you know I do. I'm just wild about you.'

He could hear her long, softly indrawn breath, more thrilling than any answer.

'I can't stop, dearest David. I only wanted you to know that I'll never marry Walter. Never – never. I didn't ever want to, I just let myself be talked into it. And then, when I thought you didn't want me. . . . But now I'll tell him, first thing tomorrow.'

He could not let her face this alone.

'I'll come with you, Mary. I'll ask Drummond for time off.'

'No, David,' she said firmly. 'You have your exam. That's the important thing, for you to get through. After that, come straight away. I'll be waiting for you.' She hesitated. 'And . . . and if you've a wee minute you can write to me in the meantime.'

'I will, Mary. I've already begun a letter.'

'I can't wait till I get it. Now I must go. Goodnight, Davie dear.'

The receiver was replaced. Now she would be creeping upstairs in the silent house to the room beside Willie's. Seizing pen and paper he dashed off a long and fervent letter; then, undressing in a kind of trance, he flung himself into bed.

Next morning, like one inspired, he redoubled his work for the finals. In the intensity of this last spurt time flew. When the day of the examination arrived he entered the Eldon Hall, tense but confident, and took his place at one of the desks. The first papers were distributed. He saw, after a rapid run through, that the questions suited him. He began to write, never once looking up, covering the pages with a flowing legible script. During the next three days, coming and going between the hospital and the University, he took his place at the same desk, set himself to do his utmost, not only for his own sake but for hers.

Then the clinical examination began. In medicine he spotted his case at once: a bronchiectasis with secondary cerebral abscess. He believed he was doing well. On the last day of the examination he went in for his oral. Drummond, sitting with old Murdo Macleish, Regius Professor of Midwifery, known as the Heiland Stot, and Purvis, the external examiner, gave him a friendly nod, remarking to his colleagues:

'This is the fellow with the bedside manner.'

'He's got rather more than that,' said Purvis, glancing through Moray's case-report.

They began to question him, and Moray – fluent, ready to agree, to smile respectfully, and always, always deferential – felt he was giving of his best. Yet the Stot worried him. This formidable character, both a terror and support to generations of Highland students, was already legendary for his brutal frankness and bawdy humour. At his opening lecture of the session it was his habit to summon some shrinking youth to the floor before the entire class, throw him an end of chalk and, pointing to the blackboard with a grim smile, indicate in the coarsest terms his wish to have a pictorial representation of the female private parts. At present he was not saying much but watching Moray intently, with a suspicious look in his small red eye. However, the interview was soon over and Purvis said with a smile: 'I don't think we need keep you.'

When Moray had gone and the door closed behind him he added: 'Nice young fellow.'

The Stot shook himself irritably.

'Smart enough,' he grunted. 'But a bluidy young humbug.'

The other two laughed. At his age, no one took old Murdo seriously.

The results were to be posted on Saturday morning. As Moray walked up the long hill to the University, all his assurance left him. He had been mistaken, he had not done well, he had failed. He scarcely dared approach the notice-board beside the main archway. Bracketed with two others, his name was at the head of the list. He had passed with honours.

He felt faint. After all his years of striving and self-denial the triumph of that moment was beyond belief. It was all the greater because of the sweet knowledge that he would soon share it with her. Barely waiting to receive the congratulations of the others gathered round the board, he went directly to the branch post office at the foot of Gilmore Hill and sent off a telegram.

Arriving Ardfillan 5.30 p.m. train today.

He hoped she would have returned from Craigdoran at that hour, and indeed, when he arrived, she was at the station to meet him. Quickly, quickly, her eyes shining, looking pale yet prettier than ever before, she advanced and, breathlessly unheeding of the others on the platform, offered him her lips. If, in these last hectic days, he had forgotten the warm freshness of her kiss, now it was renewed. As they went out of the station and started towards her home he still held her hand. Overcome, neither had so far spoken a single intelligible word. He saw that she dared not ask the question uppermost in her mind, and though he had planned a long and suspenseful recital of his success he merely said, humbly, not looking at her:

'I've passed, Mary . . . at the top, with honours.'

A sudden nervous tightening of her fingers on his; then, in a voice stifled by feeling, 'I knew you'd do it, Davie dear. But, oh, I'm so glad, so terribly glad you have. Now we can face up to things together.'

He bent towards her in concern.

'It's been difficult for you here?'

'Not exactly easy.' She softened the words by a tender upward glance. 'When I went to tell Walter, at first he thought I was joking. He couldn't believe his ears, that any woman would turn him down. When he found I was in earnest . . . he wasn't . . . nice. Then his parents came to see Father. That was bad too.' She smiled wryly. 'I was called a few fancy names.'

'Oh God,' he groaned, 'to think of you having to suffer that and me not there. I'd like to break that damn fellow's neck.'

'No,' she said seriously. 'I suppose I was to blame. But I can only thank Heaven for being spared the awfulness of getting into that family and,' she pressed close to him, 'for finding you.

I love you, Davie.'

'And I you, Mary.'

'That's everything,' she sighed. 'Nothing else matters.'

'But didn't your own family stand up for you?'

'In a way,' she said. 'But except for Willie they're not too pleased with me for all that. However, here we are, and first we'd better see my father.'

Through an entrance in the near side of the yard she took him into the bakery. It was low and dark, hot from the glow of two draw-plate ovens, and honey-sweet with the smell of a batch of new bread. Douglas, with his foreman, John Donaldson, was shelving the heavy board on which the double Scotch loaves, black crust upwards, were ranged in rows. The baker was in his shirt sleeves, wearing a floury apron, and old white canvas shoes. Over his shoulder he saw Moray enter, yet he finished the shelving, then slowly divested himself of the apron before coming forward.

'It's yourself, then,' he said, unsmiling, offering his hand.

'Father,' Mary burst out, 'David has passed his examination with honours, and come out top of the list.'

'So you're a doctor now. Well, that's something gained.'

He led the way out of the bakery and upstairs to the front parlour, where Willie was at the cleared table doing his lessons and Aunt Minnie seated knitting by the window. The boy gave Moray a swift welcoming smile but the aunt, frowning at her flashing needles, did not once look up.

'Sit down, man, sit down,' said the little baker. 'We've had our tea earlier nor usual today. But . . . well, maybe afterwards, if ye're hungry, Mary'll get you a bite.'

David took a stiff chair by the table. Mary drew another over and sat down by his side.

'Leave the room, Willie,' the aunt said, finally forking her needles into the knitting and favouring Moray with a chilly scrutiny. 'Did you hear me, Willie!'

Willie went out.

'Now, David,' the baker began, 'yet must understand that this has been a bit of a shock to us . . .'

'And to everybody else,' Aunt Minnie cut in, her head shaking with indignation. 'The whole town is ringing with it. It's a positive scandal and disgrace.'

'Ay,' Douglas resumed. 'It has placed us in a most unfortunate position. My daughter had given her plighted word to a worthy man, well connected and highly respected in the borough. Not only was she engaged to be married, the wedding day had been set; when suddenly, without rhyme or reason, she breaks the whole thing off in favour of a total stranger.'

'There was a very good reason, sir. Mary and I fell in love.'

'Love!' exclaimed the aunt in an indescribable tone. 'Before you appeared on that blessed bike of yours, like some – some half-baked Lochinvar, she was in love with Walter.'

'Not at all.' Moray felt Mary's hand steal towards his under the table. 'She never was. And I'm convinced she would never have been happy with him. You've called Stoddart a worthy man. I think he's a pompous, conceited, unfeeling ass.'

'That'll do now,' Douglas interposed sharply. 'Walter may have his peculiarities, but we know he's sound enough underneath.'

'Which is more than we know of you!' threw out the aunt.

'I'm sorry you have such a poor opinion of me.' Moray glanced deprecatingly towards Minnie. 'I hope later on you may change your mind. This isn't the first time an engagement has been broken. Better late than never.'

'It's true,' Mary murmured. 'I never wanted Walter.'

'Then why didn't you say so before, you wicked besom? Now you've put the Stoddarts against us. They'll hate us for ever. And you know what that means to your father.'

'Ay, it's not a pretty prospect. But the least said on that score the better.'

'But I will speak, James.' The aunt bent forward towards Moray. 'You may think everything is easy osey with us here. But it's not. Far from it. What with the big combines and their machine-made bread and their motor delivery trucks rampaging the whole countryside, to say nothing of the alterations we're supposed to make under the new Factory Act, my brother-in-law's had a hard fight this many a year, and him not in the best of health forbye. And Walter, through his father, had definitely promised . . .'.

'That's enough, Minnie.' Douglas raised his hand. 'Least said soonest mended. I've aye managed to stand on my own two legs in the past, and with the help of Providence I hope I'll keep on them in the future.'

A silence followed; then Moray, pressing Mary's hand,

addressed himself to the baker. He had never shown to better advantage, his fresh, clever young face alight with feeling and sincerity.

'I realise that I've caused you a lot of trouble, sir, and pain. I'm truly sorry. But some things just can't be helped. Like lightning . . . they strike you. That's the way it happened with Mary and me. You mayn't think too much of me now,' he half turned towards Aunt Minnie, 'but I'll show you. You'll not regret having me as a son-in-law. I have my degree, and it's a good one. I'll get a job in no time, and it won't be so very long before I've a first-class practice. All I want is to have Mary with me, and I'm sure that's what she wants, too.' He smiled, from one to the other, his diffident, taking, heart-warming smile.

There was a pause. Despite his determination to be firm, the baker could not restrain his nod of approval.

'That's well said, David. And now ye've spoken out I'll allow that from the first . . . like my daughter here . . .' he smiled at Mary, 'I was real taken with ye . . . and wi' all ye have done. Since what maun be maun be, I'll agree ye can be engaged. As for the marriage, there maun be a decent interval, ay, a decent interval to prevent scandal in the town. Take a job for three or four months, then we'll see. What do you say to that, Minnie?'

'Well . . .' the aunt temporised. 'There's no use crying over spilt milk.' Even she had softened, impressed by the tone of Moray's moving little speech. 'Maybe you're right. We mustn't be too hard on them.'

'Oh, thank you, Father . . . thank you, Aunt Minnie.' Mary jumped up a little wildly and kissed them both. Her cheeks were flushed, a lock of hair hung loose across her forehead. She tossed it back triumphantly. 'I knew you'd make everything all right. And now will I get Davie something to eat, Auntie?'

'Fetch him in biscuits and cheese. And some of the new batch of cherry cakes. I ken ye likes them.' She shot a wry glance at Moray. 'He ate six of them the last time he was here.'

'Just one thing more, Father,' Mary pleaded, angelically. 'Can Davie stay the night? Please. I've seen so little of him lately.'

'Well, just for tonight. Tomorrow he'll have to be off seeking that job.' A thought struck the little baker. He added severely: 'And if you're thinking of walking out tonight, Willie'll have to go with you.'

Hurrying between the kitchen and the parlour she put a choice little meal before him, but in the wonder of this magic day, food had become a sordid thing; he had little appetite. When he had finished, she put on her hat and coat. Every movement that she made seemed to him special and significant, precious, unique, adorably feminine. Then they went out and, arm in arm in the darkness, walked along the Esplanade with Willie at their side. The boy, excited by the turn of events, was in a talkative mood, putting all sorts of questions to Moray, who had not the heart to tell him he was in the way. Mary, on fire with an equal longing, was more resourceful.

'Willie dear,' she said sweetly, as they reached the end of the promenade, 'I've just remembered I forgot to get Auntie's black striped balls for tomorrow. Here's a threepenny bit. Run back to McKellar's for twopence-worth and get a Fry's chocolate bar for yourself. There's a good boy. Davie and I'll be sitting here when you get back.'

When Willie had scudded off they went into the wooden shelter. It was empty. Seated in the corner, protected from the wind, they clung to each other, the beat of the tide lost in the beating of their hearts. The waves rolled in, a star flashed unseen through the sky. Her lips were dry and warm; the innocence of her kiss, in its ardour and passion, moved him as never before.

'Oh, Davie darling,' she whispered, her cheek against his. 'I'm so happy I could die. I love you so much it's like as if my breast would break.'

CHAPTER VI

THE GRADUATION CEREMONY took place a few days later. Immediately he had turned in his hired cap and gown, Moray set about finding a suitable job. At least two house appointments were his for the asking in the Infirmary. But here, not only was the salary a pittance, he had long ago wisely decided against the long toiling road of academic promotion. Again, several, assistantships were available, mainly from country practitioners, but these he dismissed on sight. These rural G.P.s, he well knew, were not looking for honours graduates; they wanted husky youngsters who would eat anything and, unencumbered by a wife, get out of bed for a midwifery call at any hour of the night. No, he would be lost in such a situation, nor would he accept any stopgap offer: locums, dispensary work, temporary employment with one of the shipping companies, all were rejected. For his own sake and Mary's he must find something better. Intently he scanned the columns of the *Lancet* and the *Medical Journal*, pored over the advertisements of the local newspapers in the reading-room of the Carnegie Public Library. He found nothing that would do. He was worried stiff when at last he came on an unobtrusive panel in the appointments column of the *Winton Herald*.

Wanted for Glenburn Hospital, Cranstown. Resident Phsyician. Salary £500 per annum and unfurnished cottage. Engagement to commence January 1st. Apply the Secretary to the Board Winton-shire Public Health Department.

He drew a long, deep breath. It was right, exactly right, except perhaps for the date of the appointment – but that, balanced against the other advantages, was a detail, immaterial. He knew the hospital and had often admired it on his weekend excursions from the city. Situated in pleasant rolling country, within a long tram ride of Winton, it was known locally as the 'Fever Hospital', having at one time been devoted exclusively to infectious diseases. Now, however, it was mainly given over to the treatment of tubercular children. It was small, of course, no more than four isolated pavilions, holding about sixty beds, with a central office and laboratory, nurses' quarters, and a neat, red-tiled gate lodge. Nothing could be better: the salary was generous, a house was available, obviously they wanted a married man, and the laboratory would afford him facilities for research. A gem of a place, he kept repeating to himself. He knew, of course, that competition would be severe, cut-throat in fact, and as he got up from the reading-room bench he had the look of one going into battle.

The campaign which he forthwith conducted was indeed, in Its resourcefulness, subtlety and consummate adroitness, fit to be honoured and recorded as the classic example of job-getting. From his University professors he got testimonials and letters of recommendation, from Drummond a personal introduction to the Wintonshire Medical Officer of Health, and through Bryce's father, who was a baillie of the city, a complete list of the members of the board. He called first on the Medical Officer, whose attitude, though noncommittal, was pleasant, then on the Secretary, who, as a friend and brother Mason of the senior Bryce, was distinctly cordial. Next, he began discreetly, in the evenings, to canvas all the board members at their homes. Here he did well, was even introduced to the sonsie wives of several of these substantial citizens in whom, by judicious shyness, he started warm springs of maternal sympathy. Finally, he cadged a ride in a delivery van to the vicinity of the hospital, made friends with the retiring doctor who was going into practice, shook hands with the head sister and, after a really hard beginning, completely won over the stubby little martinet of a matron. She invited him to tea. The difficulties of his student days, his romantic meeting with Mary, his honours degree, all had by this time been composed into a modest, yet free-flowing tale. In her own cosy sitting-room, over the teacups – it was, he noted, first-rate tea and a delicious homemade sponge – she listened with growing sympathy.

'We'll have to see what can be done,' she finally declared, throwing out her well-starched bust until it crackled. 'And if anyone has influence with that wrong-headed committee, it's yours truly.'

He murmured thanks.

'Now I'll be off, Matron. I've taken far too much of your precious time.'

'Not at all. How are you getting back?'

'As I came,' he said, offhandedly playing an inspired lead. 'On Shanks's mare.'

'Ye *walked* out from Winton! All that way?'

'Well, to be perfectly honest, Matron,' he smiled confusedly, winningly, looking into her eyes, 'I just didn't have the tram fare. So I'll walk back too.'

'You'll do nothing of the sort, doctor. Our driver will take ye in.' She rang the bell. 'Nurse, slip down to the gate lodge and fetch Leckie.'

He rode into the city on the front seat of the old Argyle ambulance. When Leckie returned and reported to the matron, he remarked: 'I hope we get Dr Moray. He's such a nice likeable lad. And keen, forbye. If only I get appointed, says he to me, I'll work my fingers to the bone.'

No opposition could stand against such a virtuoso, pulling out all the emotional stops. A week later his name appeared on the 'short list' of ten candidates and, at the meeting of the board on August 21st, he was unanimously appointed.

Beyond indicating non-committally that he had a possibility in view, Moray had said nothing at Ardfillan of the marvellous prospects offered by Glenburn. Because he had lived so much alone, it was his nature to keep things to himself. Besides, he had been horribly afraid of missing the job. Now however, with the thrill of anticipation, he prepared for the joys of triumphant revelation.

He made his plans with characteristic thoroughness. He went, in the first place, to Gilhouse, the University Bookseller at the foot of Fenner Hill, and sold all his text-books, also his microscope. Since he had spotted a fine oil-immersion Zeiss in the lab. at Glenburn, he would no longer need his own second-hand Wright and Dobson. With a tidy sum in his pocket he crossed Eldongrove Park to a less salubrious neighbourhood and entered the pawnshop at the corner of Blairhill Street where, over the past five years, he had occasionally been an unwilling client. Now the position was reversed. Taking his time, and wisely rejecting the dubious diamond pressed upon him, he selected from the unredeemed pledges a thin gold ring mounted with a nice little aquamarine. Set in velvet in a red leather case it looked extremely handsome, and it was genuine. With this in his pocket he borrowed Bryce's bike and set off for Craigdoran. He arrived at eleven in the forenoon.

'Mary,' he exclaimed, walking straight into the refreshment room and putting his arm round her waist. 'Shut up shop. Now. At once.'

'But, Davie, I still have two more trains . . .'.

'Hang the trains, and the passengers in them, and the entire North British Railway Company. You're coming with me, this very minute. And while you're about it, put a few buns and sandwiches in a bag.'

She gazed at him, half doubtful, half smiling, yet conscious of something compelling behind the lightness of his tone.

'Well,' she conceded finally, 'I don't suppose it'll ruin the company, or Father, this once.'

Ten minutes later they were off together on the bike. He took the Stirling road, turned east at Reston, and about one o'clock, swinging round the outskirts of Cranstoun, came to rest a quarter of a mile along the Glenburn lane.

'This is where we take a stroll, Mary.'

She was confused, vaguely disturbed, did not understand why they should be here, but she accompanied him obediently down the lane. Presently they reached the sweep of ornamental railings which enclosed the hospital. He halted, wise enough to know that at this stage they must penetrate no further. They both peered through the neat, painted railings. The sun was shining on the enclosure, some children in red jackets were seated with a nurse on a bench beside the green stretch of lawn, a blackbird sang in a nearby forsythia bush.

'What a dear wee place,' Mary exclaimed.

'You think so?'

'Who wouldn't, Davie? It's like a picture.'

'Then listen, Mary,' he said, drawing a deep breath. 'This is Glenburn Hospital. These four buildings among the trees are the wards. That's the administrative block in front of them. And over there, with the garden at the back, is the medical superintendent's residence. Not a bad house, is it?'

'It's a sweet wee house,' she answered wonderingly. 'And such a nice garden. Do you know someone there?'

Ignoring her question he went on, pale now and breathing rather fast. 'The medical superintendent has sole and complete charge of the hospital. He has full facilities for research in the hospital laboratory. His salary is £500 per annum, plus the produce of the garden and a free house, that house over there, Mary, in which he is lawfully entitled to keep his own lawful wife.' His voice was cracking with excitement. 'Mary . . . as from the 1st of January they've appointed a new medical superintendent. You're . . . you're looking at him now.'

CHAPTER VII

HE TOOK THE return journey slowly, making a wide detour at Overton that would bring them through the Carse of Louden, along the south shore of Loch Lomond, and up across the moors of Glen Fruin. This was a noted route, one of the prettiest in the West, but Mary saw nothing of it . . . nothing . . . nothing . . . not even the majestic crest of Ben Lomond, towering above the shimmering loch. Dumb with happiness, still stricken by all the thrilling wonder of the miracle he had worked for her, she closed her eyes and hugged him to her with all the grateful love of her overflowing heart.

And he was happy too – how could it be otherwise? – excited by the effect he had so carefully planned and so successfully produced. Yet to his credit, he had regained calm, he did not seek praise, his natural air of modesty remained unchanged. He was in love and had wished to impress less from a sense of self-importance than from the desire to make her suddenly rejoice. Unlike Walter, who, exacting the utmost in adulation, pressed the last drop of juice from every favourable situation, he disliked being fussed over – it offended his fastidious sense and made him uncomfortable. Besides, had he not still another surprise in store for her?

As they topped the long hill which led from the loch to Glen Fruin, he checked the machine and turned off the road into one of the grassy sheep tracks which criss-crossed the moor. Following the path for about a quarter of a mile he drew up at the river beside a bank, deep in heather and bracken, sheltered by a clump of silver birches. Beneath them the moor fell away in a great sweep of purple and gold. Now she could see the mountain and the loch, a shimmering landscape that seemed to her of heaven and which she interpreted in her own fashion.

'What a braw spot, Davie.'

'Braw enough for us to eat our grub.' He teased her. 'All this chasing around should have given you an appetite.'

'I'm too carried away to eat.'

But when they seated themselves and spread out their lunch upon the checked tablecloth she had brought, he made her eat her share, the more so since, amplifying his instructions, she had packed a substantial lunch. Besides buns and sandwiches there were hard-boiled eggs, Clydeside tomatoes and a sausage roll, with a big bottle of that famous local 'mineral', Barr's Iron Brew, to quench their thirst. She had even remembered to bring the wooden plug that knocked down the glass marble in the bottle-neck.

'Oh, Davie,' she murmured, between bites. 'That bonnie wee house . . . I can't get it out my head. Just wait till ye see how I'll look after you there.'

'We have to furnish it,' he warned. 'But we have time before January. Now we're all settled I'll take a locum or something over the next four months, which should give us enough cash for a start, anyway.'

'Dearest Davie. You think, of everything.'

'There's one thing I nearly forgot.' Offhandedly, he dived into his jacket pocket. 'Here it is, lass. Better late than never.'

Watching her as she opened the little red box, he had never been so deeply moved. Completely still she looked at the ring which, like her, was simple yet beautiful. She did not praise the ring, she did not thank him for it, but, turning, she looked into his eyes just as she had done after that day at Gairsay, and in a trembling voice, that he was to remember all his life, she whispered: 'Put it on for me, dear.' Then with a little sigh she reached out her arms towards him.

They lay together on the soft bracken under the hot afternoon sun. Bees were droning faintly amongst the heather flowers, a lark sang its way into the blue, the scent of thyme and the wild orchids filled the air. From far off came the whirr of a risen grouse, then again stillness, but for the quiet ripple of the stream. Her skirt had risen as she lay back and his hand fell upon her knee. Caressingly, he stroked it. Her lips were parted, slightly swollen from the sun, and almost purple against the soft pallor of her face. Her eyelids, masking her doe-soft eyes, had a fainter, bluish tinge. Warm in his arms, she trembled as his fingers, moving upwards, came to rest on the soft bare skin above her long stocking.

His heart was thudding against his side so hard, the sound of it made a rushing in his ears. Another gentle movement, and his hand would find what it sought. He longed for her, but was afraid. Then, close to him, she breathed:

'If you want . . . take me, dear.'

The sun passed behind a cloud, the bees ceased their hum, a circling curlew uttered its mournful cry. They lay still, until at last he whispered humbly:

'Did I hurt you, Mary?'

'Dearest Davie.' She burrowed her head into him. 'It was the sweetest pain of all my life.'

When at last they stirred and gathered up the picnic things, he drove off slowly, a trifle sad and sorry, touched by a rueful sense of regret. Had he not been premature, crushing so much joy into so short a time, snatching so early at the first fruits-of happiness? She was so young, so innocent. A fresh surge of tenderness swept over him: should he not have shown restraint and waited? Indeed, from the beginning, had he not rushed on too fast and heedlessly? No, a thousand times no: he banished the thought and lifted a hand from the controls to press once again the softness of her thigh.

'I'm all yours now, Davie.'

She snuggled against him, laughing softly in his ear. No mournful, injured wistfulness for her! She was renewed, confident, more than ever alive. Half turning, he saw that her eyes were fresh and dewy; he had never known her so radiant. She seemed to sense instinctively his vague depression, and gaily, tenderly, possessive as a mother, she lifted him up.

They had reached the summit above Ardfillan when suddenly the heavy cloud that obscured the sun broke upon them in a drenching shower. Hurriedly he slipped the gear lever into neutral and coasted rapidly down hill. He was at the shop in no time, but not before he was unpleasantly damp. Mary, behind him, had escaped the worst of the rain.

Upstairs she insisted that he change into a suit of her father's, but he passed the matter off. He was not really wet he said, there was a good fire in the room, he would soon dry off. In the end they compromised: he put on the baker's carpet slippers and an old tweed jacket Mary found in a cupboard.

Presently the shop was shut and Aunt Minnie appeared, followed a few minutes later by Douglas. The four sat down to the evening meal. Willie, it appeared, was away, spending the weekend at the Boys' Brigade Camp at Whistlefield. At the outset, as

70

the teacups were passed in silence, Moray was painfully embarrassed, asking himself if some intangible evidence of guilt, a lingering aura of those delirious moments of consummation on the moor, was not observable in Mary and himself. Mary's cheeks were flushed, his own, he felt, were pale, and Aunt Minnie was directing oddly suspicious glances from one to the other. The baker, too, seemed unusually reserved and more than usually observant.

But when Mary ended the silence the general tension relaxed. Moray had promised to let her break the news of his appointment in her own way, and she did so with a brio and a sense of drama which far surpassed his own effort of the morning.

First she displayed her ring, which was admired – though grudgingly by the aunt, who remarked, aside: 'I hope it's paid for.'

'I don't think we need worry about *that*, Auntie dear,' Mary answered kindly, with just a hint of patronage. She began forthwith to describe the hospital at Glenburn, painting it in colours rather more glowing than reality, and working without haste towards the climax, which was tremendous.

A long pause followed, then Douglas said, deeply pleased:
'Five hundred pounds and a house . . . and the bit garden for your vegetables. . . . It's fine, man, it's downright handsome.'

'Not to mention the laboratory and the chances of research,' Mary put in quickly.

'This,' the aunt drew in her lips with a hiss of satisfaction, 'will be gall and vinegar to the Stoddarts.'

'Hush, Minnie.' The baker offered his hand to Moray. 'I congratulate you, David. If ever I had a doubt about you and this whole affair, it's gone now, and I can only ask your pardon. Ye're a fine lad. I'm proper glad my daughter is marrying you, and proud to have you as my son-in-law. Now, Minnie, don't you think this calls for a celebration?'

'Without a doubt!' Minnie was won at last.

'Run down then, Mary, to the wee back press – ye'll find the key in the top drawer – and bring up a bottle of my old Glenlivet.'

The bottle was brought and the baker, using sugar and lemon, and with due regard to the varying dilutions of the aged spirit, mixed for each of them a glass of good hot toddy. It was a comforting drink but it came too late for Moray. All evening he had

71

felt his shirt clinging damply to his chest. The toddy made his head hot but his feet were leaden cold. He was relieved when they persuaded him to stay overnight, but when he went to bed he was shivering. He took his temperature, 101°, and knew he had caught a chill.

CHAPTER VIII

MORAY SPENT A restless, fevered night, and when he awoke from the snatch of sleep into which he had fallen, towards morning, he had no difficulty in diagnosing his own case; he was in for a bout of acute bronchitis. His breathing was tight and painful, even without a stethoscope he could hear the râles in his chest, and his temperature had risen to 103°. He waited with commendable self-control until nearly seven o'clock, then knocked on the wall which separated him from Mary's room. He heard her stir, and a few minutes later she came into his room.

'Oh, dear, you're ill,' she exclaimed at once in dismay. 'Half the night I was worrying you'd caught cold.'

'It's nothing much. But I'll be laid up for a bit and I can't make a nuisance of myself here. You'd better ring the hospital.'

'I'll do no such thing.' She had taken his hand, which felt so hot to the touch that her heart contracted with concern. 'You'll stop with us in this very room. And I'll look after you. Who else, indeed!'

'Are you sure, Mary?' Suddenly he wanted her to care for him. And what a bore it would be getting the ambulance, trundling back to the Infirmary as a patient. 'I'll only be a few days. If it's not too much trouble, I'd far rather stay.'

'And so you shall,' she said firmly. 'Now, should I send for the doctor?'

'No, no, of course not. I'll prescribe for myself.'

He raised himself on his elbow and wrote a couple of prescriptions. The effort made him cough.

'That's all I need, Mary. And occasional hot fluids. . . .' He forced a smile. 'And you.'

He was worse than he made out. For ten days he was quite ill, with a high fever and a racking cough. She nursed him devotedly and, for one untrained, with surprising talent. With Aunt Minnie, she poulticed him, brewed him nourishing beef tea, fed him calf's foot jelly with a spoon, made up his bed, exerted to the full her practical mind and housewifely skill to ease his distress. At the crisis of the attack, when he was obliged to have a steam kettle, she sat up half the night tending him. The dislocation of the household was, of course, acute. Meals were upset; sleep lost; service in the shop disturbed; Willie, back from the camp, had to be farmed out with Donaldson, the foreman. When, at the end of the second week, he was able to be up, and to sit in a long chair by the window, he apologised shamefacedly to Douglas for the trouble he had given them all.

'Not another word, Davie,' the little baker interrupted him. 'Ye're one of the family now.' He smiled. 'As good as, anyhow.'

When her father had gone out of the room Mary came over and knelt beside his chair. She gripped his knee tightly.

'Don't ever say you were a bother, Davie. What do you think would have happened to me if I hadn't got you well?'

His eyes filled with tears, he was still rather weak.

'What a perfect wife you'll make me, Mary. Don't think I haven't noticed every single thing you've done.'

Presently he was out, walking with her on the Esplanade, slowly at first, then at a faster pace. Finally he pronounced himself recovered, and ready to look out for a locum tenens that would carry him through the next few months. He still had a stitch in his side that worried him, but he did not speak of it. To complain now would be a poor way to reward their united efforts on his behalf. However, on the following Monday when he travelled by train to Winton to leave his name at the Medical Employment Agency, he had a sharp bout of pain, and decided it might be wise to look in at his old ward and have his chest gone over by Drummond.

It was unexpectedly late when he arrived back at Ardfillan, and Mary, who was serving a woman customer in the shop, read at once the dejection in his expression. The moment she was free, she came towards him, looking up into his face.

'No luck, Davie?'

He tried to smile, but the attempt was scarcely a success.

'As a matter of fact I didn't manage to get to the agency.'

'What went wrong, dear?' she said quickly. She saw that he had something on his mind.

At that moment the shop door pinged and a child came in to buy sweetie biscuits. He broke off, relieved by the interruption.

What a cursed nuisance it all was, and what a damned sickly nuisance of a fellow they would all think him.

'Now, Davie?' She turned to him.

'It's hard to explain, Mary,' he said feebly. 'I'll tell you upstairs.'

It was just on closing time. Hurriedly, she drew the blinds and turned off the lights, then followed him to the upper room. Her father and Aunt Minnie were there with him. He did not know how to begin. There was nothing for it, he had to reveal the reason for his visit to the hospital. Bending forward with elbows on his knees he kept looking at the floor.

'So when I got there Professor Drummond screened me – X-ray that is – and apparently I have a patch of pleurisy on my left lung.'

'Pleurisy!'

'It's very localised,' he said, refraining from mentioning Drummond's insistence that neglect would induce tuberculosis. Striving to keep the despondency from his voice, he added: 'But apparently it knocks out any possibility of a locum.'

'What's to be done then?' Douglas said, looking rather blue, while Mary sat silent, her hands pressed together.

'Well, I could go into the country . . . somewhere not too far away . . .'.

'No, Davie,' Mary intervened nervously. 'You're not to leave us. We'll look after you here.'

He gazed at her dismally.

'Impose myself on you for another two months? Impossible, Mary. How can I hang around here, bone idle, just being a confounded nuisance, on top of all the fearful bother I've given you? I'll . . . I'll get a job on a farm.'

'No farmer in his right mind is going to employ a sick man,' said Douglas. 'Surely the doctor . . . the professor ordered something definite for ye?'

There was a pause. Moray raised his head.

'If you must know, Drummond did say that I need a sea voyage – as a ship's doctor of course. In fact, he insisted on ringing up the Kinnaird Line. . . . He knows someone there . . .'

Now there was a prolonged silence. Finally the baker said:

'That sounds like sense at last. And if it's a question of your health, lad, that's all important. We would keep you here gladly. But would you get better, with the winter coming on? No, no.

75

Your professor's advice is sound. Did he manage to find ye something?'

Moray nodded, unwillingly.

'There's a boat, the *Pindari*, leaving next week from the Tail of the Bank – for Calcutta – a seven weeks' round trip.'

Another pause followed, then Douglas reflected:

'A voyage to India. Ye'd get sunshine there.'

'Do you want to go?' the aunt asked.

'Good God, no. . . . Sorry, Aunt Minnie. It's the last thing I want. Except that if I must go the pay is good, ninety pounds in all. We could furnish our house with it, Mary.'

All that evening the matter was threshed out and at last was definitely settled. Despite the divergence of opinion, all, even Mary, yielded in the end to the baker's simple argument: health came before all other considerations.

'What good will ye be to anyone – to Mary, yourself, or to Glenburn – if ye don't get yourself well? Ye maun go, lad, that's all about it.'

On the following Tuesday he crossed to Greenock with Mary. It was a wet, stormy afternoon. He looked and felt ill, and the misery of the coming separation lay upon him. And upon her too, yet she was brave, resolved not to give way. Under her windblown tweed hat, raincoat buttoned to her chin, her face was set in a mould of resolute cheerfulness. The *Pindari*, which had arrived overnight from Liverpool to take on a cargo of woollens and mill machinery, lay in the estuary veiled by a driving mist. The wind swept in staggering gusts across the docks, but she insisted on coming to the pier end to see him off, her hand beside his, under the handle of his old leather suitcase, sharing its weight. As the tender plunged and bumped in the strong tide beneath, they held each other closely, passionately, under the grey and dismal sky. Rain, like tears, ran down her cold cheeks, but her lips and breath were warm. Sick at heart, he could not bear to part from her.

'I'll take a chance and stay, Mary. God knows I don't want to go.'

'But you must, dear, for both our sakes. I'll write to you, and count every minute till you're back to me.' Just before she broke away and ran back along the jetty, she took a small package from her raincoat pocket and pressed it into his hand. 'Just so you'll mind me, Davie.'

In the cabin of the heaving tender, on the way out to the ship, he undid the wrappings and looked at what she had given him, It was an old thin gold locket, smaller than a florin piece, that had belonged to her mother. Inside she had placed a little snapshot of herself and in the back, carefully pressed, a single flower of the bluebells he had picked for her at Gairsay.

HE CLAMBERED UP the swaying gangway and came aboard. The merchandise from Winton had already been loaded; he had barely time to report to the captain before the tugs were alongside and they began to nose cautiously down the Firth. He stood on deck, striving to penetrate the mist that shrouded the vague line of the shore where Mary would be standing, watching the departure of this spectral ship. His heart was filled with sadness and love. There were few people on deck – he knew they were returning to Tilbury to pick up the main body of passengers – and the damp emptiness and dripping stanchions increased his melancholy. The deep, despondent sounding of the fog-horn gave him a strange sense of foreboding. As the mist closed down, obliterating the shore, he turned and went below to find his quarters.

His cabin was aft, on the starboard side, next to the chief engineer's, furnished in polished teak wood with red curtains to the ports, a fitted locker and book rack, and a red-shaded bunk lamp, all particularly snug. A washstand with a metal basin that tipped up to let the water away stood in the corner, and above, on a guarded bracket, an electric fan. His consulting room and dispensary, conveniently situated across the alleyway, were both equally well equiped. Although the *Pindari* was an old ship, originally the *Isolde* of the Hamburg-Atlantic Line taken over after the war, she had been reconditioned from stem to stern and was now roomy, comfortable and notably seaworthy, capable of a modest seventeen knots, making a slow, sure run to India with cargo and passengers, touching en route at various ports.

When Moray had unpacked his suitcase, containing his own few things, all washed and ironed by Mary, and the two stock uniforms provided by the company's head office in Winton, he felt completely done; his side was hurting too. A rough Irish Sea and a bad passage up the Channel did not help him. He had difficulty in carrying out his first duty, a medical examination of the native crew, and at nights his cough was so troublesome he got little sleep. Concerned not only for himself but for his engineer neighbour, an elderly Scot named Macrae, whom he must have disturbed, he dosed himself with codeine. However, at Tilbury, where they spent two days at the docks, a letter from Mary put fresh heart in him, and when they cleared the Nore and were actually on their way, he began to feel more himself. The ship had life in her now, the screws thrust forward with a stronger throb, voices and laughter echoed along the companionways.

In the dining saloon each officer took his place at the head of his own table. Moray, at his, was allotted only five passengers, all somewhat elderly and, he had to admit, dull: two well-seasoned Scotch tea planters, Henderson and Macrimmon, returning to Assam, a Mr S. A. G. Mahratta, the Hindu manager of a cotton mill in Cawnpore, and an I.C.S. official and his jaundiced, severe-looking wife, Mr and Mrs Hunt-hunter. Except for the planters, who, particularly after a session in the bar, were inclined to jocularity, and Mahratta, a fussy, hypochondriacal little man with a bad stomach, who was sometimes unintentionally funny, the general tone of the conversation was restrained and promised to be difficult.

But now they were through the grey turbulence of the Bay, sunshine suddenly blazed, sky and sea were blue as they passed through the Straits and cruised up the south-east coast of Spain towards Marseilles, where more cargo was to be taken aboard. Deck games were being set out and Moray was advised by the first officer, a long, lean, goodnatured Irishman named O'Neil, that part of the doctor's duty was to organise them. So Moray, taking paper and pencil, approached the task of rounding up the passengers, at first with a sense of his unfitness for large-scale social intercourse, yet, after some preliminary self-consciousness, with success. His official position made things easier than he had imagined. He need not seek, he was sought after – a ship's surgeon was apparently a position of some consequence. When they arrived at Marseilles, lists of competitors for deck quoits, shuffleboard and table tennis had been drawn up and Moray, with a grimace, began to overhear himself referred to as 'our nice young doctor'.

At Marseilles a long, five-page letter from Mary awaited him. In his cabin he read it eagerly, smiling at her little bits of news, touched by the simple record of all she had been doing, through which there breathed a constant solicitude for his health. She hoped that his pain was gone, his cough less, that he was taking good care of himself. She sent him all her love. Dear Mary, how he missed her. In the surgery, squaring up to his desk, he wrote his reply, telling of all his activities, and was able to catch the outgoing mail before the sack was closed. The *Pindari* was no more than twelve hours in port. Loading completed, the hatches were battened down; then, almost at the last moment – the night train from Paris was late – three new passengers came on board. Since most of the tables in the saloon were fully occupied they were seated with the doctor, and their names added to the passenger list: Mr and Mrs Arnold Holbrook, Miss Doris Holbrook. Surreptitiously, Moray examined them, as they sat down to lunch.

Holbrook was a man of about sixty, not tall, but so heavily thickset as to be short of breath, with a red, porous, mottled face partly covered by a short grizzled beard, and small, bloodshot, genially knowing eyes. He was badly dressed in a greenish ready-made suit, grey flannel shirt and a stringy maroon tie. His wife a little homely woman with small features and a gentle expression, was, in contrast, wearing heavy, fashionable clothes and an elaborate black-sequined toque. Yet she carried them without ease, as though they encumbered her and she would have preferred much simpler attire – instinctively Moray thought of her in an old loose print wrapper, busy with her household duties in a well-stocked kitchen. She wore also so much jewellery that he erroneously assumed it to be paste. The daughter appeared to be not more than twenty. She was tallish, of a pale, dull complexion, with a good figure, dark hair and slate-grey eyes which, sitting erect and silent, she kept lowered sulkily during most of the meal.

Not so Holbrook. In the accents of Manchester, genially, expansively, with an air of experience, he broke the introductory ice, tactfully set conversation going, jollied the Tamil table boy until he had him grinning, started Mahratta off on a diverting account of his recent gastronomic difficulties in London that brought a smile even to the meagre lips of Mrs Hunt-hunter. When he had awakened the table to life, he casually revealed that his son was in Calcutta opening a branch of his business, that Dorrie – he looked towards his daughter, who ignored the affectionate glance – had just left Miss Wainwright's Finishing

School in Blackpool, and that their voyage to India was pleasure and business combined. It was only when he proposed ordering champagne all round that a reproving glance from his wife drew him up.

'Ah, well, Mother,' he deferred humorously, 'we'll have it at dinner tonight. That suit you, Dorrie?'

Doris gave him a pettish glance.

'You stop it, Dad. The story of your life will keep.'

'That's my girl.' He laughed indulgently, with a note of pride. 'I like to have you keep me right.'

'And about time.'

'Now, Doris,' her mother warned gently: then, looking round the table, she added, as though in extenuation: 'Our daughter hasn't been too well lately. And the night journey was real tiring for her.'

That same afternoon, as Moray came along the companionway towards his surgery, he found Holbrook standing before the notice board with his hands in his pockets, studying the sports lists.

'It looks as though you've got everyone pretty well booked up, doctor.'

'I've gone through the passenger list fairly thoroughly, sir.'

'Our Dorrie likes a game,' said the other in a reflective tone. 'And she's a dab at most of them. Surely you could find her a partner, doctor.' He paused. 'How about yourself? You're an active young fellow.'

Moray hesitated.

'I'll be glad to, sir,' he said, adding quickly: 'If it's permitted. I'll . . . I'll speak to the first officer.'

'Do that, lad. I'd appreciate it.'

Moray's impressions of Holbrook's daughter had not been favourable; he had no wish to be let in for this job. Besides, as a ship's officer, he doubted if he could participate in the competitions. However, when he had finished his consultations he found O'Neil on the bridge and explained the situation; the big Irishman had already been friendly and helpful, casually tipping him off on his more important duties.

'Sure ye can play, doc,' said O'Neil, in a Belfast accent you could cut with a knife. 'Ye're expected to be nice to the women. Besides, I saw this little bit come aboard. She looks as if she has something.' O'Neil's blue eyes twinkled. 'With luck ye might get a tickle.'

'I wouldn't be interested,' Moray said flatly. His pure-minded feeling for Mary made the suggestion, however goodnatured, unutterably distasteful to him.

'Well, anyhow, be civil – it'll do ye no harm and may do ye some good. The old boy's rolling. Holbrook's Pharmaceuticals. Began in a back street chemist's shop in Bootle. Made a fortune out of pills.' He grinned. 'Moving the bowels of humanity. The answer was in the purgative. Say, that reminds me. Did you ever hear this one?' O'Neil, a brave and gallant soul who had been torpedoed in the war, swimming for five hours in the Atlantic Ocean before being picked up, had a positive mania for telling off-colour stories. Submitting, Moray prepared his smile as the other went on: 'A Yank was coming tearing along the street in Chicago when another Yank standing on the sidewalk stopped him. "Can you direct me to a good chemist?" says he. "Brother," says the other, in a raging hurry, "if ye want God's own chemist just . . .' At the unprintable punch line O'Neil topped his cap to a more rakish angle and lay back on the binnacle, roaring with laughter.

Moray remained on the bridge for another half hour, pacing up and down with the first officer, watching the French coastline slip away, his cheeks whipped by the invigorating wind, which was always keener up top. Drummond had been right; there was health in the tang of the open sea. How much better he was feeling now, and how agreeable life was on board. He had forgotten his promise to Holbrook but when he went below it came to mind, and, with a shrug, he entered Miss Holbrook's name and his own in the doubles events.

CHAPTER X

THE WEATHER CONTINUED fine, the sea calm, the sky brilliant by day, shading through violet sunsets into velvet and luminous nights through which the *Pindari* traced its phosphorescent wake. This was the sea of Jason and Ulysses; at dawn the ship seemed suspended between sky and water, timeless and unreal, except that there, on the starboard bow, was Sardinia, the healthy fragrance of the island borne on a soft and fitful breeze.

Drawing deep, free breaths of this aromatic air without pain or hindrance, Moray knew that his pleurisy had gone. No need now to put his stethoscope on his chest. His skin was tanned, he had never felt better. After those years of prolonged grind, the present conditions of his life seemed altogether too good to be true. Awakened at seven by his cabin 'boy', who, padding barefoot from the galley, brought his *chota hazri* of tea and fresh fruit, he got up half an hour later, took a plunge in the sports deck swimming-pool, then dressed. Breakfast was at nine, after which he made his round of visits or, once a week, accompanied Captain Torrance on the official inspection of the ship. From ten-thirty till noon he was in his surgery. Lunch came at one, and thereafter, except for a nominal surgery at five o'clock, he was free for the rest of the day, expected only to make himself agreeable and obliging to the passengers. At seven-thirty the melodious dinner gong boomed up and down the alleyways – always a welcome sound, since the meals were rich, spicy and plentiful, the native curries especially delicious.

On the following Monday the tournaments began, and just before eight bells, recollecting his engagement, Moray closed the surgery and went up to the sports deck for the first round of the deck-tennis doubles. His partner was already there, wearing a short white skirt and a singlet, standing beside her parents who rather to his embarrassment, had taken deck chairs close to the court so that they might miss nothing of the game. As he apologised for keeping her waiting, although actually he was not late, she did not speak, and barely glanced at him. He scarcely knew whether she was nervous or, as he had suspected at table, merely perverse.

Their opponents arrived, a newly married Ditch couple, the Hendricks, who were on their way out to Chittagong, and the match began. At first Doris was carelessly erratic but, although he had never played the game before, he had a quick eye and managed to cover her mistakes, which he made light of, with his usual good humour. At this, she began to try, and to play brilliantly. She had a straight yet well-developed figure – round, very pretty breasts and hips, and long, well-shaped legs, revealed in motion by her short skirt. The Hendricks, a plump and heavy-footed pair, were no match for them. They won handsomely by six games to two. As he congratulated her, saying, 'Your father told me you were good at games, and you are,' she gave him one of her rare direct looks, fleeting and unsmiling.

'Yes,' she said. 'I've been taught a few tricks, and picked up some on my own. But aren't you going to buy me a drink? Let's have it up here.'

When the deck steward brought two tall lemon squashes, filled with ice, she lay back in her deck chair, with half-closed eyes, sipping her drink through the straw. He glanced at her awkwardly, at a loss as to what to say, a strange predicament for one who could invariably find the right word in the right place. The heat of the game had brought a faint colour into her pale complexion, and caused her singlet to adhere to her breasts, so that the pink of her nipples showed through the thin damp cotton. She's an attractive girl, thought Moray, almost angrily, but what the devil is the matter with her? Had she lost her tongue? Apparently not, for suddenly she spoke.

'I'm glad we won. I wanted to knock out that sickening pair of Dutch love-birds. Can you imagine them in bed together. "Excuse my fat, dear." I'd like to win all the tournaments. If only to spite our delightful passengers. What a crowd they are. I hate them all, don't you?'

'No, I can't say I do.'

'You can't mean it. They're an appalling lot, especially our table. Mrs Hunt-hunter – what a horse-faced hag. Makes me sick. She's common as mud, really. And the ship's lousy too. I never wanted to come on this damn trip. My devoted parents dragged me on board by the hair. My cabin is supposed to be one of the best on A deck. Dad paid through the nose for it. You should see it. A dog kennel, with a bath like the kitchen sink. That's the worst, for, if anything, I like to wash. And can you imagine, natives serving one's food. Why can't they have white stewards?'

'Our table boy seems a very decent jolly sort.'

'Haven't you noticed how he smells? It would kill you. I'm very sensitive about smells, it's something to do with the olfactory nerves the doctor told Mother. Phooey to him – smarmy wind-bag. The point is, I like people to smell clean.'

'Do I?' he couldn't help asking, ironically.

She laughed, stretching her long legs widely apart.

'Wouldn't you like to know? Frankly, you're the one faint gleam on the horizon. Didn't you notice me taking you in that first day at lunch? I either take to a person or I don't. I can tell at a glance. To be quite frank, I asked Father to get you as my partner. He's not a bad old bird though he is a bit of a soak. And Mother is passable, if only she'd stop clucking over me. But I have to keep them in order, quite often I absolutely *freeze* them, to get them to do what I want. I'm talking an awful lot. Sometimes I talk all the time, sometimes I say nothing, absolutely nothing. I like to treat people that way. I'm proud. I used to drive old Wainwright out of her mind. When she'd start lecturing me I'd simply look at her and throw myself into a coma.'

'She's your headmistress?'

'Was,' she said idly. 'She threw me out.'

'What on earth for?'

She gave him her slow smile.

'That may be revealed in a later instalment.'

On the following afternoon Doris and the doctor successfully played two rounds at bull board and one at deck quoits, and Doris's parents were again spectators. Moray quite enjoyed the games. He'd never met anyone like her before, so amusingly prejudiced and intolerant, so sure of her own privileged position, and yet with a streak underneath of commonness, of vulgarity almost, that redeemed her absurd pretensions. The fact that she liked him was flattering. It was now apparent that the Holbrooks doted upon their daughter, unresponsive though she might be, and he was less surprised than he might have been when they rose and came towards him, quite unusually pleased by the triple victory. Mrs Holbrook gave him a noticeably kind smile.

'You brought our Dorrie out, doctor,' she remarked. 'And did very well yourself, too.'

Doris herself, who was on the point of leaving, said nothing, but meeting his eye she gave him her peculiar half-smile. He talked to her parents for a bit; then as he left to go down to his surgery he observed them put their heads together, Mrs Holbrook apparently urging her husband to action. Indeed, some minutes later, Holbrook rolled into the dispensary, lush, genial and garrulous.

'Nothing the matter with me, doc. Nothing at all. Just felt like a sup of bishmuth. Nothing like bishmuth to ease the stomach. Where do you keep it? I'll help myself.'

Moray indicated the bottle of bismuth, wondering, as he watched the other nudge a generous helping into his palm, if he ought not to alert Holbrook to the state of his liver, which was palpably cirrhotic. Most days with Henderson and Macrimmon, the two tea planters, the old boy, except for his ventures to the sports deck and his chat with the captain on the bridge, was practically a fixture in the bar.

'That's the stuff,' Holbrook exclaimed, licking up the heap of white powder with prehensile thrusts of his furred tongue. 'And here's your fee, doctor.'

'Good heavens, sir, I couldn't take all that. It's . . . it's far too much.'

'Doctor,' said Holbrook, slowly fixing Moray with his small, knowing, injected eye. 'If you want the advice of a man who's seen a lot of this wicked world, when you get the chance of a good thing, take it!'

With warm generosity he pressed a five-pound note into the doctor's hand.

Thoughtfully replacing the bottle on the shelf when Holbrook had gone, Moray, who had been infected by O'Neil's vocabulary, caught himself smiling: 'We'd bloody well better win all the tournaments now.'

This, however, was no more than a pose. The girl had begun to interest him, as a study. At times she seemed far more mature than her years, at others almost backward. One day she would be moodily taciturn, the next full of amusing and provocative talk. What he rather admired in her was her complete indifference to what people thought of her. She never sought popularity and, unlike those who were already first-naming each other in tight little groups, seemed actually to enjoy being an outsider. She had a particular gift for taking off people and could be offensively rude to anyone who tried to flatter or make up to her. Her careless attitude extended even to her personal belongings, of which she had an endless variety. She was always leaving a bag, scarf or sweater on deck, mislaying and losing valuable things without turning a hair. These complexities in her character aroused his curiosity. When at lunch and dinner she would look towards him with her concealed and puzzling smile, he was more at a loss than ever. Oddly enough he was inclined to feel sorry for her.

All this gave an added spice of interest to what the mother had so inaptly phrased as 'bringing Dorrie out' in the tournaments. There was not, in fact, much competition in the games, since many of the passengers were elderly. Only one pair seemed to offer serious opposition, the Kindersleys, a couple with two young children who were returning to Kadur in Mysore after three months' leave. He was about thirty-five, excessively hearty and downright, manager of a small coffee estate that had been hit quite badly by the slump caused by excess production in Brazil. His wife, reputedly a fine lawn tennis player, was a pleasant little woman with a frank, rather serious expression. They sat at the first officer's table. As the *Pindari* drew near to the Suez Canal, Moray and his partner, playing well together, were in all three semi-finals. So also were the Kindersleys.

On the eve of their arrival at Port Said Mrs Holbrook, reclining on the promenade deck, beckoned the doctor, indicating the vacant chair beside her. On several occasions he had been honoured by this invitation and, in response to her gentle questioning, had disclosed enough of his early 'struggles' – comparable in some degree to her own – to win her sympathy and approval. Now, after a comment on the admirable weather and a query as to when the ship would dock, she leaned towards him.

'We're going ashore tomorrow to see the sights, and do some shopping. We expect you to come with us.'

He shook his head.

'I'm terribly sorry, Mrs Holbrook. I have to stay on board. I've all the health papers to attend to with the port M.O.H. And a sick man in the crew who may have to go to hospital.'

'What a pity,' she said, upset. 'Couldn't Mr Holbrook have a word with Captain Torrance?'

'Oh, no,' he interposed hurriedly. 'That's out of the question. The bill of health's most important. The ship can't sail without it.'

'Well,' she said at length, 'we were counting on you. Dorrie will be proper disappointed.'

A short pause followed, then in an intimate manner she began to speak about her daughter. Dorrie was such a dear girl, just the apple of her father's eye, but she had been – well, sometimes a bit of a worry to them. It wasn't as though they hadn't given her the best – yes, the very best education that money could buy; Miss Wainwright's was one of the most select schools in the North of England. She spoke French and could play the piano beautifully, really classical pieces. She'd had all sorts of private lessons in tennis and such-like, elocution and deportment. Father wanted her to have all the advantages. But she was such a highly strung girl, not exactly difficult, but, well, kind of moody and, though, mind you, she could be very lively and outspoken at times, inclined occasionally to get depressed – quite the opposite of her brother Bert who day in and day out was the jolliest chap in the world. Mrs Holbrook paused, her eyes lighting up at the thought of her son. Well, she concluded, she would say no more except that she was really and truly grateful, and Father was too, for the way he had taken an interest in Dorrie, and done her so much good – really, as one might say, wakened her up.

Moray was touched. He liked this homely little woman who, weighted by the expensive trinkets and unbecoming clothes heaped on her by her husband, made no bones about her origin, and was, despite Holbrook's wealth, entirely devoid of social pretensions, yet was so eagerly and, indeed, anxiously solicitous for her daughter. But he hardly knew what to say, and was compelled to fall back on mere politeness.

'Doris is a fine girl. And I'm sure she'll grow out of her little difficulties. Just look how she's doing in the tournaments. And of course, if there's anything I can do to help . . .'.

'You are good, doctor.' She pressed his hand maternally. 'I needn't tell you we've all real taken to you.'

CHAPTER XI

ON THE FOLLOWING day at ten o'clock they were off Port Said,
passed the breakwater with the great de Lesseps statue and, after
an hour's wait in midstream till the yellow quarantine flag came
down, drew into the dock and began to take on oil and water.
All the passengers who intended going ashore had left the ship
by noon. The Holbrooks waved to Moray as they went down
the gangway and he regretted not being with them. Viewed from
the boat deck, the town had an enticing and mysterious air.
Beyond the huddle of dock sheds it lay yellow and white against
a flat horizon made hazy by the heat. Bright tiled roofs and
balconies gleamed in the sun. The pencil shapes of twin minarets
rose delicately above the narrow crowded streets filled with colour,
sound and movement. A pity he could not have accepted Mrs
Holbrook's invitation.

However, he had much to occupy him. The Lascar in sick
bay was a suspect case of osteomyelitis, and when the port
medical officer confirmed the diagnosis there were papers to be
signed and irritating delays to be overcome before the man
could be moved into the ambulance and transferred to hospital.
Then the drinking-water tanks must be checked, after which
the captain sent for him, and so it went on. The ship was full
of hucksters, policemen, stevedores, Egyptian visitors, and
company agents. Four bells struck before he was temporarily
free, and as the outgoing post closed in half an hour he scarcely
had time to finish and bring up to date the letter to Mary he
had been writing at odd moments during the past few days.
He felt guilty about this, the more so since, when the agent came
aboard at six o'clock, three letters were in the mail sack from
her, with one, he judged by the handwriting, from Willie.
Rather than skim through these now, when he was so pressed
for time, he decided to leave them on his locker and enjoy them
at leisure after he turned in tonight. He still had to make out
duplicate medical supply sheets for the extra emetine which,

since an epidemic of amoebic dysentery was reported in the town, he had obtained from the port M.O. as a precautionary measure. When he had completed the company forms, he took them to the purser's office. Only then did he remember that he was due in the smoke-room, where the Holbrooks had asked him to meet them for a drink before dinner. Aware that he was late he hurried off along the promenade deck, meeting passengers, many in a state of hilarity, wearing fezes and laden with purchases from the bazaars: boxes of Turkish delight and Egyptian cigarettes – made, according to O'Neil, from camels' dung – terracotta models of the Sphinx, brassware covered with hieroglyphics: for the most part junk. Macrimmon, drunkenly draped in a white burnous, had bought a foetus in a glass bottle.

The Holbrooks had returned earlier and were there, all three, when he pushed through the glass swing doors, father, mother and Doris, surrounded by a score of packages. Holbrook, in high good humour, ordered the drinks: double Scotch for himself, champagne cocktails for the others; Mrs Holbrook, who rarely 'indulged' and usually tried to restrain her husband, allowed herself to be persuaded on the plea of a special occasion. Then they began to speak animatedly of their expedition. It had been a great success: they had taken a car and driven out along the shore of Lake Manzala, visited the great Mohammedan mosque, watched the performance of a snake charmer, inspected a collection of scarabs in the museum, lunched in the garden of the Pera Palace Hotel, where they had been given a wonderful fish curry served with sunflower seeds and green chillies, and finally, on the way back to the ship they had discovered a marvellous store.

'Not a trashy place like the bazaars,' said Mrs Holbrook. 'It's owned by a man called Simon Artz. We had a proper time, shopping with him.'

'Artz is a man of parts,' Doris laughed. 'He keeps everything from everywhere.' Holding up the mirror from her bag, she was putting on lipstick. Either from the sun or from excitement her cheeks were faintly flushed, making her eyes brighter. She had never looked more alive.

'So we bought ever so many things for our friends,' Mrs Holbrook resumed. 'And we didn't forget you, doctor. Working hard for us here while we were off enjoying ourselves.' With an affectionate smile she handed him a small oblong package.

Reddening, he took it awkwardly, not knowing whether or not to open it.

'Go on, have a look,' Holbrook urged slyly. 'It won't bite.'

He opened the case, expecting to find some trivial souvenir. Instead it was a red gold wristlet watch, with a delicately plaited gold strap, a Patek Phillippe too, the best and most expensive hand-made Swiss movement. It must have cost the earth. He was speechless.

'You are quite the kindest and most generous people,' he stammered, at last. 'It's the very thing I want and need . . .'.

'Say no more about it, lad,' Holbrook broke in. 'Our Dorrie happened to notice you didn't wear one. 'Twas her that chose it for you.'

Looking suddenly towards her, Moray caught her gaze fixed directly upon him, that challenging, intimate look which somehow bound them together in a kind of conspiracy.

'Don't make a song about it, Dad. Let it pass. Or I'll tell how you asked about the belly dancers.'

Holbrook laughed, drained his glass, and stood up.

'I'm famished. Let's have the steward move this stuff to the cabin and we'll all go right down to dinner.'

When the ship was in port dinner became an elastic meal served at almost any hour, and they were the first to arrive at their table. The sense of intimacy begun in the smoke-room was thus maintained and they made a lively party, of which Doris was the liveliest. Her attitude towards her parents, that of a spoiled only daughter, always superior, and varying between sulky and tolerant contempt, was replaced by a sort of bantering raillery, directed mainly towards her father, who responded in the same style. At first Moray assumed, unkindly enough, that Holbrook had bought her something particularly nice ashore. But no, now he was teasing her for having refused all his offers. Some of her remarks, though perhaps too pointed, were very amusing, especially when she began to take off their absent table companions in malicious little impersonations. This, however, drew from her mother a restraining, 'Now, Dorrie dear, remember . . . not too much.'

At this Doris did give up with a side glance at Moray, which made him party to the entertainment. Meanwhile the engines had started to vibrate and the ship was now clear of the dock. As it began the slow passage through the canal, Mrs Holbrook, obviously pleased by the resurgence of family harmony, suggested that they take their coffee on the upper deck and watch the sunset over the desert. A word from Holbrook to the head steward was enough to overcome every difficulty, and presently, sheltered by an awning on the starboard side, they were sipping hot coffee at a round table set out with a dessert of fresh fruit, chow-chow, and preserved ginger. As the great molten disc slid into that vast waste of sand, palm trees were outlined in the limitless light, a string of camels slowly plodding, Bedouin tents, a nomad tribe. Then in the indigo sky a moon was revealed, brightening as the night advanced. In the main lounge beneath them the ship's orchestra began softly to play a medley of the popular tunes of the day. Moray, who was sitting next to Doris, heard her take a restless breath. Lying back in the deck chair with her arms behind her head, she moved about as though unable to find a relaxed position.

'Aren't you comfortable?' he said. 'Let me get you a cushion.'

'A cushion! Pardon me if I smile. I'll be all right – just a bit worked up tonight.'

'Who wouldn't be? You can feel we're in the East. What a sky.'

'And with music.' She hummed a few bars of 'My Heart Stood Still', stopped, hummed again, then exclaimed: 'If this goes on I'll go half-cocked.'

He laughed.

'Before you do, let me thank you for choosing such a beautiful watch.'

'I know what I like. I liked the watch and quite frankly I like you. D'you mind?'

'Not at all. I'm pleased, and grateful.'

Neither spoke for a minute; then she broke out again.

'Doesn't it do something to you up here? Like bathing in warm milk. Not that I ever have, though it's an idea. The milky way. But you'd keep losing the soap. I wish we were going swimming. Not in the sickening little pool. On a deserted beach, where we'd have it to ourselves, no need to bother about bathing suits.' She laughed again. 'Don't look so shocked, you fool. Don't you ever feel that you're all wound up and excited, right on top of the world?' Tapping her shoe on the deck, she sang: ' "I'm sitting on top of the world, singing a song, rolling along . . .". Such a marvellous sensa . . . shun. When I

get it I'm ready for anything. I have it tonight, if you're interested.'
She stretched at full length, hummed again, then sat up. 'I can't
get that damned tune out of my head. What a slouch you are!
Surely you want to dance. Come on and take a turn.'

There was an awkward pause, then he said:

'I'm afraid I wouldn't be much good to you.'

'Why not?'

'It will probably surprise you. I don't dance.'

'What! Tell me another. You're having me on.'

'No.' He had to smile at her expression. 'I was too busy
shoving myself through college to learn any parlour tricks.'

'Well, now's your big chance. It's dead easy if you have a good
teacher. And that's just what I am.'

'No, really. I'll only walk all over your feet and make a complete ass of myself.'

'Who is there to see you up here? The old man's gone to the
bar and Mother's dozed off. We've got the music, and the moon.
It's a perfect opportunity. And all free, gratis, and for nothing.'
She stood up and held out her hand. 'Come on, I'll put you in
the mood.'

He rose and, rather gingerly, placed his arm round her waist.
They started off.

'It's a foxtrot,' she told him. 'Just keep time. Short steps.
Now turn. Swing round. Hold me closer, I won't break. Closer,
I said. That's better. Strange as it may seem, we're supposed to
do this together.'

It was surprisingly easy. The tune was so catchy, she was such
a good dancer, so responsive, with such an easy laxness of posture,
that he found himself instinctively following the beat of the
rhythm, improvising steps, letting himself go. When the band
below came to the end of the number she gave him a meaning,
condescending nod.

'Didn't I tell you?'

'It's tremendous,' he admitted. 'I'd no idea. And good exercise
too.'

She gave a short odd laugh.

'That's one way to look at it.'

'Of course, you're an expert – wonderful, in fact.'

'It's one of the things I'm really gone on. In my last year at
school I used to sneak out with another girl on Saturday nights
and go to the local Palais. We'd pretend we were pros, you know,

sixpence-a-timers. We had some larks, I can tell you, kidding and carrying on – until one night there was a regular shindy . . .'.

'Was that why you had to leave school?'

Unexpectedly she tossed her head back with an injured air.

'That's a very personal question. I don't like it brought up just like that. It was no blame of mine. Actually, if you want to know, I've danced mostly with Bert, my own brother. And he's respectable enough.' Suddenly she laughed. 'Or, is he? Well, never mind, I forgive you. Now get me a cigarette, and bring the lighter. They're in my bag beside the chairs.'

She leaned against him while he flicked her gold lighter.

'You don't use these?' He shook his head when she offered a cigarette. 'What a lot of things you seem to have done without.'

'I'll get them all one day.'

'Don't put it off too long. I always go straight for what I want.'

They stood with their backs to the taffrail until the band struck up again, then she threw away her half-smoked cigarette and turned to him.

'We're off again. Put some feeling into it. Imagine you've just picked me up on the prom at Blackpool and we've really clicked.'

'Good Lord,' he grinned. 'That's not my line at all.'

'That's why you're so nice,' she murmured, pressing a little closer to him. 'But try all the same.'

They danced the next three dances and with each he could feel his improvement. This was a new experience, and exciting that he could pick the steps up so quickly. But with an eye to the proprieties he felt that it must not be overdone. As they approached her mother he drew up.

'Thank you so much, Doris. It's been simply grand, and now,' he looked at his new watch, 'I must say goodnight.'

'Goodnight nothing, it's quite early and we're only beginning to have fun.'

'No, really, Doris, I have to go below.'

She stared at him, her slate-blue eyes clouding with anger and disappointment.

'How stupid can you be? Wasting everything, with this moon and when we're just getting in the mood. We'll sit out for a bit if you're tired.'

'I'm not tired. But I do think it's time we both turned in.'

Mrs Holbrook, who, awakening from her nap, had been watching them indulgently, seemed to think so too. She rose and came towards them.

'Time for bed,' she announced. 'We've all had a busy day.'

'You've certainly made mine a pleasant one,' Moray said gracefully.

'You'll be sorry you let me down like this,' Doris said in his ear, not moving her lips, as he passed her. 'You just wait!'

She's joking, he thought – can't really mean it. Goodnights were exchanged, Doris's a violently sulky one; she looked really put out. Then, with the last bars of 'Desirée' still ringing in his ears, he went below to his cabin, switched on the light, and there, on his locker, confronting him like a reproach, were the letters from home.

Instantly his mood changed. Shocked at his own forgetfulness, he undressed quickly, climbed into his bunk and, swept by compunction, settled himself to read. There were in all half a dozen sheets to Mary's letters filled with her large round careful handwriting. She began by acknowledging his letter from Marseilles, expressing her joy at his improved health. Yet she begged him to be careful still, especially of the night air, and she hoped that his duties were not proving too severe. As for herself, she was well, though missing him badly, marking off the days on her calendar until he would be back. But she was keeping herself busy, with lots of sewing and crochet work. She had bought material for curtains for their house, and also some remnants with which she had begun a patchwork quilt. There was the chance of a nice second-hand parlour suite, very good value, at Grant's just off the Esplanade. She only wished that he might see it, but he would soon, they had promised to reserve it. Unfortunately her father had been somewhat poorly lately, but she had been able to help by doing a bit with Donaldson, the foreman, in the bakery. She signed herself simply: your own Mary.

He finished reading with a worried frown and an odd constriction of his heart. Did he not detect a note of anxiety, an undercurrent of despondency even, in her words? She wrote naïvely, always from an open heart, yet it might be that she had not told all. Hastily, he turned to Willie's letter.

Dear Davie,

I hope you are well and having a good voyage. I wish I was

with you. I would like to see all these foreign countries, especially Africa. Things have not been doing too well here since you left. The weather has been cold and wet and Father had a bad turn with his heart, it was after a man came to see him one day. I think he is bothered about the business. I heard Aunt Millie say that the Stoddarts have fairly got their knife in us. Mary is doing the scones now in the bakehouse. I am sure she is missing you an awful lot. I am too. So tell the captain to get a move on and hurry back.

Affectionately yours,

Willie.

He put down the letter in concern, recognising from the brief and boyish phrases that Mary was having her troubles at home, and missing him too, so badly. His heart melted anew with love and longing, and with contrition, too, when he thought of the comfort, yes, the luxury, of his own pleasant life here. He wished suddenly that he had never taken this voyage. If only he could be beside her now to console and caress her. He must do something . . . something. The need of swift response, of immediate action, grew upon him. He thought for a few moments with knitted brow, then took up the officers' intercommunication phone. He asked for the wireless room. Saving though he was for their future, he must mortgage a little of his pay to reach Mary at once.

'Sparks, I want to send this radiogram.' He gave the address. '*Letters just received Port Said. Don't worry. Everything all right when I return. All my love David.*'

When Sparks had repeated this, word by word, he thanked him and hung up, smiling faintly. How thrilled and delighted she would be to get his message soaring to her across the ocean, and how comforted too! His mind now more at ease, filled with loving thoughts, he switched off the light and settled himself to sleep.

CHAPTER XII

THEY WERE IN the narrows of the Gulf of Suez, the peaks of
Sinai shimmering above in a humid haze. For three days it had
been hot, a harsh, insufferable heat. In the Red Sea the sun
blazed down upon the *Pindari*; the rocks of Aden, grilled to a
torrid ochre, cracked and fissured by the heat, were truly barren,
and the port itself looked so uninviting that few passengers went
ashore. The Holbrooks were amongst those who remained on
board. Doris, indeed, since the night of the expedition at Suez,
had not appeared on deck, being confined to her cabin with a
slight indisposition, Mrs Holbrook explained to Moray. He was
on the point of offering his services when a certain reserve in her
manner, perhaps a hint that this was a delicate subject, deterred
him. He decided it must be some mild monthly upset, a conclusion strengthened when Mrs Holbrook murmured intimately:
'Dorrie occasionally gets these turns, doctor.' So he merely sent
his regards adding that the inhuman heat was enough to knock
out anyone.

The weather had suddenly made him extremely busy. Apart
from a rush of surgery patients suffering from the usual complaints of dhobie itch, prickly heat and over-zealous endeavours
to acquire a tan, he had several quite serious cases. He was particularly worried over the two Kindersley children, who had
both gone down with acute colitis. Following on the Suez scare of
amoebic dysentery, Mrs Kindersley was in a state of near panic,
and as the twins were at one point critically ill he had himself
begun to fear the worst. But after being in almost constant
attendance for forty-eight hours, there was a sharp improvement
just before dawn on the third day, and with an inward sigh of
relief he was able to relieve the distracted mother. Red-eyed from
weariness, collar undone, hair dishevelled, he straightened stiffly,
read his clinical thermometer at the light.

'They'll be up and around . . . making a nuisance of themselves

'. . .' he smiled and put his arm round her shoulders, 'the beginning of next week.'

She broke down. She was a reserved, self-contained woman but, like Moray, she had barely slept for two nights.

'You've been so completely wonderful, doctor. How can I ever thank you?'

'By turning in and getting some rest. You've got to get fit for our tournament finals.'

'Yes.' She dried her eyes, trying to answer his smile. 'I should like that nice tea-service for our bungalow. But isn't your partner ill?'

'Oh, nothing much, I imagine.'

She had come with him to the cabin door. Now she hesitated, looking at him intently, then she made up her mind.

'Bill and I think a lot of you, doctor – especially after this. . . . We've often wondered if you were, well, beginning to get – mixed up with Miss Holbrook.'

'Mixed up?' he repeated blankly, then with a sudden flush, realising her meaning: 'Of course not.'

'I'm glad.' She pressed his hand. 'She's attractive, and she's obviously completely gone on you. But there's something odd about that girl, something I could never like – Bill says she's a split personality, she gives him the creeps. Now you do forgive me for having spoken?'

'Quite all right.' He tried to speak easily, although he was both embarrassed and offended. 'Now take that triple bromide I gave you and off you go to your bunk.'

Uncomfortably, he went back to his cabin, shaved and showered, drank two cups of coffee, and set out on his round of visits. He had begun to realise that Doris was not popular on the ship. She was often rude, kept a great deal to herself, and doubtless, since she wore an expensive new dress every other night, provoked feminine envy with her nice clothes. Moreover, it seemed to him that their continued success in all the competitions was arousing unfavourable comment. Was this the reason of Mrs Kindersley's dislike? He could scarcely believe it. Her intervention was well-meaning. Even so, he resented it. What right had she to interfere in his affairs, especially since he had been blameless in the matter? And what the devil did Kindersley mean, with his cheap sneer? He was no paragon – a beery, social type that probably hung around the club at Kadur all day; no wonder his wife was so surprised. All morning Moray brooded, and his train of thought, rather than turning him against Doris, swung him in her favour. Admittedly she was not an ordinary, run-of-the-mill type, but was she any the worse for that? There was something to her. Instinctively he rose to her defence. Still, he decided it might be wiser to cut down their efforts in the tournaments.

At the end of the week it suddenly turned cooler, his work and the weather became less hectic. He had time to write a long, loving letter to Mary, with an enclosure specially for Willie. And that same afternoon he was given a further lift when O'Neil took him aside to say:

'I thought you'd like to know, Doc, the skipper had a good word for you on the bridge this morning. In fact, when he heard about the Kindersley kids, he said you were doing a hell of a nice job. The only sawbones we've had yet that didn't get corns on his behind.' The big Irishman paused, took a long look at Moray's new watch, and grinned. 'Present from a grateful patient? Go to it, my boy. You'll soon reach pay-dirt or I'm not from County Down.'

'Haven't I told you I'm not interested,' Moray said, irritably. 'I'm only rather sorry for her because she's such a little outsider.'

'Then why aren't you a little insider?' said O'Neil, and roared with laughter. 'Ah, now, don't be so backward in coming forward, my boy. We're all looking for a bit of skirt on this bloody tub -- otherwise it would bore the arse off us. Say, did you ever hear this one . . .'

Moray had to laugh. What a decent sort O'Neil was. There wasn't a bit of harm in his remark, he didn't really mean it -- like his profane limericks, it was just fun. Why couldn't the Kindersleys see it that way?

On the following day, when it was even cooler, Doris appeared on deck. He came on her reclining in a sheltered spot, her hair bound with a silk scarf, a light cashmere rug over her knees, looking dull and with dark lines beneath her eyes. She did not move, merely flickered her lashes towards him.

'Hello, stranger, where have you been hiding?' He took the chair beside her. 'Feeling better?'

Injured by his brightness, she did not reply.

'Quite a few people have been laid out by the heat,' he continued. 'But now it's really lovely.'

They were in the Indian Ocean where the soft monsoon made songs in the rigging and a school of young whales, disporting gaily, blew temperate fountains about the ship.

'You've seen our escort,' he went on. 'I thought whales were only found in the Arctic, but O'Neil tells me they're a regular feature of this run.'

She took no notice of the remark, making it sound fatuous. Head pillowed sideways on the chair, she watched him with flat eyes as if she were drugged.

'You're a nice one,' she said.

'Why, Doris, what's the matter?'

'Don't pretend, after what you did. It was an insult. I haven't forgiven you yet. Who have you been dancing with while I was away?'

'No one. I've been waiting on my own special teacher.'

Her expression lightened faintly. She gave him a languid smile.

'Why didn't you come to see me? Oh, well, there wasn't any need. And I can't bear anyone when I have these turns. I don't get them often, mind you, not more than once in six months.'

He looked at her curiously; it wasn't what he had imagined. She went on:

'But they're not exactly fun. Even when the headache goes, they leave me so blasted low.'

'That's not you, Dorrie.'

'Don't give me that, like Mother. When I'm this way I keep thinking what's the good of anything, why go on, what's the use. I feel I'm a terrible person, different from other girls, all so full of sweet ideas. You know what I mean. Clapcows!' She laughed suddenly. 'Where did I get that word?'

'Well, it's good to be a little different from the ordinary.'

'Glad you think so. I used to try to work it all out, that time I was off school for a bit, wanting to be respected, to have everything just right. But I couldn't do anything about it. So now I just do as I feel, you know – what I feel like doing. I can't fight it. Don't you agree? You kill everything that's in you if you don't give way to your feelings.'

'Well . . .' He stared at her perplexedly. Why was she going on like this? He didn't follow her at all.

'You know the motto, be yourself. It's a challenge. I'm glad

I'm feminine, made for love, so I just want to be myself. Did you miss me? But you wouldn't, you beastly rotter, you make friends so easily and get on with everybody. I've never made any real friends, I just don't seem to get on with people, except you.' She paused, said in a low voice: 'Can't you see I've a frightful crush on you?'

He was touched by the admission. Her apathetic voice and unusual depression went to his heart. And of course he was flattered, too.

'Come now, Dorrie, you mustn't give way.' He reached out and pressed her hand. 'If you want to know, I did miss you.'

Inclining her head a little more to one side, she looked at him intently; then, retaining his hand as he made to withdraw, she tucked it beneath the cashmere rug.

'That's cosy. I missed *you* so much.'

Moray was fearfully embarrassed, not only by the unexpectedness of her action but because, undoubtedly without her knowing it, she had pressed his fingers against the warm softness of her thigh.

'Now, Doris,' he tried to speak lightly, 'you can't do that there here – not to the ship's surgeon.'

'But I need a little petting. Mind you, I don't let anybody into my life. Oh, I've been around with boys, some of them high, wide, and handsome, but you're different. I've such an unselfish feeling towards you.'

'Please . . . someone is sure to come along.'

'You can say you're feeling my pulse.' She gave him a malicious caressing look. 'Or else I'll tell them it's what the doctor ordered. Oh, you're doing me so much good. I feel less of a washout already.'

At last with a laugh she released him, but not before a wave of heat brought the blood to his cheeks. Quickly he countered it, forcing a reproving smile.

'You mustn't try these sort of tricks, my girl, or you'll come to a sticky end. In the first place you're too damned attractive, and in the second you might pick the wrong man.'

'But I've picked you.'

'Now listen, and be serious.' He turned the conversation determinedly. 'There's something I've been thinking. It's this. As you're not quite up to the mark, I feel we ought to scratch from the tournaments.'

'What!' she exclaimed, losing her air of indolence. 'Pack up. After we've gone all the way to the finals and are practically sure to win?'

'If we do, and scoop in all the prizes, we're sure to be blamed for pot-hunting.'

'I don't care about the prizes – that plated tea-service and cheap Woolworth china I frankly wouldn't touch with a barge pole. But if I start something I have to finish it, convince people I amount to something – especially that prissy Kindersley bitch. I got my self-respect to think of. I want to show that we're the best in the ship.'

'Well, we may be, but why rub it in?'

'Because I want to rub it in. And when I want a thing I usually get it. I may be a bit down now but I pick up quick. I'll be on top of my form in no time.'

'All right then,' reluctantly he pacified her. 'Have it your way. But we must play Saturday at the latest. It's the captain's dinner that night and the presentation comes before the concert.' He rose. 'Now I must get on with my round. See you anon.'

Saturday came, they did play – in the afternoon – and, as Moray had anticipated, won all three events. Mrs Kindersley and her husband fought hard in the deck-tennis match, but as Doris, quite herself again, played a fast aggressive game they were scarcely good enough. The climax came in the final set when Kindersley, reaching too far, missed his footing, skidded, then upended himself on the deck with a fearful thud.

'Oh, do be careful.' Doris leaned over the net with mock solicitude. 'You're rocking the boat.'

Not many spectators attended the event and a hollow silence greeted the remark. Indeed, when the match ended the applause that greeted the victors was less unenthusiastic than perfunctory. Moray was annoyed although Doris, who was again in high spirits, did not appear to notice any lack of warmth. Nor did her parents who, inevitably, were present. When Moray came off the court Holbrook took his arm and drew him into the smoke-room.

'I thought you and me ought to have a chat, doctor,' he remarked, with an approving smile, when they had found two armchairs in a quiet corner. 'And the better the opportunity the better the deed. Will you have a spot of something? No?

You'll not refuse a lime-juice then. And I'll just take a chota peg of Scotch and soda.'

When the drinks were brought he raised his glass.

'Good health! You know, lad, you remind me of my own young days. I was àmbitious too – a chemist's assistant in Bootle, making up prescriptions for ignorant G.P.s who didn't know an acid from an alkali. Many's the time I had to ring up and say: "Doctor, you've prescribed soda bicarb, and hydrochloric acid in the same stomach mixture. If I make it up it'll blow the bottle to bits." Maybe 'twas that sort of thing first gave me the idea that there was money in pharmaceuticals that actually worked. When I'd saved a bit and married the wife and opened my own bit of a shop in Parkin Street, I started off with a few of my own prescriptions: Holbrook's Headache Powders, Holbrook's Senna Paste, Holbrook's Anti-Sprain Liniment. I remember that liniment, it cost me three farthings a bottle, and I sold it for one-and-six. Damn good stuff too, all the Rugby League teams used it, it's still one of our lines today. Well, that was the beginning, lad.'

He took a slow swallow of his drink, then resumed, explaining the growth and expansion of his business, not boastfully, but with the quiet North Country assurance of a man who has built up an immensely successful enterprise and amassed a fortune from it. Holbrook's were now one of the biggest manufacturers of chemists' supplies in the United Kingdom, but the bulk of their profits came from the marketing of a large number of highly profitable proprietary medicines ranging from cough cures to anti-bilious pills.

'And don't you despise them, doctor, they're all first-rate prescriptions, I can show you testimonials by the thousands. I've kept a personal file of grateful letters that would warm your heart.' Holbrook nodded confidingly and warmed his own cockles with another swallow. 'So as we stand now we have the main factory in Bootle, a secondary unit in Cardiff, and big distributing warehouses in London, Liverpool, Glasgow and Belfast. We do a tremendous export trade with the East, and that's why my son Bert is out opening up new offices and larger stockrooms in Calcutta. But that's not all, lad,' Holbrook continued, knowingly prodding Moray with a forefinger. 'We have plans, big plans, for extending to America. Once Bert gets through with Calcutta I'm sending him to New York. He's already spied out a good factory site there. Mind you, it'll be a different kind of trade in the States. Times are changing and we'll go in for high class stuff, vitamins and such-like. We might even have a go at some of the new barbiturates. But believe me, whatever we do we'll make a slap-up success of it.'

He sat back, pulled out a cigar and lit up, wheezed a little, then, his twinkling eyes still holding Moray, he smiled.

'These are my prospects, young fellow me lad. Now what about yours?'

'Well, sir,' Moray had coloured slightly at the directness of the question, 'when I get back from this trip I have a hospital job waiting on me. A good one too, with opportunity for research work and . . . a salary of five hundred a year.'

'Ay, that's a job, lad, right enough and, saving your presence, a pretty ordinary one. I asked about your prospects.'

'Naturally, I'm hoping for advancement . . .'.

'What kind of advancement? A move to a bigger hospital? I'm pretty familiar with that line of country. It'll take years. Once you're in the hospital service you're bogged down in it for life. And for a smart young fellow like you, with brains and personality, that would be a crime.'

'I don't regard it as such,' Moray said stiffly.

'Well, I do. And I wouldn't tell you so if the missus and I didn't think the world of ye. Now look here,' he tipped the ash off his cigar end, 'I'm not a man to beat about the bush. We could use a young medico like you in our business, especially in the American plant. You could advise us on technique, work out new prescriptions, lay out our advertising and, since ye speak of research, get busy in our new laboratory. There would be plenty of opportunity for you. And from our point of view it would help us to have a professional man on the board. As to salary,' he paused, riveting Moray with a friendly, bloodshot eye, 'I would start you at fifteen hundred quid a year, with a possible bonus, and annual increases. Furthermore, I'll go so far as to say that, in time, if things went well between us, there might even be a partnership in store for ye.'

Thoroughly taken aback, stunned, in fact, Moray averted his gaze. The nature of this startling offer, while it had a sound basis of commercial logic, was in reality as transparent as the port-hole through which he now viewed with embarrassment the slowly heaving sky. And Holbrook meant it to be transparent.

104

How to refuse gracefully, without hurting the old boy's feelings, without indeed alienating the entire family, that was the problem At last he said:

'It's extremely generous of you, Mr Holbrook, and I feel deeply honoured by your good opinion of me. But I've accepted the hospital appointment, given my word. I couldn't break it.'

'They'll get somebody else,' Holbrook countered easily. 'Ay, without the slightest trouble. There'll be a regular hard-up rush.'

Moray was silent. He knew that he had only to mention his approaching marriage to kill the offer dead. But for some obscure reason, perhaps an over-sensitivity, an exaggerated delicacy of feeling, he hesitated. He stood so well with this worthy family that he did not relish the thought of shattering – as he undoubtedly would – a very pleasant and satisfactory relationship. Besides, the question of his engagement had never once come up during the voyage. It was not his fault if he had been mistaken for an unattached young man; he had simply not had the opportunity to introduce the subject. How painfully odd it would seem if he were forced to do so now. He'd look an absolute idiot, or worse, as though he had almost been ashamed to speak of Mary, No, with the end of the trip almost in sight, he could not place himself in so invidious a position. It wasn't worth it. In a few more days the Holbrooks would be gone, he would never see them again. And on the voyage home he would take good care to declare his position early so that this kind of contretemps could not possibly recur. In the meantime his best course would be to temporise.

'I needn't say how much I appreciate your interest in me, sir. But naturally, with such an important decision to be made, I'd have to think it over.'

'Do that, lad,' said Holbrook with an encouraging nod. 'The more ye think on it the better you'll like it. And don't forget my bit of advice. When a good thing comes your way, take it.'

Moray went below to his cabin, and shut himself in. He wanted to be alone – not to consider this extraordinary offer, for he had not the slightest intention of accepting it, but, simply for his own satisfaction, to reason in detail how the thing had come about. In the first place, there was no doubt but that Dorrie's parents had taken to him from the start. Mrs Holbrook especially had shown great partiality and had lately become almost maternal in her attitude. Old Holbrook was a tougher article, but he too had been won over, either through his wife's persuasion, or through an actual liking for Moray. In the second place, so far as could be gathered, there would be a definite advantage to Holbrook and his son Bert in the acquisition of an active and clever young doctor for this new American venture. So far so good, thought Moray; but the answer was not yet conclusive. A third decisive motive must have operated to bring the two other factors together.

Moray shook his head unconsciously, in self-disparagement, in immediate renunciation of all conceit, yet there was no escaping the fact that Doris herself must have had an important part in the development of this wholly unexpected situation. Even if he had not the evidence of Mrs Kindersley's recent remarks, there was proof enough in Dorrie's own behaviour. She was not the love-sick type, she would not sigh and moon around, but that look in her eye had a specific meaning that only a fool would misconstrue. Add to this the influence which, as a spoiled only daughter, she exercised over parents who were accustomed to yielding to her wishes, and in this instance willing to see her settled in a suitable marriage, and the answer was complete.

During these reflections Moray had been frowning. Now, looking at himself in the glass, he gave a short, troubled laugh. Doris had really gone in off the deep end – head over heels. No, no, it wasn't funny, not a bit of it. On the contrary – adjusting his expression – he felt put out and embarrassed, although no doubt it was flattering to be sought after and to have a rich, attractive girl so 'completely gone on him' – Mrs Kindersley's absurd phrase came to him again, making him smile – particularly when those moments on the upper deck, and others, came to mind, as they did now, with a sudden disturbing rush.

He checked himself, looked at his watch – that fine Patek Philippe – which showed five minutes to six. Good Lord! He'd forgotten about his surgery hour. He'd have to rush. Life was really exciting these days.

But before he left the cabin he went to his bedside chest and took out the locket Mary had given him. Gazing at her dear sweet face in the little snapshot, a rush of tenderness overwhelmed him. He murmured emotionally:

'As if I'd give you up, my own darling girl.'

Yes, her image would protect him. In future he would be calm and composed, pleasant and agreeable of course, but inflexible to any of *that* nonsense. Only ten days remained before they would be in Calcutta. He swore by all he held dear that he would maintain this attitude of discretion until the danger was past, and the voyage over.

CHAPTER XIII

THE TEN DAYS had passed, they were now in the delta of the Hoogly, and Moray, alone in his surgery, viewing that period in retrospect, found every reason to be satisfied with himself. Yes, he had kept his word. At the captain's dinner, a hilarious affair of paper streamers, toy trumpets, and false noses, he had been a model of discretion. Indeed, he had done better. Resolved not to allow Doris to make an exhibition of herself, and him, before the entire ship, when O'Neil read out the sports prize winners he stood up, diffidently yet calmly, and with an unexpectedness that took everyone by surprise.

'Captain Torrance, Mr O'Neil, ladies and gentlemen, with your kind permission may I say that Miss Holbrook and I fully understood from the start that as one of the ship's officers I was not really eligible to compete in these events. We only went in for the fun of the thing and although we were lucky enough to win, we've both completely agreed we couldn't possibly accept the prizes, which should go in all the events to the runners-up.'

When he sat down, instead of the few desultory handclaps that might have broken out, there was a sudden and sustained eruption of genuine applause. The Holbrooks were delighted, for even they had at last begun to sense the general feeling; Mrs Kindersley went up, smiling, for her tea service; and afterwards the captain actually gave him a word of approval. Only Doris reacted unfavourably with a very dirty look.

'Why the devil did you do that?'

'Just for a change I thought you might like to be popular.'

'Popular my tits. I wanted them to boo us.'

He danced only two dances with her, drank no more than a single glass of champagne, then, on the plea of having letters to write, excused himself and retired to his cabin.

After that, while never easy, it was less difficult. He avoided the boat deck where she usually sat, and when they did meet adopted a tone that was light and jocular. Beyond that, he kept himself strictly busy – the approaching landfall made his plea of extra work a plausible excuse. What Doris thought he did not know: following the dinner she had developed a habit of looking at him with narrowed, almost mocking eyes. Occasionally she smiled, and once or twice, when he made a simple remark, burst out laughing. Certainly her parents suspected nothing; they were more marked in their attentions to him than ever.

He sighed suddenly – it had really been quite a strain – then, rising, he locked up the surgery and went on deck. On the starboard side a group of passengers had gathered, viewing the river bank with an interest made greater by long days at sea. Tall coconut palms rose above the muddy shore lit by a flash of tropical birds, natives knee deep in the yellow water were throwing and drawing their circular nets, catamarans heeled and rippled past, the ship was barely moving, almost stationary, awaiting the river pilot. Amongst the others were the Holbrooks, and finding safety in numbers, Moray joined them. Immediately Mrs Holbrook excitedly took his arm.

'We're so hoping that our Bert will be coming aboard with the pilot . . . not that it's easy . . .'.

As she spoke a motor launch shot from the sandy, palm-lined shore and bobbed alongside the ship, and another figure was observed, looking upwards and waving, beside the uniformed pilot.

'It *is* our Bert,' joyfully exclaimed Mrs Holbrook, and she added proudly to her husband: 'Trust Bert to have managed it.'

He was on board and hugging all three of them within a few minutes, a fair, fattish, pink-faced, jolly fellow of about thirty-one or two, wearing a sportily cut, tight-waisted tussore silk suit, solar topee at an angle, fine two-tone buckskin shoes and a startling club tie. Bert, indeed, though inclined to flesh and, as now appeared when he removed his topee, rather thin on the top, seemed something of a dandy, exhibiting gold in his teeth and, on his person, certain articles of unessential jewellery. His eyes, alight with good-fellowship, were agreeably blue though they protruded slightly and had a faintly glassy sheen. His ready laugh, full of bonhomie and sportsmanship, a real back-slapping laugh, echoed across the deck. Too much thyroid, but a good sort, thought Moray, who had been standing some paces away, as

Bert came forward to be introduced to him.

Their meeting was cordial – anyone, Moray surmised, might be an old friend of Bert's within a couple of hours – but he could see that as yet Dorrie's brother had no inkling of his close friendship with the family, so he soon took off tactfully for his cabin. At lunch, however, when Bert and his father came down from the bar, Moray, already seated at table, discovered a fraternal arm around his shoulders while a well-primed voice exhaled into his ear:

'Didn't rumble you were *with* us, doc. Couldn't be more delighted if I'd won the Calcutta Sweep. We'll have a regular old chinwag later.'

The slow progress up-river gave them, as Bert put it, plenty of time to get together, and it was not long before Moray realised that while Bert might be a sport, a dasher and a josher, just a little flashy perhaps, and with a strong tendency towards pink gins at any hour of the day, he had, like his father, a good heart and a strong sense of family feeling. Moreover, it became equally apparent that for all his gush and gusto Bert had, as his mother put it, a head on his shoulders. He soon revealed himself as a thoroughly knowledgeable fellow, and when it came to business would certainly be a very cool customer with a capacity for getting things done. He had travelled extensively for the firm, had recently spent three months in the United States, and was full of the opportunities and excitements of New York. He talked well, with a man-of-the-world air, a kind of easy intimate verve that exuded cheerfulness and good-fellowship.

In his company Moray found the river passage all too short. He felt an actual disappointment when they reached Calcutta and the *Pindari*, churning the muddy water, began manoeuvring into Victoria Dock while the usual pandemonium of debarkation descended upon the ship. Amidst the uproar Bert remained cool and collected, everything was arranged and under control, speed and efficiency were the order of the day. As they came into the dock his long open Chrysler car and a truck were drawn up, waiting alongside. With his parents and Doris he came down the baggage gangway, first off the ship. Three stewards followed with the luggage. In the customs shed, while other passengers hung about interminably, a nod from Bert to the chief babu saw the Holbrooks through without formality. Then off they rolled in the big car to their reservations at the North Eastern Hotel.

All this happened so fast it left Moray somewhat dashed. There had been goodbyes of course, but hurried ones, given with such preoccupation as to leave him with the unsatisfactory and slightly painful impression of having been rather summarily discarded. Naturally, he was not at liberty to accompany them, yet he felt there might have been definite mention of a future meeting. However, as the *Pindari* would be two weeks in harbour, loading teak, tea, rubber and cotton goods, he told himself that he would have an opportunity to be with them later on. In any event, was it not best that they should have gone, leaving him free of all conflict, his mind undisturbed, at peace? He began to busy himself with his official duties. He was occupied most of the forenoon and when the last passenger had finally quitted the ship his first reaction was one of mild relief. The pressures exerted on him had been exacting: it would be good to relax.

By that evening a sudden inexplicable depression descended upon him, nor did it lift during the days that followed. The captain had taken up his usual quarters on shore and O'Neil, departing gaily for a trip along the coast to Kendrapara, had left Jones, the second mate, an elderly uncommunicative Welshman, to supervise the routine operations. Jones, a frustrated man, stuck with a master's ticket in a subordinate position, had never had much time for Moray, and now he more or less ignored him. He spent much of his day bent over paperback thrillers in the dock canteen, reading and picking his nose, leaving the work in hand to the quartermaster. In the evening he shut himself in his quarters and played his accordion with mournful unction. He never went ashore except to buy ivory elephants to take home to his wife. Already, he assured Moray, he had a glass-cabinetful in his semi-detached house in Porthcawl.

The empty ship, moored to the filthy, mosquito-infested dock, exposed to the racket of unloading, the endless high chatter of the native stevedores, the scream of winches and the rattle of cranes, was unrecognisable as the noble vessel which had so buoyantly breasted the blue water. It made a miserable lodging. The heat was sweltering, mosquitoes swarmed into his cabin, kept him awake at night with their shrill menacing ping, obliged him to take precautionary measures against malaria. Fifteen grains of quinine a day lowered his spirits further. To make matters worse, the agent had issued an advice that the mail boat had been delayed by a strike at Tilbury and would not arrive until the following week. Moray felt himself even more deserted through the absence of letters, and more and more his melancholy thoughts turned towards his departed friends.

Why on earth did he not hear from the Holbrooks? Why ... why ... why? First with irritation, then with anxiety, and finally with all the heart-sinking of hope deferred, he kept asking himself that question. It seemed inconceivable that they should have forgotten him, cast him off as a reject, someone they had used on the voyage but had now decided they did not want. Yet this mortifying thought grew within him. He pictured them in their de luxe hotel, every moment of their day delightfully filled with entertainment and sight-seeing, new faces and new friends around them. Amidst such distractions it might after all be easy to forget. And Doris: no doubt she had quickly found another interest, she who had been crazy about him. He winced jealously, between apprehension and anger. This was the most tormenting thought of all. Only his pride and the dread of a rebuff kept him from ringing her at the North Eastern.

In an effort to occupy himself he essayed a tentative expedition ashore. But the docks were miles from the city proper, he could not find a gharry, and after losing himself amongst a huddle of ramshackle huts where squatting natives squirted scarlet betel juice into the pervading dust, he finally acknowledged defeat, and plodded back to the ship, with the wretched sensation that he had reverted to the drab and dismal days of his youth.

It was then that he began really desperately to miss the Holbrooks, and all that he had enjoyed in their society. What a wonderful family they were – how hospitable, generous, and – now he made no bones about it – so rich! He'd never have the luck to meet such people again. Mrs Holbrook was sweet, so kind and motherly. Bert was such a good sort; they had taken to each other on sight. And the offer the old man had made him, admitting that he couldn't accept it, was fantastically favourable, the chance of a lifetime. Never would such a golden opportunity recur. Never. By comparison his future at the little Glenburn Hospital was dimmed to drab insignificance. And he had called himself ambitious.

And Dorrie, did he not regret her most of all? What a damned attractive girl she was – even her variable moods were somehow fascinating. One could never be bored by her. On the contrary, just to be with her was an excitement. At night, sleepless in his stifling cabin, which lay close against the high dock wall, he tossed about in his bunk, thinking of their dances together, of how, looking into his eyes with that intent and silent invitation, she had pressed against him, of that afternoon on the boat deck when all sorts of possibilities had opened to him. A wave of hot longing swept over him. What a fool he had been to reject that seductive offering. How O'Neil would laugh, if he ever came to hear of it. What a clot she must have thought him. Could she be blamed for having written him off altogether? He buried his face in the pillow in an access of misery and self-contempt.

CHAPTER XIV

AT THE END of that week, on a sweltering, gritty forenoon, as Moray leaned idly over the deck rail, his spirits at their lowest ebb, he saw, as in a mirage, the big shining Chrysler enter the dock and roll alongside the ship. Stunned, he raised his hand to his eyes. It couldn't be real, the sun and his imagination had produced a visual hallucination. But no, there, gracefully reclining in the rear, one arm negligently along the upholstered seat back, plump legs nonchalantly crossed, Burma cheroot poised airily between ringed fingers, topee at a rakish tilt, was Bert.

'Do my aged eyes deceive me, or do I perceive the medical officer of the good ship *Pindari*?' Bert called up with a grin: then, in a different voice, 'Bring out your gear, old boy. You're coming to us.'

Moray's heart leaped. They had not forgotten him. Pale with excitement and relief he rushed down to his cabin. What an idiot he had been – of course they wanted him, it couldn't have been otherwise. In less than five minutes he had changed out of his uniform and was in the car with his suitcase, which the native chauffeur bestowed in the boot. As they purred off towards the city, Bert explained the reason for the delay in calling for him – a hitch in the warehouse lease that had taken several days to straighten out. But now the agreement was signed and they were free to let themselves go in a proper good time.

'This is a lively old burg once you savez your way around,' he confided easily. 'Some geezer called it the City of Dreadful Night, but I've found the nights full of something better than dread. There's a couple of little Eurasian nurses – hot stuff and pretty as you find them.' He blew an explanatory kiss into the air. 'I speak with the voice of experience, m'boy. But there, I know you're only interested in our Doris. And believe me, though she's my sister, Dorrie's a pretty good number herself.'

Clear of the outer straggle of dilapidated shacks, they entered the city proper by the wide, crowded stretch of Chowringhe Road, swept past the broad maidan, green with ficus trees and studded with lamentable equestrian statues, then drew up under the tall portico of the North Eastern Hotel. They were bowed in, through the high marble pillared hall, whirling with ceiling fans, and Bert led the way upstairs to the room he had reserved for Moray adjoining their own apartments on the first floor.

'I'll leave you to get straight for half an hour,' he said, looking at his watch. 'Ma and Dad are out, but we'll all meet at tiffin, meaning lunch, Dave.'

When he had gone Moray looked round the room. It was most luxurious – large and cool, tastefully tiled, with latticed jalousies and fresh, draped mosquito curtains shading the large high bed which had been turned down to expose fine spotless linen. The furniture was painted a pale shade of green, and a bowl of roses stood on the dressing table. Beyond was the bathroom, white and gleaming, lush with towels, soap, bath salts and a soft white bath robe. He smiled delightedly. What a difference from his small, stuffy, mosquito-ridden cabin: this was the real thing. He unpacked his few things, had a wash, and was brushing his hair when the door opened and Doris came in.

'Hello,' she said briefly.

He swung round.

'Dorrie . . . how are you?'

'Still breathing, if it interests you.'

They gazed at each other in silence, he with admiring ardour, she with an almost expressionless face. She was wearing a smart new clinging frock in soft petunia colours, fine beige silk stockings and high-heeled suède shoes. She had on a lipstick that matched the predominant pink in her frock, and her hair had been freshly set. She looked different, smarter even than on the ship, older, more attractively sophisticated, and, alas, less attainable. Her scent came towards him.

'You look . . . stunning,' he said huskily.

'Yes,' she said coolly, reading his eyes. 'I believe you're slightly glad to see me.'

'More than slightly. The question is . . . what about you?'

She gave him a long direct stare, then barely smiled.

'You're here, aren't you? That seems to be the answer.'

'Good of you to have me,' he murmured, submissively. 'It was rather miserable down at the docks.'

'I thought it might be,' she said with cold knowledge. 'I wanted to punish you.'

He looked at her blankly.

'What on earth for?'

'I just wanted to,' she answered noncommittally. 'I like to be cruel sometimes.'

'What a little sadist,' he said, trying to catch the facetious note he had once used towards her. Yet as he spoke he had the odd sensation that the balance of their relationship had altered, passed to her. He felt suddenly, dismally, her wish to establish that on shore he had ceased to be the dashing, sought-after young ship's surgeon in his natty company uniform, and was no more than an ordinary young fellow in a worn hand-me-down suit that did not fit and was quite unsuitable for the climate. However, although aware of the effect she had created, she had dropped the subject as though it no longer interested her.

'You like my new dress?'

'It's a dream,' he said, still striving for lightness. 'Did you get it here?'

'We bought the silk in the bazaar yesterday. They have lovely native material there. It was made up in twenty-four hours.'

'Fast work,' he commented.

'And about time,' she said coolly. 'I can't stand waiting, or being put off. To be quite frank, I've had about enough of that in the last two weeks, the way you've been giving me the air. And incidentally, because I've told you off, don't imagine we're all straightened out. I haven't forgiven you yet by a long chop. I'll want a word with you later,' As she turned to go she seemed to relent. Her expression cleared slightly. 'I hope you like your room. I put the roses in myself. I'm just across the corridor –' she flashed him a sly glance, 'if you need anything.'

When she had gone he remained staring at the panels of the closed door. She was offended, and no wonder, after the way he had cold-shouldered her. How stupid and unmannerly he had been to hurt her feelings. He hoped she would come round in the end.

Below, in the great marbled lounge, his welcome by the Holbrook parents was altogether different, almost that of a returned son. Indeed, Mrs Holbrook kissed him on the cheek. Luncheon was more than a reunion, almost a festival. They had a table by the window, overlooking the gardens, four native servants in white tunics with red sashes and turbans stood behind their chairs, the food, chosen by Bert, was rich, spicy and exotic. This was the first time Moray had been in an hotel since that eventful day at the Gairsay Grand, but if a recollection of that other, so different, lunch crossed his mind it was swiftly gone, swept away by Bert's explosive laughter. Exuberantly bent on showing them the town, he was, while juicily disposing of a succulent mango, outlining his programme for the coming week. This afternoon he proposed to take them to the Jain Temple and the Gardens of Manicklola, to see the famous fish in the ornamental lake.

'They're quite remarkable,' he concluded. 'They come to the surface and swim over to you when you call them.'

'Now, now, Bert,' Mrs Holbrook smiled in fond protest.

'Seriously, Mater. I'm not joking. They'll eat out of your hand if you want to feed them.'

'Imagine that! What do fish like best?'

'Chips,' Doris said in a bored voice, then went into fits of laughter.

After a siesta, when the sun had begun to decline, they set off, driving through thronged bazaars where the sacred cattle, garlanded with marigolds, wandered amongst the stalls, butting through the crowds, browsing at will on the fruits displayed. Strange sounds, high-pitched and remote, struck the ear above the high keening of native tongues, a distant temple bell, the booming of a gong, a sudden shrill cry, that lingered, vibrating on the nerves. The air was charged with aromatic scents, heady and provocative, that stung the nostrils and drugged the senses. Moray felt as though he were lifted up, absorbed to a state of extreme excitement and beatitude. His individuality had been extinguished, he was not himself, but had become an altogether different man, entering upon a new and thrilling adventure.

Arrived at the temple, they removed their shoes and entered the incense-misted dusk where the great gold Buddha wore eternally that impassive and ironic smile. They wandered in the gardens of the court jeweller, a network of ornamental filigree, called and fed the huge obedient carp. Moray's intoxication increased. Doris, wearing her new petunia frock and a little plaited straw hat with a double ribbon that fell over the brim in two tantalising little tags, had taken on the special glamour of the afternoon. Seated beside her on the way home, he turned towards her with a surge of gratitude.

'It's all been so wonderful, Dorrie . . . and to see it with you . . .'.

She had sensed the change in him, and while her manner since lunch had been increasingly possessive, whenever he advanced she had chosen to retreat. Now she gave him a grudging little nod, as though prepared at last to relent.

'So you've decided I make a difference.'

'All the difference,' he murmured fervently, then added disconsolately: 'Only you've been so cold. I don't seem to make much difference for you.'

'Don't you?'

Her eyes seemed to cloud. Then, unobserved by the others, she suddenly lifted his hand and set her teeth in his forefinger, a sharp painful bite that went through the skin.

'That ought to show you if I'm cold,' she said. Then, at the sight of his face as instinctively he nursed the hurt, she began to giggle. 'Serve you right, for insulting me these last two weeks.'

Next day Bert took them to the races. He had tickets for the paddock and the club enclosure, also a stable tip for the big race. Nothing could go wrong, nothing, nothing. The horse, Maiden Palm, which Moray backed on his advice, romped home, a winner by three lengths. This was living, this was life! And Doris was being nicer, much nicer, to him. It was as though, having suitably punished him for his past defections, she had finally made up her mind to forget them.

On the day after, they visited the famous Zoological Gardens, crossed to Howrah, and viewed, at a discreet distance, the burning ghats by the Hoogly, drove out to the Royal Calcutta Golf Club for tea, finished with a trip down-river to Sutanati. Money opened the door everywhere. Bert on holiday was a spender, a lavish tipper; Moray saw hundred-rupee notes materialise inexhaustively from Bert's wallet, pass expertly to expectant palms. How wonderful not to pinch and scrape, to count every miserable coin in a penury he had known all his days, but instead to have money, real money, more than enough to enjoy all the good things of life.

Time flew past as one exhilarating event followed another in swift succession. Moray simply let himself go, inhibiting every warning thought, blocking out the past and the future, living only in the present. Yet always the date of the *Pindari's* departure drew near. When it was announced that she would sail on the following Tuesday, the fever in his blood was at its peak. Everything he had longed for all his life was here, ready to his hand, if only he would reach out and take it. Holbrook, suave and amiable, had not again pressed his offer: this had been made and still stood, the solid offer of a man of substance, awaiting Moray's reply. Mrs Holbrook, through increasing hints and promptings, strongly wished and hoped that he would accept. Bert, however, had no doubts whatsoever on the subject. On Friday afternoon when he came in from the Bengal Club, where he had a guest membership, he found Moray in the hotel lounge and drew up a chair beside him.

'I've got a spot of good news, Dave.' They had almost from the beginning been on terms of first-name intimacy. 'I've been trying to find someone who might sub for you on the return voyage. Well, just now at the club I ran into an I.M.S. doctor going home on leave, fellow by the name of Collins. He jumped at the chance of a free trip with pay. He's our man.'

As though stung by a wasp, Moray sat up in his chair. Bert's unexpected announcement, and the assumption of accomplished fact with which he made it, had finally brought the matter to a head. A sudden wave of weakness went over him and, yielding limply, he felt he must at long last unburden himself. After all, to whom could he better disclose and explain his predicament than to a good fellow like Bert?

'Look here, Bert,' he said, haltingly. 'You know I'd naturally . . . very much like to accept your father's offer . . . and especially to work with you. But . . . I wonder if I ought . . .'.

'Good Lord, why not? Dorrie apart, we need a medico in the business. We like you. You like us. I hate to stress it, old boy, but for you it's an absolute snip. You know how dear old Wagglespear put it – "There is a tide in the affairs of men." '

'But, Bert . . .' he went on abjectly, then broke off. Yet he had to say it, though every word was dragged up from the pit of his stomach. 'There's someone . . . a girl . . . waiting for me at home.'

Bert stared at him for a long moment, then went into fits of laughter.

'You'll kill me, Dave. Why, I've got girls waiting for me all over Europe – and pretty soon my little Eurasian fancy will be waiting for me in Calcutta.'

'But you don't understand. I've promised to . . . to marry her.'

Bert laughed again, briefly, rather sympathetically and under-standingly, then he shook his head.

'You're young for your age, Dave, and still a bit green behind the ears – that's partly why we've all taken to you, I suppose. Why, if you knew girls as I do . . . You think they'll pine away and die if you give them the soldier's farewell? Not on your sweet mucking life – excuse my Hindustani. I'll lay you a level fiver your little friend will get over her disappointment and forget all about you in six months. As for your own feelings in that direc-tion, which haven't struck me as too full of cayenne, remember what Plato or some other old Roman geezer said: "All women are alike in the dark." Seriously, though, I've talked it over with Ma and the old man. We all think you're just the fellow for Dorrie. You'll steady her down. She needs a bit of ballast, for off and on she's,' he hesitated, 'she's had a spot of trouble with her nerves. And she'll give you a bit of tiddley-high which in my humble opinion will knock some of the wool off you and do you a power of good. She's had fellows before, mind you, she's no angel, but you're the one she's gone right overboard on, she damn well means to have you. And let's face it, old man, you've gone so far with us as a family, it would be a crime if you backed out now. So why don't you pass the word and we'll start ringing those old wedding bells? And now we'll have a couple of chota pegs and drink to the future. Boy – boy!' Leaning back in his chair, he shouted for the khidmutgar.

CHAPTER XV

ALTHOUGH TEMPORARILY lulled by this jovial dismissal of his scruples, Moray did not find Bert's arguments altogether convincing or conclusive. He spent a troubled night and, awakening next morning still tense with indecision, decided he must at least go down to the ship and have a talk with Captain Torrance. It was only proper for him to enquire if Dr Collins might be an acceptable substitute, in the event . . . well, in the event that he was unable to make the return trip. The skipper was a sensible man whose advice was worth having; and besides, no one need know of his intention, the moment was favourable. Since Dorrie's mother had pleaded fatigue, nothing definite had been arranged in the way of sightseeing, and he had no engagement with the Holbrooks until the evening, when he was to meet them for the gala dinner and dance which was a regular Saturday night feature at the North Eastern. He got up, shaved and dressed and took a taxi to Victoria Dock.

The sight of the *Pindari*, now almost clear of dunnage, solid and familiar, struck a note of reality that was reassuring, even comforting, suggestive that once on board he might be safe, even from himself. He hastened up the gangplank. But when he reached the chart-room deck both cabins were locked, the quartermaster on duty told him that neither the captain nor Mr O'Neil was aboard. Going below, he could find only the assistant purser, who explained that none of the senior officers would be back from leave until Sunday evening.

'The second mate's on the dock if you want to see him.'

Moray shook his head, turned slowly away.

'By the by,' said the other, 'there's some mail for you.'

He went to his desk and fingered through a bundle of letters from which he handed over two. Moray, with a sudden constriction of his heart, recognised that one, rather thin, was from Willie, the other, thick and bulky, from Mary. He could not bring himself to open them. Later, he told himself. As he stepped off the ship to the dock, where the taxi still awaited him, he stuffed them into his inside pocket.

All that day Moray tried to summon up sufficient will, yet he could not bring himself to read the letters; the reproach of their pure and loving contents was more than he could face. And because he did not open them, because he feared them, he was no longer touched and contrite. Instead there crystallised in his mind an exasperation, almost a resentment, that they should have reached him at this crisis in his life. The letters, still sealed, swung him subconsciously towards Doris and all that the Holbrooks could offer him. Defensively, under the twin urges of money and sex, he set out to construct from his earliest beginnings a logical argument in his own favour: the loss of his parents, the unwanted child, the miseries of impoverished dependence, the superhuman efforts to get his medical degree. Surely he was due a rich reward, and now it was within his grasp. Could he be expected to throw it away, as though it were worthless?

True, there was Mary – he forced himself at least to think the name. But hadn't he been rushed into that affair, carried away by his impulsive nature, inexperience, and the romantic back- ground in which he had discovered her. She too, no doubt, had been swept off her feet by those same untrustworthy and transient influences. He didn't want to hurt her or to leave her in the lurch, but he did owe something to himself. And who knew but what, later on, he might be able . . . well, to do something for her, to make up for his defection. He didn't quite know what, but it was a comforting possibility. Young men made mistakes, repented of them, and made amends – were forgiven. Must he be the excep- tion?

This was his frame of mind when, still uncertain and undecided, he went down somewhat broodingly at eight o'clock to join the Holbrooks in the restaurant. Clearly his mood was not keyed to enjoyment, yet it was amazing and in the circumstances doubtless commendable how, not to put a damper on the party, he cast aside his personal problems and reacted to the lively welcome of his friends. Bert especially was in tremendous form, and the moment he set eyes on Doris he knew that she was in one of her sultry, over-charged moods. She had prepared herself with thoroughness and was wearing a short, sleeveless white dress, cut low in the neckline and embroidered with little crystal beads. It looked what it was, a most expensive piece of flimsiness. It did a great deal for her, and she knew it.

The dinner, which was luscious and prolonged, proved a further reviving influence, and when, after the dessert – a delectable compote of pineapple and persimmons served with chapattis – coffee and cognac were brought, Moray saw what an idiot he had been to mope and worry all day. Now he hadn't a care in the world. Presently they went into the ballroom where the old man had, as usual, done things in style. Champagne stood in an ice-pail beside their orchid-strewn table on the edge of the dance floor, facing the palm-fringed platform occupied by the scarlet-coated band.

'We like to see the young folks enjoying themselves, don't we, Mother?' As they took their places Holbrook made the remark in a sentimental tone induced by several double brandies. 'Couldn't you have found yourself a nice partner too, Bert?'

'I would have, Dad, only I'm sorry I can't stay long,' said Bert, with a wink to Moray. 'Got to see a dog about a man.'

'Have a drop of bubbly before you go.'

The cork popped. They all had a glass of champagne. Then the lights were dimmed, the band struck up a waltz. Bert got to his feet with a theatrically formal bow to Dorrie that exposed and bisected his tight plump buttocks into two full moons.

'May I claim family privilege, and have the honour, Miss Holbrook?'

They danced this first dance in brother-and-sister fashion, then, after downing a second glass of champagne, Bert breezily consulted his watch.

'Good Lord, I must push off or that little poodle will be barking up the wrong tree. Be sure you all have a good time. Cheerio, chin-chin!'

'Don't be too late, Bert dear,' remonstrated Mrs Holbrook. 'You were last night.'

'Certainly not, Mater.' He bent and kissed her. 'Only let's face it, ducky, Bert's a big boy now. See you bright and early in the morning.'

He's off to the little Eurasian, thought Moray. The band struck up a snappy one-step. Mrs Holbrook glanced at Moray, then at Doris, not smiling this time but with serious meaning, as though to say: You two now, and while you're about it make up your minds. Moray could not take the floor with confidence. Besides, he had sampled the cognac thoroughly after dinner, and it seemed to be going well with the champagne.

'If I may say so, my dears,' Mrs Holbrook commented, when they returned, 'you make a very handsome couple.'

Holbrook, smiling indulgently, just a trifle fuzzy, poured them both another glass of champagne. Then they danced again. They danced every dance together, and it seemed as though each time his arm encircled her she drew closer to him, so that every movement of her body provoked an answering movement of his, until they moved as one in a corresponding rhythm that throbbed along his nerves. He could feel that she was wearing very few clothes. At first he had made pretence at a few remarks, commenting on the other dancers and on the band, which was first rate, but she silenced him with a pressure of her arm.

'Don't spoil it.'

Yet if she maintained silence, there was in her wide bright greedy eyes, which she kept fixed unremittingly upon his, something communicative, not an inquiry now, a message rather, impossible to misunderstand, both possessive and intense. Only once did she speak again when, with an impatient glance towards her parents, she murmured restively:

'I wish they'd go.'

They did not, in fact, stay late. At half past ten Mrs Holbrook touched her husband, who was half asleep, on the shoulder.

'Time we old folks were in bed.' Then, with a restraining smile: 'You two can stay just a little while. But don't wait up too long.'

'We won't,' Doris said briefly.

For the next number the lights were lowered, and as they swung round behind the band she said, a trifle unsteadily:

'Let's take a turn outside.'

It was warm and still in the garden and dark under the high screen of greenery. She leaned back against the smooth bole of a great catalpa tree, still looking up at him. Trembling all over, he placed his arm behind her neck and kissed her. In response she pushed her pointed tongue between his lips. Then, as he pressed closer, the button on his cuff caught the string of seed pearls round her throat. The clasp gave way and pearls dropped into the low front of her dress.

'Now you've done it,' she said, with a queer strained laugh, passing her hand across her throat. 'You'll have to find them for me.'

His head was whirling, his heart pounding like mad. He began to search for the necklace, first in the yoke of her dress, then moving between her firmly nippled breasts, further down over the smooth flatness beyond.

'I'll tear your dress.'

'Never mind the dress,' she said, in that same choked voice.

Then he discovered that she was wearing nothing beneath her frock and, since all the time she had the broken necklace in her hand, what he found was not the pearls. He forgot everything; all the suppressed desire of the past weeks went through him in a blinding rush.

'Not here, you fool.' She broke away quickly. 'In your room . . . in five minutes.'

He went straight upstairs, tore off his clothes, switched off the light and flung himself into the bed. A shaft of moonlight pierced the darkness as she came in, closing the door behind her. She took off her dressing gown, stood stark naked, then parted the mosquito curtains. Her body had an almost sultry warmth as she wound her arms tightly round his neck and drew him towards her, fastening her mouth on his so that her teeth edged into his lower lip. She was breathing quickly and under her crushed breast he could hear the hot pulsing of her heart.

'Quick,' she breathed. 'Can't you see I'm dying for you?'

If he had not at once realised that she was not a virgin, now he would have known it by the nature of her response. When at last she lay back, though not releasing him, she gave a long-drawn-out sigh, then pulled his head down beside her on the pillow again.

'You were good, darling. Was I?'

'Yes,' he said in a low voice, and meant it.

'What a lot of time we've wasted. Couldn't you see I wanted you, wanted you like mad, right from the start? But it's going to be perfect from now on. We'll tell them in the morning. Then we'll both be off with Bert to New York. Oh, God, couldn't you have seen how gone I am on you? I'll never have enough of you – you'll see.' With her tongue she touched, played with his lips, stroked his body with her finger tips. A sudden rigor passed over her. 'Again,' she whispered, 'only longer this time . . . and the next. It's so lovely, make it last.'

She remained with him till the first grey light of dawn.

That morning, after hilarious congratulations at breakfast, he took a walk to clear his head. He felt a trifle listless, but she was really the goods, he could scarcely wait until tonight, and of course there was the job, the money, and the future all secure. Damn it all, a fellow had to look after himself. In the dulled state of his mind, it was less difficult to shut out the past and think only of the future. Passing across the Howrah Bridge he leaned suddenly over the parapet and without looking, taking his hand from his inside pocket, dropped the two letters, still unopened, into the filthy, corpse-polluted waters of the sacred Ganges.

PART THREE

CHAPTER I

DAWN COMES EARLY in the Swiss Oberland. Its hurtful brightness and the clanging of the cowbells awoke him. As he had feared, the pheno-barbitone had failed to act, and in those hours of wakefulness he had relived every moment of those fatal, youthful months until, tortured, at three in the morning he had fumbled for a capsule of sodium anytal, which had given him a brief respite of total blackout. Now, with throbbing temples, deadened by the drug, he faced the situation dully yet with almost desperate resolution, aware that, at long last, he must take the decisive step.

Wilenski had told him so, at that last consultation in New York, smiling down encouragingly, as he always did, with one arm across the headrest of the couch and lapsing into that caressing Southern accent which he used to untie the inner tangles of his patients.

'You may have to go back one day, just to break that little old guilt-complex for keeps. Actually, you want to go back, partly because you've got a suppressed nostalgia for home, but of course mainly to see your – your friend and straighten things out with her. Well, why not? Better late than never. If things haven't gone too well for her, you're in a position to help. Why,' his smile took on a genial slyness, 'now you're a gay widower, if you find her still attractive, you could clear the whole thing up by marrying her – provided, of course, she's free.'

'She will never have married.' He had no doubts whatsoever on that score, though he hoped she might have found happiness.

'Keep what I'm telling you in mind, then. And if you feel you're getting into trouble again, take my advice and go back.'

Yes, he would do it, and at once. Relief came to him with the reaffirmation of his decision. He pressed the bell and, after consulting the Swissair schedule, told Arturo to ring Zurich and reserve a seat on the two o'clock plane for Prestwick. He got up, shaved, dressed, breakfasted downstairs. Afterwards, while Arturo packed his valise, he smoked a pensive cigarette. He was taking only a few things, returning quietly, humbly, without the slightest fuss or ostentation, no Rolls, no signs of wealth, nothing. The thought, arousing sombre anticipation, injected his melancholy with a transitory gleam. As for the villa, in his absence, with a household so well organised, staffed by such trustworthy servants – he had hinted to them of an urgent business appointment – it was simplicity itself to leave, even at a moment's notice.

The phone rang: he rose and went to the instrument. As he had expected, it was Frida von Altishofer.

'Good morning. Am I disturbing you?'

'Not at all.'

'Then tell me quickly. Are you well . . . better?'

His frightful night made him long for a word of sympathy, but he knew this to be unwise.

'Definitely better.'

'I am so glad – and relieved, my friend. Shall we go walking this morning?'

'I wish we could. However . . .' he cleared his throat and delivered the polite fiction he had prepared: yesterday there had been a telegram, purely a matter of business, but upsetting, as she had observed, which he ought to put right by a visit to his British lawyer. He must leave this morning.

There was a sharp silence in which he sensed surprise, disappointment, perhaps even a hint of dismay, but quickly she recovered herself.

'Of course you must go – such a man of affairs. But do not tire yourself. And come back soon, before I leave for Baden. You know how much you will be missed.'

Arturo drove him to the airport in the Humber utility car, thus setting the tone of moderation for the entire journey. In Zurich it was his custom to lunch at the Baur-au-Lac, but today he passed by that admirable hotel, telling Arturo, who expressed concern, that he would probably get some sort of snack on the plane. They were early at the airport but fortunately the plane was on time, and at two o'clock precisely it took off. As the D.C.7 soared through low cloud into the blue his fixed expression did not relax, yet a strange elation took possession of him. He was going back, at last, back after thirty years to the country of his birth. Why in God's name had he delayed so long? – for there alone could he find peace of mind, a final liberation from that remorse which from time to time had fallen upon him like a dark oppressive cloud. A word came to mind, edifying and full of promise. He was not a religious man, but there it was: Redemption! He repeated it to himself, slowly, earnestly.

Suddenly, elevated though they were, his thoughts were interrupted. The pretty stewardess was smiling down at him in her smart blue uniform, serving the snack he had deprecated and which now appeared as an excellent meal appetisingly arranged on a tray: smoked salmon, a wing of chicken with braised celery, peach melba, and a glass of excellent champagne. After this, despite his wretched night, he felt more himself, and drowsed over the Irish Sea, but always with an eye for the landfall of the Scottish coast. Prestwick was sighted at half past six, in the indigo haze of an early twilight through which pinpoint lights had begun to sparkle. Their landing was smoothly perfect and, only a few moments after, he was hearing with quickened pulse the almost forgotten burr of his native tongue. Bareheaded, on the tarmac, he drew deep breaths of the soft lowland air.

Home, at last . . . home. Unconsciously he murmured the famous words of Rob Roy Macgregor: 'My foot is on my native heath.' Emotion flooded him.

Outside the customs shed the coach was waiting, and presently it set off, running smoothly through the Ayrshire farmland. Eagerly he kept rubbing the moisture from his window in the effort to snatch glimpses of the darkened landscape, scarcely realising the passage of time until the noise of traffic alerted him: they were at the air terminal in Winton.

He took a taxi to the Central Hotel where he secured a room on the quiet side, away from the station platforms and the noise of trains. Now it was late and he was tired. He ordered milk and sandwiches brought to him; then, after a hot bath in which for fifteen minutes he soaked, relaxing his tense nerves, he went to bed. He slept immediately.

CHAPTER II

NEXT MORNING, AWAKENING early to the thrilling awareness that he was actually in Winton, physically present, in the city of his youth, scene of his homeric strivings as a student, he had to damp down a great sweep of sentiment. He must be calm and judicious in his approach to this great turning point of his life. Yet as he rose quickly, dressed, and went down to breakfast in the warm, red-carpeted coffee-room, where for the first time in thirty years he tasted with relish real Scottish porridge and cream, followed, to the accompaniment of tea and toast, by an authentic finnon haddock, he was increasingly alert to the momentous prospects of the day.

Immediately he had finished his third cup of excellent tea he went to the lounge, took up the *Winton Herald* and, running through the advertisements, obtained the name of a motor hire agency. A small car, while inconspicuous, would facilitate his journey to Ardfillan and any subsequent movements which might be necessary. A curious inhibition withheld him from the obvious course of asking the head porter to arrange the hire, and instead he telephoned the agency personally. Could he have explained this vaguely irrational act? He was not known at the hotel, it seemed altogether unlikely that he would be recognised, yet all his instincts impelled him to concealment. At any rate, after requesting that the car, a small standard model, be delivered at the Central at the earliest possible moment, he was promised it, after some pressing, for one o'clock.

Restlessly, he looked at his watch: it was now just past eleven. With two hours to spare he went out, surrendering to the impulse to make a brief pilgrimage to the familiar places of his youth. The city, grey, cold, and soot-encrusted as ever, still with its overcast of smoke, showed few alterations from the days when he walked its drab and bustling pavements. At the corner of Grant and Alexandra Streets he boarded the yellow tram that would take him to Eldongrove Park. Outside the Park gates he got off, walked slowly through the gardens and, with increasing melancholy, up the hill to the University. But here, wandering through the shadows of the old cloisters, recollections of his student days were so painful and acute that, after a brief survey, he hastened from the precincts, passing at the lower gates the Gilhouse shop where he had sold his microscope to buy the ring with the little blue stone for Mary. His eye moistened. What a pitiful gift, compared to all that he could shower upon her now. Yet it had taken every penny he possessed. No one could have accused him of meanness or of the least foreknowledge of all that was to follow.

From Eldongrove it was not far to the Blairhill tenement and, driven by his mood, he took the road over the hill down to the docks. Yes, his old lodging still stood, a disreputable barrack, grimier, even more sordid, than before. Gazing upwards he saw himself, as a youth, bent over his books behind that narrow garret window. How he had battled and endured, fitting himself for a great and wonderful career.

And what, in God's name, had he made of his life? After noble beginnings, what had been the result? As he stood there, gazing upwards with an air of vacancy, a shaft of sincere compunction pierced him and he experienced not only genuine and bitter regret, but also an overwhelming sense of the futility of all that he had done since he left that attic room.

He had made a fortune, a large fortune, but how? Not as a brilliant surgeon, a specialist of the first order, esteemed and revered in his profession, but as a wretched pill-maker, a time-serving purveyor of popular remedies, of slight clinical significance, advertisements for which debased the landscape, and all sold at such profit over cost as to constitute a further imposition on the public. No, he must not be too hard on himself; some of his work – the group of analgesics he had developed from the phenothiazines, for instance – had been of value. Yet on the whole, what a burlesque of the career he had planned. Why, under heaven, had he done it? Why, above all, had he been such a fool as to marry Doris Holbrook?

Surely, on that fateful voyage, he might have foreseen her psychotic tendencies, realised that the moods he found so entertaining on board would be insufferable later on, that the physical excitements she offered him would quickly pall. His mind went back to the neat little Cos Cob house her father had set them up

133

in, convenient to the new Connecticut offices in Stamford. She had adored it – for six months – then suddenly hated it. Their move to nearby Darien, at first an immense success, was soon an equal failure. She seemed incapable of settling down or of adapting herself to a new environment, and his refusal to move again had started her off on daily trips to New York, almost a commuter on the morning and evening trains. Then came her futile art and sculpture classes, her style of dress increasingly extreme, her new, ever-changing, dubious acquaintances with whom he soon suspected she was deceiving him. When he remonstrated there were recriminations, estrangements, shouts through locked doors, hysteric reconciliations. She wanted to go back to Blackpool – could one believe it! More incredible still was the fact that now she actually seemed to hate him. When, after a long interval, he had smilingly attempted to resume marital relations, she had picked up her ivory hairbrush and practically brained him!

But he was getting on fast. Divorce might mean a break with the Holbrooks; he managed to put up with her. After five years in Darien an act of appeasement by old Holbrook had given them Fourways, a handsome property in the Quaker Ridge district of Greenwich. Quieter, conservative people here, the garden club – he persuaded her to join – their modest entertaining; he had hopes that she might settle down. All an illusion. Gradually, through increasingly erratic and intractable moods, fits of violence and periods of amnesia, she passed into depressive delusions. Finally the moment when Wilenski, called in consultation, put a consoling hand on his shoulder.

'Paranoid schizophrenia. She will have to be certified.'

And then, for fifteen years, he had been the man with a wife in a mental clinic, awaiting the results of the insulin and electro-shock treatments, the slight improvements and deeper relapses, enduring the whole hopeless muddle, until the unmentionable relief of that terminal hypostatic pneumonia.

Was it surprising, in these tragic circumstances, that – himself walking the tightrope of nerve tension – he had needed, had thrown himself into, his work with Bert. There was nothing wrong with Bert, good, decent, genial Bert, who had always stood by him fair and square, helped him repeatedly in dealing with Doris, even admitted liability in the matter for having glossed over her adolescent attacks, and who, after old Mr Holbrook's death, had given him outright an equal partnership in the rich and expanding American firm.

And work apart, as a man sorely victimised, had he not been justified in devoting himself *to himself*: to set out to cultivate his personality, to study the arts, acquire languages, French, German and Italian to be precise, to dress with taste – in short, to develop himself into a finely mannered man, consciously dated in his style – in his reading he favoured the gracious Edwardians – a veritable 'man of distinction' who with his natural charm and ability to please could command, even in this appalling age when all sense of values had gone by the board, immediate interest, attention and respect. And of course, in his position, he had a physical obligation to himself, which as a well-read man he could sanction – if this were necessary – by quoting Balzac's pointed letter on the subject to Madame de Hanska. He too had no intention of allowing himself to degenerate into impotence and imbecility! Naturally he recoiled from promiscuous adultery, from those brief and unreliable encounters that took place after cocktail parties in cars parked in the country club shrubbery. Chance threw him in the way of a quiet little woman – he had always preferred the small-boned type – a widow in her early thirties, blonde and of Polish extraction, her name Rena, who worked, humbly enough, as a binder in a Stamford commercial publishing house. His tactful approach produced surprisingly agreeable results. He found her both soothing and satisfying, neat, clean in her person, undemanding, and absurdly grateful for his, help. Soon a discreet and regular arrangement was reached between them. He even grew quite fond of her, in her own way, and though she was fearfully broken up when he left America, he had done the right thing with a generous settlement.

Yes, there had been good reason for the pattern of his life, yet though self-exoneration brought some relief his thoughts were still painful as he turned away and, descending Blairhill, made his way back to the Central. Here he could not even think of lunch. But, feeling the need of something in preparation for his journey, he took a glass of dry sherry and an Abernethy biscuit in the bar, after which he felt better.

The car arrived at the specified hour and when he had signed the necessary papers and paid the deposit he drove off. No need to ask the way. Free of the busy streets, he took the main western road, past the Botanic Gardens and the Westland playing fields, then on to the highway leading from the city outskirts to the lower reaches of the Firth. This, since his time, had been widened and improved, yet while now it bypassed the shipyards and steel works of the riverside industrial towns it still was the road that had taken him to Mary. He drove slowly, prolonging his sensations, though almost overcome by them as, one after another, known sounds and scenes broke upon him. That steady rat-a-tat from the yards, the hoot of the Erskine ferry boat, a long-drawn rusty wail from an outgoing tramp – these blended to a haunting dissonance that fairly ravaged him, as did the fleeting vistas of green woods and gleaming water, of distant purple mountain crests that sudden outward, upward sweeps of the way revealed to him. All, all brought before him, in sweet anguish, the image of the one woman he had truly loved.

Some thirty miles from Winton he reached the village of Reston and, turning off the main route, took the winding, narrow road that followed the widening estuary towards Ardfillan. His heart was beating like those shipyard hammers as he entered the little town, all so unchanged, as though he had left it only the day before. Still the same narrow strip of esplanade lapped by quiet waves, the iron bandstand, the tiny pier, the curve of low grey houses, the square church towers. So blurred was his vision, he had to stop the car momentarily. Oh, God, he had stopped exactly opposite that same wooden shelter where, when Willie was sent on the errand, he had taken Mary in his arms. He was in a turmoil, confused thoughts poured through his mind: would he find her greatly altered, would she recognise, let alone forgive him, was it even possible that she might refuse to see him?

At last he took himself in hand, drove further along the front and parked the car. Then, with lowered head, he walked up the lane giving access to the Douglas shop. He reached the familiar back street, lifted his head, then suddenly drew up. The shop was no longer there. Instead, a high brick frontage from which a whirring of machinery emerged, confronted him. He had built with such irrational confidence on finding everything as he had left it that he was less disappointed than stupefied. After a few blank moments he moved further along the narrow cobbled way, and saw that a wide new cross street had been cut at right angles to the old, giving access to a large double-fronted glittering establishment with a neon sign: *Town and Country Bakeries Ltd.*

Motionless, he stood gazing at the trays of starkly coloured cakes which filled the windows, then he crossed the street and went into the shop. Two pert-looking young girls in mauve dresses with white collars and cuffs were behind the counter.

'Excuse me,' he said, 'I am seeking a family who once owned a shop in this vicinity. The name is Douglas.'

They were of the age that construes the unusual as the absurd, and seemed prepared to giggle. But something, perhaps the excellence of his clothes, restrained them. One glanced at the other.

'I never heard tell of any Douglas, did you, Jenny?'

'Me neither,' Jenny said, with a shake of her head.

There was a pause, then the first girl said:

'Maybe old Mr Donaldson could help you. He's been here a long time.' Now she did giggle. 'A lot longer than us.'

'Donaldson?' The name touched a chord of memory.

'Our caretaker. If you go through the van entrance on the left you'll find his wee house opposite the bakery.'

He thanked her and, following her directions, found himself in what had once been the Douglas yard, greatly enlarged now, with the big machine bakehouse on the left, a garage for motor vans facing him, and on the right the old stable converted to a small one-storey apartment. He rang the bell and after an interval slow steps were heard within. The door opened, revealing the stooping, steel-spectacled figure of a man of seventy in a cloth cap, worn back to front, a black alpaca apron and carpet slippers. When Moray questioned him, he remained silent for a moment, soberly reflective.

'Know of James Douglas?' he answered finally. 'I think I should. I was his foreman for more nor twenty years.'

'Then I hope you can give me news of him, and his family.'

'Come in a minute,' Donaldson said. 'It's nippy by the door, this time of year.'

Moray followed him into a small dark kitchen with a faint blink of fire in the grate, the stuffy, untidy room of an old man living alone. Donaldson pointed to a chair, then, still wearing his cap, shuffled to his own corner and sat down below the wooden pipe rack.

'You're a friend of the Douglases?' he inquired, with caution.

'Of long ago,' Moray said hurriedly. 'And now almost a complete stranger here.'

'Well . . .', the other said slowly, 'the story of the Douglases is not a very cheery one. James, poor man, is dead and in his grave, lang syne, and Minnie, the sister-in-law, too. Ye may as well know that for a start. Ye see, James failed in his business and was made a bankrupt – there was queer work behind it, to do with condemning the property and making the new street, all by order of the town council. Anyhow, the disgrace just fair killed James, for he was an upright man and as honest as the day. Minnie, who was aye an ailing sort of body, soon followed him up the road to the cemetery. So that was that, and in place of James's shop we got these grand premises, and pastries that would rot your bowels – not that I have anything against the company, mind ye, they kept me on and gave me this bit of a job.'

He broke off, lost momentarily in the past. Intently Moray pressed forward.

'There was a daughter, was there not?'

'Ay,' the other nodded. 'Mary . . . and she had her troubles too. When she was a lass she got engaged to some fly-by-night that away and left her. A sore, sore heart she had for many a day. When I cam' out the auld bakehouse I used to see her greetin' by her window. But in time she come to, got verra religious in fact, and some years later when the new young minister, Urquhart by name, came to the Longend church, and a fine man he was, she had the luck to marry him. And 'deed, a nice bairn she gave him a year or so after.'

Stunned, Moray sat rigid in his chair. She had married, forgotten him, or at least betrayed what he had believed to be a unique and lifelong love: more painful still, had borne another man a child. In his present state of mind it seemed a desecration. And yet, for all his chill dismay, reason had not entirely left him. Who was he to deny her the right to happiness, if indeed she had found it?

At last, in a strained voice, he said:

'She is here, then, in the town, with her husband?'

'No. She left Ardfillan with her daughter not long after the husband died.'

'Died?' he exclaimed.

The old man nodded.

'He wasna' one of the strongest, ye ken, and when we had the big Spanish 'flu epidemic in thirty-four he was taken to his eternal reward.'

Unconsciously, Moray relaxed slightly, drew an easier breath.

The situation was suddenly and to some degree ameliorated. Dreadful, of course, to have lost a young husband whom he, on his part, would never have wished the slightest harm. Still, the unfortunate fellow had apparently been weakly from the start; the motive on Mary's side might well have been pity rather than love. Partially restored, and with renewed feeling, he put his final question.

'Where did they go, Mary and her daughter?'

'A village in the Lothians. Markinch they call it. The daughter wanted to train for a nurse and they sought a place that was near to Edinburgh. But what's come of them since I cannot tell ye. They werena' in the best of circumstances, and they've never looked near Ardfillan since the day they left.'

A long silence followed while Moray, with bent head, tried to reassemble his thoughts. Then, still visibly affected, he stood up and with a word of thanks pressed a note into Donaldson's hand. The old man, after feigning reluctance to accept it, was peering at his visitor across his spectacles with growing curiosity.

'My sight isna' what it was,' he remarked, as he accompanied Moray to the door. 'But I have an odd notion that I've seen you before. I'd like fine to ken who ye are?'

'Just think of me as someone who means to do well for Mary Douglas and her daughter.'

He made the statement firmly, with the consciousness of a new honesty of purpose and, turning, made his way back to the car. Now he perceived how illusory his hopes had been, how all his imaginings had been falsely based on a romantic re-creation of the past. Had he actually expected, after thirty years, to find Mary as on the day he had abandoned her, sweet with the freshness of youth, tenderly passionate, still virginal? God knows he would have wished it so. But the miracle had not occurred and now, having heard the history of a woman who wept for him late and long, who married, though not for love, then lost an invalid husband, who suffered hardships, ill-fortune, perhaps even poverty, yet sacrificed herself to bring up her daughter to a worthy profession – knowing all this, he had returned to reality, to the calm awareness that the Mary he would find at Markinch would be a middle-aged woman, with work-worn hands and tired, gentle eyes, bruised and beaten by the battle of life, but because of that the more willing, perhaps, to forgive and accept his generous attentions.

His heart warmed to these thoughts as he drove back to Winton through the fascination of the deepening river dusk. Then, all at once, it occurred to him that he had forgotten to ask Donaldson about Willie. Inexcusable omission! What, he now wondered, had happened to that bright little boy, the eager inquirer of their evening hours? Well, he would find out soon enough, and from Mary herself.

Seven o'clock was striking when he reached the hotel, and having eaten little all day he was thoroughly sharp set. After a quick wash and brush-up he descended to the grill room, ordered a double rump steak, onions, baked Arran Chief potato, and a pint of the local Macfarlane's ale – all with such aplomb that he might never have been away. Afterwards he proposed to yield to the rich seductions of golden syrup tart. How good these native dishes were. He attacked them hungrily, secure in the knowledge that he would leave for Edinburgh and Markinch first thing tomorrow.

CHAPTER III

ALTHOUGH THE CAR was not running particularly well, misfiring occasionally on one cylinder, he decided to retain it rather than face a chafing delay at the agency, and at eleven o'clock on the following morning, having settled his bill at the Central, he set out for Edinburgh. According to his road map, Markinch lay some five miles inland from Dalhaven on the east coast, a small village apparently – at least he had not heard of it – and its limited population would undoubtedly facilitate his search.

The day was grey and breezy, with woolpack clouds tumbling about the sky, but in the early afternoon, when he reached Edinburgh, a low sun broke through, sending shafts of brilliance from the Castle ramparts across the gardens of Princes Street. A good omen, he thought, setting his course along the eastern road to Portobello. Here the traffic was held up for a few minutes at the Cross to let the Portobello Girls' Pipe Band go through, on their way, he fancied, to some local gathering. It did him good to see the bonnie Scots lassies swing past to the strains of 'Cock o' the North', their kilts swishing about their hurdies, Glengarry ribbons streaming in the blast of the chanters. Scotland's natural resources, he told himself, with a smile, his discriminating eye singling out several most promising little pipers. But the hooting of cars behind recalled him and he drove on, through Musselburgh and Newbigging. He struck the coast beyond Gosford Bay and, drawing up beside a deserted beach, ate the sandwiches they had packed for him at the Central. Then he was off again. The sea had a sparkle, and a keen wind blew across the cropped links and the yellow dunes fringed with sharp-edged, bleached grass and tangled aromatic wrack. Offshore on his left the Bass Rock came in sight, and far ahead, on the landward side, the green cap of Berwick Law. Gulls were wheeling and calling above the blowing sands. He could taste the salt in the spray-filled, gritty air; the tang of it against his teeth was the very feel of home.

He had fixed on Dalhaven in advance, as a convenient centre, but when he arrived and circled the town seeking an inn, he could find nothing that looked suitable. The low, windswept houses, built of red sandstone, cowered about the fishing harbour with an inhospitable air, while the inhabitants, confronted with a stranger, proved dourly uncommunicative. Eventually, however, he found a friendly native and was directed with strong recommendations to the Marine Hotel, which stood above the golf course two miles beyond the town. This he discovered to be altogether superior, an establishment of the first class, where he was quietly welcomed by the manageress and shown to an excellent front room.

When he had washed he made inquiry as to the exact route, and after a short drive inland through winding country roads lined with hawthorn trees came to the village of Markinch, which as from an inner voice, he knew suddenly to be his true and final objective.

This conviction calmed his nerves, as he drove slowly down the single deserted street. Whitewashed cottages stood on either side, climbing nasturtiums still flowering against their walls. Not a soul in sight, only an old collie half asleep, one eye open, by the kerb. There was a general store and post office combined, then came a smithy, an oldfashioned shop with bottle-glass window panes and the sign: *Millinery* above, then across the way what looked like a small dispensary with the notice outside: *Welfare Centre*. In which of these should he make his inquiry? Perhaps the store and post office, although this would, unfortunately, bring notice of his arrival into the public domain. At the end of the street he was about to turn when some distance ahead he saw the village church and the adjoining manse. A thought struck him, induced by the recollection of a remark of Donaldson's, and by the desire also for privacy and discretion. He continued towards the church, which was of Scots baronial design with a square tower instead of a steeple, parked the car opposite, then advanced towards the manse, a small but decent greystone dwelling, and pulled the brass handle of the bell.

After a considerable interval the door was opened, and by the minister himself, a small sallow man with extremely short legs and an oversized head topped by a bush of grey hair. His old black suit and the frayed edge of his clerical collar gave him a disheartened appearance, confirmed by the cast of his features. A pen in one hand and a heavily corrected manuscript in the other suggested that he had been disturbed in the preparation of his sermon, but his manner was civil enough.

'What can I do for you, sir?'

'If I may trouble you, I am seeking a lady by the name of Urquhart.' Now the new name came more easily to Moray; at first it had wounded him to think of her as other than Mary Douglas. 'I understand she lives in your parish.'

'Ah, you must mean our excellent district nurse.' The little man's expression cleared, showed willingness to assist. 'She lives above the welfare centre you've just gone by. She is a very busy young person but if she's not at home you will find her in the dispensary from five until six.'

'I'm much obliged to you,' Moray said, well satisfied. 'You are obviously speaking of my friend's daughter. I presume that her mother lives with her?'

'Her mother?' The minister paused, studying the other. 'You are a stranger in these parts?'

'I've been away for many years.'

'Then you'd no idea how ill she had been.'

'Ill?'

The minister made a gesture of affirmation.

'I fear I must prepare you for sad news. I buried Kathy's mother in our churchyard just nine months ago.'

The words, spoken with professional condolence, were reinforced by the church bell which now, like a passing knell, struck the hour with a harsh cracked note. There could be, there was, no mistake . . . it was the finish of his seeking, the end. Not disappointment alone but actual shock must have shown in Moray's face, painful shock, that drove the blood from his heart and forced him to lean against the lintel of the door.

'My dear sir . . . come in and sit down for a minute. Here in the lobby.' Taking Moray's arm he led him to a chair in the hall. 'I see it has affected you deeply.'

'I had hoped so much to see her,' Moray muttered. 'A very dear friend.'

'And a truly worthy woman, my dear sir, among the chosen of my flock. Don't grieve, you will meet her in the hereafter.'

The afflicted man had not much confidence at that moment in the promise of the hereafter. She was gone, carrying with her to the grave the memory of his unfaithfulness. To the end, he had remained for her despicable, a festering wound in her memory. And now he could never redeem himself, never break the hateful complex which perpetually threatened his peace of mind, must continue to bear the burden of his guilt. Bowed with sorrow, disappointment, and a welling self-pity, he heard the parson run on, extolling the dead woman.

'Her daughter, too,' the other continued, 'has the same high standards, a most devoted girl. But now, if you're more composed, perhaps my wife could offer you a cup of tea.'

Moray straightened and, though still not master of himself, had the wisdom to decline.

'Thank you, no.'

'Then I feel sure you would like me to show you where she lies.'

They went to the graveyard behind the church. The grave, marked by a simple Celtic cross, was indicated, and the minister, lingering a moment, between sympathy and curiosity, said:

'You are of our persuasion, I trust. If so I hope we may see you at divine service on Sunday. The Word is a great healer. Are you residing in the neighbourhood?'

'At the Marine,' Moray mumbled.

'Ah, an excellent hotel – Miss Carmichael, the manageress, is a good friend of ours.' The credentials of the stranger thus established, he introduced himself with an almost pathetic eagerness to be of service. 'My name is Fotheringay – Matthew Knox Fotheringay, B.A. of Edinburgh, at your disposal, sir, should you require me further.'

With a bow, he moved discreetly away.

Alone, Moray still gazed down upon the green sward of which a long rectangle, the turf annealed yet still slightly elevated, presented a sad, significant outline. There lay that sweet body which in youth he had caressed. And in the form of sweet youth he now visualised her – as on that day upon the moor, while the lark sang above the heather, and the stream rippled over its fretted, pebbled bed. Clearly he saw her, fresh and glowing, with her trim figure, her red-brown hair and peat-dark eyes, with youth, youth pulsing through her, alive. Overcome, he supported himself against the granite monument and closed his smarting eyes.

How long he remained bent and motionless he never knew. A slight sound, a footstep on the gravel path, disturbed him. He turned, raised his head, then almost collapsed. There, risen from the grave, Mary Douglas stood before him, Mary, exactly as

144

he knew her, as he had dreamed of her a moment ago, the fearful, ghostly illusion heightened by the spray of white flowers clasped to her breast. He tried to cry out, but he could make no sound. Dizzily, with swimming head, he realised that it was Mary's daughter, the mortal image of her mother.

'I must have startled you.' She came towards him, concerned. 'Are you all right?'

'Yes,' he said, confusedly. 'But thoroughly ashamed of myself . . . behaving so stupidly.' And seeking an excuse, he added: 'I – was quite unprepared . . . You see . . .'.

She look at him understandingly.

'I met our minister, on the way in. You were a friend of my dear mother's.'

He inclined his head, indicating respectful sadness.

'And of all your family. They were very good to me when I was a poor . . . and homeless student.'

Her face expressed sympathy and kindness. It was evident that his grief at the grave had strongly predisposed her in his favour.

'Then you knew James, my grandfather?'

'A wonderful man . . . I could see that, though I was a heedless young fellow then.'

'And Uncle Willie?' she asked, with a warmer sympathy.

'Willie and I were the best of friends,' he said, with a half sigh of recollection. A sudden inspiration led him to validate their association. 'We often bunked together. Long talks we had at night. He was a fine boy.'

'Yes,' she said, 'I can believe that.'

There was a pause, during which he could not bring himself to look at her. His mind was not yet clear, not fully adjusted to this extraordinary turn of the wheel. He still regretted the mother and all that her loss entailed, yet it had begun to dawn on him that in the daughter he might still find the opportunity he sought. Perhaps, after all, it wasn't the end of his journey; at least, in sudden anxiety, so he fervently hoped. With an effort he maintained an air of calm.

'I must introduce myself. My name is Moray – David Moray.'

Her expression did not change. As she took the hand he held out to her, he could barely suppress a sharp breath of relief. She did not know of him, nor of his unedifying history. Why had he doubted? Mary would never have told her, the secret was still locked up in that poor broken heart, now stilled for ever, down there, six feet under his expensive hand-made shoes.

'You have my name,' she was saying shyly, while he still held her hand. 'Kathy Urquhart.'

He gave her, though still with quiet sadness, his most winning smile.

'Then, if I may, as an old friend of your dear mother, and of all your family, I shall call you Kathy.' He said it kindly, almost humbly, anxious to put her at ease, to make her feel at home with him. Then, standing aside in subdued fashion, with a sense of compunction and responsibility, conscious of his defects and deficiencies, of all his misdeeds of the past, he watched her as she placed her few chrysanthemums in a green enamelled vase before the Celtic cross and began, with a few touches, to move some fallen beech leaves from the sward.

She was bareheaded, wearing a dark blue, noticeably shabby coat over her denim nurse's uniform of lighter blue, and one of her shoes, he observed with a pang, was patched, a neat patch to be sure, yet an actual cobbler's patch. These little economies, so apparent to his expert examining eye, moved him. We will change all that, he told himself, with a sudden burst of feeling. Yes, his opportunity *was* here, certain and predestined, he felt it in his bones.

'There!' she exclaimed, straightening herself with a confiding smile. 'We're all tidy for the Sabbath. And now,' she hesitated shyly, scarcely daring, yet venturing to say it, '. . . would you like to come away home with me for a nice cup of tea?'

They walked down the pathway of the graveyard together.

CHAPTER IV

SEATED BY THE window in the room above the dispensary while she went into the kitchenette to infuse the tea, he glanced about him, surprised by the want of comfort, the bareness of all that met his eye. Not even a rug on the scrubbed and polished wooden floorboards, the furnishings scanty, little more than a square deal table and some horsehair covered chairs, the fireplace blackleaded yet lacking coal, the walls white-distempered, relieved by only one picture and that a religious subject, a reproduction from the *Christian Herald* of a bad copy of Valdez Leal's *Transfiguration*. There were a few books, mainly nursing manuals and a Bible, on a shelf. A hart's-tongue fern in an earthenware pot stood on a blue saucer on the window-sill beside a work basket holding a piece of knitting, ready to be picked up. But while admitting its spartan neatness, and the touch of brightness which a vase of wild asters on the mantelpiece, caught in the yellow light of sunset, gave to it, he saw in the room, as in the little alcove bedroom, the door of which on entering she had quickly closed, disturbing evidence of straitened circumstances. On the tray, too, which hospitably she now brought in, the china was of poor quality and the single plate held nothing more than buttered slices of cottage loaf. He could not altogether understand it, yet with a sudden lift of mood he reasoned that the more help she needed the more would he be able to give her.

'If only I'd known you were coming,' a little flustered, pouring the tea, she reproached herself as she handed him his cup, 'I'd have had something nice. When I'm busy I don't bother about shopping till the Saturday. But never mind me, tell me about yourself. . . . You've been abroad.'

'Yes, for many years. You may imagine what it's meant to me, coming home.' He sighed, then smiled. 'Now that I am here I mean to make an extended stay.'

'Where were you?'

'Mostly in America.'

147

'I almost hoped you'd say Africa.' She half smiled to him, though her gaze, passing beyond, was remote. 'Uncle Willie is out there – at Kwibu, on the border of northern Angola.'

Although he gave no sign, he nevertheless experienced a strong sensation of relief. Willie would certainly have known him; any premature meeting might well have induced a most undesirable crisis.

'You don't surprise me a bit,' he said pleasantly, with a light note of interest. 'Even as a boy Willie was wild about Africa. Why, he and I walked practically every mile of the way with Livingstone, to Lake Victoria. And when Stanley found him you should have heard us cheer. But Angola, isn't that rather primitive country?'

'It's all that. Since Uncle went out he's had some terrible rough years. But things are going better now. I've all sorts of interesting snaps I can show you. They give a good idea of the conditions out there.'

At this stage he thought it wise not to enlarge on the question of Willie's pioneer activities – whether mining or engineering he could not guess – so he refrained from pressing the matter.

'When you've time I'll enjoy seeing the photographs. But what I really want to hear about is your own work here.'

She made involuntarily a shy, disclaiming gesture.

'Oh, it's nothing much. Just the usual run of district nursing, health visiting, and the like. I go round the countryside on my bicycle, sometimes on foot. Then there's the Welfare Centre for pre- and post-natal care, with a clinic – we call it the milk bar – for the babies. And odd times I do a turn at the Cottage Hospital in Dalhaven.'

'All that sounds as if they work you much too hard.' He had already noticed that her hands were rough and badly chapped.

'It's nice to be busy,' she said cheerfully. 'And they're very decent. I have Thursday afternoons off and three weeks' holiday in the year – I still have two weeks of it to go, in fact.'

'Then you like your job?'

She simply nodded, with a reserve more convincing than any outburst of enthusiasm. 'At the same time, there isn't quite enough scope here. But – well, I have something much better in view.'

At this remark, and the reserve with which she made it, a disconcerting thought crossed his mind. Although he knew it to be bad taste, he had to say it.

'You mean to get married?'

She laughed outright, showing even white teeth against healthy pink gums, a wonderful laugh that fell sweetly, reassuringly on his ears.

'Good gracious, no,' she exclaimed, composing herself at last. 'Who would I find round here but a few farm laddies that think of nothing but their Saturday night dances and the movies in Dalhaven? Besides,' she continued, slowly and very seriously, 'I'm – well, so set on my work, I scarcely think I could ever give it up for anything – or anyone.'

All this was exactly as he would have wished it. Quite alone and without encumbrances, sensibly though not permanently attached to a worthy but dull and unrewarding profession, she could not have been a more perfect subject for his affectionate and philanthropic attention. His thoughts flashed ahead. Unacquainted with the law, he wondered if she might be made his ward: adoption seemed to him unfeasible, reminiscent of orphanages and partaking of frustrated parenthood. Be that as it may, his heart swelled with genuine feeling. He was, always had been, a most generous man, no one could deny him that slight virtue. What couldn't he do for her! He mustn't force things unduly least he alarm her, since it was apparent that she had taken him for a man of moderate means. Yet this was an aspect of the situation which struck him as being rich, in the double sense of that word, with the most delightful possibilities of revelation and fulfilment.

In the silence that had fallen between them, he considered her as, with lowered gaze, she put together the used tea things on the tray. She was, after all, not quite the living replica of her mother he had fancied in that first emotional shock. She had the same fresh complexion, dark brown eyes and short slightly thickened nose, the same soft chestnut hair clustering naturally on her neck. Yet her expression was different, reflective, almost reserved, the mouth wider, fuller, more sensitively curved, and in the set of the lips he saw evidence of a nature less given to gaiety. There was a certain aloofness about her that he liked – a sense of detachment. She smiled rarely, yet when she did it was the sweetest thing he had ever seen. But what struck him most was her touching look of youthfulness. Mary had been a sturdy lass with rounded breasts and well marked hips. This girl was slender, almost undeveloped – an immaturity contrasting with her serious air that strongly aroused his most protective instincts. He meant no injury to the dead when he concluded that this sweet child, equal in looks, had more depth, perhaps even greater capacity for feeling. . . . He came to himself. A hint of emabrrassment, something in her manner which she was unwilling to express, made him suddenly recollect that Fotheringay, the minister, had told him her dispensary began at five. Glancing at his watch, he discovered it to be ten minutes past the hour. He rose precipitously.

'My dear Kathy, I've stayed much too long,' he apologised. 'I'm keeping you from your patients.'

'They'll not mind waiting a few minutes. It's not every day I have visitors.'

'Then just let me say quickly what a joy it's been for me to . . . to discover you. I hope this fortunate meeting will be the first of many, for you must understand that I've much to repay for the kindness of your family.'

When she had seen him to the door he walked to his car, and drove back to the hotel meditating emotionally on the events of this extraordinary, this memorable afternoon. Sadness mingled with a kind of exhilaration. Here he had come, from the highest motives, and instead of an ageing woman who might have met him with reproaches, even rancour, remaining unresponsive to his offers of amendment and assistance, he had found a poor, hard-working girl who stood in need of, and must benefit by, his help. He deplored the loss of the mother, it had been a blow, yes, had cut him to the heart. But there was compensation in this dear child, who might, but for unavoidable circumstances, have been his own daughter, and on her, in reparation for the past, he would bring to bear, readily and freely, a benign influence, wise, helpful, paternal. The ways of Providence were indeed wise and inscrutable, beyond the mind of man.

CHAPTER V

THAT EVENING AFTER dinner he arranged with the manageress of the hotel to have a sitting-room. Fortunately there was one adjoining his bedroom, a large comfortable apartment with a good fireplace which Miss Carmichael confidently assured him 'drew well'. This settled, he put through a trunk call to his villa, in Switzerland.

When Arturo answered, almost comically delighted to hear his voice, Moray instructed him to dispatch golf clubs and additional clothing by air freight from Zurich. As to mail, he should use his discretion and forward those letters which seemed important. Was there any news? Everything was going well, Arturo replied, the weather kept fine, they had picked the damsons and the plums, Elena had made ten kilos of jam, one of the pier-master's children had been sick but was well again, and Madame von Altishofer had telephoned twice asking for his address: should he give it? Although gratified by her solicitude Moray, after considering for a moment, indicated that he would be writing to Madame himself.

But later, as he prepared for bed, his mood changed unexpectedly. Reviewing this eventful day he was struck, suddenly, by a chilly wave of self-condemnation. How quick he had been to find consolation in the prospect of exercising his charity on Kathy. How wrong to forget his own dear Mary, to accept the daughter and forget the mother, with no more than momentary sorrow. *An ageing woman who might have received him with rancour* – had he actually thought of her in such terms a bare hour after viewing her lonely grave? Never, never, would she have met him with anything but forgiveness and love. Standing in his long silk monogrammed sleeping-jacket, one of the individual coats specially tailored for him by Gruenmann in Vienna, he raised his eyes to the ceiling and swore he would make reparation openly, tomorrow. The thought comforted him.

Next day, true to his vow of the previous evening, he obtained from Miss Carmichael the name of Edinburgh's premier florist and telephoned his order. Presently there arrived by special delivery a great gorgeous wreath of arum lilies. This he took personally to the cemetery and placed reverently beneath the Celtic cross. Then, setting forth freely, swinging his stick, he turned towards the sea and walked upon the links, taking deep breaths of the bracing air. Resisting all inclination, he did not go near Markinch, wisely reflecting that whatever Kathy might be to him he was to her still more or less a stranger. However, on the day after, which was Sunday, he dressed in a dark suit and sombre tie, ascertained the time of morning service from the invaluable Miss Carmichael, and set out for the village kirk.

He had not been to church for more years than he could readily remember. On Sundays in America he had played golf with Bert Holbrook, gone through the routine of the usual exurbia weekend at the local Country Club, where the course bore the surprising name of Wee Pinkie Burn. The members, for the most part New York executives who bedecked themselves in remarkable sporting attire, ranging from chartreuse shorts to scarlet tam-o'-shanters, were a friendly and congenial group. But he had never felt quite at home there. He was not the type who could readily be at ease in the exuberant bonhomie of mass masculine society; and besides, he felt that they all knew of his unfortunate domestic situation and must therefore pity him. Still, it was a good course and he enjoyed the golf, at which he excelled. When the Sunday was too wet for play he usually went to the laboratory at the works. On one rainy and fortunate Sunday he had come up with the formula for, of all things, a new perfume, which Bert, with his unerring instinct for a selling name, had immediately christened *Church Parade*, and which, marketed as a sideline, had made a small fortune for the firm. It must, he estimated, be a matter of fifteen years since, on that Friday when Doris was finally certified and taken away to Wilenski's clinic at Appletree Farm, he had sneaked into the back seat of St. Thomas's Church on Fifth Avenue. On his way to the University Club almost next door his eye had fallen on the sign: 'Open all day for prayer and meditation.' He was feeling so abject, almost psycho himself, that he had thought it might help him to go in. But it hadn't: although he had crouched in a back seat, gazing furtively towards the dim altar, and had even shed a few miserable tears – for he could weep on appropriate occasions – he emerged without the faintest sense of benefit or improvement, obliged to fall back on his original intention: a Turkish bath at the Club.

Now, however, his state of mind was altogether more propitious. He approached the little country church, to which a sparse congregation was being summoned by the discordant pealing of a cracked bell, in a mood of keen anticipation. And immediately, as he entered, he had the satisfaction of Kathy's swiftly lowered glance of recognition. When the service began with a hymn, sung rather uncertainly, and later, during Fotheringay's sermon, which was long and dull, a truly laboured effort, he had the privilege of observing her, though always discreetly, as she sat with the village children. He was struck by the competence with which she controlled her restless charges and by the patience she brought, sitting very erect, to the tedious discourse. Her profile had a purity of outline that reminded him of an Italian primitive – Uccello, perhaps, No, no – her sweetness of expression suggested a much later canvas – Chardin's *The Young Teacher*, he decided finally, pleased to have hit it exactly, but wincing at an increasing volume of disharmony from the choir.

His reward came afterwards when, outside the church doors, he waited for her. She came out with Mrs Fotheringay. The minister's wife was a short, stout woman with a downright manner and a broad, plain, honest face, her lined but keen blue eyes set behind highly coloured cheekbones – a Raeburn face, Moray thought instinctively. She wore her 'Sunday best,' an antique black feathered hat and a dark grey costume that had seen much service and was now too tight for her. Moray was introduced and presently, after a few moments' conversation, they were joined by Fotheringay. Immediately, Moray congratulated the minister on his sermon.

'Most edifying,' he said. 'Listening to you, sir, I was reminded of a spiritual experience I had in the church of St. Thomas's in New York.'

At the implied comparison with the great city Fotheringay reddened with pleasure.

'It was good of you to come to our country service. We are a small congregation and our poor old bell does not attract many people from the outside world.'

153

'I did notice,' Moray raised his brows deprecatingly, 'that the tone was not particularly clear.'

'Nor loud,' the other said, glancing upwards towards the church tower with sudden irritation. 'The bell fell last year from a rotted cross-beam. It will take near to eighty pounds to recast it. And where is a poor parish to find that siller?'

'At least there is nothing wrong with your voice,' Moray said diplomatically. 'I found you most eloquent. And now,' he went on agreeably, 'I'm going to take the liberty of inviting all three of you to Sunday dinner. I've made arrangements at the hotel. I hope you are free to come.'

A brief, rather blank pause ensued: such invitations were not current in the district. But almost at once Fotheringay's expression cleared.

'You're very kind, sir. I must confess that when I come out of the pulpit I always seem to be sharp set.' He glanced almost jocularly at his wife. 'What do you say, my dear? Our little roast will do tomorrow, and you won't have to wash up today.'

From the start, with the blunt look of a woman who must be convinced rather than persuaded, she had been openly taking stock of this newcomer who had arrived so dramatically from the unknown. But her first impressions seemed not unfavourable and the prospect of emancipation from those menial duties imposed by the meagreness of her husband's stipend was a mollifying one. She gave Moray a dry sort of smile.

'It'll be a treat for me. If Matthew gets his appetite in the pulpit, I lose mine by the kitchen stove.'

Kathy looked pleased, less perhaps at the prospect of her own visit to the Marine than at this hospitable treatment of her old friends. After Moray had settled them in the car, the minister and Kathy behind, Mrs Fotheringay beside him in front, he drove off. From the outset he had realised that the Fotheringays must be won over, if necessary propitiated, and everything seemed to be going well.

At the hotel they were welcomed by Miss Carmichael. As the season was virtually over – only a few visitors remained in the hotel – half of the main restaurant was closed and she had given them a table by the fire in the cosy breakfast room, a privacy especially pleasing. The food, simple and unpretentious, was of the first quality: a Scotch broth, saddle of Lothian lamb with roast potatoes and garden beans, home-made trifle laced with sherry and topped with double country cream, then a native Dunlop cheese and hot oatcakes. Moray had hoped the parson and his spouse would enjoy this repast and they did, especially Mrs Fotheringay, who ate with hearty and honest appreciation of the good things. The more he saw of this plain, outspoken woman, the more he liked her. But what gave him most satisfaction was the fine blood that the nourishing meal – so different from the meagre fare which, he was convinced, awaited her at home – gradually brought to Kathy's cheeks, making her eyes brighter, her smile warmer. Thank heaven, he thought, she isn't all spirit, and pressing her to another helping of trifle, he set out to ensure that the flesh was not neglected. Indeed, with that flexibility which enabled him to attune himself to any society, he was the perfect host. Kindly and serious rather than gay, he charmed them all. Keeping the conversation moving with discretion, he spoke briefly of his business in America, of his early retirement and return to Europe, finally of the home he had made for himself above the Schwansee; and, since Kathy was listening with attentive interest, he took pains and, with feeling, described the lake, the village, the surrounding landscape.

'You should see it under snow, as it will be soon.' He concluded on a high note. 'A mantle of the purest white.'

'It sounds a braw spot,' Mrs Fotheringay said. Assured that her first doubts had been unjustified, she had long since thawed towards him, revealing an unsuspected archness. 'You're a lucky chiel to live amongst such beauty.'

'Lucky, yes.' He smiled. 'But lonely, too.'

'Then you're not married?'

'I have been a widower for some years.'

'Oh, dear,' she exclaimed, concerned. 'But you have children?'

'None.' He raised his eyes, looked at her gravely. 'My marriage . . . was not a particularly joyful one.'

The painful words, so obviously the understatement of a perfect gentleman, produced a sudden silence. But before this became prolonged he rallied them.

'That's all past. And now I'm happy to be back in my own country and in this present company.' He smiled. 'Shall we go into the lounge for coffee?'

Regretfully the minister looked at his watch.

'I'm afraid we must decline. Kathy has her Sunday School class at three. And it's after half-past two.'

'Good gracious,' said Mrs Fotheringay. 'How time has flown. And so very agreeably too. We're most indebted to our new friend. Come, dear, we'll leave the men for a wee minute.' She rose and took Kathy's arm, adding with her usual directness, 'Miss Carmichael will show us where to tidy up.'

Left alone with the parson, who had also risen and was standing by the window viewing the sea, Moray seized the opportunity to take his cheque book from his inside pocket. A few strokes of his ballpoint pen and he got to his feet.

'As a token of friendship and good will, permit me to offer you this so that your congregation may be summoned fittingly.'

Fotheringay turned sharply. A dejected little stick of a man, with more bile than blood in his veins, he was now completely overcome. Staring at the cheque, all taken aback, he stammered:

'My dear sir . . . this is more than generous . . . it's . . . it's *munificent*.'

'Not at all. It's a pleasure. One I can well afford.' Moray placed a finger on his lips. 'And please – not a word to the others.'

As he spoke the two ladies returned and Mrs Fotheringay, struck by her husband's attitude, cried out:

'Matthew! What on earth's the matter?'

He took a deep breath, swallowed the dry lump in his throat.

'I cannot help it. I must speak. Mr Moray has just given me the eighty pounds to recast our bell!'

There was a sharp silence. A deeper colour had rushed into his wife's cheeks, already flushed by the substantial meal.

'Well, I never,' she said in a low voice. 'That is most extraordinar' handsome.' She came slowly towards Moray and took his hand tightly in both of hers. 'That wretched bell has had my poor old man worried near out of his wits. I just cannot thank you enough. But there, I hadn't been five minutes in your company before I kenned ye were *one of the best*.'

He was not often at a loss but now the genuine feeling in her voice unexpectedly embarrassed him.

'Nothing . . . nothing,' he said awkwardly. 'If I'm to get you back in time we ought to be on our way.'

Ignoring their protests he insisted on taking them back in the little car. This time the Fotheringays were in the rear seat, Kathy beside him. During the short run she did not speak, but as he said goodbye outside the manse she remained behind the others to thank him – quickly, shyly, but with unmistakable sincerity.

CHAPTER VI

ON MONDAY AFTERNOON his golf clubs and two valises arrived by special delivery van from Prestwick Airport: he had known that the good Arturo would not fail him. The sight of his beautiful leather bag and shining true-temper clubs stimulated him, and although it was late in the day he went to the clubhouse, introduced himself to the secretary, and arranged for a temporary membership. Then he got hold of the professional and had just time to play twelve holes with him. The open, rolling course suited Moray, he was in excellent form, and when fading light forced them to stop he was actually one up on his opponent, a dour and stocky Scot, who had started with all the expert's disdain of the amateur, but rapidly and rather comically changed his views.

'Ye hit a verra sweet ball, sir,' he conceded, as they walked back to the clubhouse for a drink. 'It's not often I come up against a visitor that can beat me. Would ye care for a return tomorrow?'

Moray accepted.

'Ten o'clock sharp,' he said, slipping a pound note to the other. 'And perhaps we'll go out again in the afternoon.'

Firmly, he was controlling his persistent wish to go to Markinch. Not only was discretion imperative, lest his motives be misconstrued; he well knew the wisdom of delay, the advantage of an interlude in which expectation could develop and recollection could have its way.

He took no action until noon on Wednesday, when he wrote a note, which he dispatched by the hotel boots, a lad of seventeen.

My dear Kathy,

I have to go to Edinburgh to do some shopping tomorrow. As I believe you are off duty that afternoon, if you have nothing better to do would you care to come with me? Unless I hear to the contrary I will call for you at two o'clock.

Most sincerely yours,

David Moray.

His fear that she might not be free was quickly removed; a verbal message of acceptance was brought back by the boy, and on the following afternoon when he drew up at the dispensary she was waiting for him outside, dressed in a clean white blouse, a speckled grey Harris tweed skirt which, at a glance, he decided she had made herself, and, as the breeze was keen, the rather shabby coat in which he had first seen her. Though her fresh young face redeemed everything, exhaling an innocent smell of brown soap, it was an unbecoming outfit, little better than that of a country maidservant on her day out. Nevertheless it pleased him, especially the worn coat, since it might present the opportunity he sought. She would be difficult to convince, but he meant to try.

How delightful it was to find her beside him after those three days of self-enforced abstinence. Not only had she been glad to see him, her mood was lighter than before, she seemed full of expectation for their expedition. He sensed that she was becoming less shy of him. After they had driven for some time in silence, she said:

'This is much nicer than the bus. It was good of you to ask me. And convenient, too. It so happens I have an errand in Edinburgh.'

'Then we'll do it whenever we arrive,' he said heartily. 'Just tell me where you want to go.'

'Number 10a George Street,' she told him. 'The offices of the Central African Missionary Society.'

He glanced at her quickly. Their eyes met for only an instant before he returned his gaze to the road ahead, yet she had caught the blankness of his expression, and with a smile she said:

'Did you not know? Uncle Willie is out there for the Society? It's my fault for not showing you the photographs, but I thought you surely understood. He's been working for years in the foreign missionary field.'

It took him a few moments to overcome his surprise.

'No . . . I didn't quite realise . . .'.

'Well, he is. And doing wonderfully under the most difficult conditions. You've no idea of what he's been through.'

In spite of himself, and his lack of sympathy for Willie's spiritual objectives, he was impressed by her glowing and ingenuous tone. A sentimental recollection of the bright-eyed little boy in Ardfillan thirty years ago came over him.

'Well, well. Come to think of it, it's just the thing I would have expected of Willie. I honour him for it.'

'I knew you would,' she said in a low voice.

'I must admit . . .'. They were now in the outskirts of Edinburgh and a momentary difficulty in negotiating the traffic caused him to pause, before resuming. 'Yes, I admit I was puzzled at your asking me to take you to the – to George Street. But I see it now. I suppose they keep you in touch with Willie's movements.'

'Indeed they do. And besides, the least I can do is to send him regular parcels. I arrange it through the Society. They know what he needs and are able to buy the right things at reasonable prices.'

'You go in and leave the money?'

'Why not?' she answered light-heartedly. 'It's little enough. Uncle Willie's worth more than that. Besides, he's the only relative I've got.'

He saw then the reason for her cheap clothes, poor lodging and indifferent food, saw the purpose of her sparing way of life. This devotion touched him, yet his main sensation was one of indignation that she should be denied the things that were due her, and he had a sudden impulse to speak of the resources at his command, of all that he could, and would, do for her. But his instinct warned him – no, no, he thought, not yet; above all he must avoid too sudden, too startling an advance.

They were now approaching the centre of the city and, following the directions she gave him, he turned off Princes Street at the Scott monument, drove for some distance along Craig Terrace, then, after crossing a wide square, arrived at a grey stone building marked by a well-polished brass plate bearing the name of the Society. It had the look of an old dwelling house, Victorian in character, which, he surmised, had been donated by some deceased benefactor, possibly the pious widow of a city merchant. In the windows several posters were displayed showing representations of what appeared to be, at this distance, distressing groups of emaciated native children.

'Miss Arbuthnot will be expecting me,' she told him as she

stepped briskly from the car. 'I won't be more than a few minutes.'

She was as good as her word. There was just time to smoke a Sobranie cigarette – he had been careful to bring a plentiful supply of his special brand from Switzerland – before she reappeared. The dashboard clock, which was actually going, showed only half-past three. But glancing at it she apologised, rather breathlessly.

'Och, I have kept you waiting.'

'Not a bit of it. Was everything all right?'

'Oh, fine, thank you.'

'Now then, Kathy,' he said, decisively engaging gear, 'you've done your good deed for the day and you're in my hands for the rest of the afternoon. Let's forget Central Africa for a bit and think a little about ourselves. First of all we'll park the car, then we'll go shopping together.'

He found a garage nearby and presently, taking her arm, he guided her back to Princes Street. The sun was shining as they walked along. In the gardens opposite roses were still blooming and a cool breeze fluttered the leaves of the plane trees. Above, the battlements of the Castle were as though cut clean by a knife against a wide swathe of luminous sky. He still held her arm protectively, steering her along the crowded pavement.

'Isn't Princes Street nice?' she remarked. 'They say it's the bonniest street in Europe.'

'It *is* a bonnie street, Kathy,' he answered gaily, 'and full of bonnie shops – all with lovely things in them.'

'Ay,' she nodded soberly, 'and all dreadful expensive.'

He burst out laughing. A wonderful mood was descending upon him. The scene, the sun, the brisk invigorating air, all exhilarated him.

'Kathy, Kathy,' he exclaimed, pressing her elbow. 'You'll be the death of me. When you know me better you'll realise that the one thing I really enjoy is spending money.'

She had to smile in sympathy, though a little doubtfully.

'Well,' she said practically, 'so long as you don't waste it.'

'My dear, you're the very one who ought to know that what's spent on others is never wasted.'

'Oh, you're so right,' she agreed, her expression clearing. 'That was the most splendid and generous thing you did, giving the bell to Mr Fotheringay.'

'Yes, the old boy's got his bell. But we mustn't forget poor

Mrs F., who got nothing – and I think she's had plenty of that all her life. So we must find something pretty for her. But first of all,' he had stopped opposite Ferguson's, the confectioners, 'I want to send some Edinburgh rock to two little friends of mine in Switzerland.'

He went in with her and ordered a large box of the famous sweet to be mailed to the children of the pier-master in Schwansee. Next he sought her advice and, in a neighbouring shop, purchased a fine capacious black lizard-skin handbag for the minister's wife.

'It's a beauty.' Kathy stroked the shining leather admiringly. 'And I know it's the very thing she's wanting.'

'Then you'll have the pleasure of giving it to her.'

Emerging, he conveyed her further along the street towards an establishment which, as he drove in, he had observed to be of special merit.

'Now,' he announced in great good humour and with a rather mischievous air, 'I'm going in here to do some real shopping.'

He took a step forward, but as he prepared to lead the way in she stopped him hurriedly.

'Don't you see – this isn't a man's shop.'

'No,' he replied, looking down at her seriously. 'It isn't. But I'm going in – to buy you a new coat – and a few other things which I'm sure you need. Now, not a word. I'm an old family friend, you must learn to accept me as . . . well, someone like Uncle Willie. Or better still, as an older brother. And as such, I simply can't have you sending all your money to Angola and doing without absolute necessities – a pretty girl like you.'

A warm colour had risen to her brow. She tried to speak but could not. Her eyes fell.

'I never bother what I have on – not much, anyway.' Then, to his relief, she looked at him again and, unable to resist, after a faint tremor of her lips, she smiled. 'I mustn't pretend. I suppose I like to be as nice as the rest.'

'And you shall be, only nicer.'

They went into the shop which, as he had surmised, was of the first order. Aided by a discreet, mature saleswoman who rustled towards them, and ignoring all Kathy's whispered protests, he selected a coat of fine Shetland material, warm yet light, new gloves and shoes, a hand-blocked silk scarf, and finally a restrained yet tasteful dark green lovat suit. He wished to do more, infinitely more: nothing would have given him greater joy than to have swathed her in those rich furs past which, with a speculative glance, the saleswoman had tentatively led him. But he dared not – not yet. While Kathy retired to the fitting room upstairs he took an armchair in the elegant red-carpeted salon, stretched out his legs, and lit a cigarette, perfectly at home. Presently she came down, and, with lowered gaze, stood before him. He could not believe his eyes, so startling was the change. She looked ravishing.

'Madame is rather different in the lovat, sir.' The saleswoman, with an air of achievement, was studying him covertly.

Under that experienced gaze he restrained himself.

'A great success,' he said coolly. 'It seems to fit.'

'Naturally, sir. The young lady is a perfect thirty-four.'

He insisted that she wear the suit and the new coat: the other articles, elegantly wrapped, were easily portable, the old discarded coat could be sent to Markinch with her Harris skirt. When the bill was presented, though he was careful not to expose the total, she kept murmuring remorsefully in his ear, but as she left the shop in her new possessions he did not fail to notice the sparkle of pleasure in her eyes. He had done well, he reflected with an inward thrill, and this was only the beginning.

She remained silent as they walked back together along the street, where the low sun behind a bank of clouds cast a golden gleam, then looking straight ahead she said:

'I think you are the kindest person, Mr Moray. I only hope you have not ruined yourself.'

He shook his head.

'I told you I had something to repay. But it is you who are repaying me.'

She half turned, looking at him steadily.

'That's just about the nicest thing that's ever been said to me.'

'Then you will do a nice thing for me? Mr Moray is so stiff, won't you please call me David?'

'Oh, I will,' she said shyly.

Before the silence became awkward he exclaimed lightly:

'Good gracious! Past five o'clock. Time for tea. I've been running the show so far, but now I'm going to let you take over. Which place do you recommend?'

She named a café unhesitatingly as being not only the best but moderate in price. It was not far off and presently they were seated upstairs in a bright, warm room filled with the cheerful sound of voices and overlooking the gardens across the way. The table, in Scottish fashion, was already laden with tempting scones and buns, and with a many tiered-central stand bearing every variety of that native confection made of sponge, icing and marzipan, known as a 'French' cake. He handed her the menu which was safely anchored in a little metal ball.

'What do you suggest?'

'Are you hungry?' she asked.

'Starving.'

'So am I.' She gave him a modest, playful smile. 'You haven't forgotten what a good Scots high tea is?'

'Indeed I haven't. And the best I had were in your old home at Ardfillan.'

'Well, there's a dish they have here, fried fillet of fish with parsley sauce; it doesn't sound much but it would just melt in your mouth.'

He looked at her quizzically.

'Is it expensive?'

She laughed outright, freely and spontaneously, such a happy laugh it evoked responsive smiles from dour Edinburgh citizens at the adjoining tables.

'It'll cost a good half crown. And after the perfect ransom you've spent today I think I'd better pay.'

When the waitress approached he let Kathy give the order. The fish, as she had promised, was delicious, fresh from the sea, the toast hot buttered, the tea strong and scalding. The excitement of the expedition and the consciousness that she was looking her best had released her from shyness, giving her an animation that made her companionship the more delightful, since already he had detected an introspective strain in her nature, even a tendency to sadness, and it was good to be able to lift her to a lighter frame of mind. And how attractive she was in her new smart outfit, so transformed as to draw towards her many admiring glances, which he clearly saw but of which she remained unaware. Yes, he thought, watching her indulgently, she's worth all that I mean to do for her, she'll do me credit.

When they had finished they sat for some time in a communicative silence, then she gave a contented sigh.

'It's a shame this wonderful day has to end. But I must be back to relieve Nurse Ingram at seven o'clock.'

'Must you really?' he exclaimed with a note of disappointment.

'I'm afraid I must.'

'And I was hoping we could stay and go on to a theatre. Wouldn't you have liked that?'

She lowered her eyes, but after a moment raised them and looked at him frankly.

'It will probably amaze you, Mr Moray – I mean, David – I have never been to the theatre in my life. When Mother was alive we went every year to the Orpheus Choir's performance of "The Messiah". And I've been to concerts at the Usher Hall.'

'But the regular theatre – good plays, the opera, and suchlike?'

She shook her head with such a look it touched him to the heart.

'But Kathy dear, I can't bear to think what you've missed. Didn't you ever want to go?'

'No – not really.'

'But why?'

She paused, as if to consider his question. In the end she said, simply:

'Mother didn't care for me to go. Besides, I suppose I've been too busy . . . and had other things on my mind.'

'What a serious little person you are.'

'Don't you think we're living at a pretty serious time.'

'Yes,' he had to admit, 'I suppose we are.'

Her capacity to astound him seemed unlimited. And how withdrawing she could be at times, when that contained expression came into her eyes. Yet how wonderful, in this age of debased morality, to find such fresh unspoiled innocence.

'Come then, my dear,' he said gently. 'I'll take you home.'

He drove back slowly through the little towns on the firth where lights were already springing up against the encroaching night, and as the car purred softly he meditated on the future. Virgin soil, he repeated to himself, worthy of any effort on his part. Time was on his side of course but there was much to be done. Despite her sweetness and native wit he was obliged to acknowledge, as a man of the world, that she was a simple and untutored girl, knowing nothing of music, art, or literature. That one picture in her room – terrrible: those few text-books and the Bible, edifying no doubt, but scarcely comprehensive. Poor child, she was probably too hard-worked, too tired at night to read. That must be changed, she must be educated, taught several languages, attend a good university, Geneva or Lausanne would be suitable, take a course in, say, social science. All this, and mixing with cultured and civilised people would give her poise, smooth out her little gaucheries, bring her to perfection. Her upbringing must in a sense be held responsible – pure and spartan though it had been, it had un-doubtedly been . . . well . . . narrow. And this obsession with Willie, splendidly unselfish though it might be, was a nuisance and must be watered down. But the most pressing need was to remove her from her present work. Indeed, she had hinted that she was preparing to leave it, and with an idea of encouraging this, he said:

'I've been wondering if you'd take me on your round one day. I'd be most interested. Could it be this week?'

'Of course,' she said readily. 'Not tomorrow, for I have to see the County Medical Officer at Dalhaven, but the day after if you like.'

'Good. I'll call for you at nine o'clock.'

When they reached Markinch he collected her parcels, escorted her to her door, stilled her renewed thanks, said good-night kindly yet briefly. The day he had so carefully planned would speak for itself. A bond had been created between them; he would not risk breaking it by doorstep sentiment.

CHAPTER VII

MORAY TURNED IN early that night with an unusual sense of serenity, conscious that everything had passed off well, had indeed been perfect. And what a refreshing little companion she had proved, how supremely restful! Properly educated she could be a source of interest to him, a new objective in his life, besides affording him the long-sought satisfaction of an exercise in virtue. He fell asleep as soon as he had settled his head comfortably on the pillow.

Next morning when his early tea was brought the weather, unfortunately, had changed. Heavy rain beating on the window gave no inducement to rise in haste. Having swallowed his tea and the thin bread and butter that accompanied it, he lay back and closed his eyes, but failing to get off again rang for the morning paper. The boots, who brought it up, handed him a packet of mail forwarded by Arturo from Schwansee: a few business communications from his New York brokers, a couple of bills, several dividends, an illustrated catalogue of a sale of Daumier drawings to be held in Bern, and finally a letter from Madame von Altishofer. He opened it.

Gasthof Lindenhof
Baden-Baden.
Thursday, the 15th.

My dear friend,

I hear from my correspondents in Schwansee that you are not yet returned to your villa and I begin to fear that some mischance is responsible for your prolonged absence, especially since I have no single word from you since your unexpected departure. Has your business proved more tiresome than you foretold? Or can it be that you are ill? I trust sincerely that both of these suspicions, which have lately troubled me, are not well founded. But please, you must take time to send me news of yourself. I am sure you acknowledge that nothing could exceed my deep interest in all concerning you.

The weather has been pleasant here and I am much the better of my residence. But I am dull – dull – in fact I am becoming increasingly aware of being alone. I do not freely make new friends, and saving an old acquaintance, an invalid lady I met at the spa, I speak rarely to anyone. And how quietly I exist. I rise early, drink the waters, then take my coffee and zwieback at a little nearby café. Afterwards I walk into the hills – you know how much I love to walk – then come back to this modest pension, where they are so very good to me, and eat my simple mittagessen on the terrace under the linden tree. I then rest for an hour or so. The afternoon I sit in the gardens, still green and blooming, having selected carefully a chair not too near the orchestra which since my arrival has already fourteen times dispensed Strauss's Wiener-Walzer. Here, I pass the time partly in dreaming, partly in studying the faces of those who pass. Are they happy, I ask myself? So often I doubt it. At least I find them altogether different from the people one met and knew when first I came here with my parents in my early youth. This reflection depresses me and I hasten to the pavilion where I have my cup of tea – not, alas, so good as your delicious Twinings – and a slice of the English plum cake. In the evening I do not venture to the casino, the sight of all those greedy eyes repels me. Instead I take my nice book – now I am reading again 'Anna Karenina' – and retire to the ever open window of my room. The light of my lamp attracts an occasional môth, fireflies gleam beneath the linden tree, I begin to feel sleepy and so, in the words of your Mr Pepys, to bed.

That, dear friend, is my day. Is it not simple and a little sad? Yes, sad because I miss you, and your charming kamer-adschaft. I also need your advice, since a man from Basle – someone in chemicals – asks to buy the Seeburg. I do not wish to part with that beloved house which I know you also admire, but circumstances are now most difficult. So write me soon and let me know when you will be home. As there is nothing to take me back to Schwansee until you are there, I shall remain in Baden until I hear from you.

Forgive me for revealing my regard for you,

Sincerely,

Frida von Altishofer.

He put down the letter slowly. A nice letter he told himself, despite its rather stilted style, the letter of a well born and distinguished woman who was utterly devoted to him. Normally he would have been touched by it, but now, perhaps because of his mood, the aftermath of yesterday, it found him unresponsive. He was glad, naturally, to hear from her, flattered that she should miss him, yet at the moment he could not generate his usual interest in her activities. And was she not slightly exaggerating her solitude? She was a woman who invited and enjoyed society. That frugal lunch, too, struck an incongruous note. He well knew that she was not averse to the pleasures of the table, and on her last visit to Baden had brought back a marvellous recipe for chestnut soup. In any case, he was not in the mood to answer today. He would advise her about the Seeburg, but later; at present he had other things upon his mind.

It was almost noon when he got up and began idly to dress. After lunch the rain continued. He hung about the hotel trying to occupy himself with some ancient magazines, devoted mainly to Scottish sport and agriculture. Then an impulse took hold of him to get out the car and drive to Markinch, but he reflected that she would not be there. She had told him that she must go to Dalhaven. Still, he would have the satisfaction of passing her window. . . . At this absurdity he drew himself up with a sudden selfconscious flush. He would see her tomorrow and must wait. Gazing in bored fashion out of the blurred windows of the lounge he hoped the weather would turn fine.

But when the next day came it was still raining, the sky remained heavily overcast. Nevertheless he was in a mood of cheerful expectation as he backed the car out of the hotel garage and drove between the sodden hedgerows towards Markinch.

She had already finished the forenoon clinic when he arrived. She locked the dispensary door and, carrying her black bag, got in beside him.

'Good morning.' He greeted her, feeling how good it was to see her again. 'Or rather, what a morning! I'm glad to be driving you today. Not having you cycle around in the rain.'

'I don't mind cycling,' she said. 'Or the rain either.'

The tone of the remark mildly surprised him but he made no comment except to say:

'Anyhow, I'm entirely at your disposal. Where do we go?'

'Towards Finden. I can't promise you beautiful country. It's all poor clay land. And Finden is a poor village, built round a brickworks that's just been re-started after a long shut-down.'

'Well, it's not a day for viewing the scenery,' he said amiably, and after asking and receiving directions he set off through the village.

As they proceeded, she remained unnaturally silent, and he began to fancy a certain reserve in her manner. Not exactly a coldness. But she had lost that uplifted and responsive spirit that marked their day in Edinburgh, when he had felt the beginnings of a sympathetic understanding throb between them. After glancing sideways towards her several times, he said: 'You look tired.' And indeed she had not her usual air of well-being. 'You've been working too hard.'

'I enjoy hard work.' She spoke in that same odd, rather constrained tone. 'And I've quite a number of serious cases on hand.'

'That proves you've been doing too much. You're quite pale.' He paused. 'Surely it's time you took the remainder of your vacation?'

'In this weather?'

'All the more reason for you to get away from it.'

She did not answer. And why did she not look at him? He waited a few moments then said:

'What is wrong, Kathy? Have I offended you in any way?'

She blushed deeply, vividly, all over her fresh young face.

'No, no,' she said hastily. 'Please don't think that. Nothing could be further from the truth. It's just that . . . probably I am a little out of sorts.'

It was true enough, though very far from the full explanation. Yet how could she tell him of the mood which had followed their day in Edinburgh, or of the intensity of her reaction to it? On awakening yesterday morning she had experienced, in warm and sleepy recollection, an afterglow of happiness, but this had been succeeded, almost immediately, by a sharp pang of troubled conscience. The gay and spendthrift adventure of the day before, far exceeding all her previous experience, now took on the colours of an act of self-indulgence, almost of wrong-doing. With what silly vanity she had preened herself in her new clothes. They were beautiful, of course, but they were not for the likes of her. Be not solicitous what you put on – had she forgotten that? She felt guilty . . . guilty, untrue to herself and all that she had been brought up to believe. Remembrance of the smart saleswoman, seeing her undressed in her cheap rayon slip and darned navy blue woollen knickers, patting and patronising her in the fitting room, made her flush painfully. What would her dear mother have thought had she seen her then!

It was not Mr Moray, or rather – true to her promise she corrected herself – David, who was to blame. No one could have been kinder or more generous, he had meant well, acted from the most disinterested motives. He was so nice, too, so interesting and companionable, and had such a tactful and pleasing way with him that it would have seemed most ungracious to refuse his gifts. Yet an inner sense told her that she should have done so. Yes, the fault had been entirely hers, and she must see that it was not repeated.

She had risen quickly, washed in cold water and put on her uniform. But as she did so, trying to fix her mind on the work awaiting her at Dalhaven Hospital and the difficult interview with the M.O.H., when she must tell him of her intention to leave the Welfare Service, the prospect looked so flat and dull she could scarcely face it. Worst of all, longing came over her for a repetition of the previous unique day, not necessarily a return to the city, but something of a similar nature, under the same kindly guidance and patronage.

Abruptly, with all the firmness of a mind habituated to self-discipline, she had put the thought away, yet even now she had not altogether forgiven herself. However, as they drew near the first cottage she was due to visit she willed herself to throw off her constraint. Turning to him she asked if he would like to come inside with her.

'That's why I'm here,' he exclaimed. 'I want to see everything.'

The cottage was tenanted by a farm-worker whose leg had been caught in a threshing machine at the last harvest. He lay in the usual alcove bed in the dark little kitchen, where also were his wife, a defeated-looking woman in a torn wrapper, and three half-dressed unwashed young children, one of whom was crawling on the floor with naked buttocks, slavering over a slice of bread and jam. The room was in a state of disorder, used pots piled in the sink, greasy dishes on the table which was covered by an old soiled newspaper. Into this mess and muddle, which left him appalled, Kathy walked with an air of unconcern, said good morning to the woman and the children, calling each by name, then turned to the bed.

'Well, John, man, how are you today?'

'Oh, not so bad, nurse.' His face had cleared at the sight of her. 'It's just that, like the wife there, I never seem to get out the bit.'

'Tuts, man, don't give up. You'll be getting about in a week or so. Now let's have a look at you.' As she opened her bag, she added casually: 'This gentleman is a friend who has come along to say hello to you.'

It was a severe and extensive injury. Viewing it across her shoulder Moray could see that only by the barest margin had the femoral artery escaped. Several of the tendons had been severed, and as healing had not taken place by first intention, some of the sutures had gone septic. He watched as, having noted pulse and temperature, she cleansed the wound, renewed the dressing and rebandaged the leg, meanwhile maintaining a flow of encouraging remarks. Finally, straightening, she said:

'John here doesn't know how lucky he's been. Another inch and the thresher would have been through the big blood vessel of the leg.' In an undertone to Moray, modestly displaying her knowledge, she added: 'It's called the femoral artery.'

He restrained a smile, accepted the information with an appreciative glance, meanwhile continuing to observe her as she closed her bag and moved from the bed exclaiming:

'That's enough for you, John. Now let's give your lass a hand.' She turned to his wife. 'Come away now, Jeannie Lang, and get a move on. If you redd up the dishes, I'll see to the bairns.'

It was amazing: in fifteen minutes she had washed and dressed the children, swept and straightened up the room, dried the dishes as they were handed dripping from the sink. Then, almost in the same breath, she had rolled down her sleeves and was on her way out, calling over her shoulder:

'Don't forget now, send to the Centre for the children's milk this evening.'

Moray made no comment until they were back in the car and he had restarted the motor, then he said:

'That was well done, Kathy.'

'Oh, I'm used to it,' she said lightly. 'It's just a matter of method.'

'No, it was much more than that. You seemed to put new heart in them.'

She shook her head.

'The Lord knows, they need it, poor things.'

It continued dismally wet and windy, the tangle of country by-roads which served her district were smeared in liquid mud, the labourers' and brick-workers' rows of cottages, small, poor homesteads, all were dripping and bedraggled in the rain. Yet this wretchedness seemed never to depress her. The troubled mood of the morning was gone. As she stepped from the car with her black nurse's bag, splashing her way towards damp kitchens and attic bedrooms, there was about her an alacrity beyond professional pretence, an unforced willingness he couldn't understand. Although she wanted him to stay in the shelter of the car, he insisted on accompanying her: something unknown compelled him to do so. All that day he watched her at work; tending nursing mothers and fractious children; a schoolgirl with a painfully scalded arm, the dressing so adherent it must be removed with time-consuming care; the wife of a brick-worker propped up in bed, struggling with asthma; then the old people, some bedridden, full of their tedious complaints, one old man, helpless and incontinent, who must be washed, the sheets changed, his bedsores cleaned with spirit.

And beyond all this were the extra duties she imposed upon herself: the dusty rooms, smelling of lamp oil, to be aired and tidied, soiled linen to be rinsed, dishes washed, milk to be heated, soup put to simmer on the kitchen range; all under conditions which would have reduced him to the lowest ebb of melancholia, and all accomplished not with quiet competence alone, but with a sympathy, a sense of spirited enterprise that left him baffled.

He might, at times, have obtruded with a remark arising from his own knowledge, for this renewed contact with sickness and disease, although so long deferred, induced a strange evocation of the days when he had walked the wards of Winton Infirmary. Yet he refrained, mainly because, in an effort to interest him, she had continued to make simple little medical comments on the condition of her patients. He did not wish to wound her.

In the late afternoon, on one of her last visits, when she had been to a case in a row of cottages, a woman called her in from a neighbouring doorway. Angus, her youngest, had 'a bit of a rash,' she thought that nurse ought to have a look at him. The boy, looking fevered and uncomfortable, was lying down under a plaid shawl on two chairs placed end to end. His mother said that he complained of headache and had refused the dinner. Then she had seen his spots, some of them like little blisters.

Kathy talked with him for a minute, then, having gained his confidence, turned back the shawl and undid his shirt. At the sight of the rash Moray could see her face change. After sending the mother into the scullery on a pretext she turned to him.

'Poor boy,' she whispered. 'It's the smallpox. They've had two cases down in Berwick and I'm terribly afraid this is another. I'll have to notify the M.O.H. at once.'

He hesitated; then, for her own sake, felt obliged to intervene. In a tone which lightly parodied the professional manner, he said:

'Take another look, nurse.'

She stared at him, disconcerted at his use of that word, above all to find him smiling at her.

'What do you mean?'

'Only that you needn't worry, Kathy.' He bent forward, pointing to illustrate his remarks. 'Just look at the distribution of these vesicles. They're centripetal, none at all on the hands, feet, or face. Also they're not multilocular and show no signs of umbilication. Finally these papules are at different stages of development – unlike smallpox where the lesions appear simultaneously. Taken with the mildness of the prodromal symptoms there isn't the slightest doubt about the diagnosis. Chickenpox. Tell his mother to give him a dose of castor oil, some baking soda for the itching, and he'll be over it in a week.'

Her expression of surprise had gradually deepened until now she seemed almost petrified.

'Are you sure?'

'I am absolutely and positively certain.' He read the unspoken question in her eyes. 'Yes, I'm a doctor, Kathy.' He spoke with a kind of mild frankness, half in apology. 'Does that shock you?'

She could scarcely speak.

'It fair takes my breath away. Why did you not tell me?'

'Well, you see . . . I've never been in practice.'

'Never practised! It's beyond belief. Why in all the world not?'

'It's a long story, Kathy. And one I've wanted to tell you ever since we met. Will you hear it . . . when you've finished your round?'

After a brief but intense silence, during which she still gazed at him wide-eyed, she nodded uncertainly, then, as Angus's mother returned, she reassured her, gave her Moray's instructions, and they went out. In another half hour she had finished for the day and, without further ado, he pressed hard on the accelerator and drove fast to the hotel. As the deserted lounge was cold and draughty he took her up directly to his sitting-room, where a bright driftwood fire blazed, pressed the bell and ordered hot consommé and buttered toast to be brought immediately. Her look of fatigue, which had worried him that morning, had suddenly intensified – and no wonder, he thought bitterly, after those long hours of chill and sodden slavery. He did not say a word until she was refreshed and warmed, then he drew his chair up to hers.

'I've so many things to tell you I scarcely know how to begin, and the last thing I want to do is to bore you.'

'Oh, you won't. I must hear why you never practised.'

He shrugged slightly.

'A poor student just through college, with an honours degree. A sudden exceptional offer to work in the laboratory of a large commercial enterprise. It's as simple as that, my dear.'

She studied him earnestly for a full minute.

'But what a waste – what a dreadful waste!'

'I was doing scientific work,' he reasoned mildly, translating his adventures with the pills and perfumes into more acceptable terms.

'Oh, I daresay,' she said, with vigour. 'That's very well for some. But a man like you, with such personality. . .'. She coloured, but went on bravely: 'Yes, such gifts, to throw away the chance of helping people, the sick and the suffering, the real purpose of the doctor. It seems a crying shame.' A thought arrested her. 'Have you never thought to take it up again?'

'At this late hour!' Hurriedly, to correct any false impression the unfortunate phrase might have given her, he added with pardonable subtraction: 'I'm not far off the middle forties.'

'What of it! You're fit, healthy, in the prime of life: yes, a young-looking man. Why don't you go back to your real work? Remember the parable of the buried talents.'

'I should have to brush some of the dust off mine.'

At her gratifying reference to his youthful appearance he had smiled so engagingly she was forced to smile in sympathy.

'At least you put me right on my smallpox scare. And me trying to tell you about the femoral artery. What a cheek!'

There was a brief silence. How sweet she was with the firelight playing upon her earnest young face against the darkness stealing into the room. A wave of protective tenderness, almost, but not quite, paternal, swept over him. He half rose.

'Let me get you another cup of that soup.'

'No, no, it was really good, made me much better, but I want, I would like to . . . go on with our talk.'

'You feel strongly on that subject?' His brows were raised humorously.

'I do, oh, I do. It's my idea of what life should be – helping people. It's what we're here for, to do our best for one another. And the greatest of all is charity – that's what I was brought up to believe. That's why I trained as a nurse.'

The spiritual content of her words was mildly discouraging but he accepted them kindly. Then, with firmness, he said:

'Kathy, you're a wonderful nurse – haven't I seen you in action? I admire and respect you for the work you're doing, though frankly I don't think you strong enough for it, but we'll let that pass. What I do feel, however, is that you could exercise *your* talents on a different, let's say a higher level, with much broader and rewarding results. Now, now, wait a minute.' Gently, he stilled her interruption and resumed. 'Ever since we met there's something which I've hidden from you, deliberately, because I wanted you to take to me, to like me on my own merits, if I have any.' He smiled. 'And I hope you do like me?'

'I do, very much,' she answered, with impetuous sincerity. 'I've never met anyone who's made such . . . such an impression on me.'

'Thank you, Kathy dear. So now I'm free to tell you, with all the humility in the world, that I am rather well off. I'm sorry I can't put it less crudely, for in fact, I'm lamentably and outrageously rich – for which I was never more grateful than at this moment, because of what it'll enable me to do for you. No, please,' he raised his hand again, 'you must let me finish.' Then after a pause, in a graver manner, he went on. 'I'm a lonely man, Kathy. My marriage was unhappy . . . well, let's face it, a tragedy. My poor wife was for years confined to a mental institution, and she died there. I have no children, no one like you to occupy me. All my life I've worked hard. Now, at an early age, I've retired, with ample leisure and more material possessions than I need, or deserve.' He paused again. 'I've already told you that I owe a great debt to your family – don't ask me what it is, or you'll remind me of my graceless and ungrateful youth. All I need to say is that I must repay that debt, and I want to do so by interesting myself in you, by taking you out of this drab environment, giving you a fitting background, and all the things that you deserve. A full, rich, and rewarding life, and not of course an idle one, for as you have humanitarian ideals you may fulfil them with my co-operation, and with the resources I can put at your disposal.'

While he was speaking she had been looking at him with growing agitation, and now that he had finished she lowered her eyes and for an appreciable moment remained silent. At last she said:

'You are very kind. But it is impossible.'

'Impossible?'

She inclined her head.

'Why?' he asked, persuasively.

Again there was a silence.

'You have probably forgotten . . . but that first day I told you I was giving up the district work for something better. At the end of next month I'm going out to Angola . . . to work with Uncle Willie at the Mission.'

'Oh, no,' he exclaimed in a loud, startled voice.

'But I am.' Smiling faintly, she looked up and met his eyes. 'Uncle Willie is coming home to fetch me on the 7th of next month. We'll fly back together on the 28th.'

Almost stupidly he asked:

'And how long do you mean to stay there?'

'For good,' she answered simply. 'I gave my notice to the M.O.H. yesterday.'

A prolonged stillness descended on the room. She was leaving – he calculated quickly – in five weeks' time. The news devastated him – his hopes blasted, plans fatally ruined – no, he could not, would not accept it. The projects, so well considered, which he entertained, had reached possessive force, not only for her sake, but for his own. She was to be *his* mission in life. Nothing so inane as this wild desire for self-immolation in the wilds of a

177

tropical jungle must interfere. Never, never. But his wits were coming back to him, he saw the danger of opposing her outright and risking an immediate break. He must work for time and opportunity to change her mind. When he spoke his voice was calm, with the right note of regret.

'This is a severe disappointment, Kathy, a blow in fact. But I can see how intensely, how close this lies to your heart.'

She had been prepared for opposition. At this quiet acceptance her eyes brimmed with grateful sympathy.

'You understand so well.'

'And I'll help, too.' The thought seemed to revive him. 'Willie will have a donation for the Mission – and a handsome one – by the next mail. You've only to let me have his address.'

'Oh, I will, I will. How can I thank you!'

'But that is only the beginning, my dear. Didn't I tell you how much I want to do for you? And the future will prove it. As for the present – let me think. When did you say Willie would return?'

'In about a fortnight's time. We leave three weeks after.'

He was silent, his brows contracted in thought.

'I believe I have it,' he said at length. 'As you're to disappear so unexpectedly and so soon I think you might reasonably give me a little of your remaining time. Furthermore, I'm worried about your health. You're quite run down and if you're to stand up to hard work in tropical heat you owe yourself a holiday, or at least a rest. So I suggest, with all reserve, that you take the two weeks' vacation still owing to you and spend it at my home among the mountains. Willie, on his return, will join us there, and even though neither of you can stay long, we'll have the happiest reunion in the world!'

For five fatal seconds he thought she would refuse. Surprise and doubt clouded her open expression, but this, merging through indecision, was followed by a hesitant smile. He saw that his inclusion of Willie in the invitation had been sheer inspiration. But was it enough? Doubt had returned to her eyes.

'It would be nice,' she said slowly. 'But wouldn't it be too much trouble for you?'

'Trouble! I don't know the meaning of the word.'

'The mountain air would be good for Uncle Willie,' she reflected, 'coming beck from Kwibu.'

'And for you, going out there.' With an effort he maintained

178

a matter-of-fact tone. 'So you'll come?'

'I want to,' she said in a low voice, looking small and un-protected in the deep armchair. 'But there are difficulties. My work, for instance. Then as I've given notice I might not be allowed my vacation. I'd have to see Matron or the M.O.H. about it.' She took a long breath. 'I'm on duty at the hospital for the rest of this week. Will you please let me think it over till then?'

At that moment he saw there was nothing he could do but agree.

CHAPTER VIII

HE DROVE HER back to Markinch for the evening clinic. When they arrived, afraid of saying something injudicious in his present state of mind, he confined himself to a few words of good-bye and a restrained though speaking glance. Then he started back slowly towards the hotel.

The rain had ceased, and, with that perversity of Scottish weather which occasionally at the end of a drenching day affords an illusory promise of better things, a bar of clear light appeared on the horizon. But this transient brightness did little to raise his spirits, and presently he drew into the side of the road to think things over and switched off the ignition.

Yes, it was a nasty set-back, made worse since it was the last thing he'd expected. Who could have foreseen it? A sweet young girl bent on throwing herself away on a pack of primitive, painted savages who could no more appreciate her than – well, than they could the lovely little Bonnard that hung in his study at Schwansee. His hand shook with vexation as he thumbed at his gold lighter and drew deeply at a cigarette. Of course, he could not deny that he had heard or read of such extraordinary cases. Hadn't some rich young society woman renounced her fortune recently and gone to live on bananas with some eccentric doctor in the Brazilian jungle? Then again, nuns went out as nursing sisters, but that was part of their vocation. And he supposed that the wives of missionaries, if they felt it their duty, might accompany their husbands. Yet in this instance there was no need for renunciation, no moral or matrimonial obligation; in all its aspects the project appeared to him preposterous and futile.

What could he do about it? – that was the question. Lighting one cigarette after another, an excess completely foreign to his moderate habit, he applied himself to the problem with a concentration made possible by the force of his indignation. The simplest solution, of course, would be to abandon his plans, to give up, spare himself all further trouble, and go home. No, no, that he

180

could never do: he rejected the thought outright. Apart from his tacit obligation to her and to himself, he had in the short time become fond, yes, extremely fond of little Kathy. The mere idea of never seeing her again was too defeatist, too dismal to be entertained.

The more he reflected, the more he became convinced that his best chance of winning her from her obsession lay in showing her, even briefly, the fullness and richness of the life he could give her. Brought up so strictly, isolated, one might say, from the world, she hadn't the faintest idea of what he could do for her. If only he might take her to Europe, demonstrate the charm and elegance of the great Continental cities he knew so intimately: Paris, Rome, Vienna, with their art galleries, historic buildings, famous monuments and churches, their choice restaurants and fine hotels, and introduce her thereafter to the comfort and resources of his home, she must surely swing to reason and be convinced. His invitation, then, made on the spur of the moment, had been a brilliant stroke, which now after serious deliberation he could not improve upon. All that remained was to ensure that she accept. But how? Casting around for assistance and support, it was not long before the obvious person came to mind.

At this, he stubbed out his cigarette, pushed hard on the starter button, then swung round and drove back through Markinch to the manse. Within five minutes he was there. As he parked the car and entered the drive he made out a rough scaffolding on the upper part of the tower and heard Fotheringay's voice raised commandingly within, all of which seemed to indicate that the bell was in process of being removed. But he had no wish to meet the minister, to be embarrassed by further expressions of gratitude; and with relief, as he passed through the overgrown laurel shrubbery, he saw Mrs Fotheringay in the vegetable garden at the side of the house. He went straight towards her. She wore a man's battered felt hat, an old stained mackintosh and heavy tackety boots, and in her hand she held a pair of garden shears.

'You have really caught me in my braws,' she exclaimed, with a wry though welcoming smile, as he approached. 'I've been slaughtering slugs. After the rain they fairly go for my cauliflowers. But I seem to have done for most of them. Come away ben the house.'

'If you don't mind,' he hesitated, 'might I speak to you here?' She studied his expression frankly, then without a word led the way to a green-painted trellis summer-house that stood at the foot of the garden. Seating herself on the wooden bench, she indicated a place beside her, then, after a further scrutiny, she said:

'So Kathy has finally told you?'

Her penetration surprised him, but it was helpful, giving him a lead.

'I heard only an hour ago.'

'And ye don't approve?'

'Who would?' he said in a suppressed voice. 'The very idea, a young girl burying herself for life in that wilderness. I'm . . . I'm inexpressibly distressed.'

'Ay, I thought you might be upset.' She spoke slowly, wrinkling up her broad weatherbeaten brow. 'And ye're not the only one. My guid man is against it, though as the minister it's hard for him to speak out. But I'm just the minister's wife and I say that it's an awfu' pity.'

'It would be bad enough at any time. But now especially, when trouble seems to be stirring in Africa . . .'

She nodded soberly, restrainingly, but he was not to be held back.

'She's not fit for it. After her work today she was quite done up. Why is she going? What's the reason of it all? Is it this uncle of hers that's responsible?'

'Ay, in a way, I suppose she's going for Willie's sake. But for her own too.'

'You mean from religious motives?'

'Well, maybe . . . though not entirely.'

'But she is religious?'

'She's good, in the best sense of the word.' She spoke with feeling, lapsing more and more into the doric. 'She helps us in the church, teaches the bairns, but – she's not the kind that aye has a Bible under her oxter and the whites of her eyes turned up. No, to understand her reasons for going, ye must understand Kathy. I don't have to tell ye that she's unusual in this shameless day and age, different as chaff from good Lothian corn from the horse-tailed, empty-headed sexy little besoms ye see gaddin' around, wi' their jazz and their rock and roll, out for nothing but a good time, or a bad one I might say. She's a serious, sensitive lass, quiet mind ye, but high strung, with a mind and ideals of her own. Her upbringing – for her mother was unco' strict – has had a deal to do with it. And living away out here in the country has kept her very much to herself. Then, since Willie went out to Angola, where apparently there's baith sickness and starvation, she seems, as was only nat'ral, to have become more and more taken up with this idea of helping him. Help where it's maist needed – service, that's her word for't. It's become the one thing, ay, the mainspring of her life.'

He was silent, biting his lip in protest.

'But she can be of service without burying herself.'

'Hav'na I told her that, again and again.'

'Why doesn't Willie tell her? He must realise that the whole thing is utterly impractical.'

'Willie is not practical.' She seemed about to say more but merely added: 'He doesna' really live in this world.'

'Well, I do,' he exclaimed, with nervous feeling. 'I'm interested in Kathy. You must have seen that. I want to *do* things – for her own good. Give her all that she needs and deserves.'

She made no reply but continued to look at him with questioning eyes, in which also there was such open sympathy that he was seized by the sudden emotional necessity to unburden himself, to justify his motives and win her completely to his side by a full admission of the past. The impulse was irrestible. Yielding, he took an agitated breath; then rapidly, at times almost inarticulately, and sparing himself considerably in the narration, he told her all that had brought him to Markinch.

'So, you see, I've every reason, every right, to make up for the past. Why, if I hadn't taken that unlucky voyage, Kathy,' his voice almost broke, 'might well have been my own daughter.'

In the pause that followed he kept his eyes lowered. When he raised them her smile was kinder than before.

'I guessed as much from the start. Kathy's mother was a reserved woman, but once she was showing me an old album, and there, on a page, was a spray of pressed flowers. In my usual style I made a bit joke about them. She looked away and sighed, and said just enough to let me know there was someone she had cared for dearly before her marriage.'

He flinched slightly at this too vivid evocation of his desertion, but recovered himself quickly.

'Then you'll help me! I've asked her to come to Switzerland to meet Willie in my home. If I can get them both there, Kathy especially, in a fresh environment, I believe I can make them see reason. And she does need a holiday, poor child. Will you persuade her to come? She's sure to ask your advice.'

She did not immediately answer, but continued to consider him with a reflective, womanly air. Then, as though giving expression to her thoughts:

'It's a strange thing. I've hoped, ay, and prayed, that something would turn up to save Kathy from this step in the dark. It's not just the danger, which is bad enough, for Willie, the crazy loon, has near been killed half a dozen times, it's the fact that she's so intense, she'll wear herself out in a twelvemonth in that ungodly climate. And she's such a dear sweet lass, made for different things. Well, it seemed hopeless, and then at the very last, when I've given up and she's on the point of going, you come along like a second father, since ye've put it that way, and it's plain to me why ye've been sent.' She paused, reached over and put her large roughened hand on his. 'We all do heedless things when we're young. It's no matter that ye made a mistake then. I believe you're an upstanding, generous-hearted man. There's not many I would trust with Kathy, but I trust *you*. If only you can take her out of this rut, get her to travel a bit, mix with people, and, best of all, find her a braw steady young husband who'll give her a good home and children to look after, someone who'll look after *her*, then you'll have more than made up for things.' She pressed his hand firmly. 'I believe in the intervention of Providence. Although you may not know it, I've a sound notion you're the answer to what I've been seeking, and I'll help you all I can.'

His eyes were still moist as he left the manse. He felt restored, purified by his confession and, aware of the worth of that good woman's promise, sufficiently reassured to wait patiently for word from Kathy. She had warned him that she would be fully occupied at the Dalhaven hospital until the end of the week. He must not, he told himself, expect an answer till then. Yet when the first day merged into the second, and the second into the third, a restless uncertainty began to torment him, his concern returned and his mood grew less hopeful. There was nothing else to engage his attention or to relieve the monotony of waiting. The weather had turned cold and windy, the sea raged, spume and blown sand whirled across the dunes and links. Even if he had been in the mood, golf was out of the question. Finlay, the professional, had shut up his shop and gone back to club-making in Dalhaven. The hotel, too, had suddenly contracted, more rooms were closed with windows shuttered, the last of the autumn guests had taken their departure, and only two permanent residents, both elderly ladies, remained with Moray to share the rigours of the north-eastern gales. Since he could no longer offer the excuse of a vacation, people both here and abroad were beginning to wonder at his prolonged stay. Miss Carmichael had twice asked him if he could give her some idea of his plans, while in Schwansee his admirable servants were becoming uneasy about him. Yet all this was as nothing compared with his increasing anxiety, the realisation that time was going on, shrinking the limited period at his disposal.

On Saturday, in an effort to distract his mind, he decided to spend some hours away from the hotel and to make inquiry in Edinburgh regarding the possibility of plane reservations. He passed the forenoon in the city; then, as the sky had brightened, rather than return early he set off idly in the car to explore the northern countryside. He lost his way, not unpleasantly, a couple of times in rural surroundings, stopped to ask directions and drink a glass of milk at a small farm-steading, started off again to get his bearings, and in the end must have wandered further than he knew, for suddenly, as he began to think of turning back, he found himself in a strangely familiar landscape. Looking about him with a tightening of his nerves, he marked one feature after another. There could be no mistake. Perhaps it was not chance but some strange subconscious prompting that had brought him here. He was in the Fruin valley, on the deserted side road that led up from the loch, through that same stretch of lovely heathland where, on the day they came back from the hospital at Glenburn, all those years ago, Mary had given herself to him.

A strange weakness took hold of him, made him want to turn back, but he resisted it. With a set expression he drove on for a few miles, then, pressing hard on the foot brake, skidded to a stop. Yes, it was the very spot. Undecided, he sat for some moments, a rigid figure, then he got out of the car and walked across the grassy verge to the moor which, as he advanced, presently fell away into that sheltered, unforgettable dingle where the stream ran clear and strong over its pebbled bed. My God, he thought, it's exactly the same, everything so unchanged it might all have happened yesterday.

Standing there, with a hollow stomach and a fast-beating heart, the past re-created itself before him. The arrival on the bike, the picnic in the warm sunshine, the laughter and tender glances, the hum of the honey bees, and then under the blue sky, while the curlews circled and called unheeded, the joy and fear of those ecstatic moments when, irresistibly drawn, they clung together He saw it all, felt it all, lingered over it, in a bath of sentimental recollection, until with a start of panic, an actual physical shock, he pressed his hand across his eyes.

The girl in his arms was not his long-lost love. Every sensation, every burning detail of that passionate scene, he had relived not with the mother but with the daughter. It was Kathy he had held so closely in his arms, whose soft warm lips had pressed on his, who had yielded in sweet abandon. He cried out to the deserted heath. Utterly unnerved, struck by a sudden shame, he broke away, stumbled uncertainly up the slope and through the tufted heather, back to the car. Like a man possessed he drove away. Why had he not realised it before? He was in love – not with the old, but with the new. His thought of Kathy as his daughter, a ward whom he might protect, had been no more than self-deception, a protective camouflage, of his subconscious desire. From the first moment of their meeting, his original love, long cherished as the one love of his life, had been re-created, reinforced and transposed to her. Not only was the image there, fresh, young, even more beautiful, but a living, flesh-and-blood reality as well. Staring fixedly ahead, steering automatically, he tried to stem this tide of sensation. The situation was a delicate one, quite proper of course, nothing dishonourable about it, yet somehow arousing scruples, calling for second thoughts or at least restraint, otherwise the evil-minded might discover a bad odour where none existed. But how could they? His motives were of the highest, his feelings, natural, honest, and normal, could never be construed as incestuous, he had no cause for compunction, no reason to recoil. Who could blame him? How could it have been otherwise? The thought gave him release, filled him with a sudden pulsing joy, and the future, which hitherto had never exactly taken shape, now fell into place precisely, took on colours that were enchantingly sensuous and vivid. And, God, how young he felt, rejuvenated in fact, by this exciting double passion so enticingly made one.

Now, more than ever, must there be no hesitation, no more delay. Discretion always, of course – no ill-advised or premature revelation of his feelings. But he would telephone her at Dalhaven immediately he got back. Down went the accelerator, the car flew, as on wings. Arrived at the hotel he leaped out, made directly for the telephone booth in the hall, was about to enter when the porter signalled to him from the desk.

'There's a message for you, sir. Mrs Fotheringay called when you were out. She brought you this note with her best regards.'

The man handed him a plain sealed envelope with his name written on it. He dared not open it here. Hurrying upstairs to his room he tore it open and with unsteady fingers drew out the cheap sheet of notepaper within. A glance told him it was from Kathy.

Dear David,

We have been so busy at the hospital I have scarcely had any time to myself, but yesterday afternoon I was off duty and had a long talk with Mrs Fotheringay. Afterwards I spoke to Matron who has agreed to release me and let me have my remaining two weeks' holiday beginning Monday next. So I shall be free then to accept your kind offer to take me to Switzerland, and I have written to Uncle Willie telling him of your invitation to join us there.

Sincerely yours,

Kathy.

I am very happy to be going with you.

No need to telephone, of her own free will she would come with him. He sat down in a convenient soft armchair, suffused by a glow of triumph. And on the way to Schwansee, mindful of his original intention, why shouldn't they stop off at his favourite city, at Vienna, just for a few days, to give her a taste of Continental life? He re-read the letter: so she had written to Willie. A cable would be quicker, better too. Tomorrow he would send one, a long, frank, personal message that would explain things to Willie and so ease their eventual meeting. Once again he read the postscript: *I am very happy to be going with you.* There was only one thing possible for a man of such taste and feeling, a man of his particular refinement, untouched by the crudity and vulgarities of this barbarous age. He raised the shabby little scrap of paper and pressed it to his lips.

CHAPTER IX

FROM AN ALTITUDE of twenty thousand feet the Caravelle began gradually to edge down from the starry night sky into the darker plateau of cloud below. Moray glanced at his watch: half past nine. He turned to his companion.

'Not long now. You must be tired.'

Their journey had been protracted, with delays at London and Paris, but he, at least, would not have missed a minute of it. To sit beside her, so closely, in the intimacy of the de luxe class cabin, observing with amused yet tender solicitude her reactions to her first flight, anticipating what he judged to be her wishes, though she expressed none – this, and her companionship, had afforded him a rare and precious pleasure. Since it was all so strange to her, she had not said much, and because of these silences which seemed to indicate some slight degree of tension, he now struck a note of encouragement.

'I do hope you're going to enjoy yourself, dear Kathy. Forget about slogging through the mud at Markinch and have a real holiday. Let yourself go a bit.' He laughed. 'Let's both relax and be – well – human.'

'Oh, I'm only too human,' she smiled responsively. 'You'll maybe think I'm a regular nuisance before long.'

The voice of the stewardess on the inter-communication system broke in upon them.

'We are now arriving at Vienna Airport. Please fasten your safety belts and extinguish all cigarettes.'

She was still inexpert, and helpfully he guided her fingers to make the adjustment of her belt. As he touched her small trim waist and felt the warmth of her body, a sudden joy took possession of him.

The lights of the airport, now visible below, tilted sharply as the plane banked, then with a final turn and a perfect approach they were on the runway, manoeuvring towards the wooden customs shed.

'It's a poor little airport,' he told her as they descended, 'not built up since the war. But we'll soon get you through.'

With practised efficiency, he was as good as his word. In less than seven minutes they came out to the main driveway and there, as his cable had commanded, was the Rolls, gleaming under the neon lights, with Arturo, in his best uniform, all bows and smiles, in attendance. Of this he had said nothing, meaning to surprise her, and he succeeded. When greetings had been exchanged with Arturo and they purred off into the night, enclosed by a fur rug and the soft grey upholstery, she murmured, in a small voice, 'What a lovely car.'

'I've never appreciated it more than now.' He patted her hand reassuringly under the rug. 'It'll help in showing you around.'

The road to Vienna from the Flughaven was, he knew, a bad introduction to gaiety, being flanked by a long succession of cemeteries and, as though this were not enough, by mournful establishments for the manufacture and display of tombstones. But now the kindly darkness masked these grim intimations of mortality. Within half an hour the cheerful illuminated city welcomed them. They drew up at the Prinz Ambassador. It was not a large hotel but it was luxurious and he preferred it to the others as the most Viennese in character, with a delightful old-world situation overlooking the Donner fountain and the Kapuziner Kirche. Here, too, he was known and appreciated, quickly shown to a double suite on the upper floor, the sitting-room a period piece in brocade and red velvet with a dazzling central chandelier, crystal wall lights and a baroque gesso table where already the direction had set out a great vase of bronze chrysanthemums and a basket of choice fruits.

'Now, Kathy,' he said decisively, when he had approved her bedroom and adjoining modern bathroom, both done in a delightful pale yellow with dove grey hangings, 'you're quite exhausted, in spite of your protests, so I shall say goodnight. I'm going to order something nice sent up to you on a tray, then you'll take your bath and go straight to bed.'

How wise he was, how gentle and courteous. He could tell from her eyes that he had divined exactly what she wanted. Not a word more was needed, only the simple, graceful exit. He raised her wrist lightly, brushed it with his lips, nodded briskly, then with a cheerful: 'We'll meet at breakfast in the morning,' he was gone.

He rang for the floor waiter, ordered breast of chicken sandwiches and hot chocolate to be sent up, then descended to the restaurant. Before going in he lit a Sobranie, and took, bareheaded, a short stroll along the Ringstrasse. How good to be in Vienna again, to hear laughter in the streets and waltz music coming from the cafés, even to see the naughty little *dirnen* starting out on their evening promenade. Scotland was very well, if one accepted the weather, excellent for golf and fishing, but this was better, more *gemütlich*, more his style altogether. And once she found her feet, how Kathy would adore it.

Next morning came clear and fine, a crisp autumnal day, and at nine o'clock, when breakfast was wheeled in, he went through the sitting-room, tapped discreetly on her door. She was up, already dressed, occupying herself with some knitting while waiting to be summoned. They sat down together. He poured the coffee, hot, fragrant and delicious, the very best coffee; it frothed into the fine Meissen porcelain cups, white as the snowy tablecloth and decorated with a gold crown. The butter, on ice, had the colour of cream, the honey in its silver pot was a rich golden yellow. The rolls, crisp and sweet smelling, were still warm from the bakehouse.

'Try one of those,' he said informatively. 'They're Kaisersemmeln – fit for an emperor. They've been going for almost a century. So you had a good night? Well, I'm delighted. Now you'll be ready for a good day's sightseeing.'

'I'm looking forward to it.' She glanced up inquiringly. 'Shall we need to go by car?'

He saw instantly that she was shy of using the Rolls. What a dear unspoiled child she was, and so sweet this morning, all dewy fresh from sleep. He said sympathetically.

'We must drive this morning, we are going some little distance. But another time we'll use Shank's mare.'

The phrase must have pleased her. She smiled.

'That will be nice, David. Don't you think, when you walk, you see more? And more of the people, too.'

'You're going to see everything, my dear.'

Arturo was already waiting outside and could be seen from the window pacing up and down, maintaining vigil against the press of an admiring and inquisitive crowd. When at last they descended he whipped off his cap, bowed respectfully, and presented Kathy with a single rosebud and – delighted gesture – a brass-headed pin.

'You see,' Moray murmured in her ear, 'how much my good

Italian approves . . .'.

She had blushed deeply but, when they were seated in the car, submitted while he pinned the rose to the lapel of her lovat suit. Then they were off, bound for the Kahlenberg.

It was a dazzling drive, winding upwards through clean bright little suburbs to the high pine-clad greensward of the Wiener Wald. The sun shone, the air, electric with the hint of frost, was crystal clear, so that, when they breasted the ultimate slope, suddenly, far below, the whole panorama of Vienna lay revealed with breath-taking brilliance. Leaving the car, they wandered about the summit while he pointed out the landmarks of the city: the Belvedere Palace, St Stephen's Kirche, the Hofburg, the Opera House, and, just opposite, the famous Sacher's, where he proposed to take her for lunch.

'Is it a very grand place?'

'One of the best in Europe.'

At this, she hesitated, then diffidently placed her hand upon his arm.

'David, couldn't we just have something here?' With her glance she indicated the little café just across the way. 'It looks such a nice simple place. And up here it's so lovely.'

'Well,' he queried doubtfully, 'simple is the word. And the menu will be simpler still.'

'Probably good plain wholesome food.'

When she looked at him like that, her cheeks glowing in the keen air, he had to yield.

'Come along then. We'll risk it together.'

He could refuse her nothing, though his forebodings were more than justified. A bare trestle table, cheap cutlery, and the inevitable Wiener Schnitzel, tough and rather tasteless, with which, of all things, they drank apfelsaft. Yet she did not seem to mind, appeared actually to enjoy it, and so, in the end, he became good-humouredly reconciled. Afterwards they sat for some time – she was still fascinated by the view – then, towards two o'clock, returned to the car and set out for Schonbrunn.

This was the special treat he had promised himself, for, as one set inflexibly against the architectural horrors of the modern age, he had a romantic affection for the stately eighteenth century summer palace of Maria Theresa and the lovely gardens, designed in the old French manner, which surrounded it. Besides, the role of cicerone was dear to him. From the moment they passed through the massive iron gateway he laid himself out to be interesting and, since he knew his subject, he was handsomely successful. Wandering through the great baroque apartments he re-created the Imperial Court in all its luxury and splendour. Vividly he sketched the life of Maria Theresa: from the quaint demure little maiden – he paused before her portrait at the age of six – in her long gown of blue and gold brocade, reproducing the dress of a fashionable Viennese lady, who seeing her father in state array called out, to the diversion of the entire court: 'Oh, what a fine papa! Come here, papa, and let me admire you' – from that sweet child to the woman of strong and noble individuality, central figure in the politics of Europe, patron of the arts, mother of five sons and eleven daughters who, asked on her death bed if she suffered greatly, as indeed she did, answered calmly – her last words:

'I am sufficiently at ease to die.'

Time passed unnoticed. Never had he let himself go with such dramatic fervour. They were both surprised to discover that it was almost six and beginning to get dark when they came out again to the cobbled entrance court.

'Good heavens,' he exclaimed, in apology, 'I've walked and talked you to a shadow. And, what's worse, made you miss your tea. That's inexcusable in Austria where the kuchen are so marvellous.'

'I wouldn't have missed *this* for anything,' she said quickly. 'You know so much and make everything so real.'

Apparently he had given her something to think about, for on the way back to the hotel, after a reflective silence, she remarked:

'The privileged classes certainly did well for themselves in those days. But what was life like for ordinary people?'

'Not quite so attractive.' He laughed. 'It's said that in Vienna more than thirty thousand families had each no more accommodation than a single room. And if the room happened to be fairly large, two families lived in it – divided by a clothes-line!'

'How dreadful!' she said, in a pained voice.

'Yes,' he agreed, comfortably. 'It's wasn't a good age in which to be poor.'

'And even now,' she went on, 'I've seen signs of poverty here. As we came out, children barefoot, begging in the streets . . .'.

'There always have been, always will be beggars in Vienna. But it's a city of love, laughter, and song. They're quite happy.'

'I wonder,' she said slowly. 'Can people be happy when they're hungry? I was talking to the woman who came to do my room this morning – she speaks very good English. She's a widow with four young children, her husband was killed in some trouble during the occupation, and I can tell you she's had a fearful struggle, with the high cost of everything, just to keep her family *alive*.'

'Doesn't that sound like the usual hard-luck story?'

'No, David, she's a decent wee body and completely genuine.'

'Then you must give her something from your pocket money.'

'Oh, I have!'

The pleased exclamation made him glance at her sideways. After they left the airport, so that she should have something to spend, he had pressed a bunch of notes into her purse – probably some 1500 Austrian schillings, the equivalent of twenty pounds sterling.

'How much did you give her?'

She looked up at him rather timidly.

'All.'

'Oh, no, Kathy.' Then he burst out laughing. 'What a little do-gooder you are. Parting with your entire fortune at one go.'

'I'm sure she'll put it to good use.'

'Well, if it pleases you, it pleases me,' he said, still amused. 'And one has to be liberal and a little crazy in Vienna. I love this city, Kathy – so much that it hurts me to see how quickly it is changing. You must take it all in now, my dear, for only too soon, like so many of the beautiful places of the world, it will be completely ruined. Just look at that horror on your right.' They were passing a tall new working-class apartment building. 'That faceless nightmare of steel and concrete full of hundreds of little rooms like dog kennels has replaced a lovely old baroque house, a petit palais that was bulldozed down twelve months ago so they could stick up this – this penitentiary.'

'You don't like it?'

'Who could?'

'But, David,' she took a full thoughtful breath, 'the people who live in it will like it. They'll have a sound roof over their heads and comfort too, heating, hot water, proper sanitary arrangements, and privacy. Isn't that better than pigging it across a clothes-line?'

He frowned at her quizzically.

'Won't they pig it in any case? But that's not the point. What one resents is the destruction of beauty that's going on all over the world. Tractors and trucks tearing about, gouging and rooting at the lovely monuments of the past, acres of jerry buildings springing up, all identical and all so drearily ugly. England is now swallowed up by dreary suburbs. Italy is full of factories. Why, even in Switzerland they're crowding scores of tenements on to their loveliest lakeside sites – though not near me, thank God.'

'Yes, it's a new world we have to live in,' she agreed, after a moment. 'But that's all the more reason to make the best of it. And to do our best to make it better.'

She looked at him inquiringly, as though anxious to know how he would answer her remark. But by this time they had reached the Ringstrasse, where lights were springing out and people beginning to leave their offices, congregating at the pavement cafés, talking, laughing, bringing a note of anticipation to the air. It was a fascinating hour and here, at least, there was nothing to offend his eye. As they slid easily through the evening traffic he drew near to her and, in the gathering dusk, passed his arm through hers.

'I've worn you out with lectures and arguments. You must rest in your room for an hour. Then we'll go out to dinner.'

He had sensed that she was shy of going to Sacher's, yet for her own sake decided he would take her there. With a little encouragement she would soon overcome her constraint: besides, at Sacher's one need not dress. As eight o'clock struck on the clock of St Stephen's he escorted her downstairs and out of the hotel. As the night was fine, they walked the short distance along Kärntnerstrasse. The glassed-in terrace of the restaurant was crowded but he had taken the precaution of making a discreet reservation in the little side room known as the Red Bar. He could see that his choice of table gave her confidence and, glancing across the menu, which he had been studying, his expression became reminiscent.

'I hope we'll get something as nice as the fish you chose in Edinburgh. Our first meal together. I'll never forget it. Tell me, do you like foie gras?'

'I don't know.' She shook her head. 'But I suppose I might.'

'Well, then, we'll have it. With some Garnierter Rehrücken and Salzburger Nockerln to follow.' He gave the order, adding: 'As we're in Austria we must honour the country and drink a little Durnsteiner Katzensprung. It comes from the lovely Danube valley about fifty miles from here.'

The foie gras was brought, tenderly pink; he sniffed it delicately, assuring himself it was the real Strasbourg, adequately truffled, then ordered it served with raspberry sauce. When the wine was shown, sampled, approved and poured, he raised his glass.

'Let's drink a little toast to ourselves.' Then, mildly, as she hesitated: 'Remember, you promised to be human. I want to get you out of that dear little Scottish shell of yours.'

Obediently, though a trifle tremulously, she raised the long-stemmed glass, put her lips to the fragrant, amber liquid.

'It tastes like honey.'

'And is just as harmless. I think you know me by this time, Kathy.'

'Oh, I do, David. You're so very nice.'

The venison was all he had expected, served with a savoury radish and apple sauce. He ate slowly, as was his custom, and with feeling, giving to each mouthful the respectful attention it deserved. In the adjoining alcove someone had begun to play softly on the piano, a Strauss waltz of course, but in this setting how right – charming, haunting, melodious.

'Isn't this agreeable,' he murmured across the table. He loved to see the colour come and go in her fresh young cheeks. What a darling she was, arousing the best in his nature, bringing out all that was good in him.

The sweet, as he had hoped, proved to be a triumph. Reading her expression, at which he was not expert, he explained:

'It's made almost entirely from fresh eggs and cream.'

'How many eggs?' she wondered.

He turned to the waiter.

'Herr Ober, how many eggs in Salzburger Nockerln?'

The man shrugged, but with politeness.

'So many, sir, you forget the number. If Madame wishes to make good Nockerln she must not count the eggs.'

Moray raised his eyebrows at Kathy across the table.

'We'll have to start a poultry farm.'

She broke into a peal of laughter, like a schoolgirl.

'Oh, the poor hens, trying to keep up with *that*.'

Delighted with her unusual high spirits, he did not fail to notice that she offered no objection to his hint of their future association.

Presently the bill arrived and, after a casual survey, he paid it with a note of high denomination, and tipped so lavishly as to produce a succession of bows, almost a royal progress.

As they came out of the restaurant they were met on the pavement by the usual outstretched hands – the match and paper flower sellers, the cripples, fake and genuine, the ragged old man with the wheezy accordion, the old women who now had nothing to sell but flattery. With the change from the bill he gave freely, indiscriminately, just to be rid of them; then, escaping towards the hotel, he was unexpectedly rewarded. She took his arm and of her own accord came close to him as they walked towards the Neuer Markt.

'I'm so glad you did that. I'd have felt ashamed after that delicious, expensive meal if you hadn't. But then that's just you, David, to be so unsparingly kind and generous. And what a day you've given me. Everything so new and exciting. I can scarcely believe it all. When I think that only a few days ago I was washing dishes in Jeannie Lang's back kitchen, it's . . . it's like a dream.'

It was so good to see her relaxed, free of her inhibitions, actually gay. Listening in indulgent silence, he let her run on, aware that her one glass of honey-tasting Durnsteiner could not alone have induced this mood but that he was in the main responsible for it. And in a sudden flashback he remembered that with Mary he had shown the same talent, one might even say the power, of lifting her from her serious preoccupation to a new lightheartedness. It was an auspicious omen.

Only too soon they were at the hotel. Outside her room she turned to him to day goodnight.

'Thank you for a most wonderful time, David. If you won't forget our day in Edinburgh, I can tell you I'll never forget this one here.'

He lingered a moment, unwilling to let her go.

'Did you really enjoy it, Kathy?'

'Terribly.'

'Sure?'

'Cross my heart.'

'Then tell me, what did you like most of all?'

She paused in the act of closing her door, became suddenly serious, seemed to examine her thoughts. With averted head, not looking at him, she said very simply:

'Being with you.' Then she was gone.

CHAPTER X

DURING THE NEXT three days the weather, though colder, remained brilliantly fine. Conditions could not have been more perfect for the pleasures and excitements of continued sightseeing. Varying his programme with commendable skill, Moray escorted her to the Hofburg and Hofgarten, to the Imperial Museum of Fine Arts, the Rathaus, the Belvedere, the Parliament. They took tea in Demel's, made the tour of the fashionable shops in the Graben, attended a performance at the Spanish Riding School – which, however, proved rather a disappointment since, although reserving comment, she had obviously disliked seeing the lovely white horses strained into unnatural circus attitudes. He had also accompanied her on a visit to Anna the chambermaid's four children, all lined up in a row and dressed in new warm clothes with strong winter boots, and this had been perhaps the most successful expedition of all. These were, Moray told himself, the happiest days he had ever known. She had brought joy and sweetness into his life, renewed his buoyant youth. The more he saw of her, the more he realised he could not do without her.

And yet at times she puzzled him, even caused him an odd concern. Was she truly entertained by all that he so engagingly displayed? Impossible to doubt; he had seen her eyes light up a score of times, fill with interest and animation. Nevertheless there had been occasions when, while willingly attentive, she seemed troubled, nervously disturbed. At one moment she drew near, very near to him, and the next suddenly drew back. She had a strange capacity for receding into herself and could surprise him by her constancy to her own point of view.

When in the Graben he had vainly used all the subtlety he possessed to induce her to accept a gift – a necklace, simple in design but set with emeralds – which, unthinkingly and with slight knowledge of the price, she had admired.

'It's beautiful,' she had answered, with a shake of her head, 'but it is not for me.'

And nothing would move her. Nevertheless, though as yet she remained unaware, he meant to have his way.

His greatest surprise lay in the realisation that his money counted for so little with her. She had not responded to the luxury of the hotel, rich and elaborate meals were becoming merely an embarrassment to her, and he sensed that she had preferred the little hired car to the silent comfort of his Rolls. Once, indeed, when he dropped a hint on the subject she had unexpectedly replied:

'But, David, money can't buy any of the things that really matter.'

Disappointed and somewhat chagrined by this lack of appreciation, he was nevertheless comforted by the thought that he would be loved or, as he now dared to hope, was being loved for himself alone. And since the simplicities of life so obviously pleased her, he decided to divert her attention towards Switzerland and the restful quiet she would find there. Vienna had not been a mistake; not only had he got to know her better, he had made progress, great progress, in these last few days. Intimacy had been positively established, a current of vibrations now passed between them. Though she herself might still be unaware, he knew from her sudden changes of colour, the touch of her hand, the brightening of her eye when he appeared, that she was passing the point of no return. Every instinct told him so. And to see and feel this shy, intense young girl gradually expanding under the novel compulsions of love was the most delicious experience of his life.

On Saturday morning, when they had finished breakfast, he remarked lightly, but with an undertone of consideration:

'It begins to look as though we've had enough of the city for the time being. Would you like to leave tomorrow for Schwansee? If this cold continues we'll undoubtedly have snow in the Oberland and that's something you shouldn't miss.'

The warmth of her response gave immediate confirmation of his intuition.

'I'd like it better than anything – that is, if it suits you to go. I do so love the country. Not,' she added quickly, 'that I am not happy to be here.'

'Then that's settled! We'll take the Sunday afternoon plane. I'll send Arturo on ahead today – the journey by road across the Arlberg would be much too trying for you at this time of year. But before we leave,' he paused and smiled, 'there is just one

198

more hurdle for you to clear, I think you'll find it a pleasure and not a penance.'

'Yes?' she queried rather uncertainly.

'There is a gala at the Opera House tonight – *Madame Butterfly* . . . but a quite exceptional performance, since Tebaldi is singing. And the décor is by Benois. It's been practically impossible to get tickets but I've succeeded by a stroke of luck. As I'm sure you'll enjoy this particular opera, will you come?'

'Yes, David,' she answered with only a scarcely perceptible hesitation. 'But I'm worried at the way you keep putting yourself about for me.'

'Don't give it a thought.' He did not tell her that only by the payment of an enormous premium, effected through the concierge, had he been able at this late date to secure a loge. 'By the way, we'll take it easy today so that you'll be fresh for tonight.'

Both were glad of the rest, especially since the sky had become overcast and a keen wind blowing down from Semmering made passage through the streets a chilly business. However, after giving Arturo his instructions to leave for home he was out and about in the afternoon, on some affair of his own. At his suggestion they had an early dinner in the sitting-room: no more than a cup of strong turtle soup, omelette fines herbes with pommes pont neuf, pêche melba and coffee: by design a light meal, but good.

When they had finished he stood up.

'It's a nuisance, my dear little Puritan, but we have to dress up a bit for this affair. Luckily I knew your size, so you'll find something in your room. I had your nice Anna lay it out for you.' He put a comradely arm about her shoulder, bent forward close to her in his most winning manner. 'Please wear it – for my sake.'

Humming a snatch of the love duet from *Butterfly* under his breath, he changed in leisurely manner: first the electric razor until the smoothness of his cheek satisfied him, then a hot bath followed by a tepid shower, a good rub down, and a dust of plain talcum. The hotel valet had already put out his evening clothes, with the onyx and diamond links and studs in the fresh frilled starched shirt, the black silk socks half folded over, the patent shoes, trees removed and tongues turned back, set nearly by the armchair. Arturo could not have done better, he must remember to tip the man. At last he was ready. A touch of Eau de Muget and a brisk drill with his monogrammed ivory-backed, military brushes – thank God he had kept his hair – completed the picture. He studied himself in the glass. He had always looked well in white tie and tails – no one could touch Caraceni, in the Boncompagni, for perfection of cut – and tonight, in all modesty, he knew unquestionably that he made a handsome, distinguished, and amazingly youthful figure. In a spirit of some anticipation he switched off the light – the habit persisted from his youth – and went into the sitting-room.

She did not keep him waiting. Presently the door opened and slowly she came out wearing the green dress he had chosen for her and, to his delight, the thin necklet of emeralds that so exactly matched it. Literally, he held his breath as, still slowly, with lowered eyes and cheeks faintly flushed, she advanced and stood before him. If he had thought her ravishing in the lovat suit, now there was no word to fit the case.

'Kathy,' he said in a low voice, 'you will not like me to say this, but I must. You look enchantingly and unutterably lovely.'

He had never in his life spoken such absolute truth. So young, so fresh, and with that warm complexion and reddish gold hair, green undoubtedly was her colour. What he would make of her when he took her to Dior or Balenciaga! But was she trembling? She moistened her lips.

'It is the most beautiful dress,' she said haltingly. 'And, after all, you bought me the necklace.'

'Just to go with your frock,' he said gaily, determined to lighten her mood. 'A few green beads.'

'No. Anna was admiring them. She says they are cabochon emeralds.'

'Ah, well! I only hope your escort looks good enough to go with them.'

She looked at him, then looked away.

'I never knew there could be anyone like you.' He saw that she was seeking a phrase; it came with unusual awkwardness. 'You're . . . you're just out of this world.'

'I hope I won't be for some time.' He laughed. 'And now let's be off. It will delight your democratic spirit – since Arturo is away, we must take a taxi.'

'Am I to wear these gloves?' she asked nervously, on the way down. 'They seem so long.'

'Wear them or carry them, as you please, dearest Kathy, it makes no difference. You can't improve upon perfection.'

The concierge, though shocked that in such splendour they

should be denied their usual conveyance, bowed them into a respectable cab. In a few minutes they arrived at the Opera House, passed through the crowded foyer and were shown to the loge he had secured in the second circle. Here, in the privacy of the snug, red-carpeted little box, which was all their own, he felt her relax. Free of her nervousness, she gazed out upon the brilliant scene with increasing interest and excitement while he, seated close behind, looking over her shoulder through his opera glasses, had the delightful consciousness of reproducing that incomparable Renoir on the same theme, not, alas, his own, but one he had always admired.

'This is new, of course, rebuilt since the war,' he explained. 'A little too white and glittering perhaps – the Viennese tend to overdo their crystal – but still quite charming.'

'Oh, it is,' she agreed unreservedly.

'And as you see, everyone in their best bib and tucker for Tebaldi. Incidentally, as she'll be singing in Italian I ought to give you an idea of what it's all about. It opens at Nagasaki in Japan where Pinkerton, an officer in the United States navy, has arranged through a broker to marry a sweet little Japanese girl, Cho-Cho-San . . . '. Concisely he ran through the main points of the story, concluding: 'It's very sentimental, as you see, one of Puccini's lighter offerings, far from being grand opera, but nevertheless delightfully moving and poignant.'

He had no sooner concluded than a burst of applause announced the appearance of the conductor, Karajan. The lights dimmed, the overture began, then slowly the curtain went up, revealing a Japanese interior of exquisite delicacy.

Moray had already seen this opera twice at the Metropolitan in New York, where he had been for years a season-ticket holder, and where, in fact, he had several times heard Tebaldi sing. Once he had assured himself that the great diva was in voice, he was able to devote himself to the reactions of his companion, and unobserved, with a strange and secret expectation, he watched the changing expressions that lit then shadowed her intent young face.

At first she seemed confused by the novelty of the experience and the oriental strangeness of the scene. But gradually she became absorbed. The handsome Pinkerton, whom he had always found insufferable, obviously repelled her. He could sense her rising sympathy for Cho-Cho-San and a worried precognition of impending disaster. When the curtain fell at the end

201

of the first act she was quite carried away.

'Oh, what a despicable man,' she exclaimed, turning to him with flushed cheeks. 'One knows from the beginning that he is worthless.'

'Vain and self-indulgent, perhaps,' he agreed. 'But why do you dislike him so much?'

She lowered her eyes as though reflecting, then said:

'To me, it's the worst thing – never to think of others, but only of oneself.'

The second act, opening on a note of tender sadness, sustained by an undertone of hope deferred, would, he knew, affect her more acutely than the first. As it proceeded, he did not look at her, feeling it an intrusion to observe such unaffected swelling of the heart. But towards the end of the scene, as the lights dimmed upon the stage and Cho-Cho-San lit her lantern by the doorway to begin her nightly vigil, while the haunting melody of the aria 'Un bel dì' swelled then faded from the darkening room, he took one swift glance at his companion. Tears were streaming down her cheeks.

'Dearest Kathy.' He bent towards her. 'If it is upsetting you, we will leave.'

'No, no,' she protested chokingly. 'It's sad but it's wonderful. And I must see what happens. Just lend me your handkerchief, mine is useless now. Thank you, dear, dear David – you are so kind. Oh, that poor, sweet girl. That any man could be so inhuman, so – so beastly.' Her voice failed, yet she willed herself to be composed.

Indeed, during the third act, rising through unbearable pathos to the final shattering tragedy, she retained control. When the curtain fell and he dared look towards her she was not weeping, but her head had fallen forward on her breast, as though she could endure no more.

They left the theatre. Still overcome, she did not speak until they were in their taxi; then, secure from observation, she said, in a muffled voice:

'I shall never forget this evening . . . never . . .'

He chose his words carefully.

'I knew you had feeling, a great capacity for emotion. I hoped you would be moved.'

'Oh, I was, I was. . . . And the best thing of all, dear David, was seeing it with you.'

No more than that, but enough for him to sense through her still quivering nerves a melting softness towards him. Silently, gently questing in the closed intimacy of the cab, he took her small hand in his.

She did not withdraw it. What had happened to her? Nothing, ever, like this, before. Oh, she had naturally had attentions paid her. While attending her nursing classes, a student at the University, working for his M.A. degree, had been strongly attracted to her. She had not responded. At the hospital during the previous Christmas festivities, the young asistant doctor had tried to kiss her under the mistletoe, succeeding only in clumsily reaching her left ear. She had passed off the attempt with indifference, and refused, later, when he asked her to go to the New Year's dance. She knew herself to be a serious-minded person, not interested in young men, sharing indeed her mother's view, so often forced upon her until it had become her own, that they were brash, inconsiderate and undependable.

But David was none of these things, instead his qualities were exactly opposite. And his maturity, oddly reassuring, had from the first appealed to her. He was still holding her hand, quietly and soothingly, as they reached the hotel. Nor did he relinquish it then. The night concierge was half asleep at his desk as they entered and took the lift to their floor. In the corridor he paused, opened the door of their sitting-room, conscious of a quick thread of pulse in her imprisoned fingers, his own heart beating fast.

'I ordered hot chocolate to be left for us. It would restore you, dearest Kathy.'

'No.' Half turned away from him, she shook her head. 'Nothing . . . please.'

'You're still upset. I can scarcely bear to let you go.'

He led her, unresisting, into the room where, as he had said, a Thermos jug, with fruit and sandwiches covered by a napkin, had been placed upon the table. The room was faintly lit by a single shaded light that cast a soft glow on the carpet while the walls remained in shadow, and they too were in shadow as they faced each other.

'Dearest Kathy,' he said again. 'What can I say? What can I do for you?'

Still not looking at him, she answered in a stifled voice.

'I'll be all right in the morning.'

'It's almost morning now,' he reasoned gently, despite his pounding blood, 'and you're not all right. What really is the matter?'

'Nothing, nothing . . . I don't know. I feel lost somehow. I've never been like this before – sad and happy at the same time.'

'But how can you be lost when you're with me?'

'Oh, I know, I know,' she admitted, then hurried inarticulately on. 'That wretched man has made me see how different – but that's just the trouble. You're so . . . '. She broke off, tears coursing afresh down her cheeks.

Her head was bowed, but placing his fingers beneath her chin he raised her tear-stained face so that they looked into each other's eyes.

'Kathy darling,' he murmured in a tone of ultimate tenderness, 'I'm in love with you. And I believe that you love me.'

Bending, he kissed her upturned fresh young lips, innocent of make-up – which he abominated – and deliciously salt from her tears. The next instant, with a gulping sob, she was closely in his arms, her wet flushed cheek pressed hard against his breast.

'David – dearest David.'

But it was only for a moment. With a cry she broke away.

'It's no use – no use at all. I should have known it from the beginning.'

'But why, Kathy? We love each other.'

'How can we love each other three thousand miles away? You know I'm going away. We'd only break our hearts. Mine is breaking now.'

'You could stay, Kathy?'

'Never – it's impossible.'

He had caught her wrist to keep her from flying to her room. Still straining away from him like a captive bird, she went on wildly.

'I must go. All my life I've been preparing for that one thing – training as a nurse, getting experience at Dalhaven. I've thought of nothing else. I'm needed out there. . . . Uncle Willie expects it. . . . Most of all, I promised Mother before she died that I would go, and I would never fail her, never.'

'Don't, Kathy,' he cut in, fearfully. 'For God's sake – you mustn't do it.'

'I must do it for God's sake . . . for both our sakes.'

She freed herself and, half running towards her room, was gone.

He stared painfully at the closed door. Resisting an impulse to follow her, he began to pace the soft piled carpet in a state of acute agitation. Yet, with the imprint of her soft lips still lingering on his, gradually his distress passed and his main feeling became one of joy. She loved him, utterly, unmistakably, with all her heart. Nothing else mattered. There were difficulties in the way, but they could be overcome. He must, and would, persuade her. Anything else was unthinkable. At all costs he would have her.

Suddenly he felt strong, filled with vigour, and an immense potentiality for love. Hungry, too, As his eye fell upon the good things on the table, he became conscious of the hours that had elapsed since dinner – and the meal had not been notably substantial. Seating himself, he poured the chocolate, still steaming hot, folded back the napkin and began the sandwiches. Ah! Caviar, and the real Beluga, too. Absently, yet with relish, he scoffed the lot.

CHAPTER XI

HE HAD FORECAST snow in Switzerland and, as though confirming his infallibility, snow had greeted them – an early, light covering that had frozen hard and now lay glittering under cobalt skies. For almost a week they had been in Schwansee, rigidly conforming to the covenant of restraint which, as a condition of her coming, she had obliged him to accept. Throughout this horrid stalemate of emotion, in a frantic effort to sway her, he had made simplicity and calm the order of the day. Their too theatrical welcome by Arturo and Elena had been quickly suppressed, staidness imposed, and plain meals commanded, served with an absence of formality. Straining to demonstrate the desirability of his picturesque landscape, he took her walking every afternoon in the crisp, tingling air: excursions, conducted mainly in silence, which brought them into the white foothills of the Alps, seen above as soaring pinnacles made rosy by the rising and setting of the sun. In the evenings, seated in the library on either side of the crackling log fire, tired less from their long outings than from persistent strain, he gave her a programme of his records – selecting mainly Handel, Bach, Mozart – which, rising from time to time, he played upon the stereophonic radiogram, its varnished mahogany skilfully concealed in his lacquer Coromandel cabinet. No one knew of his return, there were no intrusive visitors, no distractions, just themselves alone.

How idyllic under normal circumstances such an existence would have been. But, alas, beneath that superficial control a bowstring tension quivered insufferably with, for him, a rankling sensation of frustration and defeat. With all his charm and subtlety he had tried to dissuade her from her intention to desert him, and he had failed. Persuasion and argument alike had proved futile. And time was flying – indeed, had flown. She must leave when Willie arrived in three days' time.

This inflexibility in one so young, untried and inexperienced, remained for him a perpetual source, not of anguish alone, but of stupefaction. It was not as though she did not love him. Every hour of the day presented him with evidence of her suffering through the constant suppression of her natural desires. Now when he accidentally touched her hand, as in passing a dish at table, the tremor that ran through her was physically perceptible. And how often, when she thought herself unobserved, had he surprised her glance bent upon him, charged with longing, with all the sad hunger of the heart.

One morning, although visitors were proscribed, he had felt he must introduce her to his two little friends, the children of the pier-master. So Hans and Suzy were summoned, introduced, and given 'elevenses' of cherry cake and orangeade. Afterwards all four had gone into the garden to make a snow-man from a drift blown against the thick bole of the Judas tree. This snow, beneath its hard crust, was soft and malleable, and he tied back the swing he had put up for them last summer, so they could get at it. What fun the children had, what shouts of glee, what rosy cheeks and sparkling eyes! Watching them, he had said to her, almost curtly:

'Wouldn't you like to have children like these?'

She had flushed, then paled as from a sudden hurt.

'They are sweet.' She avoided his question. 'So completely natural and unspoiled.'

Why – why – why should she refuse his love, the children he could give her, and all the immense advantages of his wealth and position? Above all, what could the alternative offer? That same afternoon, when they took their favourite walk along the high ridge of the Riesenthal, he kept asking himself these questions with a kind of brooding, desperate despondency induced for the first time by a gleam, a breaking through so to speak, a compelled recognition that there *must* be something in her point of view. And although a truce had been declared between them, as they strode along the high path between the silver-dusted pine trees he could hold back no longer.

'Dearest Kathy, I've no wish to reopen our wounds, but it would help to – to soothe mine, if only I could get a fuller understanding of your motives. Are you leaving me mainly because you have pledged your word?'

'Partly for that reason,' she answered, walking with lowered head. 'But also for another.'

'What other?'

'As I told you, because of what I believe is demanded of all of us. We're living at a terrible time, David. We just seem to be drifting towards self-destruction, moral and physical. Beneath the surface we're all terrified. Yet the world keeps moving away from God. We'll never get through unless everyone, every single person, does something about it, each his own part, no matter how small. Oh, I'm not clever, but it's so obvious, what Uncle Willie says – that we must prove love is stronger than hatred – show that courage, self-denial, and above all charity, can defeat brutality, selfishness and fear.'

Mentally he had made the state of the world taboo, except to reflect that *it would see him out*. But in spite of this he was impressed – who wouldn't have been by such ingenuous fervour?

'So because of your ideas of – of duty and service, you condemn yourself to a life of hardship and misery.'

'Misery?' Quickly she raised her head in protest. 'You can't imagine the personal rewards of such a life.'

'A life of self-sacrifice.'

'It's the only way life can be lived. Nowadays especially.'

'You can't be serious.'

'I was never more in earnest. Wait till you see Uncle Willie. He's had what you might think of as a miserable time, and a great deal of illness, but he's the happiest person in the world.'

He was silent. This hitherto had been beyond him, something outside his conception of life. Could one really be happy out there, *doing good*, in that confounded wilderness? He asked himself the question with a sense of growing agitation.

'And there's more than happiness,' she went on, with difficulty, still striving to express herself. 'There's contentment and peace of mind and a sense of accomplishment. One can never get these by enjoying oneself, by running after pleasure all the time, shutting one's eyes to the agony of others. And they certainly can't be bought. But if one does a really fine job, something to benefit other people – people in need . . . Oh, I'm no good at explaining things, but surely you understand what I mean . . . '. She broke off. 'If you had practised as a doctor you would know . . . and I think – please forgive me, David – I'm sure you would have been a much happier man.'

Again he kept silence, biting his lip, and switching with his steel-pointed stick at the iced lumps of snow turned back by the passage of farm wagons. She was enunciating, naïvely, a humanitarian cliché. And yet, wasn't there more than a grain of truth in what she said? In the pursuit of the rewards of this world, had he found anything but heartache, ennui, recurrent dissatisfactions and regrets, and a bunch of neurotic complexes which had more than once brought him to the verge of a breakdown?

'Dear Kathy!' With sudden self-pity and a rush of sentiment. 'I've always wanted to be good, and to do good, but circumstances have been too much for me.'

'You are good,' she said earnestly. 'It's – it's looking out of your face. You only need the opportunity to prove it to yourself.'

'Do you honestly believe that?'

'With all my heart.'

'My God, Kathy – if you knew what my life had been, what I've endured until . . . well, virtually, until I met you.' Emotionally, he went on: 'As a young man, in India, trapped – yes, literally trapped – into a disastrous marriage and then, for years, the American treadmill, trying to get on . . . on . . . on, finding some refuge in the arts, but only a temporary respite, make-believe, really never achieving true satisfaction though deluding myself that I had. It all springs from my poor unwanted childhood. The whole tree of my life, roots, stem, and branch, was formed then. I've been told,' he refrained from mentioning Wilenski, 'I know it too, all my present being comes from those early years when I had nobody but myself.'

'All that you've said only convinces me that you still can do great things.'

He was too moved to reply and they continued in constrained silence. But her words vibrated in his mind and he felt that she was right – the potential for high achievement still lay within him. What was that line? 'Do noble deeds, not dream them all day long.' He remembered suddenly the last advice Wilenski had given him on leaving New York: 'When you get over there, for heaven's sake find yourself something worthwhile to do, something to do with other people, that'll take your mind off yourself.' Why had he ignored, forgotten this? It had taken Kathy to remind him. Her sweetness and goodness, the purity of her being – he did not shrink from the phrase – had worked on him unconsciously, affected him without his knowing it. How could it have been otherwise?

He was about to speak when, looking up, he saw they had reached the mountain hut where on a previous occasion they had stopped for coffee. It was a poor brew made from some inferior powder, but it was hot, Kathy had appeared to like it, and the peasant woman, skirt kilted over her striped petticoat, was already welcoming them. They sat down on the wooden terrace, in the cold sunshine, both conscious of something momentous and unavoidable developing between them. Nervously, he began drumming on the table, took a quick incautious sip of coffee, spilling it slightly, for his hand shook, then said suddenly:

'I do admit, Kathy, that everyone ought to have some worthy objective in life. I had hoped to find it in devoting myself to you here. But now – it begins to seem as though something more is being demanded of me.'

'What, David?' Her lips were trembling.

'Can't you guess? You're the one who's made me feel it, not only by speaking out now, but simply by your presence. Kathy,' he murmured, in a low, reaching-out voice, 'all other considerations apart, do *you* really need me?'

She looked at him, drawn beyond endurance.

'How can you ask that?' Then with a sudden weakening of control, pitifully avoiding his eyes: 'I need you so much . . . I want you to come with me.'

It was out at last, she had been forced to say it, the unspoken longing that until now she had kept locked up within her breast. He gazed at her in a shaken silence of revelation, realising that he had wanted and waited for that plea through all these recent days of strain.

'You mean,' he said slowly, demanding more, at least a repetition, 'to take the trip out with you?'

'No, no . . . to stay.' She spoke almost feverishly. 'As a doctor, there's the greatest need for you. Uncle Willie is planning a little hospital adjoining the orphanage. You would find there the very work you are fitted for, which in your heart you are seeking. And we would be together, working together, happy.'

'To be with you, Kathy,' he conceded feelingly, 'I'd give my right arm. But think of the changes it would mean, in my – my way of living for one thing. Then again, it's some time since I took my medical degree.'

'You could brush up quickly – you're so clever. And you'd get used to the life.'

'Yes, dear Kathy, but there are other difficulties.' The inordinate desire to be pressed further made him go on. 'Financial affairs that require constant attention, responsibilities; then as regards the mission, you know I'm not a religious man. While agreeing with what you've just said, I doubt if I could surrender my mind to your spiritual convictions.'

'The work you'd do is the best kind of religion. In time, David, you would know the meaning of grace. Oh, I can't speak of such things, I never could, in words they become stiff and wooden, I can only feel them in my heart. And you would too . . . if you'd only come.'

Their hands glided together. Hers, from inner strain, was cold, a marble hand; he held it tightly until the blood began to throb. Never had he felt closer to her. All her soul seemed to flow into him.

The arrival of the peasant woman cut into this splendid moment. While he looked up at her, unseeingly, she pointed to the northern sky and said, practically:

'Es wird Schnee kommen. Schau'n sie, diese Wolken. Es ist besser Sie gehen zurück nach Schwansee.'

'She's advising us to get back home.' Returning to earth, he answered Kathy's inquiring glance. 'Snow is forecast and it's already clouding over.'

He paid the score, leaving generous *trinkgeld*, and they set off back along the ridge, now in total silence, for he was deep in thought. The air had turned grey, cold and very still and the sun was dropping fast behind the mountains like a great blood-orange. Within the hour they had descended to the flatlands and, worried for her in the chill twilight, he looked forward to reaching the villa quickly. But as they were about to cross the short stretch of main road that intersected the path to Schwansee, a red sports M.G. flew past, hesitated, screeched to a stop, and noisily reversed towards them.

'Hello, hello, hello,' came the effusive greeting in high-pitched tones. 'I felt sure it was you, dear boy.'

Jarred out of his meditation, Moray recognised with mis-giving the brass-buttoned blazer of Archie Stench. Leaning airily out of the window from the driver's seat, smiling with all his teeth, Stench extended a gloved hand which Moray accepted with the forced affability of extreme annoyance. The solemn pattern of the afternoon was shattered.

'This is Miss Urquhart, daughter of an old friend,' he said quickly, bent on extinguishing the suggestive gleam already glittering slyly in Stench's eye. 'Her uncle, a missionary in Central Africa, is joining her in two days' time.'

'But how inter-esting.' Archie split and stressed the word. 'Coming here?'

'For a brief visit,' Moray nodded coldly.

'I should like to meet him. Africa is in the news, and *how*. The wind of change. Ha, ha. Dear old Mac. It's quite a breeze now in the Congo. Are you enjoying your stay, Miss Urquhart? You are staying with Moray, I presume?'

'Yes,' Kathy replied to both questions. 'But I shall be leaving soon.'

'Not for wildest Africa?' Ogling, Stench threw out the question facetiously.

'Yes.'

'Good Lord!' Stench thrilled. 'You're really serious? Sounds like quite a story. You mean you're in the missionary racket – sorry, I mean business – yourself?'

Kathy half smiled, to Moray's annoyance, as though taking no exception to Stench's persistence.

'I am a nurse,' she explained, 'and I'm going out to help my uncle – he's opening a hospital at Kwibu, on the Angola border.'

'Good work!' Stench glowed. 'While everyone's running away from that windy area you're rushing in. The nation ought to hear about it. We British have to keep the flag flying. I'll drop over when your uncle arrives. You'll give me a drink, dear boy. just for old lang syne? Well, got to be off. I'm all in. Been down at the Pestalozzi Village doing a conjuring show for the kids. Sixty kilometres each way. Dam' bore. But decent little brats. Cheerio, Miss Urquhart; chin-chin, dear boy. Wonderful to have you back!'

As he drove off Archie called out, ensuring his prospective visit:

'Don't forget, I'll be giving you a ring.'

'He seems nice,' Kathy remarked conversationally, when they had crossed the road. 'Good of him to entertain those children.'

'Yes, he's always up to something like that. But – well, a bit of a bounder I'm afraid,' Moray answered in the tone of one unwillingly forced to condemn, adding, as though this accounted for everything, 'Correspondent for the *Daily Echo*.'

The unfortunate meeting at this particular moment, when vital soul-subduing issues surged in his mind, had thoroughly put

212

him out. Stench was a menace. Confound it, he thought, brought back to the mundane, in half an hour news of his return with Kathy would be all over the canton.

Indeed, no sooner had they got back and taken tea than the phone rang.

'Put it through to the study,' he told Arturo briefly. 'Excuse me for a few minutes, dear Kathy. Friend Stench has been at work.'

Upstairs, he unhooked the receiver, pressed the red button with an irritable premonition immediately confirmed by Madame von Altishofer's contralto overtones.

'Welcome home, dear friend! I heard only this moment that you were returned. Why did you not let me know? It has been so long. You have been missed greatly; everyone is talking about your mysterious absence. Now, how soon may I come to see you, and your exciting young visitor who has designs on darkest Africa?'

It was amazing how disagreeable he found this intrusion – not only what she said, but her manner, her inverted English, even her modulated well-bred voice. He cleared his throat, launched into a perfunctory explanation, the essence of which was simply that the demands of old family friends had detained him much longer than he had anticipated.

'Relatives?' she queried politely.

'In a way,' he said evasively. 'When my other guest arrives I hope you'll come over and meet them both.'

'But before, you must come to me for a drink.'

'I wish I could. But I have so many things to attend to, after being away.' Looking out of the window he saw that the first frail snowflakes were beginning to drift down. He seized upon the topic. 'Good gracious! It's actually snowing. I'm afraid we're in for an early winter.'

'No doubt,' she said, with a little laugh. 'But are we reduced to speaking of the weather?'

'Of course not. We'll get together soon.'

Frowning, he hung up, terminating the conversation, annoyed at her interference – no, that was totally unjust; despite her Germanic strong-mindedness she was a thoroughly nice woman and he had perhaps over-encouraged her. He was very much on edge. Again he had a strange feeling that time was closing in upon him. Downstairs he was disappointed to find that Kathy had gone to her room. She did not appear again until dinner, and then he saw that, to please him, she had put on the green dress. Touched to the heart, he knew that there was only one woman in the world for him. He wanted her with a need so extreme he had to turn away without his usual compliment, without a word. All evening, despite his efforts to entertain, he was not himself – preoccupied, obsessed rather, with the need of achieving some decision, in the ever-dwindling hours at his disposal. After he had played a few records she must have seen that he wished to be alone, for on the plea of fatigue she went early to bed, leaving him in the library.

CHAPTER XII

WHEN SHE HAD gone he stood for several minutes listening to her light movements in the room above. Then, automatically, he began to slip the long-playing discs into their polythene covers and to replace them in the cabinet. He half opened one of the three tall windows and peered across the terrace into the night. The snow, beginning with light flurries, had fallen steadily all through the late afternoon, gentle, silent, clouding the air with great drifting flakes. Now the garden was blanketed, nothing visible beyond, life seemed extinguished. No sounds disturbed the unnatural stillness but the abandoned wail of a paddle boat groping its way across the shrouded lake, and the faint whine of the *bise* springing up, imperceptible at first, but gaining in force. He well knew that wind, spiralling down from the mountains with immediate violence, and recognised through all his senses the portents of a storm. Within five minutes, as he had foreseen, the wind was howling round the house, creaking the shutters and tearing at the roof tiles. The air, turned colder, edged the whirling flakes with ice. They fell sharper, mixed with a heavy spattering hail and clots of driven snow. The trees, unseen but plainly audible, had begun that familiar mad fandango which, mingling Berlioz with the blast, he had so often dramatised for his own entertainment.

But his mood was too disturbed to permit of Berlioz. Wagner would have been more appropriate, he reflected grimly, something like the Ride of the Valkyries, but he had no heart for anything, could think only of the fateful decision he must make, and of her. He shut the window and pulled the tasselled cord that drew the pale pink quilted curtains, wondering if she were asleep, or if, as seemed probable, the storm had disturbed her. The thought of her lying there, alone, listening wide-eyed to the harsh discords of the night! If only he might go to her. But of course he could not. God, how restless he was, he must compose himself, try to clear his mind. Taking a book from the shelves, a new biography of Lord Curzon, he threw himself into a chair. But he could not settle to read, not even of Curzon, a man he deeply admired, had in fact unconsciously adopted as an exemplar. His attention wavered, the words ran together into a meaningless blur. He got up, looked at the Tompion longcase clock: only half past ten: too early for bed, he'd never sleep. Never. In the drawing-room he began to pace up and down, head bowed, without a glance towards his paintings, so often a consolation in the past. He felt unendurably hot, suppressed an inordinate impulse to go out on to the snowbound terrace, went instead to the pantry and turned down the thermostat. No sounds came from the kitchen; Arturo and Elena had retired to their own quarters. Even they had shown signs of disquiet lately, as though waiting, uneasily, for an announcement. Returning to the drawing-room, he was about to resume his pacing when forcibly he drew up short, facing at last the core of his problem.

Once it had been established, finally, that she would not stay, only one possible course of action remained open to him. Though he had stubbornly evaded the issue, he saw that from the beginning, when he set eyes on her in Markinch churchyard, the end had been inevitable, part of his destiny. It was the pressing need to amend his life that in the first instance had brought him back to his native land. Now she offered the very opportunity he sought, and with it all the wonder of her love. How could he refuse? She had become an absolute necessity to him. If he should lose her through vacillation or stupidity, life would be impossible. Hadn't he learned that lesson from his sad youthful mistake? He must accompany her to Kwibu, give himself up completely to the work ordained for him. And why not? It was splendid work. He truly wanted to be the new person she would make of him. And he would be. It was not too late. It was not impossible. Others had found that saving spark, and in comparable manner. He had read of them, tortured men in spiritual travail, who discovered themselves in strange suspenseful backgrounds, habitually tropical, and at the last gasp.

'I'll go,' he said out loud. 'It's the only way.'

When he had spoken these thrilling words, he experienced an immediate singing sensation of release. He felt lighter suddenly, freed, as if a load had been lifted from his shoulders. What a liberation – almost a transfiguration! Was it what they called a *conversion*? She had spoken of grace, and now he seemed not alone to sense its meaning, but actually to feel it flowing into and through him. A sweet ichor, a fountain of light – the words came to him as, with head thrown back, he looked upwards, deeply and genuinely moved, experiencing fully this moment of beatitude, even feeling himself, though distantly, in touch with Heaven. He could not yet ascend to the heights, he had been earthbound too long, and so he did not attempt a prayer, but that – later perhaps – might come.

Slowly, he relaxed. It was done, the die heroically cast. Gladness overwhelmed him. And how easy it had been, simply an acceptance of the truth and an offering of himself. Why had he hesitated so long, keeping her waiting in an agony of protracted uncertainty? For she had suffered, poor little thing, perhaps more acutely than he. If only he could tell her now, spare her these extra hours of suspense. Yet would it be quite proper? Right and reason were on his side. But no, he felt it might scarcely be correct. Well, at least he would rest with a mind at peace.

After standing motionless for several minutes he switched off the lights and went slowly upstairs to his room. Still inspired, warm with salvation, he took a tepid bath and his usual dust with talcum, put on his sleeping coat, morocco slippers and dressing gown, sat down on the edge of his bed. He must really turn in. Yet the excitement of his decision kept mounting within him. His good news simply would not keep, physically he could not contain it. Was she asleep? If not, it would be only Christian charity to deliver the good tidings now, in person. He got up, hesitated, speculatively opened his door, and gazed across the long upper landing. Then, holding his breath, he tiptoed cautiously, without a single creak, over the thick Wilton carpet towards her room.

The wind, still roaring outside, intensified the inner stillness of the darkened landing as he paused outside her door. He almost turned back. Then, his pulse sounding in his ears, he tapped upon the panel, gently turned the handle.

'Kathy,' he whispered, 'are you awake?'

An immediate stirring in the darkness answered him, even before her startled voice came back.

'David!'

'Don't be alarmed, dear Kathy. I thought the storm might

have kept you awake. And as you are . . . I have something important to tell you.'

Feeling his way forward, he came to the bed and knelt down beside it. Faintly, he could see the outline of her head upon the pillow, of a bare arm resting upon the counterpane. He touched it lightly, reassuringly.

'Kathy, dearest Kathy. My mind is made up. I had to let you know at once. I am coming with you.'

'David!' she said again, in a soft thrilling whisper. He could feel the sudden joy that took possession of her, every nerve in her seemed alive. 'Oh, thank you – thank you, from my heart.'

'You're not angry with me . . . for disturbing you?'

'Angry! Oh, my dear, I've been lying here, longing and longing to hear what you have just told me.'

'I couldn't bear the thought of you waiting, through what might have been a sleepless night.' He paused. 'Now I am here, may I stay a little while and talk?'

'Yes, stay, stay. I am wide awake now. Shall I switch on the lamp?'

'No, dearest. I can see you clearly now.'

'And I can see you.' She gave a low joyful sigh. 'Oh, I'm so happy. Do you know what I was half dreaming, just before you came in?'

'Tell me, dear.'

'That we were out in Kwibu together and that Uncle Willie . . . ' she hesitated, then opened her heart, 'that Uncle Willie was marrying us in the Mission church.'

'And so he will, dear Kathy.'

They remained looking at each other. His heart, swelling in his side, was a pain and a delight. With gentle fingers he began gently to stroke her arm.

'I am still thinking of our future,' she went on in a lulled, dreamy voice. 'All settled. You and I together.'

Outside rain and hail kept drumming on the window, then came a flash and a crack of thunder. He shivered slightly.

'Dear David, you are cold. Please get a rug to cover yourself.'

'It is chilly.' A lump rose in his throat, yet he spoke reasonably, with calm moderation. 'If you could share the counterpane, we could bundle – like they do in the Islands at home. There's so much we have to say to one another.'

A moment later he lay beside her, but in the semi-darkness, fumbling to lift the counterpane, almost inadvertently, he had raised also the blanket and linen sheet that covered her. Her face was close to his on the pillow. At first she had turned rigid, lying so still he thought she had ceased to breathe, then he felt that she was trembling. Quickly he reassured her.

'Dearest, you know I don't mean to distress you.'

'But David . . .'.

'I respect and cherish you more than anything in the world.'

Gradually, very slowly, she relaxed. The warmth of her young body came to him through her cotton nightdress. The rain hissed down the gutters and thunder rolled and echoed amongst the mountains. Half turning, he pressed his lips against her hair.

'David, this is wrong,' she said at last, in a breaking voice. 'Please don't let us do a wrong thing.'

'Darling,' he said, with deep conviction, 'how could it be wrong? We are already one in the sight of Heaven.'

'Yes, David, but please let us wait, dear.'

'Don't you love me enough?'

'Oh, I do – I do – so much that it hurts. But we'd be so sorry, after.'

'No, dear Kathy, love like ours is itself a forgiveness.'

'But David . . .'.

'And surely my – our mutual pledge makes this moment a sacred one.' He could feel the struggle within her. He murmured earnestly: 'It cannot be wrong, dear, when in only a few days, almost a matter of hours, Willie will marry us.'

He took her in his arms, inhaling the scent of her fresh young skin. How thin and slight she was, how young, and how violently her little heart was beating against his breast, like a bird just captured and fluttering in its cage.

'No, David, dearest.'

Then, nature overcame, released her from conscience. Sighing, she put both her hands behind his neck and kissed him fiercely. 'I cannot help it. I love you so much it's. . . like dying.'

A consciousness of rectitude welled up in him. Whispering, he sought to still her trembling. Pure unprofane sex was no sin, a sanctification rather, almost an act of worship – that had been said recently, ecclesiastically, had it not? – in a court of law. Tenderly enclosing her, he readjusted his embrace, but with prayerful gentleness. How sweet at last to taste the slow pleasure, the mounting rapture, all in the odour of sanctity. Later, as he felt her tears on his cheek, he sighed, appeased, though still exalted.

'You are crying. But why, dear child?'

'I'm afraid for what we've done, David.'

'Was it not sweet for you too, my love?'

'Yes, it was sweet,' her voice stifled in the pillow. 'But it was a sin, David, and God will punish us.'

'No, dearest. He knows. He will understand. And if you think it was just a little wrong, you know we will make up for it.'

She is different from her mother, he thought dreamily, as of a shadow passing before him. Mary had no regrets. Yet she too had turned religious, in the end.

'Don't, dear,' he said soothingly, wiping her hot sad face with the cool entangled sheet. 'Think of our work – of the happiness that lies ahead of us.'

'Yes, David.' Striving obediently to check her tears, she clung to him. 'I am trying . . . thinking of you and me, David, in the little Mission church.'

CHAPTER XIII

At ZURICH AIRPORT, striding to and fro between the flower stall and the newspaper kiosk that flanked the exit of the *douane*, Moray expanded his chest with a long deep breath, suffused by a new sense of the joy of living. The sensation was so strong he smiled involuntarily, and it was a proud smile. Often he had experienced a delightful consciousness of himself, but never before with such intensity as now. He had seen the Super-Constellation land, it could be no more than a matter of minutes before Willie appeared. Admittedly he was nervous, and for that reason, among others, had managed to persuade Kathy not to accompany him, explaining that for her so emotional a reunion was best conducted in private. In any event, she was still rather agitated, not yet quite herself. When he looked into her room before leaving for the airport, he had been concerned to find her kneeling in contrite prayer. But while he respected these tender scruples, they would pass. If he himself felt a twinge of compunction, he was sustained by the inner consciousness that he was at last on the way he had sought so long, loved for the vital decision he had taken, a man with a mission in life, soon to savour the joy of energetic action, the thrill of enthusiasm, the sacred peace of duty accomplished. Rising early, he had squared his shoulders against the task ahead. Already the latest medical textbooks had been ordered by telephone, inquiries sent out as to tropical equipment, consideration given to the adjustment and settlement of his affairs. Looking back he now regarded the emptiness, the falsity, of his previous life with shamed and scornful self-contempt. But the future prospect exonerated him, filled him with the double anticipation of spiritual regeneration and the sweetness of continued love.

He paused abruptly in his promenading. Customs examination was over, the passengers of the big Trans-World plane from Luanda via Lisbon were filing through the glass doors, and there, at the end of the line, came a tall, emaciated-looking man with sloping shoulders, carrying a small blue airlines zipper bag, dressed in an open-necked drab shirt and a thin khaki service suit, the blouse with flat pockets suggestive of the war-time pattern. He wore no hat and his streaky sun-bleached hair had the same colour as his face which, lined and sunken, was of a withered yellow. But his eyes, though hollow in their orbits, were still youthful, almost unnaturally bright, and, meeting them across the crowd, Moray knew that, unmistakably, this was Willie.

They shook hands. Then to Moray's relief – for despite his newfound faith in himself he had experienced a sudden wilting inrush of near-panic – Willie smiled.

'You knew me,' he said. 'And I knew you, too.'

'Wonderful to see you again. Kathy is expecting you at the house. Was it a good flight? Have you had lunch?' In his excitement Moray almost babbled, there was so much he wanted to say, to explain, all in one breath.

Willie did not want lunch but said he would be glad of a cup of coffee.

'You feel the cold, coming back,' he added mildly.

And no wonder, thought Moray. No overcoat and such an outfit. Aloud he said:

'We'll go immediately your luggage is brought out.'

'This is it.' Willie indicated the zipper bag. 'All I need. Some shirts and a pack of coloured slides. You know I can't stay long.'

In the café below the restaurant the waitress brought two steaming cups. As Willie applied himself to his, Moray took a painful yet purposeful inspiration.

'I want to explain everything to you, Willie . . . in the hope of your forgiveness. It's a long tragic story, but perhaps you'll listen, for it has a – I fully believe – a good ending. You see, when I . . . '.

'Don't,' said Willie, fixing the other with tired, brilliant eyes. 'That's all in the past and forgotten. Human beings should not judge one another. I had your cable and Kathy's letter. So not another word.'

An immense wave of gratitude flowed over Moray, so warm and overwhelming it left him speechless. In total silence he sat watching Willie nursing the hot cup, drinking in little gulps. If there seemed no flesh on his body, there was less on his hands; the fingers holding the cup were skeletal. He noticed also that Willie had a marked tic which periodically caused his head to jerk laterally, exposing a scar that ran from one side of the neck to the larynx.'

'I see you've spotted my beauty scratch.' Willie had caught his eye. "One of my old scoundrels was a prize spear-thrower in the early days. Now he's my chief catechist. It doesn't trouble me much, though once in a while I lose my voice. It was worth it."

All this was said in such a natural lighthearted manner as to impress Moray even more. He'd have given a lot, there and then, to announce the intention that burned inside him. But no, Kathy had claimed the privilage of imparting this sensation, linked to the news of their marriage, so with all his newfound self-denial he refrained, saying instead:

"If you're ready we may as well be off."

In the station wagon Moray turned the heating full on, but they hadn't gone far before he observed that Willie was shivering. He wanted to stop and offer his overcoat, but this, although St Francis of Assisi had set the precedent, struck him as officious in the present case. Yet his heart glowed towards Willie. Dressed as he was, with that explosive tic and his strange shivering remoteness, Willie looked odd, extremely odd, but there was something real about him, he was undoubtedly a man. Already Moray had identified himself with him and, half turning, while still keeping one eye on the road, he said:

'If I had some idea of your plans, it would enable me to make the best possible arrangements for your stay.'

'I'm due in Edinburgh on the eleventh. Let's see,' Willie reflected, 'that's three days from now. I've some serious matters to put before my committee. And a lecture to deliver in the Usher Hall. Kathy,' he added, 'had better come along to help me and collect her gear.'

'Must you both go so soon?' Moray exclaimed in a disappointed tone. 'I'd banked on keeping you for some time.'

'It's all very pressing. We shall not stay long in Edinburgh but work down to London, lecturing on the way. I'm needed at the Mission. So I've arranged to fly back to Kwibu on the twenty-first.'

'Good heavens, that's sooner than we expected – less than two weeks from today. And I did want to do something for you here.'

Already, at the back of his mind, Moray had felt the need of a definite act to mark his departure from Schwansee. He meant to go off with a bang. No hole-and-corner business, no slinking off, he'd march out with head high and flags flying. And now, under the stress of urgency, this idea took definite form: he'd have a farewell party, introduce Willie to a gathering of his friends, there would be a frank declaration by himself, an appropriate speech by Willie – ah, that suggested an added attraction.

'You say you're to deliver some lectures?'

'They call it a lecture.' Willie smiled. 'Just a little descriptive talk about the Mission, chiefly our beginnings there, illustrated by coloured slides. I only do it to raise funds.'

'Then,' said Moray warmly, 'why don't you raise some here? Give the lecture in my house tomorrow. I can promise you a substantial response.'

'I wouldn't mind,' Willie said, after a moment's thought. 'I'm not much of a speaker. At least I could run through some of it.'

'Good, then that's settled.'

They were now beyond Lachen, on the last stretch of their journey, yet the dazzling view of the mountains which presented itself brought no comment from Willie. Instead Moray became increasingly aware that his companion, drawn up in the corner of the seat and despite the fact that the station wagon had become excessively warm, was enduring a sharp return of his earlier shivering fit. Momentarily neglecting the road, Moray turned rull round to find the other's over-bright gaze bent apologetically upon him.

'Don't mind me,' Willie said. 'I felt this coming on in the plane. Just a little snatch of fever.'

Reverting to eyes front, Moray groped along the seat and found Willie's bony fingers. They were dry and hot.

'Good heavens, man, you're obviously getting a temperature. You must go to bed immediately when we get back.'

Selecting an interlude between the rigors, Willie smiled.

'If I lay down every time I had a temperature I'd never be up.'

'What is it?' Moray asked, after a pause. 'Malaria?'

'It could be. But then I've so many interesting bugs inside me – amoebae, cocci, trypanosomes, and whatnot – one never knows.'

'Surely not trypanosomes?'

'Oh, yes, I've had a go of sleeping sickness. Then I did have to be flat on my back.'

'We'll stop at the chemist's and at least get you some quinine.'

'Thank you, David, you're a goodhearted chap. However, I've had a staple diet of quinine so long it's stopped doing any good. I stoke up with atabrine and paludrin occasionally, though actually it's better to let the bugs fight it out amongst themselves. If you leave them alone the different strains go into battle and knock each other out.'

Good God, thought Moray, staring straight ahead and frowning, this man is a hero or a saint – or else he's a little bit dotty.

But now they were in Schwansee and, turning up the hill from the lake, into the winding avenue lined with acacia trees, Moray drew up at his house. Immediately Kathy rushed from the porch – she had been waiting more than an hour for the sound of the car.

Watching the reunion of uncle and niece, Moray suffered a twinge of jealousy that it should be so affectionate. But, manfully, he dismissed the unworthy sentiment – Kathy, he well knew, was all his own. He smiled at her meaningly.

'Show Willie to his room, my dear. I'm sure you have lots to say to him.'

When he had washed and restored himself with a quick glass of amontillado he went into the library to wait for her. She was a long time in coming down, and although he occupied himself by drawing up a list of the people he meant to invite to the lecture party – Arturo would telephone them later in the day – he had begun to feel anxious at the delay when the door swung open and she appeared. Her cheeks were flushed, she flew like a homing dove straight into his arms.

'I've explained everything. Uncle Willie is coming down to have a talk with you, so I won't stay. I think it's all right. I'm sure he likes you . . . And, oh, dearest David, I'm happy again.'

When she had gone, he waited with a touch of apprehension, aware of the many points on which he might be interrogated. But when Willie arrived his expression, with its mixture of patience and kindness, was far from intimidating. Standing there, with his sloping shoulders and thin, dangling hands, his bones seemed loosely strung together under the thin, parchment-dry skin. He looked at Moray from under his brows with those bright, luminous eyes, in an embarrassed manner, made evident by an exacerbation of his tic.

'Kathy has told me,' he said. 'I could be glad for all our sakes. She wants you. I want you. But . . . ' he hesitated, 'do you really want to come? I think you should consider that question carefully before you proceed.'

Moray, who had hoped for warm acceptance, perhaps even for congratulations, stared at Willie, disappointed and at a loss.

'I have considered it. And I do want to come. Of course . . . ' his eyes fell, 'I suppose you've good reason to distrust me.'

'No, no, it's not that, David. I only feel that you must be strongly attached to your own way of life. Perhaps that life may call you back in spite of yourself. You may not succeed in breaking away from it.'

'You misjudge me,' Moray protested seriously, with unmistakable sincerity. 'My life, my old life, has become obnoxious to me. For a long time, even before I set eyes on Kathy, I had felt how empty and trivial it was – a useless existence. Now I know that I needn't be a slave to the past, that it's possible for me to make what I will of myself. I'm determined to build a new – a happy life.'

'A happy life,' Willie repeated, as though reflecting on the words. 'When you say that, are you not thinking only of yourself? That kind of life has no part in our work. Happiness should never be regarded as an end in itself – it is found only in a total absence of concern about oneself. If you come with us you'll be called on to do many things which are neither pleasant nor enjoyable.'

'I recognise that,' Moray said, in a hurt voice, not without dignity. 'But with Kathy at my side, and your help, I believe I can acquit myself creditably. At least I will try.'

There was a stillness during which Willie gazed intently at Moray. His eyes were guileless but held something searching in their depths. Then he smiled and held out his hand.

'I believe you will,' he said, with sudden cheerfulness. 'And if you do, you will be rewarded in a manner far beyond your present expectation. I believe, David, that anyone who has been accorded talents such as yours must devote them to the service of his fellow men. If he does he'll achieve the ultimate purpose of every man's being. If he does not he will be consumed by unhappiness and sooner or later suffer an atrocious punishment.

So for your sake as well as my own I rejoice in your decision. It's all settled then. And I may now tell you how much your help will mean to me – you and Kathy, doctor and nurse, a team of husband and wife working together, it's a gift straight from the Lord.'

CHAPTER XIV

MORAY'S SENSE OF the dramatic had been a feature of his character even in those early days when he had so carefully built up that thrilling surprise for Mary in demonstrating the wonders of Glenburn Hospital and the little house which, alas, they were never to occupy. As a different man, and in a different cause, yet with unchanged enthusiasm, he had resolved to make his farewell party for Willie's lecture an occasion that would be remembered in Schwansee long after he had gone. His preparations had been elaborate, and now the day, the hour, and the moment had arrived. They were here, all his friends, seated expectantly in a neat semicircle in the drawing-room where, against the closed double doors, a white screen had been unrolled. A projector, hired for the occasion, stood on a Pembroke table at the other end, already connected to an electric point.

From the beginning, when Leonora Schutz arrived in a new hat with Dr Alpenstuck, quickly followed by little Gallie and Archie Stench, who had given her a lift, then by Madame Ludin and her husband, and finally, after an anxious interval, by Frida von Altishofer, the party had gone well, progressively enlivened by his excellent buffet and superlative champagne. Leonora was in a gay mood, her laugh ascending with an extra trill; Stench, wandering around, glass in hand, kept repeating, 'Lavish, dear boy. Indubitably lavish,' while little Gallie, handbag at the ready, kept smiling to herself that secret, self-contained smile of the very deaf. One did not expect an equal response from the placid Ludins but even they had responded to the current of anticipation in the air. Moray was pleased – perhaps Archie had been active, dropping hints in his usual fashion, but not enough, he hoped, to spoil his final surprise. Once or twice, glancing at Madame von Altishofer, who partook sparingly of the good things, he wondered how much she guessed of his decision, and a queer conviction came over him that already though by what means he could not decide, she *knew*. Yet her manner, pleasantly amiable, so especially nice towards Kathy, altogether so completely at ease – occasionally he had even caught her eyes resting upon him quizzically – gave no indicaton of the disappointment he might have expected of her. He could only commend her breeding and hope, charitably, that memories of their friendship would survive unimpaired.

What did particularly gratify him was the success, deserved though unexpected, of his two house guests, Kathy especially, though he might have wished her a little less nervous, more socially at ease. Still, Madame Ludin and the vivacious Leonora made much of her, while the ubiquitous Archie hovered unsteadily around, full of giggling compliments. Willie, too, though at first, because of his unclerical appearance, rather oddly regarded, had soon proved a centre of sympathetic interest. Observing them both, Moray was filled with a warm sense of comradeship. He had never felt happier. He was like a schoolboy breaking up at the end of term, going off for the holidays. How satisfying, how charged with anticipation these last three days had been, days of cosy intimacy during which they had held long talks, discussed plans, grown together into a close-knit partnership. The sweetness of Kathy's presence, the joy of knowing that she loves him, had been intensified by Willie's presence. To be with Willie was to realise the value of the work that he, himself, would do. Yes, amazing, in this short time, the effect Willie had produced upon him, by his practical, human cheerfulness, even by his silences. Inspired, Moray told himself repeatedly how glad he was to have linked his life with a character so transparently simple yet strong – and, with it all, so good. Somehow you felt that Willie loved the whole human race.

And now it was time for him to give his lecture. Moray stepped forward and, taking him by the arm, led him towards the circle of chairs. As he did so, he was swept again by a deep, sincere wave of feeling, of affection, and more, for this thin, sickly string of a man in the faded khaki suit. He rapped with his knuckles on the occasional table, causing a cessation of chatter and a polite craning of necks.

'Ladies and gentlemen, or rather good friends all, my dear friend the Rev. Willie Douglas will now deliver his address. Afterwards I may have just a few words to say to you.'

Facing his audience, who had come mainly from curiosity, in the secret expectation of an entertainment such as might be given by some eccentric performer, like a conjurer producing rabbits out of a hat, Willie stood awkwardly, a lanky and ungainly figure, his arms hanging loosely from his sloping shoulders, his neck twitching faster than usual. But he was smiling, a gentle and remote smile that humanized all his oddity.

'Don't be alarmed,' he told them mildly, 'I'm not going to preach at you, or lecture you either, for that matter. Instead, I think it might interest you to hear how, with God's help, a little Christian colony was built from nothing in the remote wilderness of Central Africa. And please don't hesitate to interrupt if you have any questions to ask, or if I'm not making things clear.'

Moving over to the projector he cleared his throat and, in an informal conversational manner, went on:

'First of all, how did we get there? It wasn't so easy, twenty years ago. Usually missionaries go out from our headquarters in Melopo two or three together, but that wasn't possible in this instance. All that could be spared me was a native catechist, but he was a fine man, baptised Daniel – I'll show you his photograph presently. Well, off we started, bound for the Kwibu district in the extreme north-east, one of the wildest parts of the borderland between Angola and the Congo. Since we wanted to take cattle with us and as the country was so rough and rocky, we had decided to use an old ox-waggon for transport instead of a truck. It was a blessing we did so, otherwise we should never have got there. I had made a few short trips around Melopo while gathering experience and learning the dialects, but this beat anything I'd ever seen. Let me give you some idea of the country we went through. It's not the sort of country you associate with the tropics, swamps and steaming jungles and such-like, but it had a few problems of its own. Of course these photographs, and many of the others, were taken at a later date.'

In succession he showed a number of slides on the screen: deep, dried-up river beds choked with boulders, precipitous slopes of sharp-edged black rocks in tangles of yellow scrub, thickets of thornbush so dense as to evoke a murmur from his audience.

'How on earth did you get through those, dear boy?' Archie voiced the general feeling. 'Didn't they tear you to shreds?'

'We lost a little skin.' Willie smiled. 'But we averaged at least fifty yards an hour. Yet that wasn't the worst. Just after we got through that last bit I showed you, because of my stupidity we lost our compass and wandered off the high northern tableland into the Cazar desert. It was a bad mistake – sand, deep sand, everywhere, and low scrubby bush, a waterless waste land. In the heat and blinding dust storms we ran out of water and would have fared rather badly if we hadn't come on three Bushmen who led us to a sucking hole – a muddy pit they had dug in the sand.'

'Aren't the Bushmen dreadful little aboriginals, with hair all over their faces?' asked Leonora, intelligently.

'These were not large, only four feet in height,' Willie answered gently. 'But they were certainly not dreadful, for if they had not humanely shared their scanty supply of water, neither my companion nor I would have survived. In fact we very nearly didn't, for presently my good catechist went down with dysentery, three of the oxen sickened and died, and I – well, by this time we were both covered with sores from tick and mosquito bites, so I got a touch of malaria. As if this wasn't enough, the waggon chains broke and it was really a miracle that we did at last reach our destination, Kwibu, the chief village of the district and tribal headquarters of the Abatu. I have an old photograph which I took shortly after arrival.' He projected another slide on the screen. 'As you see, it's just a scattered collection of conical mud hovels roofed with palm thatch, no cultivation whatsoever, and in the background you can make out a few skeleton cattle, poor starved creatures, always covered with flies, wandering miserably around on the parched ground.

'Well, we had arrived, and were feeling pleased with ourselves, when we received a nasty shock. The chief of the Abatu wouldn't let me enter the village. Here he is, all painted up for the occasion, and I think you'll agree that I was not wise to press him too hard.'

'Oh dear,' Leonora thrilled with sympathy. 'What a fearful old sinner.'

'Sometimes the biggest of sinners make the best of saints,' Willie smiled. 'And old Tshosa hasn't done so badly, as you'll see. However, at that time he wasn't too full of brotherly love, so we were obliged to up stakes and move off some distance, to higher ground above the village where there was a small clump of tacula trees and a spring. Here, first of all, we set to and built a little hut. It was hot work. I wasn't used yet to the sweltering temperature, and the tacula wood was so tough it blunted my

231

axe. We didn't have any roofing material, and by now we were running very short of food supplies.'

'I was going to ask you that,' interposed Madame Ludin. 'How did you live? Catering is my business and I'd be interested to know.'

'Our only food was a kind of porridge. I would boil my kettle and pour the boiling water into a bowl containing a handful of oatmeal. It sounds little enough, but it's good solid Scotch fare and stood by us well.'

'It wouldn't me,' exclaimed Archie. 'I'm all for the liquid Scotch.'

'Anyway,' said Willie, joining in the laugh, 'we had already started to make a garden and to dig ditches to carry the spring to irrigate the land. Properly watered, the grass grew amazingly quickly, we raised mealies, potatoes and Indian corn, and our remaining oxen began to thrive. All this time none of the tribe came near me; our only visitors were lions, cheetahs and an occasional rhinoceros.'

'Oh dear. Did you shoot them?' said Leonora. She was fascinated by Willie, his oddness, his tic, that marvellous sweet expression. A thought flashed through her giddy brain: if there was game, why not take Herman on safari, drop in on the Mission, like a Hemingway heroine? But he was answering her question.

'No,' he said thoughtfully. 'We've never had a gun. They came close too, but I scared them away by throwing pebbles at them.'

'Good heavens, weren't you afraid?'

He shook his head.

'I think we didn't fear them because we were both terribly weak and our spirits were at a low ebb, especially when the rainy season began, continuous thunderstorms followed by a plague of white ants. Daniel and I were both ill with fever. He was so weak he had to be fed with a spoon. I didn't seem to be doing any good; it looked as though our Heavenly Father had no use for us at all. But just when I felt ready to give up, Tshosa, the chief, suddenly appeared, at the head of a long line of his best warriors, all carrying spears. It was an alarming sight and I was very frightened, for of course I thought it was all up with us. But no, he had come bearing an offering.' Willie paused with a faint smile. 'Would you like to guess what it was?'

No one seemed able to advance a suggestion but they were all listening intently.

'Well,' Willie said, 'it was a bowl of blood and milk, the Abatu token of friendship. So I drank this awful brew, though it was a struggle, and communications were established between us. It appeared that they had been closely watching my gardening efforts, and now they wanted me to show them how to cultivate their dried-up land. Well, we began to work their fields for them and presently, in return, got some of the tribe – mostly women, for they did all the hard labour, poor things – to build a little church of sun-dried mud bricks. This is it.' A poor little shanty with a palmetto roof and sacking over the window and door appeared on the screen. 'Here I began my first services, trying to plant the seeds of the gospel in the minds of those poor savages. Then I went often to the cattle posts to try to explain Christian principles to the men, and especially to teach the children. It wasn't easy, we had to face primitive ignorance and ingrained superstition. And there was always the danger of a sudden mass uprising incited by those who feared the word of God because it might undermine their prestige and destroy the pagan fetishism that's the basis of many tribal customs. For instance, I had some little trouble with this fellow.' Another slide came on the screen.

'Oh, what a horrible old man,' exclaimed Leonora. 'He's worse than the chief.'

'That's the witch doctor and rain maker. When the droughts came, and they were frequent, his job was to dispel them with magic. And when his mumbo-jumbo didn't work he blamed it on the bad medicine of the new religion. During my second year we had a dry spell so prolonged and serious that things looked very bad for us. I don't think I ever prayed so hard for rain – I almost cracked the heavens.'

'And the rains came,' Leonora murmured in a dreamy voice. She already felt herself a little in love with Willie.

'No, not a drop,' Willie said calmly, and paused. 'But I had a sudden idea, an inspiration if you like – that my spring, which disappeared high on the hill, might be running down the slope *underground*. I'd never done a stroke of water divining in my life but I cut myself a mangana twig, which was the nearest I could find to hazel, asked the good Lord to help me if He didn't want to see His servant without a head, and started walking down the hill towards the village. By the time I got there the whole tribe were round me, watching, including our friend there on the screen. Suddenly, just outside the chief's hut, the twig gave a twitch. I thought it might only be my shaky nerves, but I took a chance and told them to dig. Twenty feet down we came on a rushing subterranean stream that went right through the centre of the village. I couldn't describe to you the wild scene that followed, for I was on my knees reciting the fourteenth Psalm, but since that moment we have never lacked water and it was then that I made my first converts.'

There was a ripple of interest and appreciation, a spontaneous reaction that fell warmly on Moray's ears. Now a full partner in this splendid enterprise, he exchanged a quick communicative glance with Kathy.

Meanwhile Willie had resumed, describing the further progress of the Mission, the slow and painful emergence from darkness to light of a savage, isolated tribe. There had been setbacks of course, and some bad disasters. His original church had been burned down and when, having gained a mastery of the language, he tried to change the tribal initiation rites, in which youths and young girls were subjected to indescribable indignities, he'd had a difficult time. But for the intervention of Tshosa the entire Mission would have been wiped out. As it was, three of his converts were killed and several attempts made on his life. The following year a Swedish missionary, his nearest neighbour, ninety miles away, and his wife and two little daughters were murdered – all beheaded. It was so difficult to change the hearts of men inured to brutality and bloodshed that he had determined to concentrate on the children; by early teaching he could obtain positive results, and for this reason he had built the school and, later, the orphanage. He showed several slides of these little ones grouped around Daniel the catechist, now an old man, touching photographs which caused Leonora to exclaim: 'Oh dear, aren't the whites of their eyes so divinely pathetic.'

'Their eyes are pathetic because so many of them have trachoma. And as you see, some of the faces are pitted with smallpox scars.'

'Then it's not a healthy district?' someone asked.

'Unfortunately not. Malaria is still endemic, sleeping sickness too, and we get a lot of hookworm and filariasis, even an odd case of leprosy.'

So the main necessity was now a hospital, and – with a half

smile towards Moray – he hoped to have this soon. Proper medical treatment would prove of immense benefit. Still, after nearly twenty years of continuous labour he was not ashamed of the results: the fine stone church, the school and orphanage, the proper mission house – he displayed them on the screen – all were rather different from that first mud shed. And he now had over three hundred practising church members, besides four catechists and several out-stations in the bush which he visited in rotation every month in his jeep. Needless to say, they still had their troubles. He was worried over the situation that might develop in the neighbouring province of Kasai. If the civil authority failed there, now that the Belgians were going out, there might be some disorders. And they were very near, in fact two of his new out-stations were actually across the border. Nothing had happened so far, at least nothing to speak of, but because of the possibility of trouble he must get back to the Mission quickly, to be on hand if needed.

'And now,' Willie said, with an apologetic smile, looking at the clock, 'that's about all. I only hope I haven't bored you and that you'll forgive me for having taken so much of your time.'

When he concluded there was a cordial round of applause, a tribute only faintly tempered by the slight note of misgiving on which the talk had ended. Encouraged by the general approbation which, through his inclusion in the scheme of medical reform, must apply in some measure to himself, Moray seized the appropriate moment and stood up. He was normally a confident speaker but now he was restrained, almost humble. Still, the words came to him.

'I think I speak for all of us, in offering warmest thanks to our good friend for his stimulating and moving discourse. His has been a supremely brave and unselfish accomplishment – an epic humanitarian achievement. Incidentally,' he added, striving for humorous parenthesis, 'if you should wish to express your appreciation in more tangible form, a salver has been placed for that purpose in the hall. And now,' he followed on quickly, 'if I may impose upon you for a moment, I should like to add a personal postscript to what has already been said.' He paused, almost overcome by a rush of feeling. 'The truth is . . . I've come to a decision that may surprise you . . . but which I hope you will hear with understanding.'

A stir passed over the audience, a decided stir.

'You might imagine it to be a sudden decision. It is not. Although I've been happy here I've been conscious of a prompting, an urge, one might say, towards a more active, a more useful existence, in which my medical knowledge might be utilised, not for reward but for good. And in how remarkable a manner that intention has been given effect. Early last month it so happened that I felt myself recalled to my native country. Here I made contact with a family I had known and loved in my youth, a family, in short, of which Kathy and Willie are members. Kathy I had not known, the joy of finding her was therefore all the greater. Willie I already knew. He and I, in those early days, had been friends, he as a little lad, I as a thoughtless though striving youth, and often, during our long conversations, he had thrilled me with his boyish enthusiasm for the missionary life. And now the wheel has turned full circle.' He paused, so affected he could scarcely go on. 'My friends, I don't want to weary you with the story of a soul's regeneration. I will say simply that I am going out with Willie to the Mission, as a doctor, and Kathy, my dear Kathy,' he moved over to where she stood beside the projector and placed his arm about her shoulders, 'will be there with us, as my wife.'

Now, indeed, there was a marked reaction which took the form of an immediate silence, followed by a sudden outburst. In a hurry, everyone got up and began to speak at once. Congratulations were showered on Moray, his hand was shaken, the ladies pressed round Kathy.

'More champagne,' Stench shouted. 'A toast to the bride and groom.'

Champagne was available, the toast was drunk, it seemed as though the party would begin all over again. Most encouraging of all was Madame von Altishofer's composed acceptance of the accomplished fact. He had feared trouble, some marring exhibition of pique or displeasure, but no, her behaviour had been perfect, a smile of congratulation, gently tinged with sadness perhaps, yet a definite smile for him, and for Kathy a kiss upon the cheek.

Indeed, when half an hour later the others had begun to leave and, standing in the hall, he was speeding them on their way, she stopped briefly for a final word.

'Dear friend, I rejoice in your happiness. Such a sweet child. All that – and heaven too, with this splendid new work.'

'You are most kind, Frida.'

'Ah, I had a premonition that we should lose you, even when I was at Baden and you did not write.'

'I always knew you were intuitive,' he said guardedly.

'Unfortunately, yes. But all that is past. Now is the time to be practical, to show the value of a true friend who also is, as you say, matter-of-fact. Your *déménagement* in so short a time will be most difficult. You will need help, and if you wish I can give it. Your little one tells me she leaves with her splendid Willie tomorrow. I would wish to come then, but as you may be at the airport . . . yes ? . . . very well, shall I come the day after?'

'You're most thoughtful,' he said, realising after a moment's reflection that nothing could be more acceptable. She was so capable, and already he had begun to worry about the complexity of the arrangements that must be made. 'I shall expect you. And thank you.'

She smiled, and passed through the door.

Immediately he hurried back to rejoin Kathy and Willie in the salon. He took the salver from the hall table with him.

'Well, was it a success?' he asked gaily.

'It went ever so well,' Kathy said, looking flushed and happy.

'Did you think so too, Willie?'

He nodded. He was sitting down, looking tired.

'They were all very kind.'

'Let's just see how kind,' Moray said slyly. He was in tremendous spirits. With the air of a conspirator he handed the salver to Kathy and, while she held it, began to count the money. There was a respectable heap of fifty- and hundred-franc bills and one coin – a two-franc piece.

'I bet that's from little Gallie,' Moray laughed.

'Then it means a lot,' Willie said, unexpectedly.

'Oh, yes,' Kathy agreed warmly. 'I liked her much the best.'

There was a pause, then Kathy said again:

'Haven't you forgotten that bit of paper at the bottom?'

'Have I? Good lord, don't tell me someone's chipped in with a bad cheque. Take a look, Kathy.'

She gazed at the cheque, quite speechless, then she handed it to Willie. Still silent, she looked at Moray, then suddenly put her arms around his neck and kissed him.

CHAPTER XV

NEXT DAY, AT two in the afternoon, Moray arrived back from Zurich, still rather cast down by the departure of Kathy and Willie for Edinburgh on the noon plane, yet charged with vigorous purpose. Only eleven days remained before he would join them at London Airport, and much must be accomplished in that brief span; the need for immediate action was imperative. As he let himself into the house – following the departure of his guests he had given Arturo and Elena the afternoon off – he felt glad of Madame von Altishofer's promise of assistance and hoped she would not fail to turn up next morning.

However, he had only begun to go through his mail in the study when, to his surprise, he heard the beat of her litle Dauphine in the drive. Leaving unopened the *Journal of Tropical Medicine*, to which he had just subscribed, and a parcel of lightweight nylon camping equipment that promised to be interesting, he went to meet her.

'Am I too prompt?' She spoke briskly, looking extremely workmanlike in a grey linen skirt and knitted grey cardigan. 'I happened to see you pass in the Humber and thought not to waste the afternoon.'

'You're quite right,' he agreed heartily, leading the way into the library. 'There's so much to do, the sooner we start the better.'

'Tell me then, what, roughly, are your plans?' She sat, not in the chair, but on the arm, indicating instant obedient readiness.

'The villa, of course, will be put on the market. Arturo and Elena will move into the chalet and act as *gardiens* of the property until it is sold.'

'And your things?'

'My pictures and silver must go provisionally to the bank. Their ultimate disposition will be in my lawyer's hands – Stieger is a most reliable man. My furniture and books can remain here temporarily – quite safe if the house is shuttered.'

'These lovely books,' she exclaimed, looking at the long double rows of fine Sangorski bindings. 'You cannot leave them so, in a shut-up house, or they will become altogether foxed. Every one must be separately wrapped, and that is something I can do for you.'

'Arturo . . . ' he began.

'No.' She got up smilingly. 'He will have enough on his hands. And he is so overthrown by your going, he is not fit for anything extra. Besides, I love books; my father had a famous library at Kellenstein. So off to your own work and leave this to me.' As he moved towards the door, she added, tactfully, but with a glance both ironic and approving: 'By the way, I suppose you have read Mr Stench's article in the *Tageblatt*.'

'I haven't seen today's papers. What article?'

'It is a piece about your party for the Mission, but there is much in it about you, and of your courage in going out there, in spite of this tribal affair. It is most flattering.'

He reddened, chiefly from pleasure, thinking of his friends in Melsburg and so many others in the canton who would read of him.

'Archie is rather a nuisance,' he said. 'Though basically good at heart. I hope he didn't overdo it. And what's this tribal affair?'

'Apparently an outbreak of some sort, probably no more than the general unrest your friend referred to in his lecture. Now tell me, where may I find lots of wrapping paper?'

'In the pantry. Elena has stacks of it in a cupboard.'

When she went off he stirred himself and set about his first important task, to make the inventory of his antiques. This was something after his own heart and as he toured the house with paper and pen, noting down this piece and that – the Charles II red lacquer cabinet bought at the Antique Fair in London, the exquisitely mellowed Queen Anne bureau listed in Macquoid's classic *The Age of Walnut*, the Louis XVI fauteuils he had bid for successfully at the Parke-Bernet Galleries – waves of recollection, of bitter-sweet nostalgia, flowed over him. It was hard to part with these costly trifles, yet never had he felt so spiritually elevated, so convinced of the merit of his renunciation. Archie Stench was right. He *was* doing a worth-while thing.

The tabulation was not quite complete when, at five o'clock, Madame von Altishofer found him brooding over his Elizabethan buffet in the dining-room.

'Time for tea,' she announced.

He looked up.

'Have you finished?'

'Not nearly. The books alone will take at least another half day. But workers of the world require refreshment. And I have presumed to make a few *amaretti*.'

The break was in fact most welcome.

'What good biscuits,' he remarked. 'I never associated you with the domestic virtues.'

'One learns from necessity – and disappointments, of which I've had many. Please take another.'

'I shouldn't.' He smiled deprecatingly. 'The impression I've received lately is that I'm rather over-addicted to the pleasures of the table.'

'What nonsense,' she said spiritedly. 'Now especially, to build your strength, you should be eating well. Goodness alone knows what wretched fare you will get out there.'

'I'll be all the better for it. I supped plenty of porridge in my youth.'

'In your youth, yes, dear friend.' She smiled tolerantly. 'But now?'

A brief silence followed this remark, during which she gazed round the, as yet, undenuded room, her eyes coming to rest on the lovely pastel of Madame Melo and her child.

'Do you remember the afternoon you showed me the Vuillard? It seems only yesterday, yet so much has happened in that short time. Promise me to keep your paintings on the walls until the last possible moment. You often told me you could not live without them, and certainly that you would never sell them.' A thought seemed to strike her. She hesitated, glanced away, then towards him, finally exclaimed impulsively: 'Must you really sell your home? Couldn't you keep it, well, as a kind of rest house which you could fall back on in case of need? Dear friend, I worry about you, and the last thing I wish is that you should get one of those tropical diseases that have broken up poor Willie. And what a catalogue he recited, malaria, sleeping sickness, leprosy and the rest; the poor man looks ill enough to have half of them himself. . . . But as I was saying, if you should contract something serious, at least you would have a safe place in a proper climate to recover and recuperate.'

He looked at her, at first frowning, as in doubt, then thoughtfully. The idea had never occurred to him and, at first sight, it appeared to have considerable merit. Why should he sell out in a blind rush; he had not the slightest financial need. Besides, if he took time, with mounting property values he would undoubtedly secure a far better price. But no, no, that would be merely temporising, playing around with half-measures, a dangerous procedure at all times. He was going for good, and would not return. He shook his head decisively.

'No. I prefer to make a clean, sharp cut.'

'Yes, I suppose you are right. Always you see things so clearly, never thinking of yourself. I did wrong to make such a weak proposal, but it is because I think only of you. God knows I shall never for one moment have peace once you are out there.'

'But why, Frida? It's not so dreadful at the Mission.'

'Oh, my friend, because you are brave and strong, don't pretend in order to make this easier for me. You understand, better than I, the dangers that will surround you. Last night, for thinking of that poor Swedish family whose heads were hacked off, I could not sleep. If such a cruel death occurs for a man after many years of service, what might not occur to you, a newcomer.'

He glanced at her irritably, with a touch of asperity.

'For goodness' sake, Frida, don't exaggerate.'

'Exaggerate, because I tell you of the thoughts of one small bad night. If that were all I feared for you, I should be happy. But besides the fevers, are there not beasts of the jungle, scorching sun and torrential rains, and, worst of all, this trouble in the Congo. Mr Stench says it is beginning and must spread. And you are so near. But why am I so foolish to talk of what you already fully understand?' She stood up abruptly. 'Work – work, that's what we must do, in order not to think for a moment of the future. There are some books on the high shelves of the library that I cannot reach. When I have put away the tea trolley you must hand them down to me. After that, it is time for me to rush back to Seeburg.'

He moved slowly into the library, frowning, vaguely displeased, not with her, for no one could have his interests more at heart, but rather with the manner of her presentation of the obvious. As if he did not realise what he was getting into. Absurd. The books to which she referred were mainly special full folio editions of the Paragon art series, but although his eye was cast towards them they left no conscious imprint on his retina. Finally, however, with a slight start, he came to himself, decided against fetching the step-ladder from the basement and instead brought forward the long needlepoint stool that had its place before the fireplace. Mounting, he reached up and, one at a time, began to transfer the heavy, richly clasped and padded volumes to a lower and more accessible shelf. He had almost finished when she appeared and stood watching him.

Only three books now remained at the end of the top shelf. Hurrying, he stretched up and sideways, took hold of all three. But in the effort of lifting he lost his balance and, still clutching the books above his head, was obliged to make a quick backward step off the stool that brought him safely though jarringly to the floor.

'Well done,' she complimented him. 'You saved yourself most cleverly.'

'Yes . . . ' he spoke through compressed lips, 'but I rather think I've wrenched my back.'

'You did come down sharply. You must sit down and rest.'

He seated himself cautiously on the end of the stool and, with his hand pressed against the affected part, watched while she wrapped up the Paragon edition.

'Now, you are better?' she inquired, when she had finished.

'Not altogether. But it's nothing, it'll pass.'

'If not, you must see to it. For tonight take aspirin and get Arturo to rub you. Have you some antidolor liniment?'

'I think there's some in the medicine cabinet.'

She continued to study him sympathetically, head on one side.

'I wish I did not have to leave you, but there. . . . Now do not forget, antidolor and aspirin, after your bath. No, don't get up. I will let myself out. And for tomorrow, shall we say ten o'clock?'

He nodded agreement, with as little movement as possible, and, when she had gone, remained seated for several further minutes, prodding his back with a speculative finger. Then, as everything seemed intact, he got up and began, though awkwardly, to move about. The inventory was complete, he must now arrange a meeting with his lawyer. He went to the telephone, dialled Stieger's number. It was the girl, his secretary, who answered, with that sing-song cadence which the local Swiss imparted to their school-taught English.

'I am sorree, Mr Moree, Herr Stieger is in Munich.'

'When will he be back?'

'Saturday morneeng. But if eet is important I will telephone heem.'

He reflected quickly.

'Saturday will be all right. Make an appointment for eleven a.m.'

'Very well, Mr Moree. I will myself inform Herr Stieger.'

He swung away from the phone, an injudicious movement that made him wince. Annoying that Stieger was away; he wanted everything done quickly; yes, at once. His earlier mood of vigorous confidence, a state verging on exaltation, had lapsed, he felt a longing for Kathy: the touch of her lips, her sweet glance of encouragement. For one who had always enjoyed his own society it was strange how he now disliked being alone. If only Madame von Altishofer had not been obliged to dash away – what a help she was, in his present emergency. The idea of a solitary dinner did not appeal to him, moreover he felt he owed it to himself to turn in early. He rang for Arturo, told him to prepare a tray and take it up to the study, explained the necessity of massage later on, then, passing between the piles of wrapped books, he tuned in the radio to the evening broadcast of the B.B.C. Lately he had been so preoccupied with his own affairs he had not listened to the news. But he was too late, immediately a voice said:

'That is the end of the news.'

With an exclamation he switched off and went upstairs, reminding himself to take his vitamin tablets.

CHAPTER XVI

PUNCTUALLY AT TEN o'clock next morning the door bell rang and Arturo, with an expression more enigmatic than usual, showed Madame von Altishofer to the drawing-room where Moray, seated on the sofa before the open Dutch cabinet, was pensively contemplating his collection of Chinese porcelain.

When he had greeted her and asked to be excused from rising he waved an expressive hand.

'The futile tyranny of possessions. All this will have to be packed. When I bought it with such joy, and every piece is authentic K'hang Hsi, little did I think it would be such a nuisance in the end.'

'I will pack it.' She spoke quietly. 'So it will be no nuisance. But first, how is your back?'

'No worse, I hope, though I slept badly. But I seem to have developed a queer sort of limp.'

'A limp?'

'In my right leg, when I walk.'

'Then you must see to it at once.'

'No.' He shook away the suggestion. 'It can't be serious. At least I'll give it another day.'

Turning from the cabinet he found her gaze bent upon him in a fashion so oddly concerned it gave him quite a start.

'Is anything wrong, Frida?'

'No, no,' she said quickly, forcing a smile. 'I was thinking only of your injury. I hope you will be able to go to the party this afternoon.'

'What party?'

'Why, naturally, Leonora's.'

'I know nothing of it.'

'But surely you are invited. We are all going, all our circle. It must be a mistake that you are overlooked. So you will come with me, yes?'

He bit his lip, vexed that he should have been left out, at this

244

last hour, already regarded by the others as a dead letter.

'I'm much too busy to go. Anyhow, the lecture party was my swan song. I'm no longer interested in Leonora's frivolous nonsense.'

'I am sorry, my friend. I know that all is finished for you here and that you must seek society where you are going, if indeed it is possible to find it among these – these uncivilised people.'

'I shall have Willie and my dear wife,' he said sharply. 'And my work will be to civilise the people.'

'But of course, you will be very happy,' she agreed in a conciliatory tone. 'Still, three together is a limited group after the interesting society to which you have been accustomed. But now, no more, you have enough to worry you. I must go to finish the books. Another time, perhaps tomorrow, I will see to the porcelain.'

What's the matter with her, he asked himself, when she had departed for the library. Yesterday she had been bright and brisk, today a subdued melancholy clouded her yellow eyes. He found the change in her mood and manner quite inexplicable.

As the forenoon wore on, he took time off from his desk, where he was busy with the settlement of all outstanding accounts, to look in at the library – ostensibly to inspect her progress but actua'ly to determine if her mood had changed. It had not, was indeed keyed to a lower pitch.

'Something is on your mind, Frida,' he said, on his second visit.

On one knee beside the bottom shelf, she straightened, but without looking at him.

'There is nothing, nothing.'

The evasion in her tone was only too apparent. At lunch – she had consented solely as an economy of time to remain for a light meal – he made an effort to dispel the gloom.

'You're eating nothing. May I give you some of this salad?'

'Thank you, no.'

'Another slice of galantine.'

'Nothing more, please. I have little appetite today.'

'Then if you've finished, let's take a rest on the terrace. The sun is quite strong now.'

Outside it was distinctly warm, and Wilhelm had swept away the snow and put out garden chairs. They sat down facing the marvellous skyline of the Alps.

'You have the finest view in Switzerland,' she murmured. 'At least for a few more days.'

A silence followed, then thinking to please, perhaps to placate her, he said: 'I hope you understand, Frida, that I will always have the highest regard for you.'

'Will you?'

'Always. Moreover, Frida, I don't take your help for granted. I'd like you to choose something for yourself from my collection as a souvenir.'

'You are generous, my friend, but I do not care for souvenirs. Always they invoke sadness.'

'But you must. I insist.'

'Then if I am to be sad, I shall be deeply so. You shall give me the small photograph standing on the right side of your desk.'

'You mean the little snapshot of you and me on the Riesenberg.'

'Exactly. That I will keep for remembrance.'

'My dear Frida.' He smiled chidingly. 'You sound like an obituary notice.'

She gave him a long sombre look.

'That is not surprising.' Then, her reserve breaking down: 'Mein Gott, how I am sad for you. I meant not to show you this, but soon enough you must know.'

She opened her handbag, took out a newspaper clipping, handed it to him. He saw that it had been cut from that morning's *Daily Echo*, a paper she did not usually take, and was headed:
Five Hundred Die in Congo Massacre.

Quickly, he read the dispatch:

Last night in Kasai Province, where for the past few weeks there have been signs of trouble brewing beneath the surface, tribal war at last broke loose. A savage and unprovoked attack was made on the village of Tochilenge by dissident Balubas. The village, which changed hands in fierce fighting twice, was set on fire and is now a shell. An estimated five hundred lie dead beneath the scorched palm and banana trees.

'Now,' she said, 'you know where you are going.'

He looked up, meeting her gaze which had remained fixed upon him. He was not in the least discomposed, confirmed rather, hardened and fortified.

'Frida,' he said coldly, 'I'm perfectly aware that for the past two days you have been trying to dissuade me from going – no doubt with the best intentions. But I don't think you quite understand how deeply I'm in love. I fully realise that conditions are bad out there. But I *am* going. I would follow Kathy to the ends of the earth.'

She compressed her lips.

'Yes, my friend,' she sighed. 'Is it not always like that when an elderly man is possessed by a young girl? And always the end is so tragic. How well I remember that great German film, *The Blue Angel*.'

He coloured with indignation.

'The circumstances are in no way comparable.'

'No,' she agreed, in an extinguished voice. 'The old professor went only to the circus. You are going . . .'. She turned her head, shielding her face with one hand to hide emotion. 'Yes, I feel it in my heart . . . you are going to . . .'. Even then she could not say it, merely adding in a low voice: 'To something much worse.'

An angry retort had risen to his lips but, respecting her distress, he stifled it. She had always been one to conceal her feelings, tears were not her medium of expression, yet she was clearly upset. Upright in his chair, he stared straight ahead at the distant snow-capped peaks. A prolonged silence descended upon them. Finally, in a subdued manner, but still with averted head, she rose.

'My friend, I can do no more for you today. Tomorrow I will come.'

'I'm sorry,' he muttered, put out by this unexpected departure. 'Must you really go?'

'Yes, until tomorrow. If I am to visit with Madame Schutz and our friends, first I must compose myself.'

He did not protest further, saw her to her car, waited till the beat of the Dauphine died away. Then he closed the gate and limped back to the house. Deliberately, word for word, he read the newspaper clipping again, then decisively tore it up.

During that afternoon he continued his preparations, but always with an eye on the clock. At five he was to telephone Kathy at Markinch, where she was staying at the manse: the arrangement had been made before she left. After the trials and problems of the last two days, how he looked forward to it!

After a quick cup of tea, he went to the telephone, dialled long distance and gave the Fotheringays' number. There was little traffic on the lines and within ten minutes he was put through. To his delight it was Kathy herself who answered: but of course she would be seated at the phone, waiting for his call.

'Kathy, it's you! How are you, my dear?'

'Quite well, David. And most terribly busy. It's so lucky you caught me. I was just rushing off to Edinburgh this very minute.'

Chilled slightly, he said: 'What have you been doing?'

'Oh, everything. . . . Getting ready to go .. . . Like you, I suppose.'

'Yes, I've been busy too. It's very near now.'

'Oh, it is. And I'm so happy and excited. I'll be sending you all particulars of where we are to meet in London whenever I find a minute to write.'

'I was rather expecting a letter from you, dear.'

'Were you, David? I thought, as we were to be together so soon. . . . And I've worried about Uncle Willie. He's been running quite a high temperature since we came here, and he's due to give his talk this evening.'

'I'm sorry,' he said rather perfunctorily, thinking of his own troubles. 'Give him my best wishes.'

'Oh, I will, David. And I'll write you tonight, whenever we get back from Edinburgh.'

'I don't wish to force you to write, Kathy.'

'But, David dear . . . '. She broke off. 'Are you cross?'

'No, dear. Still, I will say I've felt rather lonely. I've been hard at it here. I've hurt my back. And through it all I've been longing to hear from you, just a word to say that you're missing me.'

'Oh, I have missed you, dear . . . '. The catch in her voice made her words indistinct, ' . . . just so busy, and Uncle Willie ill . . . I didn't think . . . '.

'All right, my dear,' he said, mollified by her distress. 'But if Willie is so ill, will he be able to leave on the twenty-first?'

'He will go, David,' she said confidently. 'Even if he has to be carried on the plane on a stretcher.'

Much good he'll be in that condition, he thought rather acidly, then regretted it, for he was devoted to Willie.

'I suppose you've seen that fighting has started in Kasai.'

'Yes, and it may be serious. But of course we've been expecting it. Now, dear, I really must go. I think I hear the bus. Uncle Willie is outside calling for me to come.'

'Wait, Kathy . . .'.

'If I don't go, dear, we'll miss the bus and Uncle Willie will be late for his lecture. Goodbye for just now, dear David. We'll be together soon.'

She had gone, or at least had been obliged to go, leaving him disappointed and with a chilling impression of neglect. What an unsatisfactory talk it had been, making so much of Willie, so little of himself. No, no, he mustn't think like that – quickly he banished his unworthy jealousy. Kathy loved him, the poor child had simply been rushed and harassed, and telephone conversations were never satisfactory. He found these excuses for her, but illogically the sense of slight persisted, remained with him all evening.

At bedtime, still upset, he decided to take a sleeping pill, a thing he had not done for weeks. Fifteen centigrammes of soneryl, followed by a glass of hot milk, sent him into a deep sleep which should have lasted for at least six hours. Unfortunately this was marred, broken in fact, by a frightful yet ridiculous dream.

He was lying on a camp bed in an unknown place behind high black rocks. The air, filled with the hum of insects, was insufferably hot – the humid heat of a tropical night. Darkness was everywhere, yet he could see faintly, and gradually became aware of the tall shadowy form of a man standing some paces away, gazing ahead. The man wore a khaki shirt and trousers and short gum-boots. Although the face remained invisible, he knew the man to be Willie. He tried to call to him, but although his lips formed the words no sounds emerged. Suddenly, to his horror, he saw three enormous beasts advancing from beyond. They were lions, at least they had the size and shape of lions, but to their appearance something preternatural had been added which gave to them a ferocity that paralysed him. Behind these beasts a line of Abatu tribesmen, armed with spears, stood outlined against the further darkness. He attempted vainly to rise. He wanted to get away – anything to escape this double danger. The futile effort made the sweat pour from him. Then, as he gave himself up for lost, the man who was Willie began to laugh and, picking up some pebbles, flipped them casually at the lions, like a boy taking random shots at an alley cat. Immediately the beasts stopped, hesitated for a moment, then came on again with a terrifying rush.

'The Lord is our shepherd,' Willie said. 'A silver collection will be taken later.'

Immediately the charge ceased. The lions faced about and sat up on their haunches in a begging attitude, whereupon the black soldiers began to mark time and clap their hands. Then, with disharmony resembling that of the Markinch choir, they boomed out the hymn 'Onward, Christian Soldiers.'

The grotesque and ridiculous vision was too sudden a release. Moray tried to laugh, to howl with laughter, and finally let out a shout that woke him up.

Exhausted, yet relieved by the reality of his own bedroom, he lay for a long time gloomily pondering the reasons for this absurd and painful fantasy. What rankled most of all was his own behaviour. Was he as weak as that? God, no – he would not admit it. He set his teeth and shook the thing off. Obviously, he decided, a subconscious conflict between his admiration for Willie's heroic and self-sacrificing life and his own past indifference towards religion. With that he got up. The luminous dial of his Gubelin bedside-clock showed three o'clock. Feeling around, he stripped off his wet pyjama jacket and, having rubbed himself down, put on a fresh one and returned to bed. After turning uneasily for more than an hour he got off to sleep.

CHAPTER XVII

NEXT MORNING WHEN he awoke, only half rested, he was bitterly annoyed with himself. He rose hurriedly, prompted by a sense of shame, welcoming as a corrective the discomfort of his strained back which now seemed definitely worse. Ranging about the house, restlessly awaiting Madame von Altishofer's arrival, he checked and rechecked his preparations: the inventory was complete, all his papers were in order, the bank had been notified, his appointment with Stieger definitely arranged for the following day. All that remained, then, was to finish off his packing. Impatiently, his ears alert for the sound of the Dauphine, he looked at his watch: past ten o'clock. Why on earth did she not come? Punctuality had always been outstanding amongst her many virtues. He was on the point of telephoning when, with a disproportionate sense of relief, he heard her step on the gravel drive. The door bell rang. He answered it himself.

'You didn't drive. I wondered why you were late. Come along in. I'll take your coat.'

'Thank you, no. I will not come in. Or at least only to the hall.'

He stared at her, blankly, as she took a bare step forward across the threshold. She was not wearing her usual grey working outfit, but the faded russet costume and the *bersagliere* hat in which she went walking. Yet it was her expression, calm yet firm, that astonished him most of all, and caused him, fearing some disaster, to exclaim: 'What's wrong, Frida?'

She did not immediately answer; then, gazing at him almost pityingly with those remarkable yellow eyes, she said: 'My friend, despite my great wish to help you, I have decided I must not see you now, or ever again.'

'What!' In his confusion he brought out the word with difficulty. 'But why? You promised. I'm relying on you to do the porcelain.'

'The porcelain,' she echoed with scornful emphasis. 'What does

251

that matter? You have no use for it now. You will never see it again.'

'But I – I need your help for other things.'

'Then I must not give it.' Still with her gaze fixed upon him, she shook her head slowly from side to side. 'It is altogether too painful for me. Better, in your own words, the sharp, clean cut.'

A moment of complete silence followed, during which he could find nothing to say except 'why', and he had said that before. Then she went on, with that same solemnity, almost sounding a note of doom.

'My friend, my dear friend, my feeling for you, and it is deep beyond your knowledge, has misled me. I am a woman, and weakly I have given in, to help you. But yesterday, at the party, meeting all your friends, I see that I have been wrong, greatly wrong. For all are in dismay, all have the same opinion of you.'

'I'm obliged for their concern,' he muttered, nettled that they should have discussed him in his absence. 'But I don't see how I merit it.'

'*They* see it!' Her voice stung him. 'They were, every one, speaking of you, a man who has worked all his life to make a great success, and become rich, who has good friends, and a beautiful home. And who, no longer young, throws all, all away, for a sudden idea, so extreme that even your Mr Stench was saying, in his nasty smiling way, you had bitten more than you could chew.'

'I'm obliged to Stench, and the others,' he said bitterly. 'Nevertheless, I believe I know what I'm doing.'

'But *do* you? Now you are so busy, so obsessed, you never read or even listen to the news. Yesterday Mr Stench was telling us – it had just come in – that in another town, Kalinda, which is so near your Willie's place, hordes of these tribesmen came with flaming arrows and cutlasses, broke into the Belgian mission and massacred all who were inside. Not killed alone, first mutilated them, cutting off their hands. Mein Gott, when I think of *your* hands, so fine and sensitive, which I have always admired, and some beastly savage hacking them off, do you wonder that I, and others too, are heartbroken for you?'

He bit his lip, frowning, uneasiness and anger striving for mastery in him. Anger predominated.

"You seem to forget that Willie warned me there might be danger. I've fully considered the risks to run."

"I don't believe it."

"Do you accuse me of lying?"

"I accuse you of deliberate self-deception."

"If so, it's from the highest motives."

"So you want to be a holy martyr, perhaps be shot with arrows, for a change, like Sebastian, and win a harp and a halo after." Her eyes narrowed scornfully. "I am speaking in your true interest when I tell you . . ."

'It's no use,' he interrupted her sharply. 'You won't dissuade me.'

They faced each other during a long and, on her part, a calculated silence.

'So you are going,' she said at last, in a hard voice.

'Yes.'

'Then go. You are totally blind and devoid of sense, in fact quite out of your mind.'

'Thank you.'

They were quarrelling, creating a scene – the realisation caused him an acute distress.

'You say you do this because of a great ideal, to amend your life. You do not. It is all done for the sake of going to bed with a silly young woman, a religious killjoy, who has infatuated you, who has no maturity, no meeting of minds, a common nurse who does not know a Bonnard from a bedpan.'

Pale to the lips under these insults, delivered with a fatal, telling force, he ran true to form in his indignant reply: 'You are speaking of the young lady who will be my wife.'

'And as such, what do you delude yourself she can give you? Not passion, for it is not in her. These religious women are without sex.' He winced. 'For passion such as you demand, you need a strong, vital body. An answering force which she does not possess. She is feeble. And she is already bound to her Willie, you are for her only a father figure. Besides, you have too strong a competitor. She cannot love both you and the Lord.'

'I'm afraid I must ask you to leave.'

She was breathing with a deep, though controlled violence, a Wagnerian prima donna, splendid in figure, with fire in her eyes. Then all at once she was calm, cold as ice.

'Yes, I am leaving. But do not forget that I have warned you. And remember one important thing: if you should return to reason, I am still at the Seeburg, still your friend.'

He barely waited until she had passed the drive before shutting the door with a bang. He was furiously angry, hurt, outraged, and above all inflexibly confirmed in his intention. How dared she take such scandalous liberties with Kathy and himself! This, and the maddening fact that his friends had made him the object of their malicious gossip at the party, was in itself enough to fuse and forge his resolution into solid steel. What stung most of all, quickened by a flashback thought to that night of docile surrender, was the shameful allegation against the pudendum of his future bride. A father figure indeed, competing for affection against Willie and the Lord – could any allegation be more unjust, more unutterably shameful – blasphemous, in fact? Yet that poisoned barb, worst of all, had pierced deep and still quivered in his flesh. To make matters worse, in slamming the heavy door he had aggravated his strained back and now, blaming her all the more since the casualty was basically her fault, he found that his limp had become more pronounced.

Altogether he was so worked up, he could not bring himself to remain passive in the house. What then? It was essential that he get his back put right at once and, as he had additionally some final purchases to make, he decided to take the train for Zurich and consult his good friend Dr Muller. Having cancelled lunch, he was driven by the mystified Arturo to Schwansee station in time to take the 11.45 *schnellzug*.

Settling himself in the comfortable window seat – no other trains, in his opinion, could match the Swiss – he opened the *Gazette Suisse* which, almost instinctively, he had picked up at the bookstall. Naturally, Madame von Altishofer had exaggerated in order to alarm him; nevertheless it was true, as she suggested, that he had lately been too preoccupied to heed external events. He rarely did heed them, preferring to banish from his exclusive life the shocks and discords of a disordered world. Now, however, he felt it would repay him to sift the news. He had no need to sift. There, on the front page, were the headlines.

MASSACRE ATROCE A LA MISSION KALINDA.

Still keyed to a high intensity, he read the graphic report. More than a hundred persons, men, women and children, who had sought refuge in the mission, had been butchered with inhuman ferocity. In this blood-bath the missionaries themselves, two Franciscan priests, had been singled out for special treatment, first mutilated, then beheaded, and their bodies hacked to bits.

It was a gruesome story, yet it had the ring of truth and following on the earlier slaughter at Tochilenge, was undoubtedly part of the general pattern of frenzied outrage that had broken loose.

Frida had spoken the truth: what an end for a sensitive, civilised man. A quiver of nausea constricted his stomach as he lowered the paper and gazed out at the placid Swiss landscape, the belled, brown cows grazing peacefully in the green pastures amongst the pear and cherry trees. Perhaps, after all, in making his heroic decision he had not fully weighed the obligations and dangers imposed by it. But he killed the thought before it entered his mind. Even if he had not wanted to go, he wanted Kathy. He would never turn back.

The train drew into Zurich station and he got out, finding the step down so awkward he wished he had brought a stick. His noticeable limp drew sympathetic glances as he traversed the Bahnhofstrasse, but making an effort he managed his shopping at Grieder's which, unlike so many of the other establishments, did not close between twelve and two. Then, with scarcely a thought of the Baur-au-Lac, he lunched sparingly at Sprungli's on minced veal and noodles followed by compote and a café crême. He was, indeed, too upset, too depressed to eat, and in this chastened mood he took a taxi to Dr Muller's office in Gloria-strasse, being fortunate to get hold of the good doctor before his consultations had begun. Muller, moreover – and this seemed even more important – was unaware of his visitor's imminent departure for the Dark Continent. At this moment either con-gratulations or reproaches would have been equally unbearable to Moray, who came immediately to the point, enumerated his symptoms, and concluded: 'I'm almost sure I've slipped a disc.'

Muller, a ruddy, jovial little man in an over-size starched white coat, who looked as though he enjoyed good living, had listened to the recital in the hunched attitude he assumed at his desk, darting occasional good-humoured glances at Moray. Now he got up, made an examination which to Moray seemed brief, almost cursory.

'A slight sprain of your latissimas dorsi. Get your man to rub you with a good liniment.'

'I have, and it's no better.'

'Naturally, it will take a few days.'

'But this limp I have developed, surely that is rather a matter for concern.'

'Purely psychosomatic. A protective transference of your worry about your back – though why that should worry you I can't imagine. I suppose there's nothing else on your mind, no more pressing anxiety?'

Frowning, Moray chose to ignore the question.

'Then you don't think I should have a spinal X-ray?'

'Mein Gott,' Muller laughed the idea away, 'here we do not X-ray for a simple strain.'

Moray left the doctor's office in worse case than when he entered, trying not to limp, an effort that exaggerated the condition and made him stiffen and drag his leg.

'Confound the fellow,' he muttered to himself. 'He has this psychosomatic nonsense on the brain.'

He was tempted to seek another opinion, but the fear of making himself ridiculous restrained him. Instead, in the hope that exercise might help, he walked down the hill to the Belvedere, then wandered along the front of the Zürichsee. A pale sun, glinting on the still water through a nacreous haze, had made the afternoon tranquil and luminous. Yet this strange light flooded him with confused misgiving – a doubt of the truth of his own reality, a desolate consciousness of his own insecurity in a hostile world. What was he doing here, limping aimlessly, his mind clouded by a host of conflicting thoughts that struck at him like a swarm of hornets? The direction his life was taking suddenly seemed preposterous. He felt a loss of support, an impression of falling into an abyss. Why had Frida made that violent and upsetting attack on him this morning? It was unpardonable and yet, seeking her motive, he found much to excuse and even to forgive. She was in love with him, jealous of Kathy, broken by the thought of his departure, fearful for his safety and health. Deeply, he regretted the rupture between them. He had always liked and admired her and had been to blame, perhaps, in encouraging her hopes of a closer relationship. Yet in the circumstances it was best that their friendship should be severed.

With an effort he pulled himself together, hailed a taxi and was driven to the station. The evening paper, which he read on the return journey, amply confirmed the bad news of the morning – an official statement had been issued from the United Nations deploring the outrage against innocent civilians. There was also a report that smallpox and bubonic plague had broken out; appeals for medical assistance had been broadcast. When he got home an hour later he found nothing to alleviate his despondency: no telephone message from Kathy, not even a letter, and the house now in such a state of upheaval – stacked books on the library floor, his silver in tissue paper, curtains dismantled in the salon – that all sense of comfort and security was gone. When he was enduring all this, abandoning everything for her sake, Kathy owed him at least a few words of encouragement and support. He must speak with her at once.

He went to the library telephone and put through a call to the Fotheringay manse in Markinch. The delay on this occasion was interminable, yet he would not leave the instrument. At last, following a muddle of Scottish accents at the local exchanges, a lamentable connection was established. It was Mrs Fotheringay who spoke; he could scarcely hear her voice over the persistent hum, and once intelligible contact was made, all proved fruitless. Willie and Kathy had left on the previous day, were now on their way through England, probably in Manchester, though at what address she did not know. She could, however, give him the number of the mission centre in Edinburgh, where they might be able to help him.

Cutting short the conversation, which she would have prolonged indefinitely, he rang the Edinburgh number, and was more successful in getting through. But here also he drew blank. Mr Douglas had delivered his lecture in Edinburgh and departed for London with his niece. They had no knowledge of his present address.

He ate a poor dinner and afterwards moved to the study, the only sitting-room which still remained habitable. Almost an hour later, while he sat brooding, suddenly the telephone rang.

His pulse missed a beat. He knew that it was Kathy, compelled by love and an instinctive awareness of his present need. He was at the phone in a second.

But, no – his heart sank sickeningly – it was not the sweet expected voice that came from the void, but the glottal accents of Stieger, his lawyer, who, detained in Munich, asked for a postponement of their appointment until Monday.

'Naturally, if the matter is urgent, I will fly back tomorrow morning and return to Munich in the evening.'

'No,' Moray said, struggling to recover himself. 'There's no immediate need. Don't put yourself out. Monday will suit equally well.'

'Then we will meet in three days' time.'

Three days, Moray reflected, as he hung up the phone; no harm could come of this brief postponement. At least it would afford him a breathing spell to recover and consolidate his forces. He was conscious of a vague feeling of relief.

CHAPTER XVIII

A WEEK HAD passed. Was it a week? Waiting like this, ready to go off, everything settled, it was difficult to keep track of the days. But of course, today was Sunday, and a wet one, drenching rain turning the snow into muddy slush, the mountains invisible behind swollen, dropsical clouds. God, what a horrible day, so damnably depressing to anyone, like himself, susceptible to weather. He turned from the window and for perhaps the twentieth time took Kathy's letter from his pocket, her solitary letter posted on the morning after she had been to Edinburgh. She must have written and mailed it immediately she got back to Markinch.

Dear David,
It was wonderful to hear your voice on the phone, and truly I have not had time to write you before. As I told you, Uncle Willie has had a real bad attack of fever. But he won't give up the lecture tour and we'll be leaving soon for our journey through England. When we get to London we'll be staying with Mr and Mrs Robertson, Scottish friends of Mrs Fotheringay's. Their address, if you are writing is, 3 Hillside Drive, Ealing, N.W.11. It is handy for London Airport. Everything is now arranged. Uncle Willie has got all three tickets and made the reservations. The flight number is AF 4329. The plane leaves on Tuesday the 21st at eleven p.m., so we shall meet you in the assembly hall one hour before the time of departure. We will be there from nine o'clock onwards so that there will be no mistake, and there must not be, for Uncle Willie is desperately anxious to leave. Things have been going from bad to worse at Kwibu and if we are to save the mission out-stations in Kasai we must get back at once. I am so much looking forward to working with you out there, and to the rewards it will bring us. Dear David, this is the first time I have written you and it is difficult to say all that I mean. But you

259

know my hopes are centred on you and that I will soon be your own true wife.

Kathy.

PS. Uncle Willie says be sure and be in time.

With a renewed sense of disappointment, Moray put down the letter which, when it arrived, he had opened so eagerly. Surely he might have expected something better than these few brief, restrained lines. Instead of the bare schedule of their departure, couldn't she have dwelt more freelingly on her love, said that she was missing him, that she longed to be once again in his arms? In all her vocabulary was there no stronger word than 'dear'? He admitted that she was shy, poor child, troubled by the consciousness of their intimacy – so he construed the phrase 'I will soon be your own true wife' – and limited by the small size of the notepaper. Yet she had found space to devote to Willie – his lectures, his fever, his anxieties and arrangements, his request not to be late. Not a word, not a single inquiry as to his own state of mind and body, or the distress and difficulties he might be experiencing, away from her. Really, it was too bad. He loved her, he wanted her, and all she could do was to throw Willie at his head.

This strange feeling that he had been deserted was intensified by the isolation of his present existence. His normal routine was broken, he had said goodbye to his friends in Schwansee, no one came to see him, they had all written him off as a departed member of their group. And Frida – for more than a week he had not set eyes upon her, although on several occasions, in the hope of meeting her, he had essayed a halting walk in the rain round the lake shore towards her domain. He missed the companionship she had so freely given and which, now above all, when certainty and uncertainty chased each other across his mind, he so sorely needed. Bitterly he regretted the rift between them, the result of a few outspoken words on her part which, realising their purpose, he had already condoned. Surely he could not leave her without attempting to resolve their differences. Time was getting so short, so very short; in two days he would be off. He ought to go up the hill to visit her. Yet something, pride perhaps, a restraining gleam of caution, had hitherto intervened.

The summons to lunch recalled him. He ate in abstracted silence, without appetite; then, as was his Sunday habit, took a short nap. Awakening about three he saw that the rain poured down more mercilessly than ever. He got up, moved about the house, checked his packed suitcases, smoked a cigarette, tried to kill time, but gradually his spirits sank, reached their lowest ebb and, after resisting during the hours of daylight, as the miserable grey afternoon turned to sodden evening, he succumbed to the craving for one word of human comfort. Frida would give it. She was, had always been, his friend. They would not argue, would discuss nothing involving controversy, would simply spend in sympathy one last quiet restorative hour of human intercourse.

Hurriedly, before he could change his mind, he put on his Aquascutum, took an old golf umbrella from the stand and, letting himself unobtrusively out of the house, hobbled off. The ferry took him across the lake, but for a lame man it was a long walk and a stiff climb up the steep, winding path to the schloss. Yet he was there at last, trembling at the knees like a horse after a stiff pull. God, he thought, what a wreck I've become.

Almost lost in the low clouds, the tall Seeburg towered above him. Built of rough mountain granite in the seventeenth century Swiss style, with a machicolated roof and twin pepperpot towers, it had, in the swollen darkness, a spectral, haunted air, an impression heightened by the harsh croaking of drenched ravens sheltering beneath the overhang of the eaves. Advancing on the mossy terrace outside the narrow double windows that gave on to her sitting-room, he drew up with a catch of breath. Yes, there she sat, alone on the sofa, beside the antique tiled stove, working at her needlepoint under a single shaded light that barely illuminated the large and lofty apartment, sparsely furnished with heavy high-backed walnut chairs and a great Bavarian armoire. Her favourite little weimaraner, Peterkin, lay on the rug at her feet with his nose between his paws.

The sombre domesticity of the scene touched Moray. With an agitated hand he tapped on the pane. Immediately she raised her head, turned towards the outer darkness; then, putting down her work, she came slowly forward and opened the tall window. For a long moment she looked at him fixedly, then in a calm, firm voice, totally devoid of solicitude, she said:

'My poor friend, how ill you look. Come! I will help you. So.' Taking his arm she guided him towards the sofa. 'Here you must sit and rest.'

'Thank you,' he muttered, breathing with difficulty. 'As you see, I'm rather under the weather. You may remember I hurt my back. It hasn't quite cleared up.'

'Yes,' she said, standing over him. 'Three times I have seen you by the lake, attempting to take your walk. I said to myself, unfortunate man, soon he will come to me.'

No note, no sign of triumph was evident in her tone or manner, but a kind of calm protectiveness, as though she were dealing with a favoured yet refractory pupil.

'I felt I must come,' he defended himself hurriedly. 'I couldn't bear to leave the breach between us permanently unhealed. I . . I am due to go the day after tomorrow.'

She did not answer but sat down beside him on the sofa and took his hand, holding it with strong, compelling fingers. For several moments there was absolute silence; then, gazing at him intently and speaking with the calm conviction of accomplished fact:

'My poor friend, you are not quite yourself. And now it is for a woman who knows and understands you, who has for you the best and strongest feelings, yes, it is now time for her to save you from yourself.'

'From myself?' he repeated, confused and startled.

'You have been led foolishly into a bad situation. Because you are an honourable man and, although ill, would wish to be a brave one, you want to go through with it. Even when it is plain you will not survive.' She paused quietly. 'But for that I will not stand aside.'

In the ensuing silence, compelled by a strange mixture of attraction and revulsion, he forced himself to raise his head and look at her.

'I must admit,' he said, trying to assert himself, 'with this lameness, I'm . . . almost in doubt. I mean, it has crossed my mind as to whether I'll be *able* to go as arranged, or whether I should follow later.'

'You are no longer in doubt, my friend. I do not intend to let you go.'

A complex shock passed through him, a combination of opposites, positive and negative charges of electricity perhaps, anyhow a decided shock.

'But I'm committed . . . in every way,' he protested.

'Yes, you have been wrong.' She lifted a forefinger in admonition. 'And stupid also. But listen. When you are walking in the mountains and discover yourself upon the wrong road, do you continue and fall into a crevasse? No. When you have asked directions of someone who knows better you turn and go back. That is what you will do.'

'No, no. I couldn't. What would Kathy and Willie think of me? Even the people here, after all the talk, my speech at the party, the publicity in the *Tageblatt*. I'd be the laughing-stock of the canton when they still saw me around.'

'They will not still see you around,' she answered, almost casually. 'For you must go away for a long holiday . . . with me.'

Again he started visibly, but she held him silent with a faint calm smile, went on in the same even, conversational tone.

'First we go to Montecatini, where there are wonderful baths for your back, and also, once you are better, a fine golf course where I will walk with you and admire your play. After, we take a cruise on that nice select little ship the *Stella Polaris*. Only then, in the Spring, do we return here, by which time all the silly business is finished and long forgotten.'

Immobilised by those hypnotic eyes he stared at her as though in a trance, yet perceiving, for the first time, that her hair had been freshly rinsed and set, that – as if she had expected him – she wore a new mauve silk dress, high in the waist, full and pleated in the skirt, a dress at once classic and correct, which enhanced her natural distinction. Certainly a fine figure of a woman and still beautiful – at a distance. Yet from close range his dilated pupils mirrored the commencing stigmata of middle-age; the faint reticulated network beneath the orbits, the slight sag of the muscular neckline, the speckled discoloration of the strong even teeth. How could this be compared with that other sweet face, that frail, fresh young body? An inward sigh shook him. And yet – in his present lamentable state – wasn't she a haven, an anchorage, a lady too, cultured, distinguished, and, in the ultimate analysis, not unbedworthy? He drew a sharp breath, was about to speak when, with a gleam of ridicule, she forestalled him.

'Yes, I am a reasonable bargain. And I will be the proper wife for you – by day and by night. Have I not also had strong longings during the years I have lived alone? We shall fulfil together. And what an interest for us both to restore and redecorate the Seeburg, to fill it with your beautiful things! We shall have a salon more famous than was Coppée in the days of Mme. de Stael.'

He still mumbled a protest.

'I'm terribly fond of you, dear Frida. But ... '.

'But, yes, my poor man, and I of you. For once and all, I will not let you go out there to destroy yourself.'

A silence. What more could he say, or do? He felt overpowered, dominated, possessed, yet filled with a slow, creeping tide of comfort. The plan she presented was so sane, so agreeable in all respects – vastly different from that dark future which, during these last few days, he had come to dread. Acceptance would be like sliding into a warm bath after a long exhausting journey. He closed his eyes and slid. The relief was indescribable. He lay back on the sofa.

'Oh, my God, Frida ... I feel I want to tell you everything ... from the very beginning.'

And he did, at length, with feeling.

'Ah, yes,' she murmured, sympathetically if ambiguously, when he concluded. 'I see it all.'

'You're the only woman who has ever understood me.'

As he spoke the dog stirred from sleep, looked up and, with a bark of recognition, jumped on to his knees.

'You see,' she nodded, 'Peterkin accepts you also. Now you are tired. Rest while I bring something to restore you.' She was soon back, glass in hand. 'This is from your own country, very old and special. I have kept it for you for a long time. Now, to please me, you must drink all.'

The one spirit he detested was whisky – it always disagreed with him, soured his stomach, upset his liver. But he did need a stimulant, and he wanted to please her; besides, he hadn't the will to resist.

'Well done,' she commended him, resuming her place beside him. 'Now we will sit quiet as two mice in church until you feel better.'

As he had expected, the whisky went straight to his head. His face became flushed and in no time at all he felt, not better, but stupid and inflamed. Presently, observing him, she said thoughtfully: 'I have been considering the best way to arrange our marriage. It must be done not only most quietly, but also quickly, if we are to get away before all the fuss, which you fear so much, becomes known. Yes?'

'The sooner we clear out the better.'

'Then it is best that we go to Basle, leaving early tomorrow. It will take altogether three days, for there are several formalities. But we can be back here on Wednesday evening.'

'And then, dear Frida?'

'Off on our long holiday next morning.'

Hazily he saw her smiling down at him. Damn it, she wasn't a bad-looking gammer, with those wonderful eyes and that solid, Wagnerian body which gave promise of well sprung resilience. What was she saying?

'You were sweet a moment ago. You called me dear Frida.'

'You are rather a dear, you know.' Unexpectedly, he sniggered. 'A regular Brunnhilde.'

'It is for you to know – in the future. You have never seen the upstairs of the Seeburg. My room, that will be our room, is nice. That we shall not look at this evening. But after? So? You will not find me cold. Some people do not need the love of the body, but with us it will be natural and frequent. Yes? And necessary also, for it puts one at ease. Now let us talk about our so pleasant future.'

An hour later, the Dauphine bore him triumphantly to the villa. In the close darkness of the little car she patted his cheek and gave a meaning little laugh.

'Now, like me, you will have happy dreams. Goodnight, mein lieber Mann, tomorrow I will come to you early. We must start for Basle before nine o'clock.'

Dead beat, but dulled and comforted, he stumbled into the house, thankful for the fact that he was so extinguished he must instantly fall asleep.

'I'm going straight to bed,' he told Arturo, in a voice he made an effort to keep normal. 'See that you lock up before you turn in. And I'll want breakfast at eight sharp.'

'Yes, sir,' said Arturo, somewhat blankly. 'And tonight, will you have your hot milk and sandwiches upstairs?'

No, he thought, not after the whisky, he was still not quite sober.

'Nothing tonight.' He paused, confronted by the necessity of conveying the change in his plans. Well, with Arturo it would not be so difficult; he had been quite broken up at the prospect of his departure.

'By the way,' he sought for the words, 'something quite unexpected has come up. I shall not after all be obliged to leave for good, but only for a matter of perhaps three months.'

Several shades of expression passed over the other's face before radiance shone from it.

'Oh, sir, I am so happy, so filled with joy, so thankful to the good God and Santa Philomena to whom I pray for you to stay. Only wait till I tell Elena.'

Arturo's extravagant delight was an added solace. Such loyalty, such affectionate devotion he thought, on his way up the stairs, and from Elena too, both so deeply attached to him. And now for bed.

Gazing upwards with a queer expression, Arturo watched him enter his bedroom, then he turned and went back to the pantry. Elena looked at him expectantly. He responded with an affirmative gesture and a significant grimace.

'You were right. The German has hooked him. Got him by the short hairs.'

'Madre d' Dio.' She let out the exclamation and broke into broad Neapolitan. 'Lu viecchio 'nzannaluto.'

'He's that, all right.' Arturo shrugged in agreement. 'And how he will suffer.'

'But so also will we,' said Elena despondently. 'That squaldrina will watch the money like a Swiss tax collector. Goodbye to our little ribasso from the market when she gets her claws on the bills.'

'Still, it's better than having him go. We can still milk him.'

'Llecca 'o culo a chillu viecchio 'nzannaluto?'

'That's it, lay on the butter thick.' He went to the cupboard, took out a bottle and drew the cork. 'He's the softest touch I ever handled.'

'Watch out though, with her around.'

'I know what I'm doing. Besides, we have to make the most of him while he's got it. Before she finishes, that *culo* will take everything off him.'

'Chella fetente va a ferni c' 'o mette 'nterra,' said Elena, with meaning.

At this prediction of complete emasculation for their employer they looked at each other and burst into fits of laughter.

CHAPTER XIX

THREE DAYS LATER, at the hour of twilight on Wednesday afternoon, the Humber utility car, mud-bespattered as from a journey, slid unobtrusively through the village of Schwansee, swung discreetly into the familiar acacia drive and drew up at Moray's villa.

'Well, here we are, Frida.' Pulling off his driving gloves he stated the obvious with a congratulatory smile, adding, with a glance at the dashboard clock, 'and dead on time.'

The successful secrecy with which they had invested their wedding gave him a distinct glow of achievement; it had all gone exactly according to plan. He squeezed out of the driving seat and, hurrying round the car, helped her with uxorious solicitude to alight. At the same moment the door of the villa swung open and Arturo appeared, advanced with a determined smile of welcome.

'Everything all right?' Moray asked aside, as the man removed the suitcases from the boot.

'Quite all right, sir. We have the salon in order again with the china all arranged. But the library and the other rooms will take more time.'

'You'll have time. We shall be off tomorrow for quite a long spell.' He seemed to hesitate. 'There were no messages of any kind?'

'None, sir.'

Impossible to repress that involuntary breath of relief. He had feared the possibility of a last-minute telephone call, a distressing message awaiting his return. But no, they had gone off, without a word, exactly as Frida had predicted, off to the Mission, to their work – not his, it had never been his – yes, their life's work, which, by its very complexities, its difficulties and dangers, would absorb them, make Kathy speedily forget. How misguided he had been ever to imagine that he could beneficially link his future to that dear dedicated girl, yet how wise, in her interests and his own, to realise his mistake before it was too late. And now there would be no more idealistic nonsense, no more reaching after spiritual moonbeams: safely married to a mature and distinguished woman he experienced a warm feeling of security, a sense of having at last reached journey's end.

'Bring tea quickly, Arturo,' he said, following Frida into the drawing-room. Seating himself beside her on the Chesterfield settee, he glanced round appreciatively. Yes, everything was in order, exactly as *before* – the word had now a definite historic import, like A.D. or B.C., denoting the demarcation between his pre- and post-redemption periods. His pictures bloomed more attractively than ever – God, to think he could ever have existed without them – his silver shone, his porcelain, freshly washed and arranged, gleamed in the light of a heart-warming fire of crackling cedar logs.

'Isn't this *gemütlich*?' He gave her an intimate smile. 'To be back, together, and to have managed it all so cleverly.'

'But of course, David. You will find I manage things always well.' She gave him a short pleasant nod. 'You will see later, when we are established at the Seeburg.'

He was about to answer – a compliment was on his tongue – when Arturo came in, wheeling the tea trolley, so instead, rubbing his hands, he said: 'Ah, tea. Will you pour, darling?'

Meanwhile Arturo, having adjusted the trolley, was offering him the salver from the hall.

'Your mail, sir.'

'What a lot of letters,' she exclaimed, lifting the silver teapot – George I, 1702. 'It appears that you are an important man.'

'Mostly business.' He shrugged, running them through. But one, apparently, was not. With a shrinking of his nerves he recognised Kathy's round, even writing. But, glancing covertly at the date stamps on the envelope, he was immediately reassured. The latter had been posted on the 17th, four days before her departure, and received at Schwansee on Monday the 20th, the day he left for Basle with Frida. As such, thank heaven, it could contain neither reproaches nor regrets. With a cautious side glance at Frida, who was still pouring tea, he slid it unobserved into his side pocket – he would read it later, when he was alone.

'Since we speak of business,' she added sugar and lemon and handed him his cup, 'you must one day soon tell me of your affairs – perhaps when we are at Montecatini, yes? I have a very

268

good head for these things. The actions of the German chemicals, for example, these are strong at this moment.'

'They are,' he agreed, tolerantly, as he leaned forward to cut the cake. 'And we're comfortably supplied with them.'

'That is nice. And German bonds. These also are affording a high rate of interest.'

'I see you're going to be a great help, dear. Now try this. It's Elena's special recipe and she's baked it in your honour.' He watched while she sampled the slice of cherry cake he handed her. 'Good, isn't it?'

'Yes, it is good – quite good. But it can be better, much better. For one thing there is too much vanilla and too little fruit. Afterwards I will show her properly.'

'You'll have to be tactful, dear. Elena is terribly touchy.'

'Oh, my poor David, you make me smile. As if I was without great experience! Why, at Keilenstein we had a staff, in and out, of fifteen persons, all requiring to be overseen. Here, I am sure, you have been ill served and also well cheated. No doubt your good Elena has many private arrangements, besides taking out fresh butter and eggs, while your wonderful Arturo – don't I know these Neapolitans – is all smiling in front and all stealing behind.'

A momentary misgiving troubled him, gone when she patted his hand with a protective smile.

'Another cup of your nice Twinings. That, at least, I shall not change.'

How gracefully she managed the tea things – to the manner born, neither nervous like Kathy nor clumsy like Doris, who in those distant almost forgotten days had always upset things during her attacks. Yes, after all his troubled years he had been right in this, his ultimate decision. He had always aspired to a well-bred woman, not only for the social advantages she would bring him, but also for that extra refinement with which, from her breeding, she would enrich their conjugal intimacies. Ah, yes, Frida would remake his life. And how restful the immediate prospect: Montecatini, the *Polaris* cruise – she had already made their cabin reservations at the American Express in Basle – and then all the interest of restoring the Seeburg. Comfortable though his villa was, it would never be more than a bourgeois little house, really unfitted to hold his treasures which would now adorn and transform the big schloss above the lake.

Yet, through his complacency, as he sipped his tea in the warm comfortable room, he could not restrain his thoughts from reverting, not exactly self-accusingly, but with a kind of pricking discomfort, to that plane, which even now, after its overnight stop at Lisbon, must be winging towards Luanda. Surely by now she must have got over the worst of it. She was young, she would recover, sorrow did not last forever, time was the great healer. . . He consoled himself with these and other profundities.

'I believe you are asleep.' A half-chiding, half-amused voice recalled him.

'No – no – not really. But on that subject, Frida, must you really spend the night at Seeburg? Why not stay here? After all, we *are* married.'

'Yes, we are nice married people, and for that reason must be sensible.'

'But why, dear Frida? It's been quite, well, difficult for me, away with you two nights . . . and separate rooms.'

She laughed, well pleased.

'I am glad you have the same feeling as I. But for newly-weddeds it is better to make the honeymoon away. For me there is more novelty. And for you, especially, it is better to be free of recent associations that might trouble you.'

'Yes,' he agreed, unwillingly. 'I suppose there's something in that. Still . . . '.

Assuagingly, she pressed against him imprinting the edge of her corsets upon his short ribs, then, before he could encircle her, withdrew.

'So . . . our need will grow if held back. I promise I will be nice for you at Montecatini. The Freiherr, my late husband, was a strong man in the bed, yet never did I fail to answer him with equal vigour. Since we are married, I can openly speak of these things. And now I will go upstairs. After that long drive I have much need to wash.'

When she left the room he sat half-dozing before the hot fire, as though drugged by the scent of the burning cedar. At times his mind became an absolute blank; then, recovering, he enjoyed a moment of calm relaxation. Five, ten, fifteen minutes passed. What was she doing upstairs? Taking a bath? He had not liked that reference to the late lamented baron, but at least it showed she wasn't frigid. He thought drowsily of her ample dugs, those extensile mountaineering thighs. Then absently, through his euphoria, he remembered the belated letter. Whatever his reluctance, he owed it to Kathy to read and cherish it as a last sweet message. Feeling in his pocket he withdrew it and after considering the envelope again, and confirming the date stamps, he manfully opened it.

As he did so he became conscious of the ringing of a bell. The front door? Yes. He sat up suddenly, hoping to high heaven that it was not a caller. If one of their friends, Stench particularly, burst in upon them at this precise moment, it would be a fatal embarrassment, would in fact ruin all their plans for a discreet departure. He should have warned Arturo to say he was not at home. Too late now, the fellow was answering the door.

He got up, parted the curtains of the side window and peered out at the dark driveway. No car – it couldn't be a caller, must be a tradesman or a travelling pedlar; he had no need to worry. Yet the conversation at the door appeared to be prolonged. Straining his ears he heard Arturo say, almost entreatingly: 'Please, if you will wait here, I will see.'

'But there's no need,' a thin voice answered, with a strained note of urgency. 'I'm expected. I'll go straight in.'

Moray's heart contracted. My God, he thought, it can't be. I'm dreaming, or out of my mind. Instinctively he took a few steps backwards. Futile retreat. There came the sound of hurried footsteps in the hall and the next instant Kathy was before him.

'David!' she cried, in sheer relief. 'I thought from Arturo you weren't here.' All her body seemed to incline towards him: then, running forward, she put her arms round him and laid her head against his breast.

He had turned deathly white, his face blank with horror and amazement. It was a nightmare, unreal, couldn't be true. He stood frozen into paralysed stillness.

'Oh, David, dear David,' she kept murmuring. 'Just to be with you again.'

He could not speak, the skin around his mouth had suddenly become tight. But at last he gasped: 'Kathy . . . what . . . why are you here?'

'Because I need you now . . . so much more . . . '. Still close to him, she looked up as though uncomprehending. 'You know that Uncle Willie sent me?'

'Willie?' he echoed, like a parrot.

'Didn't you get my letter?'

271

'No – yes – at least . . . I've been away.'

'Then you don't know. Oh, David, it's too terrible. The entire Mission is destroyed, burned to the ground. There's been a fearful outbreak by armed terrorists. They're fighting all around, and almost all of our people are dead. All Uncle Willie's work, the labour of twenty years, destroyed.' Tears were beginning to flow down her cheeks. 'Uncle Willie has gone out to see the worst, if they'll allow him to get there, but he knows it's finished. He wouldn't let me go with him. He's broken-hearted. I think he'll have to give up. And for me, there's nothing out there now . . . I have . . . only you, dear David. Oh, I thank God for that. But for you, I think I would have lost my mind.'

Silence. A cold sweat of panic beaded his forehead; his heart kept banging irregularly in his side. He broke away slightly, hand pressed against his brow, still struggling for speech.

'This . . . dreadful, Kathy. A great shock. If I had only known . . .'

She looked at him with faithful, uncomprehending eyes.

'But, David, when you didn't come to the airport I felt sure you had my letter telling you everything.'

'Yes, precisely . . . it's just . . . so difficult . . . having been away.' What he was saying he scarcely knew, and she had begun to look at him strangely, nervously too, with a sudden anxiety in her tired, thin little face.

'David, is anything wrong?'

'Nothing, except . . . it's all so unfortunate . . . so unforeseen.'

Now all the joy that was in her died. She showed real alarm, seemed to shrink into herself.

'David, please, for pity's sake.'

Oh God, he thought, this can't go on, I must, I'll have to tell her. He tried to pull himself together.

'Kathy . . . '. He braced himself. 'Dear Kathy . . . '.

He could not go on, could not to save his life have spoken the words. There followed a moment of complete and frightful silence. His mouth filled with bitter water, and through it all he kept thinking, I could have had her here, on my own terms, if only I had waited. It was agony. And as he stood rigid with clenched hands, unable to meet her frightened eyes, the door opened and Frida came into the room. Arrested by the scene, with one comprehensive glance she took it in; then, without change of expression, came quietly forward.

'Kathy, you are here,' she said, and kissed her on the cheek. At the same time she made towards Moray a brusque gesture of dismissal which said decisively, go, this you must leave to me.

Still rooted, he seemed unable to set himself in motion, but somehow, stumbling forward, he got himself out of the room. Kathy was very pale, but had stopped crying. Bewilderment and alarm had dried her tears.

'What is wrong with David? Is he ill?'

'I think he is unwell slightly, at this moment. The shock, you see. But come, dear child, we must sit down and be composed and have a little talk together.' Persuasively, an arm round Kathy's shoulder, she led her to the settee. 'Now first, my dear, how did you arrive here?'

'By plane to Zurich, train to Melsburg, then the little steamboat to Schwansee.'

'What a tiring journey. Wouldn't you like to rest or have some refreshment?'

'No, thank you, no.' Kathy was shivering slightly, her teeth pressed together to prevent them chattering.

'At least a cup of tea. It can be brought so quickly.'

'Oh, nothing, please. I only want to know about David.'

'Yes, of course, we must speak of David, for he is, like that nice book says, the heart of the matter. But we must speak plainly of him, for even if it gives pain we must establish the truth.' She paused and took Kathy's hand in hers. 'You see, dear child, this David whom you love is a very nice man, so full always with good intentions, yet, alas, not always with the strength to perform them, which is often sad for him and for others. Have you not an English proverb, the pavement of hell is made of good intentions? Did you never ask yourself, dear little Kathy, for what real reason he came back to discover your family in Scotland? You thought, to repay a youthful kindness. That was not so. It pains me to tell you, and it will pain you to hear. It was because as a young man this David was the lover of your mother, really her lover if you understand me, had promised marriage, then cruelly left her, for a rich man's only daughter.'

'No – no.' She took a sharp anguished breath, her pupils wide with shock. 'It's impossible. You're making this up.'

'How do I make it up when I have heard it all from David himself? Yes, he is the kind of man who seeks to discharge his guilt by an emotional confession. And succeeds. With weeping too, for, like other great men, he weeps easily – like a woman.'

'I won't . . . I won't listen to you.'

'But you must, dear Kathy, for your own sake. So our David came back full of the best intentions to make his wrong completely right. And when your mother was unfortunately not available, you became the object of his kind attentions. And it was all good in the beginning, yes, beautifully good and proper, but then things changed a little, he wished very nobly to do even more for you, and so – for those soft charming men have so much a way with women – on the promise to marry and go to your mission he became your lover, as with your mother.'

'Stop!' Distractedly she covered her ears. 'I can't – I'll not hear any more. It's too horrible.'

'Certainly it is not a nice thought, to seduce first the mother, then the daughter, and all with the highest intentions. Yet I assure you he is not altogether bad, compared with others, for I know men, dear child, and some are by far more horrible, as you say, than David, who is only selfish and weak, avoiding trouble and difficulty for himself at all costs. No, do not run away.' Detainingly, as Kathy tried to rise, she held her arm. 'Can't you see I speak for your own good. I must show you your mistake. If you had married this famous David he would have tired of you and in six months broken your heart. You are altogether different, not of the same kind. You would never convert him to religion, or even to work again as a doctor. Nor could he have made you like his stupid antiques or his famous pictures, all a mode created by the dealers. Your marriage would have been a fatal disaster.'

Kathy sat quite still, her expression blurred, as though the structure of her face had given way. There was something terrifying in her immobility. She felt feverishly sick, stripped of all that she had prized, degraded and unclean. She wanted to get away but there was no strength in her, only weakness and self-disgust.

'So, is it not evident? The wife this David needs is not a sweet, gentle girl such as you, but a woman strong enough to master him, one who will make him obey, and do always, always what is needed.'

Kathy's eyes widened suddenly, great pools of darkness in her small white face.

'You,' she gasped.

'Yes. Today we were married in Basle.'

Silence again. Kathy's brows, knit in pain, gave her a twisted look. What thoughts raced through her tortured mind! Her head drooped, could not contain or combat them – the meeting at her mother's grave, that charming, serious smile, a friend of your family, the day in Edinburgh, so gay and generous, the round of visits, what a wonderful nurse, but quite worn out, a cup of soup, my dear, so tenderly, and then Vienna, strange and whirling confusion of lights, sounds, music, Pinkerton, dear David, you could never be like that, Switzerland next, a mantle of purity, yes, I will come with you, the little mission church, one in the sight of heaven, and then, like her dear dead mother. . . . Oh God, she could not bear it. She jumped up, wildly, frantically, bent only on escape.

But Frida had risen quickly and stood at the door, blocking the way.

'Wait, Kathy, you must be sensible. Believe me, I mean well by you. There is much we can do for you.'

'Let me go. All I want is to go away . . . to go home.'

'Kathy, the car will take you to the hotel.'

'No, no . . . I'll take the boat . . . I only want to go home.'

The doorway was still blocked. She looked feverishly round, ran to the french window, flung it open.

'Stop, Kathy.'

But she had already dashed across the terrace and the lawn to the narrow garden path that led to the village. Down the steep path she ran, into the darkness, mindless of the unseen steps, falling to her knees in her desperate haste, rising again, straining through the vicious shadows, seeking only to escape. Dark shapes of bushes whipped against her like things alive, stinging her with all the malice of mankind. Shocked out of sorrow, she was no longer herself, not altogether living, moving in a confused and tragic dream. In the dim world in which she ran, everything within her drifted away but pain, all was gone. She was lost.

Frida could not follow. Standing silent and distressed at the open french window, which threw out a following beam, she watched, watched until the stumbling, wavering little figure was lost as the brutal night took possession of it. Then, turning slowly, she shook her head, closed the window and, advancing into the hall, called upstairs. He came down slowly, nervously, with watery eyes and a veal-white face. He had been seated on the upper landing, trying to steady himself with one of his monogrammed Sobranies.

'It is all settled,' she told him calmly. 'She has gone.'

'But where ... and how ' His voice shook.

'I offered the car but she prefers to return as she came, by boat. She goes home at once. All she wishes is to go home.'

'But Frida ... ' he faltered. 'She has given up her job. She can't go to Willie. Where is her home?'

'You have put the question. You had better answer it.'

A pause.

'Was she – much hurt?'

'Yes.'

'In – in what way?'

'Cannot you guess?'

'What did you tell her?'

'The truth. For her sake and ours it was necessary to perform a surgical operation. And I did so.'

'You told everything?'

'Yes.'

'But you – explained that I had meant well.'

'All was explained.'

'And yet – she was hurt – badly?'

'Yes.' With increasing sharpness: 'Have I not already said it.'

'Surely she understood I couldn't go out there.'

'She did not come here for you to go.'

He threw up his hands.

'But how in God's name was I to know the Mission would burn down.'

'In the present circumstances it was more than a possibility. They are making bonfires of all the missions.'

'My God, Frida, I feel horribly upset. I worry about her getting back.' He looked at the clock. 'She may have missed the boat – and it's the last to Melsburg. I should go after her ... if she's still on the pier.'

'Then go.'

She said it cuttingly. The look in her yellow eyes, with their narrow slits of pupils, made him flush and wilt.

'No,' he said. 'You're quite right. It wouldn't be wise.'

Silence again. Then firmly she put her hand on his shoulder.

'For the sake of pity, pull yourself into something like a man. She is young and, like her mother, will get over it. You can afford to make a settlement to her, and a large one. Later you must send it in proper legal form.'

'Yes.' His face lifted slightly. 'I can do that, thank God, and I will. Make her comfortable for life. But, Frida ... '. He hesitated, then, after a longish pause, said pleadingly, 'I don't want to be alone tonight.'

She seemed to study him, with almost a clinical curiosity, seemed about to refuse, then relented.

'Well, then, though you should be punished, I shall stay. You must go upstairs and take your bath. Then to bed, for you are tired. I will speak with the servants and have a tray brought to you. Afterwards I will come.'

He looked at her abjectly.

'Bless you, Frida.'

She waited until he had climbed the stairs; then, passing through the drawing-room, she went out upon the terrace. The moon, behind ragged clouds, shone faintly. It was thawing, the snow on the lawn had turned a dirty yellow, a damp sensual smell of leaves filled the air. She gazed out across the lake. Yes, there was the steamer, a little fountain of light, cosy and bright, already on its way, quite far on its way, to Melsburg. A faint thrum of the engines came back to her. Kathy must just have managed to get on board. Turning, she looked down at the little pier. Yes. All quiet and deserted. The single yellow lamp that was kept alight all night shone upon the solitary wooden bench. No one was seated there.

CHAPTER XX

STARTING PAINFULLY FROM a restless snatch of sleep. Moray awoke to the muddled consciousness of unfamiliar darkness. Where was he? And why alone? Then, through the oppression clamped on his forehead, the first dulled glint of consciousness brought the humiliating answer.

God, it had been frightful, his inability to find consolation in Frida's arms! She had tried to help him, at first with desire, then with encouragement, and finally in a state of weary patience. All useless – he could not succeed. And then, sorely tried by his futile fumblings, she had said, in a tone which concealed contempt but not bitterness and frustration: 'We both need some rest if we're to be off tomorrow morning. Would it not be wise if you moved to another room?'

And so he was here, in the guest room – a guest, almost, in his own house. Why, he agonised, had his normal virility deserted him? Had the sudden shock of Kathy's reappearance induced a depressive impotence? It might well be so – the oversized female in his antique bed, her musky odours and muscular anatomy, had brought paralysing images of the slender young form he had once possessed: Kathy, whom he could easily have had, and instead had hopelessly lost.

Kathy ... Stretched out on his back, he groaned. If only he had not failed her, everything would have turned out as he had wished. Oh God, what a fool he had been, in his weakness, his craving for sympathy, to marry Frida. She had caught him: he had swallowed the bait, hook, line and sinker, and was now landed, gasping, on the bank. And how skilfully she had angled for him: first that resigned acceptance of his departure, congratulations, sweet offers of assistance; then the gradual dissemination of doubt, working up to a frontal assault upon his fears; and finally, when he had been sufficiently reduced, that determined stand, a command virtually, to take her. Miserably he acknowledged her strength. She would possess him body and soul.

God, what a horrible situation! Weak rage flooded him, followed by a spasm of self-disgust. Tears came burning to his eyes at the thought of his disloyalty to Kathy. Yet it had not been a deliberate betrayal, he told himself, simply a moment of aberration, a lapse for which he had already been punished, and for which he would eventually make amends.

Amends – yes, that was still the key, the imperative word. At all costs he must not lose contact with Kathy. No matter what had happened she was still his responsibility, his charge, as essential to him as he to her. He must, yes, he must get in touch with her at once. A letter, explanatory, contrite yet constructive, was the immediate necessity, not only to outline his plans to make provision for her, but also to express the hope that when sorrow had been tempered by compassion they might meet again. He would pour out his heart in it, and since he must leave early with Frida tomorrow it was essential for him to write it now. A faint and wavering gleam dawned in the grisly prospect of his future. There was always hope – one need never give up; with his money especially there were many ways and means. Perhaps in due course everything might be straightened out. He began even to envisage, though dimly, an amicably arranged divorce that would set him free. Surely he could rely on his dear child's forgiveness.

Stirring himself with an effort, he got up, switched on the light and, while struggling into his dressing gown, looked at his wrist watch. Twenty minutes to twelve – he couldn't have been asleep for much more than an hour. Guardedly, he felt his way across the landing. Rhythmic unmelodious crescendos, percolating from his room, now hers, made him wince. He hastened past. Downstairs in the library, he sat at the bureau by the window, switched on the shaded lamp, and took notepaper from the central inlaid drawer. Then, pen in hand, he stared into the outer darkness, anxiously seeking the most appropriately touching form of address. Should it be 'Dear Kathy,' 'My Dearest Kathy,' or even 'Darling Kathy,' or simply the restrained, sombre, but oh, so significant, 'My Dear'?

After some thought he had decided on the last when, through his abstraction, he became conscious of a glow, shining distantly through the opacity of the night. The moon is rising, he thought, seeing a hopeful omen in this sudden brightness; he was indeed in a mood receptive to signs and portents. Yet it could scarcely be the moon, for the sky still remained darkly unbroken and the light itself seemed less a radiance than a strange coruscation, a shifting sparkle of pin-point lights dancing like wildfire against the unseen waters of the lake below. What on earth was it? Accustomed to the wildest elements unleashed amongst these unpredictable peaks, he was unlikely to be startled by any terrestrial phenomenon. Yet so overwrought and unstable was his present state of mind, he could not repress a faint shiver of distrust. He got to his feet, opened the french window and, despite the lightness of his attire – he had always had a tendency to catch cold – went out on the terrace.

The night, as he had suspected, was pitch and unexpectedly chill. Clutching his thin dressing gown about him he peered down towards the lights. They were near, mysteriously and disconcertingly near. But suddenly he understood, and in a reflex of absurd relief could have smiled, though he did not, at his own foolishness. It was the little fishing fleet, half a dozen boats bouncing gaily on the waves, the men casting their nets, night fishing with naphtha flares. The felchen must be running, and in shoals, to have brought them out so late.

He was about to turn back into the comfort of the house when a thought arrested him. Surely the felchen didn't run in winter and never, to his knowledge, in this part of the lake? They always swarmed at the mouth of the river where it flowed in through the Reisenberg gorge. And shading his eyes – though this was unnecessary – for a more particular scrutiny, he saw with amazement that a number of people were gathered on the pier. At this hour of the night! He hesitated. He wanted to leave it, leave the matter as it stood, but something impelled him to run into the house for his field glasses, the splendid Zeiss binoculars he had bought in Heidelberg.

At first he could not find them, but after rummaging untidily through several drawers, they came to hand. Back on the terrace, he focussed them hurriedly. Then, just as he saw that all the flares were now congregated round the pier, one by one all of them went out and a curtain of darkness, barely relieved by the feeble pier lamp, cut off his view.

He lowered the glasses uncertainly. He had a splitting headache and for some extraordinary reason his heart was fluttering against his ribs. He ought to go in, he had the letter to write, the letter beginning simply and movingly, 'My Dear.' And he would have gone in, but the sound of approaching footsteps detained him. He swung round. Two men, at first dimly seen, then gradually taking recognisable shape, were coming up the path from below. The pier-master and Herr Sacht from the village Polizeiwache.

It had always been for him a source of mild entertainment that the cantonal police, in entire outward look – their stiff helmet, blue uniform and capacious boots – bore so close a resemblance to the London bobbies: perhaps a delicate compliment, he had surmised, contrived in earlier days to make the visiting English milords feel safe and more at home. But now Moray was not entertained, nor did he feel safe and reassured as Herr Sacht and his companion advanced towards him. He felt instead a sinking of his heart that was the sickening premonition of unknown yet inevitable disaster.

'Grüss Gott, mein Herr.' Respectfully, apologetically almost, the pier-master made himself spokesman – Sacht, a slow and stolid man, was at all times sparing of words. 'We have some trouble down below, and have come for your advice – though not wishing to disturb you. A young woman . . .'.

'No . . . no . . . ' said Moray, barely breathing.

'Alas, yes. We have just found her.'

'But how . . . ?' He could say nothing more. Pale and rigid, he had ceased to breathe.

'After the night boat I heard a splash – like a springing fish. Of it, I thought nothing. But when I made my last round of the pier, there was a handbag, fallen down, and in the water, floating, a lady's small brown hat. I thought it wise to alarm the Polizei.' He glanced at Sacht, who nodded in heavy confirmation. 'We got the boats out and after dragging, just two hours, we found the young person – of course completely dead.' He paused in respectful sympathy. 'I fear it is – may be a friend to you. . . . The young Englische girl, she who came this afternoon on the five o'clock boat.'

He drew back, staring at them, horrified. Then, all at once he was crying hysterically.

'Oh, my God, it can't be. But yes, a young lady . . . she did come . . . Kathy . . . Kathy Urquhart . . . a friend, as you say, daughter of an old, very dear friend. . . . She left us, running,

running to catch the last boat ... '.

'Ach, so?' Sacht said, with a slow comprehending nod. 'She was running, in the darkness. Perhaps – or surely, then, this has been an accident.'

Moonfaced, Moray looked from one to the other, grasping towards the chance of exoneration, dizzily seeking a way out of the impact of this atrocious disaster.

'But what else could it be?' Struggling, he forced himself to bring out explanatory words. 'She was on her way home, looked in to visit me again ... briefly ... to say goodbye. She was a nurse, you understand ... fully trained ... a fully trained nurse ... meaning to work with her uncle in Africa ... a missionary. I wanted to send her back by car ... but she had her ticket and liked the boat. She must have slipped, missed her footing ... it had been raining, the melting snow is very treacherous. .... And now ... '. He covered his face with his hand.

'It is sad for you, Herr Moray,' said the pier-master, 'and we do not wish to cause you inconvenience. But you could help. Herr Sacht says, if only you will come to identify the body, he can then complete his report.'

'Yes, of course. .... Yes, I will come.' His tone was expressive of assistance, complete willingness to co-operate.

'First you must put on warmer clothes, so you do not get chilled. We will wait here until you are ready.'

He had not realised his state of undress. In the hall cupboard he found a coat, cap and scarf, a pair of felt-lined snow boots. Hastily rejoining the other two, he went down the path. Still in a state of shock, he was instinctively, protectively, acting a part, but as they approached the little pier, where a silent group stood gathered outside the low wooden shed that served as waiting-room, he could not repress a shudder of numbed and silent dread.

The group parted, still in silence, as they drew near. They went into the bare waiting-room, where they had laid her on the pitch-pine table under a single hanging electric globe. There was no sheet; she lay half covered by a fisherman's jacket which Sacht now discreetly withdrew. At first Moray could not look. Frozen. Too much to demand of him. A physical impossibility. He stared woodenly at the near end of the table, seeing only the worn sole of one small brown shoe, hearing a slow steady drop of water from the upper edge of the table. The room smelled of the drifted fume of the paraffin flares and of stale cigarette smoke. Wandering away to safety, his gaze caught an ashtray, stamped Melsburg Bier, on the floor. It was filled with stubs and had been removed. But the pier-master was speaking to him; he must look or they would begin to think something was seriously out of order. Slowly and with great effort he raised and twisted his head, still protecting himself, not looking at the face, not yet, making only a swift and limited survey.

Her total stillness was astounding, and her extraordinary immaturity. God knew he had reason to know that she was small and slight – but never had he dreamed her to be so – so young as this. The sodden clothes moulded her thin body, cupped the tender breasts, bisected the slender limbs, nakedly revealing the delicate swell between, the mons veneris – the phrase came – he was a doctor – and all, all with the stark indecency of death. One of her stockings had come down, wrinkling about the ankle, a button on the blouse was undone; one hand, the palm upturned receptively, the soaked skin already blanched, hung over the table edge.

A faint convulsion went through him as, knowing it must be done, he forced himself to look towards her face. Once he had looked, he could not look away. Upturned to the light, the face was shrunken and of a greenish colour, the blue lips flattened and fallen away, the drenched hair plastered back from the brow, hanging in dank switches about the thin white neck, still exuding the trickle that kept drip, dripping to the floor. Almost unrecognisable in its dead ugliness, the face was wrapped in a strange unbearable enigma. Most mysterious, most unbearable, were the eyes, still open, expressionless, gazing directly at him. Within their unfathomable depths, suddenly, in a moment of truth, he saw himself, exactly as he was, without illusion, naked under the watchful sky.

'Ach so? It is the young English lady?' It was spoken in a low voice of sympathy.

Moray turned, made a slow, melancholy gesture of assent. Revelation might have shattered him, but habit, the style and form of years, persisted.

'Alas – yes,' he said, with careful articulation. 'It is too painful for words. Cut off so suddenly – and so young. Only an accident could account for it. Did you observe the shoe, the sole – worn smooth? On the wet planks of the pier – the slippery edge . . . '.

'Yes, it is always bad in such weather.' The pier-master spoke defensively. 'But not possible for me to dry it.'

'Oh, I only pray God she did not suffer.'

'Ach, no,' Sacht said, crudely, yet trying to be kind. 'The cold of the water would kill quickly.' He had taken out his notebook.

'Well, you will want particulars,' Moray said, and standing erect, he gave them calmly, name, age, nationality, while Sacht indited in the dog-eared book with a moistened stub of pencil.

When it was all done, the pier-master, presuming in his sympathy, pressed Moray's arm.

'You do not look well, Herr Moray. Come to my house for a cup of coffee.'

'You are most kind. But, thank you, no.' He turned to Sacht. 'You are finished with me now? I suppose you have no further need of me.'

'For the present, no. But of course we will require you at the *Leichenschau*.'

'Ah, the inquest . . . '. Moray said, in an extinguished voice. 'You consider it will be necessary?'

'It is for you only a formality, Herr Moray, but officially required, for the records of the Stadt.'

'I see.' He drew himself up. 'You understand, of course, that it will be my privilege to defray all expenses of the interment.'

Was there anything more to say? Apparently not. He shook hands with both men and, not looking again, went out.

Though he went slowly, sparing himself with many enforced stops, his breath suffocated him as he went up the hill. He was sweating too, despite the cold, an abject sweat that ran from his armpits and the back of his knees, sweating from the ghastly futility of his effort at self-deception. All part of the usual sham, the impressive front, the grand façade. He knew the truth now, the truth about himself. And soon they would all know. Yes, it would all come out, all, all, the party for Willie, his engagement to Kathy, the heroic announcement of his departure for Africa. And now, within a few days, he was still here, married to Frida, and Kathy dead. God, what would they think of him? The gossip, the scandal, the odium that would fall upon him. And he couldn't escape it, not this time, couldn't leave with Frida in the morning, couldn't slide away and conveniently forget. He must stay for the *Leichenschau*, stay till it all came out, and afterwards stay bound hatefully to Frida, who would never let him go, but

284

would grind him down remorselessly to an ultimate subjection. And all this when he might have had Kathy, when even at this moment she might have been alive, warm and loving, in his arms.

In a spasm of sweltering despair he clenched his teeth and hung on to the railings for support. It was a bad dream, a nightmare, impossible to grasp how it had come about. He had meant well, tried to do the right thing, oh God yes, he had tried so hard, he had wanted to do well for everyone. It simply wasn't in him to hurt even a fly. He couldn't be blamed if, with the best intentions, he had over-estimated his strength, broken down and been obliged to withdraw. It had not been a deliberate betrayal, simply a moment of ... no, he'd said that before, it was no use any more. Simply wouldn't work. The instant of illumination when he stared into those dead eyes had shattered his self-constructed image. The hollow shell had broken, there was nothing left, nothing. In destroying her, he had destroyed himself.

Amongst the ruins, the clearness with which he viewed the stale imposture of his life was amazing, stereoscopic, four dimensional. All that had happened was his own doing, springing not from accident, but from something within, always his propensity for taking the way he thought most advantageous for himself. A genius at dodging responsibility, trouble, unpleasant issues, he saw with a sudden access of reason that he had developed to his logical conclusion. And yet, such a nice man, a charmer, cultured too, patron of the arts. How often had he heard, and merited, these compliments. Pity it was all gone – or would shortly go: reputation, position, freedom, happiness, hope in the future, and, naturally, his belief in himself. A queer logic had begun to take hold of him, comforting almost. He nodded twice in complete agreement. Imprisoned, walled in, every outlet sealed.

He reached the top of the hill and paused, exhausted but, strangely, more reasonable than ever. What a view! And a lovely night! A faint air stirring, the moon, alive again, drifting from the clouds, a soft mist rising from the lake, a nocturnal barge, unseen, chugged distantly. His thoughts strayed. A man had once told him that chugging note was his earliest childhood memory. Who? He had forgotten. It would have been interesting to ask him what he meant by it. Elusive shapes, records of his own past, swelled and faded in his mind. Say what they liked, he'd had an interesting life. An owl hooted in the orchard.

Suddenly he caught sight of a hedgehog, a small brown ball, moving into its own shadow across the lawn with painful lack of speed. Of all things, a hedgehog; amused, he almost smiled, recollecting how Wilhelm had reviled the little creature for its shallow rootings. He lost contact momentarily, then suddenly became aware of where he stood.

'*Cercis siliquastrium* . . . ' he murmured. 'The leaves are used for salads in the East.'

Yes, a lovely tree in summer, dangling its purple drops that fell staining the lawn. A winepress. He had always been poetic.

He ceased to mediate and, under the moving branches of the tree, raised his head in a sudden, upward glance. The swing, with its long ropes, was oscillating gently in the breeze. Seductive, the motion – it fascinated him. Following the gentle movements across the face of the moon, he simply couldn't take his eyes away. The faint rhythmic creak of the metal cleats began to beat a little tune inside his brain. Reality had left off, illusion was brightening his eys. He was beginning to understand everything in a peculiar and interesting way. This extraordinary calm was the most marvellous sensation he had ever experienced. And now he was talking to himself, in a quiet, confidential manner, carefully forming the words: restitution, complete vindication, the court of last appeal – absolving all guilt, restoring his ideal self. He stood there for a long time smiling to himself, enjoying his triumphant acquittal in advance, before he decided it was time for him to produce the evidence.

Next morning, just after seven o'clock, directed by the new Madame, Arturo went to the guest room, knocked on the door and brought in the breakfast tray: fresh orange juice, toast and boiled eggs, mountain honey, delicious Toscanini coffee in the silver Thermos. Arturo was in an unhappy frame of mind, almost convinced now that he would not keep his situation, but he said good morning, put the tray down on the oval occasional table by the window. Then he drew the lined silk curtains and flung the shutters back into their automatic catches.

The morning was cold, grey with mist, the raw air made his eyes water, and the wine he had drunk last night had left him with a thick head. He was about to close the window when he straightened suddenly, wondering if he were still not quite himself. He peered into the mist, not seeing clearly, yet held by an extraordinary mirage. Turning his head, slowly, he saw that there was no one in the bed. He caught his breath, slewed round again, more slowly, then convulsively stepped back, knocking over the tray with a crash. A breeze from the lake had stirred and thinned the luminous haze. Now he saw quite clearly what was hanging in the tree.

NEL BESTSELLERS

Crime

T027 821	GAUDY NIGHT	*Dorothy L. Sayers*	75p
T030 180	UNNATURAL DEATH	*Dorothy L. Sayers*	60p
T026 663	THE DOCUMENTS IN THE CASE	*Dorothy L. Sayers*	50p

Fiction

T029 522	HATTER'S CASTLE	*A. J. Cronin*	£1.00
T030 199	CRUSADER'S TOMB	*A. J. Cronin*	£1.25
T031 276	THE CITADEL	*A. J. Cronin*	95p
T029 158	THE STARS LOOK DOWN	*A. J. Cronin*	£1.00
T022 021	THREE LOVES	*A. J. Cronin*	90p
T022 536	THE HARRAD EXPERIMENT	*Robert H. Rimmer*	50p
T022 994	THE DREAM MERCHANTS	*Harold Robbins*	95p
T023 303	THE PIRATE	*Harold Robbins*	95p
T022 986	THE CARPETBAGGERS	*Harold Robbins*	£1.00
T031 667	WHERE LOVE HAS GONE	*Harold Robbins*	£1.00
T023 958	THE ADVENTURERS	*Harold Robbins*	£1.00
T031 659	THE INHERITORS	*Harold Robbins*	95p
T031 586	STILETTO	*Harold Robbins*	60p
T025 268	NEVER LEAVE ME	*Harold Robbins*	50p
T025 292	NEVER LOVE A STRANGER	*Harold Robbins*	90p
T022 226	A STONE FOR DANNY FISHER	*Harold Robbins*	80p
T031 640	79 PARK AVENUE	*Harold Robbins*	80p
T027 945	THE BETSY	*Harold Robbins*	90p
T031 241	EVENING IN BYZANTIUM	*Irwin Shaw*	75p
T029 557	RICH MAN, POOR MAN	*Irwin Shaw*	£1.25

Historical

T023 079	LORD GEOFFREY'S FANCY	*Alfred Duggan*	60p
T024 903	THE KING OF ATHELNEY	*Alfred Duggan*	60p
T023 125	FOX 11: FIRESHIP	*Adam Hardy*	35p
T024 946	FOX 12: BLOOD BEACH	*Adam Hardy*	35p
T027 651	FOX 13: SEA FLAME	*Adam Hardy*	40p

Science Fiction

T029 492	STRANGER IN A STRANGE LAND	*Robert Heinlein*	80p
T029 484	I WILL FEAR NO EVIL	*Robert Heinlein*	95p
T031 462	DUNE	*Frank Herbert*	£1.25
T022 854	DUNE MESSIAH	*Frank Herbert*	60p

War

T027 066	COLDITZ: THE GERMAN STORY	*Reinhold Eggers*	50p
T025 438	LILLIPUT FLEET	*A. Cecil Hampshire*	50p
T026 299	TRAWLERS GO TO WAR	*Lund & Ludlam*	50p

Western

T020 754	EDGE 15: BLOOD RUN	*George Gilman*	35p
T022 706	EDGE 16: THE FINAL SHOT	*George Gilman*	35p
T024 881	EDGE 17: VENGEANCE VALLEY	*George Gilman*	40p

General

T021 009	SEX MANNERS FOR MEN	*Robert Chartham*	35p
T023 206	THE BOOK OF LOVE	*Dr David Delvin*	90p
T028 828	THE LONG BANANA SKIN	*Michael Bentine*	90p

NEL P.O. BOX 11, FALMOUTH TR10 9EN, CORNWALL:

For U.K.: Customers should include to cover postage, 19p for the first book plus 9p per copy for each additional book ordered up to a maximum charge of 73p.

For B.F.P.O. and Eire: Customers should include to cover postage, 19p for the first book plus 9p per copy for the next 6 and thereafter 3p per book.

For Overseas: Customers should include to cover postage, 20p for the first book plus 10p per copy for each additional book.

Name ....

Address ....

....

....

Title ....
(NOVEMBER)

Whilst every effort is made to maintain prices, new editions or printings may carry an increased price and the actual price of the edition supplied will apply.